SOVEREIGN JUSTICE

CHOCTAW TRIBUNE SERIES, BOOK FOUR

SARAH ELISABETH SAWYER

Editors: Lynda Kay Sawyer, Catherine Frappier, Mollie Reeder

Cover Design: MiblArt. Capitol Building photograph courtesy of the National Archives. Background image ("Great Medal Mingoes," Mount Dexter treaty) courtesy of Lynda Kay Sawyer.

Author Photo by R. A. Whiteside. Courtesy of the National Museum of the American Indian, Smithsonian Institution

Print ISBN-13: 978-0-9910259-9-2

LCCN: 2021916225

To my five brothers who have encouraged me in their own ways —
Wes, Doug, James, Clint, & Jon

With special appreciation to James,
for believing in and encouraging my writing
like our daddy did.

Mihma chim olbvlaka ya chi haksobish vt haklashke, "ilvppakosh hina, iakaiya, ibbak isht impa imma pit ish folotakma micha afvbekimma ish folotakma, achi tok. (Isaiah 30:21)

And thine ears shall hear a word behind thee, saying, This is the way, walk ye in it, when ye turn to the right hand, and when ye turn to the left." (Isaiah 30:21)

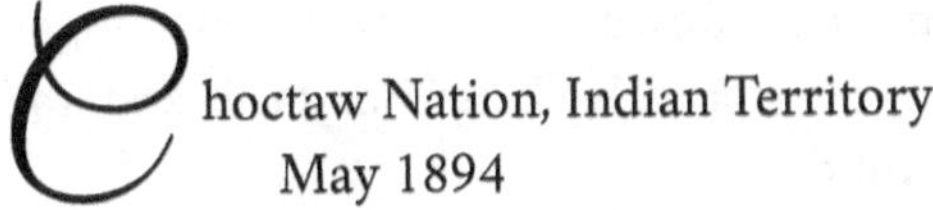

CHAPTER 1

Choctaw Nation, Indian Territory
May 1894

Ruth Ann dug her fingers into the webbing of grass and dirt on her father's grave. The dirt, the grass, both oddly cold this late-spring morning. The coolness touched her heart before hot pain seared it. Searing, ripping pain like she'd never experienced, not even when the news came about the deaths of her father and brother.

This was the pain of betrayal.

Wind whispered through the oak tree above Ruth Ann, whispered and mocked and cooled her hot cheeks. Overwhelmed her. She ripped a fistful of green blades and threw them into the wind, watched them swirl away. Just as her peace had gone that morning.

She ripped another handful and another. Another. Screamed above the quiet breeze. She wailed and began yanking at her hair, trying to relieve her inner pain, pulling all the pins loose from her fine, womanly updo.

So fashionable. So proper. So sensible. Nothing of what she was in this moment. Nothing she would ever be again. Her soul had shifted, a minuscule shift, but one like the earth itself moved, changing the very atmosphere.

Ruth Ann dug her nails into the dirt, gouging the well-settled plot of land under the oak tree. Why wasn't it a pine tree? She loved pines.

Her daddy had loved pines.

She pressed the dry dirt between her fingers and rubbed. Nothing but dust. She scraped it into a small pile and spat on it. Her hair fell forward and mixed with the mud she created. She mashed it with her fingers, then rubbed it between her palms.

Hands trembling, she raised the mixture to her cheeks and smeared it across them, then down her neck to her high-buttoned blouse. Her fingers traced back up her face, and she rubbed her tears into the mud.

"Daddy. Daddy. Daddy!"

The breeze died over the minutes that passed. A presence had joined her. She raised her head with a nod. She wanted anything or anyone who could quiet the grief that rattled her soul.

A shadow fell over her. Tall, strong, sure. She whispered, "Daddy."

Uncle Preston knelt beside her. He put a hand on her hot shoulder, the sun raising a sweat there already. She trembled, and only then did she realize it was from anger.

Her gaze trailed across her daddy's grave with its fine stone marker.

JAMES TELLER
BORN June 10, 1845
DIED Oct 3, 1888
"Be thou faithful unto death, and I will give thee a crown of life." Rev
2:10

Beside his stone was…Philip's.

PHILIP TELLER
BORN Feb 8, 1867
DIED Oct 3, 1888
"…toward the sunrising." Jos 1:15

Only Philip wasn't dead. Was he truly a betrayer of her family and people?

Ruth Ann kept her eyes on her daddy's stone. She could look nowhere else. She whispered, "Did you know?"

Uncle Preston's hand dropped to his knee. He clenched it before speaking.

"I suspected. But I figured if Philip were somehow alive, he'd have come back to us or sent word quick." He paused. "Otherwise, it was best for us all to believe he was dead."

"But…but the bodies…"

"We found bloody clothes. Some bones. Philip's fancy boots. It made sense, what with the panther tracks and all. None of us said nothing."

Ruth Ann plucked a grass blade and shredded it. "Matthew should have told us right away, right when I went to find him in McAlester. He knew then. He's known about Philip for days. Why didn't he tell us? Why!"

Her anger blinded her when she tried to look beyond her daddy's headstone.

Uncle Preston pulled her tight against him, halting her from taking out her vengeance on the grave, as though she could unearth the past and set it right.

"Shhh, now, hun," he said. "Don't blame Matthew. He had a hard time himself up in that mining country and hunting down Dan Holder and Lester Cotten. He'll explain things soon. Everyone is just going to have to hang on through this. *Chihowa* will make a way."

Ruth Ann closed her eyes, remembering the day, that day on the ranch six years ago. She had run up from the lake. Tools were tossed aside in the yard. The laundry kettle boiled over. Her mother wailed. Someone told Ruth Ann that Philip and her daddy were dead. The sky above turned a surreal blue.

And why? What had happened?

Matthew broke the news to Ruth Ann and Della, their mother, that morning, the earth shifting news that Philip was alive after years of hiding in shame. Matthew started the story with how the outlaws who killed Jim Teller and stole money from the Choctaw Nation were in jail now. That Matthew had helped track them down and bring them in from the Sans Bois Mountains north of Wilburton. It was terrifying, and Ruth Ann thought that was all there was.

But then he said how the outlaws had blackmailed Philip into helping them with the robbery. That was when the chill started in the pit of Ruth Ann's stomach. It turned into a burn, like ice on flesh, when he finished with croaking out the fact that Philip was still alive.

The sky above the graves now was a surreal blue once again.

The outlaws were in jail. They would stand trial. Would they be found guilty of her daddy's death?

Surely! If not, Philip was. And if he was, Ruth Ann could never, ever forgive him.

"...how oft shall my brother sin against me, and I forgive him? till seven times?' Jesus saith unto him, 'I say not unto thee, Until seven times: but, Until seventy times seven.'"

The words impressed on her heart, but surely Jesus hadn't meant forgiving a brother four hundred and ninety times for ripping their family apart. The only thing that would heal them, put them back together, would be to see Philip found innocent of any wrong doing.

He *was* innocent, wasn't he? If he suffered no punishment at the hands of Choctaw justice, he could come home. Her mama's heart would be healed, and Ruth Ann could forgive her brother.

"We must get him the best lawyer in Indian Territory," she said, stating it to the world as if it would understand her meaning. As if she would.

Uncle Preston loosened his hold on her, though she didn't want him to. She wanted to be held forever.

"We'll do what we can, hun. I haven't talked about Philip with Matthew yet. When y'all came tearing in here with you and your mama crying, it wasn't a time to ask questions."

Matthew had known Ruth Ann and Della would take the news hard, but when Della insisted on going straight out to the ranch, he realized his crucial mistake. They needed family.

Ruth Ann and her mother had held on to each other on the back bench of the buggy while Matthew drove them from Dickens to Uncle Preston's ranch, apologizing for not taking them out there before breaking the news. When they arrived, the story was quickly told and Della went to her mother's bedroom, and the Grandmother, Pokni, went in with her.

Ruth Ann was left alone, lost. She wanted to be alone, lost, for a little while at her daddy's grave. She thought Matthew would come to her there, explain himself, but he went to the lake instead and launched out in a canoe. They wouldn't see him for a while.

Just as well. Ruth Ann's agitation with him keeping secrets was mixed with her anger at Philip. The jumbled of emotions left her feeling she was angry at Matthew, too. Why hadn't he brought Philip home?

Someone had asked that—it might have been her—and he said that Philip wanted to stay around Skullyville until the inquest in three weeks. What was going to happen to him?

Suddenly, Ruth Ann couldn't be still. She pushed away from Uncle Preston and to her feet.

"We need to get to McAlester and see Philip," she said. "We have to get him a lawyer who can prove he is innocent."

Uncle Preston rose with her. "Hold on there. Let's take care of your mama first."

He licked his thumbs and rubbed both of Ruth Ann's cheeks. She felt the mud smearing more.

"We'll get through this, hun," he said. "You ain't alone."

He brushed her long, brown-black hair behind her shoulders. She whispered, "Please, a few more minutes here. Alone."

Uncle Preston rubbed her cheek with the back of his work-worn knuckles before walking away.

Ruth Ann knelt between the graves to absorb her daddy's headstone. Her eyes landed on Philip's, and her heart felt very, very alone.

"Daddy, I'm going to bring him back to the family. I'll put us back together. I'll forgive him then. I promise."

She needed to make sure Philip was found innocent, or she could never keep that promise.

It took two days to convince Matthew to arrange a trip to Skullyville. He said they should wait, wait until Philip was ready to see them. Ruth Ann had no desire to wait. Time was racing past them. They had lost six years already.

Matthew gave in when Ruth Ann threatened to make the trip alone. She needed to get their mama to Philip. Della hadn't spoken a word since they'd arrived at Uncle Preston's and Ruth Ann feared the vacant look in her eyes.

It was as though the terror of six years ago was on Ruth Ann again, and she was fighting for every breath. Maybe that was why she had shouted at Matthew. She would never forget the pain she caused in his eyes.

They rode the Frisco train through territory so familiar to Ruth Ann, but it all felt foreign. Was this how the Grandmother, and all their people, felt when they arrived in their new homelands? As if they were home, yet far, far from it? Nothing about Choctaw Nation felt right today. Not the pines, not the foothills, not the rivers.

On the train ride, Matthew tried to prepare them for what lay ahead.

"Philip doesn't want you to see him, didn't want you to even know," he said. "But he knew I wouldn't keep it from you."

Matthew was looking at Della as if Ruth Ann weren't sitting next to her. He no doubt was afraid to speak to his sister, afraid of what she might do.

Ruth Ann was afraid of what she might do.

Matthew was dressed in a work shirt and trousers like he'd wear on the ranch, as though wanting to conceal his identity as a newspaper publisher. His hair was overdue for a trim like usual, and it fell over his forehead when he took his hat off and dropped it on his knee with a sigh that seemed to release a month's worth of breath he'd been holding.

"Philip's changed," Matthew said. "Six years is a long time."

When Della didn't respond, Ruth Ann muttered, "What else are you not telling us? What other secrets are you keeping?"

Her mama rested a hand on Ruth Ann's arm, though her lovely eyes remained lowered, resting somewhere on Matthew's boots across from her.

Matthew didn't respond to Ruth Ann's questions. She clenched her hands into a fist and stared out the train window.

So. He still has secrets.

When the train dragged to a halt at the Poteau depot, Ruth Ann shot to her feet. She remembered the chaos from the last time she exited a train—rioters, federal troops, a young woman with her arms around Matthew's neck. What was that about?

Matthew had said little since his return other than what pertained to the *Choctaw Tribune*. He kept himself hidden away in the lean-to at the house, writing.

Ruth Ann wondered if he'd been writing more than newspaper articles. A brash temptation to find his journal and read it struck her. She'd never done such a thing. Yet she'd never had a brother come back to life, either. Nor another brother keep the fact to himself for days.

Nothing would be the same, not for the rest of their lives.

She waited for Matthew to help their mother up. Della had aged in the past two days.

The depot was crowded with people who laughed and greeted one another. Ruth Ann scowled, then scolded herself. Her misery was her own.

God, help me to…

She didn't know what to pray.

Matthew rented a rig to take them up to Skullyville. They arrived a short time later and Matthew helped their mother down. Ruth Ann jumped to the dusty street on her own. She was being terribly harsh with Matthew, but she didn't know what else to think or do or be.

As they walked up the porch steps to the hotel, Della between Ruth Ann and Matthew, he said, "He won't be expecting us, but he won't be surprised either. He knows the stubborn family he comes from."

Family. What did that word mean to them now?

Ruth Ann hoped they wouldn't be seen by anyone who knew them, that no one would interrupt their mission. Yet when they entered the hotel, she fervently wished something would stop time. Was she really prepared to see her long-dead brother's face?

Matthew didn't hesitate to take the wide staircase leading from the hotel lobby. He held their mother's arm with one hand while the other rested on her waist, as though afraid she would collapse. Ruth Ann knew she wouldn't. Their mama had been through much. She was strong enough, even for this moment.

They halted in front of a closed door, number 18. Matthew tried the knob, but it was locked. He jiggled it once, twice.

A husky, tear-soaked voice came from the other side. "I seen you coming into town. You don't want this. Annie, take Mama home."

Ruth Ann leaned against the wall, her insides melting at the scruffiness of her brother's voice.

Matthew watched her, then banged a fist on the door. "Open up, or I'll bust it open."

"You would."

The door knob turned and disappeared inward. Ruth Ann held her breath, cheek still pressed to the wallpaper. Della fell forward into the room, wailing. Matthew followed her in.

Ruth Ann pushed herself away from the wall and stood in the center of the door, watching. Her mama held tight to her oldest son.

Philip was scraggly, like any prodigal son. Only this son hadn't come home. Why hadn't he come home?

The answer was simple. He had to face trial for his part in their father's death. If he was found guilty, after whatever prison sentence or whipping he faced, he would be too ashamed to return with the black deed cast over the entire family. Only one thing would bring him home. He had to be found innocent.

He had to *be* innocent.

Philip raised his head from his mama's hair, eyes as brown and deep and sad as an open grave digging into Ruth Ann, begging her to release the tender love he needed. But she couldn't.

When he reached out a hand to her, she stepped back, turned, and fled.

Matthew chased after her. "Annie!"

Ruth Ann made it through the front door of the hotel and

pressed herself against the outside wall, gulping air, her face tingling. She was alive. So was Philip. How could she reconcile those facts?

Matthew touched her shoulder. She jerked away, and he held back.

"Annie. Annie." His voice was strained, but the tone came straight from his heart.

She sputtered, "Why did he make us believe he was dead all these years?"

Matthew sank back on his heels. "That's the first thing I asked him. Took a night in a whale's belly for him to finally tell me the whole story."

Ruth Ann glared at her brother. She was in no mood for metaphors.

He pressed his lips together, his eyes considering her. "He was afraid of us knowing the truth, of what he'd done to get black-mailed. Mostly, he went along with the Holder gang because he was scared that they would harm his family. They promised no one would get hurt if he did what they said. But then they came in shooting." Matthew swallowed, his eyes red. "Daddy...he died well. He died defending what was in his charge, including Philip."

Ruth Ann's chest heaved with fresh tears. "I don't care what Philip did to get mixed up in it all. I just want you to bring him home with us. We have to put the family back together."

"He's under arrest by the Choctaw Lighthorsemen and has to face justice."

"There has to be a way!" Ruth Ann reached up to wipe the moisture from her hot cheeks. "It couldn't have been like it sounds. We'll prove it. I'm going to bring him home, Matt. Home to Mama, and us all. Whatever it takes, I'm going to do it."

Matthew stiffened. "Do you know what it would have cost to bring him home myself, Annie?"

Ruth Ann jerked her head up to stare at him. "No. I don't. You didn't tell me anything."

"I told you what you needed to know."

"I need to know…" Ruth Ann halted and brought her voice back down. "I need to know why my brother, who was dead, is alive but not home with us. Tell me."

"The only way to bring him home would have been…"

"Yes?"

"Would have been to compromise the *Choctaw Tribune*. To go against everything we've stood for, to corrupt what God has given us in this time, and I couldn't do it even if it meant sacrificing our family being together. And Philip wouldn't—"

"So you did have a chance to bring him home, and you didn't?"

"It's more complicated than that—"

"Well, I'm simplifying it." Ruth Ann trembled. "We are going to hire the best lawyer in Indian Territory, and he will convince everyone of the truth, that Philip never meant to betray his family or his people. That he didn't really, that what happened would have happened no matter what. First, we can print the real story in the *Choctaw Tribune*. People trust us so—"

"No!"

Ruth Ann froze. Matthew scarcely shouted in her presence. He exhaled. "No. We will not use the *Choctaw Tribune* for our personal interests. We'll write the story, but in an unbiased way, no matter how hard that is."

"Impossible, you mean."

"After what I've been through the past few weeks, I think I can handle it."

Ruth Ann narrowed her eyes. "Just what have you been through? Who was that girl? And why did you come home looking like you'd been through a fire?"

"I had been."

"And?"

"And I'll tell you all about it. Someday."

"That's not good enough, Matthew Teller."

She pushed past him and headed for the train depot. She was done waiting on her brothers. She had run the *Choctaw Tribune* herself. Putting her family back together so she could forgive Philip would be harder, but God help her, she wouldn't fail. She promised her daddy.

CHAPTER 2

With the lateness of the spring sun, Matthew still had good daylight as he traveled down the road on a horse he'd rented in Dickens. He needed to get another horse soon to replace Little Chief, whether his heart was ready for it or not.

A trip like this to Eagletown shouldn't have involved hassling with Charlie Simms, the blacksmith, about how long Matthew would be away, where he was going or why. When one involved other people in their business, it created complications Matthew hated dealing with. He didn't care for Charlie or anyone else to know he was going to a meeting at Jefferson Gardner's mansion where Choctaw Nationals were selecting delegates for a trip to Washington, D.C.

Matthew wasn't a Nationalist; he was going as a newspaper reporter for the *Choctaw Tribune*. After the spat with Ruth Ann and the drain of seeing their mother with Philip last week, he needed some distance from family troubles and home, and to get back to newspaper business after the jarring time away in Krebs.

He didn't know who all would be at the meeting at Gardner's

mansion, but it couldn't be anything worse than Ruth Ann's cold treatment, like she'd given him at supper last night. She would be fine running the shop a few days. She hadn't moved all her things off his desk yet, even though he'd been back a week. He'd have to set her up her own desk if they planned to keep producing a daily.

He couldn't blame her for being angry. It was expected after he kept back the news about Philip for even a moment after finding out the truth himself.

Topping a rise on the dirt road, Eagletown came into view. The town had moved back and forth across the Mountain Fork River over the decades since the Choctaw people settled the area. Each side of the split community fought to have the post office on their side. It was currently on the west side with Jefferson Gardner, who owned a mercantile in Eagletown. The community had a courthouse, whipping post, and a flat stone known as execution rock where Choctaws used to come for their own execution by bullet.

With a U.S. federal court now in Indian Territory, the old ways and the right of self-government were fading far and fast. Men like Jefferson Gardner, an experienced Choctaw statesman who was running for chief in the upcoming election, would set the coming direction for the tribe.

And men like Pepper Barnes.

Matthew tightened his lips when he saw Pepper dismounting in front of the mansion. Not the person he wanted to tangle with today. Pepper reminded Matthew too much of Philip—brash and bent on getting his own way. Always more than ready for a fight.

The problem was, Pepper had saved Matthew and Ruth Ann's lives not so long ago, on the road outside of Finley when Cub Wassom ambushed the Tellers.

Pepper greeted Matthew with a frown. "Thought you'd still be curled up in bed after fighting with the mine strikers against our people."

"Good to see you, too, Pepper." Matthew dismounted and strung the reins through the iron ring on the same hitching post with Pepper's Choctaw horse, a fine-looking animal. "I see you're ready for battle as usual."

Pepper turned his back on Matthew. "Some of us choose to fight *for* our people."

Pepper never hesitated to say what he thought about the *Choctaw Tribune* not siding with the Nationals, and accusing Matthew of doing more harm than good with the newspaper.

Matthew decided not to respond. No use getting in fisticuffs in the first two minutes. He was still sore from his battles in the coal mining country of McAlester and Krebs.

He followed Pepper to the front porch of the mansion, where a half-dozen men stood. He knew all the men there, including Jefferson Gardner, a short, slender man. Yet his slim face exuded his determination, showing that nothing would move him if he didn't believe it was right. His Van Dyke beard—a stylish mustache and goatee—was trimmed neatly. He wore a white shirt, short tie, and starched collar beneath an unbuttoned vest and jacket.

Gardner's fine house was built less than ten years before. It was set a short distance from the Lower Mountain Fork River where droves of Choctaw people crossed on their final steps after walking hundreds of miles from the homelands in Mississippi.

Here, many of them decided to walk no more, and settled the area. Jefferson Gardner's mansion faced the old Military Road that had led his grandparents to their new home.

As men in the group turned to greet the newcomers, Matthew bumped into Pepper's back when the young man halted suddenly. Matthew saw why.

Tecumseh Shoemaker.

Matthew felt a rare twinge of intimidation. Tecumseh was a Choctaw full-blood whose family had crossed the trail later than most, opting to remain in Mississippi in an attempt to claim a piece of their homelands through U.S. citizenship when the majority of the people removed. Tecumseh grew up in the Ouachita Mountains, isolated from the influences of white settlers and formally educated Choctaws, his family practicing the old ways of their people.

Nearing forty years old, Tecumseh had witnessed great changes among their people, but he remained unchanged. His dark-skinned face was carved from clay, emotionless as he stared at Pepper Barnes.

Tecumseh Shoemaker could neither read nor write, but he was respected among Choctaws as a leader in the Nationals Party and an accomplished lawyer. In ten years of trying cases, he'd never lost a single one.

He was the best lawyer in Indian Territory.

Matthew moved past Pepper and climbed the porch steps, greeting the other men as he approached Jefferson Gardner. Matthew reached out his hand to the candidate. "Halito, and thank you for the invitation to cover this meeting."

Gardner shook Matthew's hand. "Our people need to know where the Nationals stand while representing them on the trip to Washington. Your paper has good writing, shows that our people are civilized and able to tend their own matters without the U.S. government getting invited in, like Chief Jones did with the strike, calling in federal troops. I wouldn't trust no other news-paper around here further than I could pitch a cow."

Matthew nodded in appreciation, then stepped away. He made room for Pepper, who had charged up the steps like he owned the place. Pepper greeted the man running in his party's bid for chief. Matthew turned to Tecumseh Shoemaker, extending his hand. Tecumseh folded his arms.

Forbis Kanitobe, another prominent full-blood leader, stood beside Tecumseh. His round face didn't betray his emotions as he offered a semi-hostile greeting. "You wrote a powerfully interesting story about the strikers and how that polecat Progressive Jones called in the U.S. troops to tame our land, Teller. Wouldn't have happened if we'd been in charge, and that is what we're telling them in Washington. You hear?"

He said it like he expected Matthew to whip out his pad and write a favorable story about their upcoming D.C. trip before the delegates even made it.

"I hear," Matthew said flatly.

Forbis Kanitobe shifted his jaw toward Pepper, who was bent on winning a staring match with Tecumseh Shoemaker.

"You, young Barnes, I got a letter from your daddy saying he thinks you're man enough to go with this delegation," Forbis Kanitobe said. "You ain't even married yet. What do you know about what's best for our people?"

Pepper gave up the match with Tecumseh Shoemaker to meet the new challenge. "Man enough to defend my home and family against a mob of polecat Progressives who shot up my daddy's mansion. And I'll get married soon enough. Got to make sure there's a strong Choctaw Nation to raise my offspring in first."

"Humph."

A dinner bell clanged, ending the debate as Jefferson Gardner called for everyone to meet in the dining room for supper. Matthew held back, accepting one last condemning look from Tecumseh Shoemaker as he passed. The lawyer must have heard about Matthew's brother who had betrayed their people.

Ruth Ann said she wanted the best lawyer in Indian Territory to defend Philip. She wasn't going to get him.

The dinner conversation wasn't fluffy. Matthew kept his tablet in his lap, saying nothing. Everyone else had plenty to say about the upcoming D.C. trip, Chief Jones, and the Dawes Commission.

One thing they all agreed on: They wanted Jefferson Gardner elected as chief that summer. Gardner took a strong stance against the Dawes Commission, one reason he was in the running for chief. He vowed to ignore requests from Senator Dawes to discuss allotting the communal land—the end of sovereignty for the Choctaw Nation.

"Only way to deal with them," Forbis Kanitobe boomed. "If we don't let 'em in our nation, nothing they can do."

Pepper huffed. "We've got to get politicians in D.C. on our side. Senator Newman of Georgia sympathizes with our cause and I can get him to—"

"You can nothing," Forbis Kanitobe cut him off. "You're too young to be butting your nose in the middle of all this."

"Old enough to defend our people here, old enough to do it in D.C.," Pepper said.

"Eh. Your daddy's a white man. He done a lot for full-bloods, but that don't mean he or you got the stake we do. What you say, Tecumseh?"

Tecumseh Shoemaker hadn't spoken except when asked a question. Matthew wasn't sure what had nurtured the mutual hate between Tecumseh Shoemaker and the Barnes family, but it showed at Gardner's dinner table now.

Pepper didn't let Tecumseh answer, still focused on Forbis. "We've got plenty at stake, and a no-account lawyer isn't going to say different. Lawyers have caused most of our problems in the Nation since Removal, always grabbing money whenever they win a case our whole people have battled for. They'll do the same with the Leased Claims."

Matthew scratched notes. Pepper Barnes always had a lot to say, even if he didn't know what he was talking about.

Pepper glared at Tecumseh. "How much have you pocketed in a decade? How much you going to get from this allotment business? Answer that."

Matthew realized his pencil was the only sound in the room. He stopped writing.

Tecumseh lowered the knife he was using to slice through the roast beef. Matthew couldn't help but wonder if he imagined slicing through Pepper's fiery tongue.

Tecumseh stared Pepper down. *"Issish ittimilaiyuka yvt Hattak Vpi Homma ikono kvt issish alotowa vlheha ya yakni holittoblichi kvt ohmi kiyo."*

His gaze swept by Pepper and around the table to Matthew, seated a few spots away. His words echoed in Matthew's heart: *The mixed bloods are not Indian enough to love land like the full bloods.*

Matthew shifted. He, Pepper, and Jefferson Gardner were the only mixed bloods in the room.

Pepper clanged his fork and knife beside his plate, sloshing gravy on the white tablecloth. He answered in Choctaw. "You saying you don't think Jefferson Gardner can love our land enough to defend it? I say he can, and so can I—"

"If I had prosecuted your father over him pillaging our timber, I would have had him expelled from the Choctaw Nation as an intruder," Tecumseh said.

Matthew quietly began writing again.

Pepper snorted and switched back to English. "Robert Barnes is a citizen of the Choctaw Nation."

"Then I would have had him shot."

Matthew jerked his head up. So that was the wedge between them. Tecumseh saw the Barnes as traitors.

Pepper's face was beet red, his fist clenched around his dinner knife. He flexed and clenched again. His eyes darted to Forbis. He slowly relaxed his grip and turned back to Tecumseh.

"You think you know what's best for our people," Pepper said. "You don't. But as long as these men think you're the best one to try our cases, I'll respect that. But don't threaten me or my family."

Tecumseh didn't flinch. "I remove threats to our people."

Pepper parted his lips to retort, but Jefferson Gardner stood. "We ain't here to fight each other. We've got to vote on delegates to D.C. Everyone here, except Matthew Teller, Tecumseh Shoemaker, and myself, have thrown their hat in the ring. I know we don't all see eye to eye, but I got no objections to the proposed delegates. We need fighters, as long as they focus their fight on our common enemies." He looked at Pepper.

The young man nodded, meeting eyes with Forbis again. "Agreed."

"Any objections to the proposed delegates?"

To Matthew's surprise, Tecumseh didn't object to the vote for Pepper. Maybe he was glad to see him go off to D.C. where he'd be out of Tecumseh's way for whatever case the lawyer was working on next.

The dinner party broke up, some exiting to the breezeway between the dining room and foyer they'd crossed through after entering from the front porch. While they smoked and accepted drinks from a servant, Matthew strolled down the steps toward a road he could barely discern in the dark, one that disappeared into the woods. He knew where the road led.

It wasn't hard to follow, despite the moonless night. It was a short but lonely quarter of a mile to the river.

The road curved and dipped downward into the woods. The area turned swampy and Matthew kept an eye out for nocturnal creatures that might want a taste of him.

The sound of the river's flow reached his ears. Not far now. There. The legendary Cypress tree that had stood for what many believed to be two thousand years was ahead, near the road and close to the river. The tree miraculously survived generations of floods. It had been undisturbed by humans for most of those years. All except the last hundred onward when a band of

Choctaws crossed here on the final leg of their journey to their new homelands.

Chief Pushmataha would have known about this important landmark when he scouted this territory around 1800, bringing back news about the land. Some of his observations were favorable. Most were not. Later, he went to Washington, D.C. to argue for his people and their rights guaranteed by treaty.

He contracted the croup and died while in the great white father's city. He was granted his last request to be buried with full military honors in the Congressional Cemetery. Choctaw Chief Peter Pitchlynn, too, was buried there in 1881.

Hopefully no Choctaws would die in that city on the upcoming trip.

Matthew hopped over the massive chug holes that plagued the road. His gaze finally touched the river itself, this section of the Lower Mountain Fork River. It wasn't deep there, but wide. The clear mountain water showed the crossing his people would have made. Now the crossing was only used by those on foot or horseback when they didn't want to take the bridge between the two feuding communities of Eagletown.

Alone there, Matthew could think about his people— hundreds of miles and three months away from the only homes they'd known, crossing the icy water in bare, bruised, bleeding feet. Knowing they had gone far enough and could stop.

Matthew stood still, fingering the pencil and tablet in his pocket, the story of the evening forming in his mind. It faded and his thoughts inevitably turned to his family that now included his brother. Nothing was the same as when they lived on Uncle Preston's ranch. So much had changed in Philip's absence. Matthew had changed and now he must change again to make room in his life for his brother.

What lay ahead? Regular visits to prison? And what of Philip's daughter? Did she know who she was or the family she came from? Matthew didn't even know her name. Worse, he hadn't told his mother or Ruth Ann about her.

Matthew rubbed his eyes. Moisture from the river had gathered there, not tears. Or so he told himself.

He was an uncle who had never seen his niece. What was she like? Did she have the features of the Teller family? Or her mother? Who was her mother? What kind of woman had Philip...

Matthew stiffened. Someone was coming down the road behind him. He turned to spot a swinging light moving closer, creating shadows and dispersing them. The two thousand year old Cypress grew and then shrank as a figure came around it with the light of a lantern.

"I need to talk to you about Tecumseh Shoemaker." Pepper's tone was authoritative, as though he were Matthew's elder instead of two years younger than him.

Matthew turned back to the river. "I'm not having anything to do with your feud."

"I'm not resting until I see Shoemaker run out of the Nationals party, preferably out of the territory," Pepper went on. "There are plenty of others who feel the same way." Pepper came up beside him and held the lantern almost in Matthew's face.

Matthew gave him a warning look, and Pepper lowered the lantern. "Hear me out."

Matthew held his gaze. "If it'll make you sleep better."

"It won't for you, when you find out who's prosecuting your brother's case."

Hard as it was, Matthew kept the blow to his heart concealed. The Tellers didn't stand a chance against Tecumseh Shoemaker, who despised anyone caught betraying their people.

"Now listen," Pepper said. "If we team up, we can take care of Shoemaker and your brother at the same time. That newspaper of yours has a lot of influence."

Matthew closed his eyes. Not again. Who knew half his job as a newspaper publisher would be keeping everyone out of its business?

"The *Choctaw Tribune* has nothing to do with my brother's case."

"Tecumseh has never lost in court," Pepper said. "Not once in ten years."

Philip is guilty. Matthew almost let the words slip out, but he had no intention of saying it to Pepper Barnes.

Matthew opened his eyes to take in the calm flow of the river. "I'll get Philip the best lawyer I can."

"But he won't be *the* best."

Matthew pushed his hands in his trouser pockets. He was not going to get in a fistfight with Pepper tonight. "That's not your concern."

"You wanna bet?"

Knowing he'd get no more peace at the river, Matthew headed back up the road. Pepper badgered him all the way, talking about the upcoming delegation to D.C. and the influence Pepper would have there, and on and on, until Matthew was ready for that fistfight.

But he didn't say a word. Pepper was furious by the time they reach the mansion porch.

A servant greeted them at the door. "I have an upstairs room prepared, but you'll have to share it. Everything else is taken."

Pepper turned about-face. "I'll sleep in the barn."

Matthew thanked the girl and trudged through the foyer, picking up his overnight bag he'd left there earlier, and entered the empty parlor. Narrow stairs led from the room to the second floor where Matthew had stayed before when interviewing Jefferson Gardner after the man announced his intention to run for chief.

A bed sat near the rail of the stairs with a small sitting area at the foot. Matthew deposited his bag on the bed, heaving a breath of relief to be away from Pepper. The young man had a way of draining energy from him.

Matthew pulled a newspaper from his bag, the *Indian Citizen*. This newspaper out of McAlester sided with the Nationals in their articles, always railing against Progressives. Pepper wanted to use the *Choctaw Tribune* like that. Men in the Progressive party wanted to do the same thing with the newspaper.

Neither side was going to get their way. Not as long as Matthew Teller was the publisher.

CHAPTER 3

Before daybreak Thursday morning, Ruth Ann sleepily finished cooking breakfast. She had gone out the back to do chores, planning to skip breakfast and go straight to the newspaper shop without Matthew, but noise in the barn told her he was doing her chores. The least she could do was give their mama a break from cooking. Maybe they could have a normal family meal for the first time in weeks.

Most likely, though, Matthew was avoiding her and would go to the shop without her. He had gotten home from Jefferson Gardner's mansion yesterday, but didn't talk to her about the story he gleaned or what the plan was for the day.

Ruth Ann wanted to talk to her mother, but Della hadn't spoken much all week. She went about her daily sewing, cooking, cleaning house. In fact, the house was so clean, Ruth Ann wasn't comfortable. Was her mother preparing for Philip to come home? He could share Matthew's lean-to bedroom on the side of the house, if they could manage without fighting all night.

How odd to think of them trying to be a family again.

Della came down the stairs from the attic bedroom into the kitchen. Ruth Ann pushed the bacon skillet to a cooler spot on the stove and plopped in a chair at the kitchen table, her emotional strength gone.

"Mama."

She couldn't wrap her words into an eloquent package, couldn't make everything all right. But she'd scarcely spoken with Della since they'd learned Philip was alive. Every time Ruth Ann looked at her mother, she remembered her folded in Philip's arms, him looking over Della's shoulder at Ruth Ann, pleading for her forgiveness and understanding. Ruth Ann couldn't give it yet.

Della came behind Ruth Ann and wrapped her arms around her shoulders. Ruth Ann leaned into those soft, warm arms, resting her cheek in the crook like an infant as a hint of lavender soothed her. If only she were young enough not to understand anything. It was hard to be full grown and still not understand anything.

How could she tell her mother she couldn't stand for Philip to be under their roof again until he'd been found innocent of Jim Teller's death?

The back door opened and Matthew came in, dressed in an old work shirt and trousers. He hardly looked this way since he'd started the *Choctaw Tribune*, always ready for business. This reminded Ruth Ann of before he went to college when they all lived on Uncle Preston's ranch, when they were happy and whole and one family with Daddy and Philip.

But Matthew's eyes were ancient compared to then. What he'd experience in the past month was more than he'd seen in a lifetime. Ruth Ann could tell that much about her brother. If only he would tell her what it all meant.

Ruth Ann didn't move, not ready to give up her coveted sweet spot in her mama's arms.

Matthew washed up and sat in a chair across from them, wiping his hands on a dish towel. "There's something I need to tell you both before the inquest. Something about Philip…"

Hasty footsteps sounded from outside, then the back door flew open.

"Good morning, neighbors!"

Ruth Ann winced. The greeting was sung like it was a sunny Sunday morning. Mrs. Warren rarely got up this early. The woman had even more than her usual energy since Lance and Amarillo's courtship began.

Della released Ruth Ann, creating a vacuum of coolness and loss, and went about setting the table. "Mrs. Warren, please sit. We have enough."

Mrs. Warren waved her hands about. "Oh, never you mind about that, Mrs. Teller. I am here to demand you all have dinner with us tomorrow evening. The Levitts are coming—I'll make sure of that—and we couldn't have a big family meal without our Indian friends."

Ruth Ann noticed Matthew's small smile as he stood and moved away to lean against the wall, out of Mrs. Warren's wake. They were all grateful for the changes in the woman this past year. Not the least of which, how her understanding of their people improved. Rather than insults and jabs at the "savages" of Indian Territory, Mrs. Warren had shown a keen interest in the Choctaws as people. She even talked of defending them against "thieving white men" who needed to mind their own country's troubles.

Mrs. Warren went on. "Lance and Amarillo—how precious they are!—want to host a gathering at the Ark."

Ruth Ann stood to pull the skillet back on the hot stove burner and turned the slices of bacon. "The Ark?"

"My dear, yes, what else would you call a home with three surnames?"

Matthew pushed away from the wall. "Excuse me, I've got to get cleaned up for the shop."

He navigated between Mrs. Warren and Ruth Ann, who tried to make eye contact with him.

"But breakfast…" Ruth Ann didn't finish. He was gone, out the back door to the lean-to. He hadn't told them the news about Philip. What else had their brother done?

His abrupt departure wasn't lost on Della, who stared at the closed door.

Mrs. Warren stilled, her eyes darting between Ruth Ann and her mother.

"Did I…did I disturb something?"

Ruth Ann sighed. "No ma'am. We were already disturbed."

The smell of burning bacon forced her focus to the stove. She shoved the iron skillet to the back of it, off the main heat. Beside her, the soft swish of her mother's dress told her Della left for the living room. Mrs. Warren followed.

Ruth Ann went to the doorway to see her mother curled on the sofa, crying. Mrs. Warren perched awkwardly beside her, stroking her arm.

"Oh my friend. My dear, dear friend. Such pain."

Mrs. Warren looked over her shoulder at Ruth Ann, eyes red. "You go on about your work, my dear. I won't leave her side."

Ruth Ann backed away from the strange scene of Mrs. Warren comforting her mother instead of the other way around.

When would Ruth Ann ever find a solid foothold again, a step she could take that wouldn't crumble beneath her?

She stared at the stove and whispered one of her daddy's favorite scriptures.

"And thine ears shall hear a word behind thee, saying, This is the way, walk ye in it…"

Could the Old Testament verse in Isaiah possibly reach into her life in 1894? Could she walk in that way?

Friday came, but Ruth Ann and Matthew still hadn't spoken about his trip to Jefferson Gardner's. Her brother spent his day out back of the newspaper shop, writing. Ruth Ann continued possession of his desk. Someone had to keep the day-to-day operations going.

The small crew did well in getting the newspaper out early, and everyone left the shop for the weekend. The Levitts said they would see Ruth Ann at the Warrens soon. She didn't know where Matthew was now. That was becoming commonplace.

Ruth Ann locked up and went home to find it far too still and empty. Upstairs, her mother was in bed, covers up to her ears. Ruth Ann sat on the edge and put one hand on her mother's soft shoulder. The pain was palpable.

"It's okay, Mama. Philip loves us. That's why he stayed away. But we'll bring him home soon."

She rubbed Della's shoulder, each stroke strengthening her resolve to keep the promise made at her daddy's grave.

Della said quietly, "Go on. Mrs. Warren is waiting."

"But Mama—"

"I will rest and pray."

The kitchen door downstairs opened and shut. Matthew?

Ruth Ann reluctantly dressed for dinner and went down to find her teenage cousin Peter Frazier rummaging through a tray on the table. Sweets for the dinner.

Ruth Ann swatted his shoulder. "Not a bite. Mama made those for dinner at...at the Ark."

Peter looked over his shoulder, wide-eyed innocent. "I'm invited, aren't I?"

"How much trouble did you cause on the ranch today?"

"Not a smidgen."

"Unlikely, but if you carry the tray, I'll let you go along. Someone has to feed you."

Ruth Ann had grown used to her cousin living with them in town, staying in the lean-to on the side of the house with Matthew three or four nights a week. She didn't know how they'd gotten along without him.

Ruth Ann and Peter walked together, silently. How strange that even he was quiet. But he was only ten years old when the tragedy struck, taking Jim and Philip Teller away. Peter had been old enough to remember Ruth Ann's father and brother, yet too young to grasp the meaning of it all. Ruth Ann felt the same way.

Light and laughter came through the open door of the Warren house as the Jessop children romped around the yard, playing in the spring evening light. They greeted Ruth Ann and Peter as they went inside.

Lance Fuller had made many changes, inside and out, to the Warren home over the past months. It no longer felt like the forbidding, unwelcoming fortress of secrets it had been when Mayor Thaddeus Warren was in charge.

Beulah Levitt caught Ruth Ann's hand in the foyer and asked where Della was.

"Resting," Ruth Ann answered.

Beulah had been there for Ruth Ann in the aftermath of the news that Philip was alive, but didn't know what to say. No one did. Beulah bit her lower lip now, nodding without further question.

"Well, you are just in time to help me drag my father, Lance, Stephen Austin, and your brother...Matthew, that is...down for dinner. They are adding shelves in one of the rooms to make it more suitable for Glenrose and Belle."

Heavy footfall sounded as Mr. Levitt, Lance Fuller, Stephen Austin Jessop, and Matthew came down the stairs in the foyer, dusting off their hands and being admonished by Glenrose Jessop to clean up before they set foot at the table. The twelve-year-old was fast becoming a young lady in this home.

Mrs. Warren came up the long hallway from where Ruth Ann knew her bedroom was at the end, her dress tidy for the evening, her smile bright. When Ruth Ann saw Belle Jessop shyly coming up with her, holding hands, she knew God had brought these three surnames under the same roof for a reason.

Mrs. Warren embraced Ruth Ann, then gripped her cheeks and whispered fiercely, "We know your mother will be fine, don't we?"

Ruth Ann tried to nod as Mrs. Warren patted both her cheeks before gliding off to the parlor to play hostess, adorable Belle staying close to her side.

The oldest of the Jessops, Amarillo, shooed everyone toward the parlor. "Go on in there, now. Dinner will be ready soon. Stephen Austin, see that those young'uns are washed and quiet. Glenrose, you go on up and change Goodnight while Mabel and I get food on the table. Lance…"

She started to give him an order the way she was used to running a household with four younger siblings and a baby in the shanty they lived in not long ago. But Ruth Ann saw a tenderness in the young Texas girl's blue eyes when she turned to her beau.

"Lance, would you please come help me in the kitchen?"

Ruth Ann found herself wanting to share a secret smile with someone about the courting couple. Her eyes met Matthew's. He looked away and started talking with Peter about the ranch.

Before long Mabel, the servant who stayed on to care for Mrs. Warren, announced dinner was ready.

In the formal dining room, Ruth Ann could scarcely concentrate on the conversation around her. It felt like the dinner after a funeral, when everyone talked cheerfully yet tried to be sensitive to the grief. It was the first real social event she'd been at since learning her brother had come back to life.

Matthew and Lance were talking to her right and there was a general lull around the table when the words *Washington, D.C.* popped out.

Lance nodded. "There are people there I trust. I can send letters whenever you're ready to start reaching subscribers in D.C."

Matthew raised his gaze to Ruth Ann's and glanced around the table at the sudden attention. "We were discussing the

Choctaw delegation going to D.C. I was telling Lance that I wished I could go along and work on expanding the reach of the *Choctaw Tribune* to the nation's capitol."

"How splendid!" Mrs. Warren cooed as she buttered Belle's roll. "You must say hello to my friend, Britannia W. Peter Kennon of Tudor Place. She is a descendant of Martha Washington and such a dear!"

"I'm not going anywhere for a while," Matthew said. "Have to hire on more help for the newspaper."

Even though he was talking about something so familiar, Ruth Ann felt lost in the conversation.

Beulah laughed with her distinctive bell-like sound. "Well, if ever there was a city in need of the truths in the *Choctaw Tribune*, it is that one! Now, who is ready for dessert?"

The children leaped from the table unanimously and began clearing away the dishes.

One more day come and gone in Ruth Ann's new reality. One more day closer to the inquest for Philip.

CHAPTER 4

"*D*o you swear to tell the truth, the whole truth and nothing but the truth, so help you God?"

Help me, God, Ruth Ann prayed. "Yes."

When she lifted her shaking hand from the cover of the worn courtroom Bible, the black leather stuck to her for an instant. Her palms had broken out in sweat when the Choctaw lawyer Tecumseh Shoemaker called her as the first witness to the stand inside the small Tobucksy County Courthouse.

Ruth Ann slowly sat in the chair the bailiff indicated, trying to ignore the harsh look on Judge Kendrick's face as he glared at her. Matthew warned them the inquest would be tough, that the judge held a personal grudge against Matthew and Philip. He didn't say why. More information he was holding back.

She did not want to look ahead either, didn't want to see her mother and Matthew sitting in the front rows of the benches crammed into the room. She most especially did not want to look at the defendant table where Philip, pale as a ghost, sat staring at his hands. It had scarcely been three weeks since she'd learned he was alive and now she was called to testify at the inquest to determine if he'd be held for trial for stealing Choctaw assets—annuity payments plus a special bank bag of the chief's.

His lawyer, Nelson Cobb, scribbled notes on paper on the table before him. His papers were in neat stacks, not the scattered mess Matthew kept on his desk. Ruth Ann wasn't certain if that was a good sign or a bad. She didn't know this man whom they were trusting with her brother's, and her family's, future.

Not knowing where else to look, she settled her gaze on the man behind the prosecutor's table, Tecumseh Shoemaker. She didn't know this man well either, she just wished he hadn't called her as the first witness in the inquest for Philip. She hadn't expected to be in this chair at all. What did he want from her?

Tecumseh remained behind his table. There were no papers there, at least not in front of him. His assistant, a young man about twenty, sat in the chair next to him, taking notes. Tecumseh held her gaze, calm and steady.

Judge Kendrick barked at her, "State your full name and residence for the court."

Ruth Ann jolted in her chair, scooting away as much as possible from the judge and his small bench, no more than a table. His heavy gavel was in hand, ready to bang anyone into silent submission.

Ruth Ann moistened her lips. "Ruth Ann Teller of Dickens."

Tecumseh Shoemaker addressed her. "Miss Teller, would you please state your relationship with the defendant?"

Ruth Ann's eyes darted to Philip. "I...he's my brother."

A soft murmur went through the dozen other people in the courtroom. Most weren't there for this inquest. They had their own cases on the docket, so they were undoubtedly as surprised as she was that the prosecutor called the defendant's own sister to testify.

"And what was your relationship with the victim in this case, James Teller?"

Ruth Ann felt jolted again. This time it was her heart that moved straight up into her throat. "He's my father."

"Your *deceased* father." Tecumseh put an emphasis on the word.

Dead and buried. Partly because of her brother. Ruth Ann clenched her fist and said nothing.

Tecumseh pressed the tips of his fingers on the table, leaning forward. "What was the nature of your father's and your brother's relationship?"

Ruth Ann's vision blurred. Her family before her morphed into a memory—the night before her father and Philip left on their last run together, she'd been in the loft of the barn where she'd discover kittens. Below, Philip was loading the wagon with supplies when their father, Jim, came in. He helped Philip finish loading, then began admonishing him not to leave Jim's side during the whole trip.

"Answer the question." Judge Kendrick's voice boomed in the silence of the room. Ruth Ann's vision snapped back into place and she found herself staring into Philip's eyes, still as hollow as an empty grave.

"They got on as fine as most fathers and sons, I suppose," she said.

"You suppose?" Tecumseh did not let her thoughtless addition pass by. "Were they as close as your father and other brother?" Tecumseh half turned to motion at Matthew sitting in the front row. Matthew's fingers were intertwined with Della's as they sat side by side.

Why was Tecumseh Shoemaker allowed to ask such invasive questions? She glanced over at Nelson Cobb, but he was still busy writing. He didn't seem to think her testimony was important. But wasn't everything said this day critical to her family?

Ruth Ann couldn't look at Matthew or Philip. *Help me, God.*

"I…I can't judge that."

"Cannot or will not? Did you not live with your brothers and father your entire life until your father's death and your brother falsifying his death after helping rob the Choctaw Nation?"

"Objection, your honor."

Ruth Ann took a long, slow breath, thankful Nelson Cobb had finally spoken up, giving her a chance to breathe. When Matthew said Tecumseh Shoemaker would use whatever means at his disposal to prove his case, he'd been correct.

Judge Kendrick looked at Ruth Ann and then her family. "Sustained."

Nelson Cobb went back to writing.

Tecumseh nodded. "No more questions."

Ruth Ann rose quickly from the witness stand. Judge Kendrick banged his gavel and she plopped back down, heart beating out of her chest. He glared at her.

"You weren't dismissed, little lady."

She wrapped her hands around her reticule, the velvet fabric doing very little to dry them.

Cobb glanced up. "No questions."

Judge Kendrick said, "You are *now* dismissed."

Ruth Ann called on all her feminine graces to walk steadily across the floor, right in between the two lawyers and back to her family. She met Matthew's pained look as she took her seat on the other side of their mother.

Tecumseh spoke to the judge. "I call Matthew Teller to the stand."

Ruth Ann heard an agitated sigh, so rare from her stalwart brother. Matthew headed up to take his place at the front of the courtroom. After he was sworn in on the same Bible smeared with her sweat, he took the stand and stated his name.

Tecumseh ran the same questions as the first few he had for Ruth Ann, and she shuddered with what she felt was coming. Matthew and Philip didn't always get along back in the day.

Tecumseh asked, "Please describe what happened when you saw your brother for the first time in six years?"

Matthew looked much calmer than Ruth Ann knew he felt. He put a relaxed hand on the arm of the chair and held Tecumseh's gaze. "We got into a fistfight."

"You and your brother have a habit of fighting?"

"Not a habit, no, but it happens."

"What did you feel when you saw him for the first time after believing he was dead the past six years?"

Ruth Ann wanted to stand to her feet and object. Nelson Cobb was still bent over his paper. What was he doing, writing out all of his questions for the other witnesses?

Ruth Ann was sure the judge and everyone saw Matthew's hand tighten on the chair's arm. "My feelings are my business."

Tecumseh frowned. "Your feelings have a bearing on this case. Were you angry when you saw your long-dead brother?"

"Not at first."

"But soon after?"

"Maybe."

Tecumseh glanced at the judge who growled at Matthew, "There are no 'maybes' in my courtroom. Answer the question straight. Remember, you are under oath."

"Yes, I was angry, and then—"

"Did you know the part your brother played in your father's death?"

Matthew stared at Tecumseh. Ruth Ann wanted to scream, wanted to stop this torture of her family. Why wasn't Nelson Cobb objecting? Surely their shredded hearts shouldn't be on trial!

Matthew released the arm of the chair. "For a short time I blamed him. I don't—"

"That is all for now." Tecumseh took his seat and though Ruth Ann couldn't see his face, she imagined it held the same impassive, emotionless expression she had seen.

What made this man so hard, so calloused to the raw pain he

knew the Teller family was in? Did the nation mean more to him than individuals?

"No questions." This came from Nelson Cobb, and it infuriated Ruth Ann.

Why didn't he ask Matthew about the good times they had as a family with Philip, or how Philip helped capture Dan Holder and Lester Cotton, the true perpetrators of the crime that left her father dead and the Choctaw Nation poorer? She didn't care if it was permissible or if the judge banged his gavel to silence the truth. Nelson Cobb needed to at least *try*.

Judge Kendrick dismissed Matthew with what Ruth Ann thought was a satisfactory smile, and Matthew returned to his seat. Ruth Ann wanted to reach out to him but couldn't move. Della took his hand once again. She held onto Ruth Ann's with her other.

"I call Kathryn Russell to the stand," Tecumseh said.

On the other side of Della, Matthew took a sharp breath. Ruth Ann frowned. Who was Kathryn Russell?

Matthew whispered, surely for Ruth Ann to hear, "What is she doing here?"

Judge Kendrick nodded at the bailiff, who went through one of two doors in the courthouse that was once an old farmhouse. He reemerged moments later with a woman and a little girl in tow. Ruth Ann was sitting almost directly behind Philip and watched him drop his head into one hand.

The young woman was white as fresh linen as she pulled the little girl along. The little girl stared at the room full of people with Jim Teller's golden brown eyes.

Della crushed Ruth Ann's hand in her sudden grip and that was when Ruth Ann knew. Somehow, she knew she was looking at blood kin. They all knew. This was what else Philip had done. This was what had led to the blackmail.

Della's shoulders shook and Matthew released her hand to

put his arm around her shoulders, holding tight. "I should have… I thought there was more time."

After the woman was sworn in, she took a seat on the witness stand and pulled the little girl onto her lap. The girl was five or six years old, yet tiny enough for a breeze to sweep her away. But her unmistakable nose, eyes, and dark hair spoke of her Indian blood.

Tecumseh left his table to walk towards the woman. The little girl sank deep in her mother's lap, but stared defiantly at the tall man. Tecumseh towered over them.

"Miss Russell, what is your relationship with the defendant?"

The woman coughed, her pale cheeks flaming red momentarily. "No relationship. And it's just plain Kat."

"What was your prior relationship with him, Kat?"

She squirmed. "None. Nothing much that lasted, anyway. He got in with outlaws and I told him I didn't want nothing to do with him ever again."

"Did he tell you what happened on the day his father was killed?"

"I didn't know nothing about it until after it was all done. He come back and said he was in trouble, that he had gotten his daddy killed and helped the Holder gang steal the chief's bank bag and all the Choctaw annuity money."

There was no gentle murmur in the crowd this time. The noise behind Ruth Ann escalated.

Judge Kendrick banged his gavel. "Quiet, the lot of you. This is an inquest and there's no call to get in a ruckus. Yet."

Tecumseh moved to stand beside the witness chair. The young woman folded within herself, arms tight around the little girl.

Tecumseh pointed at Philip, who hadn't raised his head. "Is that the father of your child, the man who told you he participated in the robbery and murder of James Teller?"

The woman jerked her head up. With her staring at Philip,

Ruth Ann could see her face fully. It was aged beyond her young years and dark circles obscured her pretty blue eyes that had once allured her brother and helped destroy the Teller family.

It was Ruth Ann's turn to squeeze her mother's hand hard.

Kat nodded. "That's him."

When Nelson Cobb passed once again on questioning the witness, Ruth Ann nearly leapt out of her seat. She had questions for this woman, and only the grace of God was keeping her from charging to the front. That and her mother's hand.

Kat Russell was conducted back to the small room and Ruth Ann knew nothing would keep her mother from going in there as soon as the court recessed. Her granddaughter was in that room.

Tecumseh called a few other witnesses, clerks and a banker for the Choctaw Nation, but Ruth Ann didn't pay them any mind. Nelson Cobb asked a few questions in between his intense writing.

At the end, Judge Kendrick declared Philip be held over for a jury trial for his crimes against the Choctaw Nation, to take place in four months. The docket was full until then.

The gavel banged.

Della was first on her feet, heading for that small room. She brushed her fingertips on Philip's shoulder as she walked past. Ruth Ann saw Philip shudder and turn to watch as Della entered the room. Matthew followed.

Philip stood along with his lawyer, who was speaking to him, but Philip didn't respond. He turned to meet Ruth Ann's gaze. His eyes watered and he mouthed, *I'm sorry.*

Ruth Ann marched up to Nelson Cobb, gaining the man's full attention. "Why did you let Tecumseh Shoemaker ask us all those harsh questions? You barely objected once!"

Cobb reached for his stack of neat papers, hardly looking at her. "Miss Teller, this inquest was pointless. As I was just saying to my client, we expected this outcome and will do what we can at the trial."

Ruth Ann pinched her lips and impulsively snatched the tidy papers from Nelson Cobb's hands before he could put them in his briefcase. She read quickly down the page. They were notes about the legal ramifications of the Dawes Commission. Nothing to do with Philip's case at all!

"Why you…" Ruth Ann could think of a dozen heathen things to say to this man. Philip reached out to stroke her arm, but she jerked away, refusing to look at him.

Nelson Cobb snatched the papers back. "You may not be aware, but I am working with Chief Jones on critical issues for our people before the election takes place. Time is against our people. As far as this case, there is little hope of winning. No amount of objecting will change the facts."

Ruth Ann clenched her hand into a fist, resisting the urge to slap him and Philip both. She broke away and hurried to the small room, bumping into people who were stretching their legs during the short recess until the next case was called.

A man to her left scoffed as she passed. "Ain't enough the trouble we have with white intruders, we got our own crooking our nation every time we turn around and spit."

Ruth Ann entered the smaller room with more of a rush than she'd intended, only to find it empty of anyone except Della and Matthew. Della sat in a chair by the wall, sobbing. Matthew leaned against the wall with his hand on her shoulder. Ruth Ann noticed a back door that Kat Russell must have escaped through with their flesh and blood.

The little girl was a Teller, and the Teller family had a right to see her, to be a part of her life. Would they ever be able to? So much depended on the outcome of Philip's trial.

And Nelson Cobb wasn't the one for the job.

~

They planned to take a late noon meal with Philip after the inquest, but Nelson Cobb thought it would be best if the family wasn't seen together in McAlester. Ruth Ann was relieved, which made her feel overwhelmed with guilt. But she had no desire to try and swallow food in Philip's presence.

She couldn't hug him when they parted, either. She was the first down the steps of the courthouse and up onto the porch of a notions shop, just out of sight, where she waited for Matthew and their mother. They didn't take long.

Matthew mounted the steps, Della leaning heavily on his arm. Their train home wasn't until later in the afternoon and Ruth Ann saw no point in not laying out her grievances right then.

"Matthew, that lawyer you hired will not do," she said. "He doesn't care anything at all about the case, and is letting Tecumseh Shoemaker run the whole show, making Philip look as guilty as sin."

Matthew bit on his lower lip a moment before answering. "Philip is guilty, Annie. Not to the degree Tecumseh wants to push it, but we have to face the truth—"

"No." Ruth Ann bit off the word. "Let me tell you what is true, Matthew Teller. We were a family once with Philip, and we are going to be a family again in the near future. We knew from the beginning we needed to get the best lawyer for Philip. *Is* Nelson Cobb the best?"

"No."

"Then who is?"

Matthew rubbed Della's hand that was threaded through his arm. It was limp.

"Tecumseh Shoemaker."

All the furious energy in Ruth Ann escaped her. The trial was months away, but they were truly defeated.

"Come on, Annie," Matthew said. "Let's go to the cafe by the depot like we planned. Mama needs a place to sit and rest."

Rest was all they did, hardly touching the food they ordered before going to wait at the depot for their train home. Matthew left them to pick up their bags from the hotel where they were stored. The family had spent the night before to be on time at the courtroom that morning, though none were aware Ruth Ann would be called as the first witness.

It wasn't fair! Why hadn't Nelson Cobb at least tried to prepare them? He was already surrendering.

Ruth Ann was at a loss as to what else they could do. Tecumseh Shoemaker would never consider switching sides. He wanted her brother—her whole family—punished for some reason.

At least she could focus on the case more in the coming months. Matthew had spent the past few weeks hiring more help at the *Choctaw Tribune* to keep up the daily Ruth Ann started. A man named Jasper Smith joined Caleb Gentry in setting type and running the printing press, while Earl Caldwell took care of writing about local events at the school, church, and businesses in Dickens. Matthew wanted to be free to cover the kind of news that would attract subscribers in places like D.C.

He didn't say what he wanted Ruth Ann to do, so she was determined to carve out her own duties at the newspaper, and with Philip's trial.

Ruth Ann and Della were still waiting for Matthew to return with the luggage when the telegraph operator delivered a message to Ruth Ann. She expected it to be from Peter or Beulah. But it was from the last person on her mind.

Ruth Ann Teller: I need to speak with you about your brother. Come stay the night with Sissy.—Pepper Barnes.

CHAPTER 5

It was nearly dark when Ruth Ann got off at the Springstown stop. Della made no objection, but Matthew gave Ruth Ann a sharp look. She'd only told him and Della minutes before the stop that she planned to spend part of the weekend with Sissy Barnes. She hadn't shown him Pepper's telegram, knowing he wouldn't let her go.

But Pepper Barnes knew a lot more about what happened six years ago than he'd ever let on, probably more than Uncle Preston even. Pepper was part of the same search party that found her father and supposedly Philip.

What did Pepper really know about what happened? Ruth Ann intended to drag it from him word by word if she had to, like a dentist extracting a mouthful of teeth.

Ruth Ann caught a ride with a farming family leaving Springstown from the depot. They would pass close enough to the Barnes mansion for Ruth Ann to walk the rest of the way, carpetbag in hand.

It was dark when she approached the house on foot. Strangers wouldn't be able to pick out the bullet hole repairs done to the house after the shootout a few years ago. She and Matthew were there for the political dispute that nearly turned deadly when the two main factions, the Nationals and Progressives, tore into each other. There was no telling what would happen in any incident when the Barnes family was involved.

Dogs barked, alerting the house of a visitor. The front door opened and Pepper Barnes stepped onto the porch. Ruth Ann hoped he wasn't the only one still up.

"Finally," he said. "Did you walk all the way from the depot?"

Ruth Ann went up the steps at a brisk clip. "My apologies, Mr. Barnes. Perhaps if you'd sent a buggy for me, I would have made it sooner." She halted, having no intention of entering the house alone with him. "Where is your sister?"

Movement from the foyer caught Ruth Ann's attention and Sissy came out onto the porch.

"Who is it..." She coughed. "Ruth Ann! What are you doing here? I mean, you are most welcome, it's just I have a head cold and was about to go to bed..."

Ruth Ann raised an eyebrow at Pepper, who shrugged and spoke to his sister. "Ruth Ann and I have some things to talk about."

Sissy coughed into her fist, then shook it at Pepper. "You should have told me she was coming."

"You've been in bed."

"Which would have told anyone with a lick of sense that we shouldn't have company!" Sissy lowered her fist. "Oh, never mind. Come on, my friend, we'll get you settled in the guest room. Whatever my brother wants to speak to you about can wait until morning."

She motioned Ruth Ann past Pepper, who said, "There's no sense in waiting until—"

"Tomorrow," Sissy growled at her brother. As she and Ruth Ann mounted the wide steps leading up from the grand foyer, she asked quietly, "How did the inquest go?"

Ruth Ann shook her head. She just wanted this day to end.

Before dawn broke, Ruth Ann paced the floor of the guest room, then finally dressed and slipped down the hall to Sissy's room. She'd spent many nights in this home as a youth when she and Sissy were close friends before life carried them apart. But her more recent memory of Matthew being cared for in the Barnes mansion after being shot on the road outside of Finley was less than soothing. She was anxious to be home.

Or was she? Matthew would be mad that she'd yielded to Pepper Barnes' message, and her mother, disappointed.

Ruth Ann tapped on Sissy's door. Her friend was normally an early riser like herself.

A groan sounded inside. "Ruth Ann? Come in."

Ruth Ann cracked open the door. "Sissy?"

"I am so sorry, my friend. I'm still under the weather..." She rubbed her eyes. "I wanted you to ride Solomon's Victory this morning."

"It's all right, you rest. I'll be fine."

Ruth Ann closed the door on Sissy's mumbled warning, "Watch out for my brother."

Downstairs, Ruth Ann used the back door to leave the mansion and head for the barn. She wanted to take a ride before breakfast, and especially before her conversation with Pepper.

Morning mist still hung heavy on the grass of the paddocks where dozens of Choctaw horses grazed. Ruth Ann felt a pang for Little Chief, Matthew's bay quarter horse that he lost on the trip. That was another loss caused by Philip. Matthew hadn't mentioned getting another horse yet, though he needed one for his work. This morning, Ruth Ann just needed to be on one to calm her spirit. A ride up the foothills and back would clear her mind and build her courage.

"Morning there, pretty lady." Uncle Solomon, foreman of the

ranch, came out of the barn with pitchfork in hand. "Didn't know you were here visiting."

"I came to see Sissy. Well, honestly, Pepper sent me a telegram and…" Her cheeks flushed. That didn't sound right.

Uncle Solomon chuckled. "No manners at all, that boy. When he was born, I heard the angels singing, 'Look out below, here comes Pepper.'"

Ruth Ann couldn't help the smile that teased her lips. "Everyone should be privy to that warning."

"You looking to ride today?"

"Sissy said I could take Solomon's Victory."

Uncle Solomon grinned and beckoned for Ruth Ann to follow him. "He gets his feed before daybreak. Victory's been king of the stables since that shootout."

Ruth Ann shuddered at the memory of Uncle Solomon getting hit when he went out to save Sissy's horse. This was the first time Ruth Ann had a chance to ride the stunning black Choctaw horse.

Inside the barn, Ruth Ann rubbed the length of Victory's face while Uncle Solomon tacked him up. She said, "The Barnes breed such fine horses. I wish I could take one home for my brother."

Uncle Solomon's eyes twinkled as he tossed a sidesaddle over Victory's back. "Which brother is that now?"

Ruth Ann stilled. His humor fell on a crushed heart.

Uncle Solomon shook his head. "Well, if that wasn't a poor thing to say. I figured your family was just jumping for joy to find out Philip is alive. But I reckon the circumstances could be a lot better."

Ruth Ann smiled briskly at the ranch foreman. "It's all right. God knows."

"That He does. I'll have Victory ready in a jiffy, now."

And he did. Soon, Ruth Ann was mounted sidesaddle and headed for the foothills.

She loped along a worn rut that served as a trail to the pasture where the Barnes allowed their Choctaw horses to roam up into the mountains. The day was overcast, and Uncle Solomon had warned her to head back at the first sign of rough weather.

The trail turned upward, cutting through the pines. This was on the horse herd's way to water at the Kiamichi River. They would likely head down soon, and she'd encounter them. Victory seemed to think so. He filled his lungs beneath her and let out a whinny. A horse answered in return. Only this horse was behind her.

Ruth Ann halted the gelding and listened. Someone was coming. She clenched his mane for balance while she looked back. A lone rider emerged from the wooded trail and rode straight toward her.

"Are you going to hold still long enough for me to tell you what you came to hear?"

Ruth Ann frowned at Pepper as she nudged Victory forward. "I'm trying to decide if I really want to hear what you have to say, Pepper Barnes."

"You won't ever know with your back to me."

She kept the horse moving. "I'm riding sidesaddle. I'd hardly have my back to you if you'd come alongside me."

"Ha. Very funny." Pepper trotted until he was even with her. "You're too much like your brother."

Ruth Ann swallowed. "Which one?"

"The one that always takes a swing at me when we're in the same room."

"Is that what your telegram was about?"

"No. That was about your other brother."

Ruth Ann met Pepper's steady gaze. "Did you know Philip was alive all along?"

"I wasn't sure. Just something best left alone."

She focused on the green wall of trees in front of her, picking out the horse trail and aiming for it. "What made you think you were the best judge of that?"

Pepper reached out and grabbed Victory's reins, making the horse snort in surprise. Ruth Ann wished she had a crop to use on Pepper.

Their horses bumped shoulders and halted side by side. Pepper released the reins. His leg was close to bumping hers and she snapped, "If you so much as—"

"Listen to me, Annie. I can get Philip cleared and home like nothing happened."

Ruth Ann kept her breathing even despite Pepper's closeness. He had tried to kiss her once, not long after Matthew got shot. But no man was going to kiss her except the man she married. And that wasn't Pepper Barnes.

"What on earth are you talking about?" she asked.

"Politics. Influence. I'll take care of the details. You just do your part. I need reports sent back from Washington when we go with the delegation. We work together and everyone wins."

"When *we* go?" Ruth Ann scoffed and gave Victory a nudge with her boot heel, moving him away from Pepper. "You want me to go to D.C. with you, and compromise the *Choctaw Tribune* in your party's favor?"

He frowned. "I'm not stupid. I know Matthew would never let you do what you want, even if it's best for your family."

His arrow hit the mark, but Ruth Ann did her best not to show it. She said nothing, eyes ahead on the trail.

Pepper went on. "Philip betrayed our people. He's going to need all the help he can get. Look, you just report the stories as you see fit. That'll be enough. Your trip will be fully funded and I'll see that you are introduced to influential people in Washington. That'll make your brother happy."

Which one? The echo wouldn't leave her.

And what about Pepper paying for a trip to D.C. for a *Choctaw Tribune* reporter? That sounded dangerously close to a conflict of interest. What would Matthew say?

No, of course. He didn't trust Pepper, and wouldn't trust Ruth

Ann with him either. But then, Matthew hadn't been conscious when Pepper Barnes came roaring in on the road outside of Finley, saving Ruth Ann and Matthew from more of Cub Wassom's bullets. Matthew wasn't on the knoll above the Jessop place with Pepper, with outlaws inside the cabin, holding the family hostage.

In a sense, Ruth Ann knew Pepper better than Matthew did. She had to make this decision.

One thing about Pepper—since she became a reporter for the *Choctaw Tribune*, he treated her as an equal, not a hapless female. There were times he even showed her full respect. But then there were other times like in the parlor that day…

"That sort of trip would need strict guidelines, Pepper Barnes," she said firmly. "You cannot ask me to compromise the newspaper or…or my own integrity."

Pepper gave his horse a light kick and shot out in front of her, halting Victory again. "Then we have a deal?"

Her thoughts went to Pepper's father, Robert Barnes, being acquitted for cutting timber in the Choctaw Nation. Barnes was accused of siphoning off Choctaw resources and found innocent. Was that because he was, or was there an orchestrated reason behind it?

Could the same happen for Philip? The Barnes family held considerable sway in the Nation.

She wanted Pepper to give her more than vague information about his plan, but he wouldn't tell the whole truth. He never did, so there was little point in asking what "politics" and "influence" meant. Maybe he had clout with the judge or even Tecumseh Shoemaker.

The lawyer Matthew hired for Philip wasn't interested in putting their family back together. Ruth Ann had to do some-thing, and this was right in front of her. Literally.

Pepper didn't break his straightforward stare at Ruth Ann. He held it until she wanted to look away, wanted to go home, wanted to see her brother in jail before getting involved with Pepper Barnes like this.

Thunder sounded from the trail in front of them, but it wasn't the storm. A band of purebred Choctaw horses galloped down from the foothill trail straight toward them. Ruth Ann held Victory steady as the band divided, but didn't slow as they raced around them.

Pepper and his horse shielded her from the onslaught. It gave Ruth Ann the sense that Pepper would protect her with his life. He had before when he saved her and Matthew from Cub Wassom.

Hooves thundered and Ruth Ann had difficulty holding Victory steady. He wanted to run with his own.

Pepper turned his horse in a circle and shouted at Ruth Ann, "Scared?"

She gripped Victory's mane and met Pepper's sturdy gaze. He wasn't asking about the running herd and their deadly hooves. He was challenging her to face her fears and trust him.

Pepper Barnes was brash, brunt, and brave—not a refined gentleman, but he never backed down from doing whatever he set out to do.

Ruth Ann pulled Victory's head around to follow the band at a trot as a bolt of lightning flashed through the sky. She murmured, "There's nothing left for me to be afraid of."

Pepper galloped to her side, then matched her pace. "What did you say?"

"When do we leave?"

As soon as she said it, Ruth Ann realized the depth of her commitment. She was going to make a trip all the way to Washington, D.C. and spend weeks there with Pepper Barnes.

Why had her brothers—both of them—forced her to this point?

CHAPTER 6

Ruth Ann trudged down the stairs in the Teller home Monday morning to an empty kitchen. Since returning Saturday afternoon from the Barnes, the family had scarcely spoken to each other. People at church on Sunday noticed. Ruth Ann felt stared at the whole time and was grateful there was no picnic afterwards because of continued rain.

She hadn't dared bring up her D.C. commitment to Matthew or her mother yet, but she needed to soon. The delegation was leaving in one week!

Her breakfast was on the stove, though there was no evidence of anyone else having eaten. But her mother did the dishes lately, even when it was Ruth Ann's turn. The kitchen sparkled.

She went into the living room to see Della's sewing room door was open. Her mother was already working.

Ruth Ann turned back to the kitchen. Matthew had been working, too. She realized this when she put her breakfast plate on the table.

In her usual place was an article she'd written the day before Philip's hearing about a train wreck in Missouri. Matthew had edited it. Harshly.

Ruth Ann deserved the criticism. She'd been awful toward him since the news about Philip, but she didn't know how to apologize.

Perhaps a rewritten article with no complaints would soothe their relationship. Besides, her article *was* terribly written. With getting ready to leave for McAlester, she wasn't able to concentrate on the details, and she'd forgotten to fact-check it.

Breakfast neglected, Ruth Ann worked on the story for half an hour, then rewrote it with pristine penmanship. She took a few bites of her eggs, dumped the remainder in the compost crock, and left the kitchen spotless.

She went to stand in the doorway of Della's sewing room. Della finished cutting a straight seam down a piece of gingham, then laid her scissors aside to give Ruth Ann a strong hug.

Ruth Ann stayed in the hug an extra moment, eyes closed, cheek pressed against her mama's. *"Chim atoksvli yvt katiohmi?"*

Della didn't answer the casual question about her sewing work. She wasn't easily fooled, especially not by her children. She withdrew from the hug. Ruth Ann reluctantly let go.

Della put a hand on each of Ruth Ann's cheeks, frowned, and shook her head. "You need more rest."

Ah, how deep those words went into Ruth Ann's heart. She did need just that, but life prevented it. And now she was about to leave on a trip to Washington, D.C. Who knew how busy she'd be there?

But she knew her mother wasn't talking about physical rest alone. They hadn't sat quietly in a long time to let silence work between them until Ruth Ann's deepest thoughts surfaced and spilled out for her mother to hear and reason and love her through. They certainly hadn't done that since learning Philip was alive. Ruth Ann wanted to hear her mother's heart on that. But not now. Once they cleared Philip and brought him home and Ruth Ann kept her promise to her daddy to forgive her brother, they could talk about it.

Knowing she didn't have the time she needed to let silence do its work, Ruth Ann blurted, "Mama, Pepper Barnes is the most awful young man in the country."

Della chuckled, and Ruth Ann bit her lower lip. Well, it was no surprise Pepper was awful, but Della didn't know the whole story.

"Mama, he wants me to go to D.C. with him. With the Choctaw delegation, that is," she quickly added.

Della grew somber and put her hands on Ruth Ann's cheeks again, studying every pore in her face. It took time, but Ruth Ann knew nothing was hidden from her mother. Whatever she needed to know, she would by studying her daughter.

It took several minutes before Della sighed and dropped her hands. "Tell me everything."

Della returned to cutting the fabric while Ruth Ann stood on the other side of her work table, relating the time at the Barnes' with raw honesty.

Della continued to work after Ruth Ann finished the short tale. In that moment, Ruth Ann knew she had her mother's permission to go to D.C. Not necessarily approval, but permission. It would have to do.

She started to leave, but Della took her into her arms again and whispered, "Do what is right."

Ruth Ann nodded against her mother's hair. "I will, Mama."

And she would. The right thing was to bring Philip home.

Ruth Ann took her hat from its hook by the front door and headed for the newspaper office. It was still raining.

Inside the shop, she felt as much at home as in the box house. The scent of freshly cut lumber from the Levitts' work mixed with the tangy smell of ink from the *Choctaw Tribune* side of the building. The sounder clacked away happily in the lean-to telegraph office.

The shop was full with Peter in the telegraph office and people in for Monday's business. Beulah conversed with two sets of customers near the back of the shop while Mr. Levitt examined the chair he was repairing.

All was well, except for a new, painfully slow *click click.*

Ruth Ann removed her soggy hat and stared at an odd sight that made her giggle. Matthew sat at his desk for the first time since his return, pecking one finger at a time on the keys of a brand new typewriter. His eyebrows scrunched together in concentration, oblivious to the world around him.

Beulah excused herself from the customers now conversing with her father and said across the room, "As you can see, your brother is making yet another improvement. He claims he can keep up with a daily better since a typewriter is faster than handwriting."

Ruth Ann couldn't help outright laughing. Faster?

Matthew pecked one long finger at a time to stamp a letter on the white sheet of paper pinned in the contraption. He didn't glance up when he said, "It only works if you're here to use it."

Fire flared in Ruth Ann's stomach. So. He was upset she was late. Or that she was away most of Saturday. Well, perhaps he felt a little of the frustration she had when he was gone for so long in the dangerous coal mining country without sending word.

Ruth Ann chided herself. She was there to make amends, and it was better if Matthew was in a good mood when she announced her D.C. trip. Going to his desk, she laid the article over the keys of the typewriter.

He read it, eyes moving back and forth rapidly. The moment reminded her of the first time she'd ever given him a front-page story, and she found herself holding her breath now.

He didn't glance up as he laid the article on a pile of messy papers. "Better than it was, but not as good as it could be."

Heat rushed to Ruth Ann's face. "I made every change you marked!"

Matthew glanced up sharply at her, then at the customers behind her.

Ruth Ann lowered her voice. "I did my best. If that's not good enough, I guess you can fire me."

"If I did, who would get us new subscribers in D.C.?"

"I—how did you…?"

Her brother could keep secrets about life and death. She couldn't keep a trip she hadn't even planned out from him. No wonder he was in a sharp mood about the article.

He said, "Pepper Barnes wired the Frisco depot this morning with arrangements for your train ticket. I don't think you should get involved with him."

"I can handle Pepper Barnes."

Matthew leaned back in his chair, staring at his new typewriter. "I guess since you've been to Chicago with a fraudulent teacher, you can go to the Nation's capitol with a load of Choctaw politicians bent on getting their way, and a young Nationalist with an explosive temper and no manners."

She sighed. "Matthew, you're doing what you believe is best for this family. That's what I'm doing. You'll just have to trust me like I've trusted you."

Ruth Ann wondered if she and her brother would ever fully trust each other again.

She took the train wreck article to the typesetting cabinet. In a way, she was disappointed Matthew wasn't objecting more. She expected him to make a big fuss. Maybe Matthew was glad to be rid of her for a while.

Did neither of her brothers care about her?

She donned an apron to set type on the article. What a wreck life could become.

CHAPTER 7

$\mathcal{R}$uth Ann was working the telegraph Saturday morning when one came through from none other than Pepper Barnes.

Change your ticket. We leave Sunday afternoon.

It wasn't even addressed to her, as though he somehow knew she was on the wire that morning while Matthew finished articles for Monday's edition and Peter ran the press.

She'd heard nothing from Pepper all week, and now this scant message to be ready to leave tomorrow! Only Pepper Barnes would have such ill-regard for the Sabbath and her personal schedule.

He only had one thing on his mind—Pepper Barnes. Whatever he wanted, whatever his goals, ambition, or work, it came first.

Well, she'd fix him. She fired a telegram back.

I will be ready to leave Monday as planned.

Moments later, the reply came. *Then you need not be ready at all.*

Ruth Ann restrained herself from whacking the sounder. She

clenched her fists and pecked out another message, not caring that every operator on the line heard her.

Ruth Ann: You are impossible.

Pepper: And you are stubborn.

At least I have respect for others.

Except me.

Ruth Ann sputtered. Did Pepper think she didn't respect him? Well, now that he mentioned it...

Ruth Ann: You are right.

Pepper: Fine. Now change the ticket at the depot. The rest of the delegation is leaving a day early.

Ruth Ann stopped herself from replying. Pepper could pop off responses all day, and everyone on the wire would hear it. The gossip would spread through every town in the Choctaw Nation.

Ruth Ann satisfied herself with not responding. Let Pepper stand awkwardly in the telegraph office in Springstown, awaiting a reply that would never come. She would be ready tomorrow, but she didn't need to tell him. Give him something to *not* know, since he knew everything else.

A few minutes passed, then a message came from up the line at station *Tn.* Her friend, "D."

D: Sounded like quite a love spat, little RA.

RA: Please do not call it that. I cannot even stand to be around him.

D: That is what women say after a spat.

RA: Not you too. I do not like him, yet I am forced to work with him.

D: Your misfortune, his fortune. I know you will make out grandly. You are a sweet little thing.

RA: Thank you. At least someone thinks so.

Ruth Ann leaned away from the sounder. Nothing in this world was the same, not even chatting with D.

She was about to embark on a journey to D.C. with men in the throes of the greatest controversies her tribe faced since the forced Removal in the 1830s. And she was leaving her family behind with unresolved conflicts.

Della and Matthew had made a trip to see Philip that week. Ruth Ann couldn't bring herself to even think of him except with wondering if Pepper was right, that they could bring Philip home with nothing hanging over him. Once they did that, she could forgive him. Couldn't she?

In the newspaper office, Matthew pecked away on his typewriter, the clicks painfully slow. Was he thinking the same things she was? There was no way for her to know.

For the first time, she was glad to be going far away.

Peter entered the telegraph office, disrupting her thoughts. "Print job's done. Don't you have an appointment with Lance to keep?"

Ruth Ann frowned at him. "What? Oh, yes."

She collected herself and left the shop without mentioning the change of her travel plans to Matthew. She reluctantly went to the depot and switched her ticket for tomorrow afternoon, the first train departing after church.

She wove through the heavy Saturday traffic, heading to the Warren home. Dickens was getting too crowded for her liking, but it was good for business. Their income had grown since starting the daily, and Ruth Ann decided to take extra funds with her to D.C. She wouldn't let Pepper pay for everything.

As she approached the front porch, she noted movement at the side of the house and diverted her steps to find Lance Fuller there, kneeling by a bicycle with his back to her, fiddling with the chain.

"Sorry I'm late, Lance."

"Good timing, just finished fixing this." He turned with a grin.

Ruth Ann stared at him. A lump the size of an egg protruded from his left temple. She frowned. "You assured me riding a bicycle was safe."

"Huh?" Lance swiped greasy hands on the old trousers he wore. "Oh."

He touched his forehead, leaving a black mark, his grin turning sheepish. "Amarillo and I have some things to work out in our communication methods."

Ruth Ann cocked her head, eyebrows raised.

He laughed. "I snuck into the kitchen and came up behind her, and well, it wasn't entirely proper, but...I tickled her. I'm just glad the closest pot to her was empty, not full of hot soup."

Ruth Ann suppressed a giggle. "Indeed."

"Ready to learn how to ride around the Ark?"

"Is that truly what you call this home now?"

"Aunt Susan started it. She said this is a place where we can be sheltered from the floods of life. It's not the Warren place or the Fullers or Jessops. It's the Ark, open to shelter anyone."

Ruth Ann nodded and eyed the bicycle, chewing her lip. She wore an older gingham dress with the hem tacked higher for this occasion.

She had seen women riding bicycles in Chicago and Lance had his, but she truly wondered how it compared to riding a horse. Especially astride! It seemed scandalous, but when she told Lance she was going to D.C., he insisted on teaching her how to ride a bicycle, assuring her it was the best way to get around the city, and that it was perfectly acceptable for young ladies to do. Still, Ruth Ann asked if they could practice in the privacy of the home's backyard.

Lance showed her the parts of the lady's bicycle, built slightly different from his own. He bought this one in Paris, Texas a few days before, hoping to teach Amarillo to ride so they could take them on outings.

"Once she sees how easy it is for you, it shouldn't take much to convince her," he said.

"I wouldn't bet a pot on that."

Lance winced. "I did learn she doesn't respond well to surprises."

Ruth Ann gripped the handles of the bicycle the way Lance instructed her before carefully stepping over the low bar, eyeing the chain and pedals with suspicion.

"Suppose my skirt…"

Her face reddened at the thought of her skirt getting chewed up by the moving chain, pulling her dress right off!

"You'll be fine," Lance said. "Women ride with full skirts all the time. Now, watch how I balance and turn."

Lance retrieved his bicycle from where it leaned against the side of the house and mounted. He pushed off with one foot, then planted both feet on the pedals. He pumped them, and the bicycle wheels rolled easily over the tramped-down yard and around the large garden.

It looked so simple.

Lance rolled back to her and stopped with a confident smile. He dismounted and leaned the bicycle against the wall. "The pedals on your bicycle are easy to push and once you get going, balancing and turning is no problem. Try it."

Ruth Ann swallowed and glanced over her shoulder to make sure no one was watching. She placed her left foot on the pedal, all her weight on her right foot. She gave a hard push off the ground and lifted her right foot, struggling to find the pedal.

She never did. The ground rushed toward her.

Lance broke her fall, but she still hit her side and the handlebar banged her hand.

"Are you all right?" Lance sounded breathless, like he'd been the one to take the fall. He quickly pulled the contraption away.

Ruth Ann's hip hurt, but she couldn't dare say so in front of Lance.

"I…I suppose so. I believe the lesson is over for today."

He helped her to her feet. "Let's try again. I'll stay closer next time."

God willing, there would never be a "next time." She would do well to walk home with the soreness. "Thank you for trying."

"Ruth Ann." Lance stepped in front of her. "I've been thinking about your trip, and I'm worried."

She chuckled. "There are other means of transportation around a city, Lance."

"No, I mean about the city itself." He lifted the bicycle upright and rolled it to join his beside the house. "I grew up there. You're walking into a lion's den with those politicians…I wish I were going with you, not that Pepper Barnes."

"You think I'm incapable of handling him and politicians at the same time?"

"You're one of the most capable women I know." He shrugged. "But I still don't fancy you roaming around there alone."

"I did well enough in Chicago."

"Don't forget, I was with you."

"Exactly. I know how to handle scoundrels."

He smiled. "That, you do."

"I'll be alright." *God willing.* "You just keep an eye on everyone in the Ark, and please take my family in as often as you can. We need sheltering right now."

Ruth Ann asked her family not to see her off at the depot. She wanted everyone to stay at church for fellowship while she slipped quietly away after goodbyes.

When the time came, she began making her rounds with Uncle Preston's family and close friends from the Ark. It took an hour, which she planned for, with hugs sawnd advice and requests for Ruth Ann. They wanted her to take note of certain sights, bring home a special gift, caution her not to walk about alone at night.

She took this in stride, knowing she could digest it later. Her mind was on her steamer trunk and travel bag at home, wondering what all she'd forgotten to pack. Oh well, whatever it was would simply be forgotten.

If only the bad things could be forgotten as easily as the good.

Ruth Ann kissed her mother's cheek last, and Matthew accompanied her to help with the baggage. He hauled her trunk across the road from the box house to the depot.

At church, he'd said little, and she wondered if he would admonish her to do a good job as a reporter, tell her what all he expected in her articles.

He didn't.

That took a restraint from him that discouraged Ruth Ann. He didn't care that she was going, which left her with the feeling he didn't care at all.

Mounting the steps to the depot platform cast in a shadow by the sun overhead, she halted out of foot traffic, though there weren't many travelers today. The train whistle blew in the distance. In minutes, she'd be loaded and on her way.

Matthew lowered Ruth Ann's steamer trunk he'd born across his back. Four weeks was a long spell, and she couldn't be seen wearing the same dress more than twice. Actually, she shouldn't wear a dress more than once, but no one would know except the Choctaw delegation she was with. And they wouldn't notice her much.

Ruth Ann's stomach felt queasy, her resolve weakening as she thought of four solid weeks of close contact with Pepper Barnes. How much easier, how much better it would be to remain home —to live at Uncle Preston's awhile and forget about Philip being alive, forget her resolve to bring him home. If Philip wanted to come home and make things right with the family, he could find a way on his own. She couldn't do this!

But where did that leave her mother, and her promise at her daddy's grave?

And thine ears shall hear a word behind thee, saying, This is the way, walk ye in it...

The train pulled in and Matthew made sure her trunk was loaded in the baggage car. He came back to her as she put one hand on the passenger car rail. She looked back. Why didn't he stop her?

He stared into her eyes a long moment, then said, "I'll be here when you get back."

Matthew took her elbow to help her on board. She gave in. There was no stopping now.

CHAPTER 8

At the Springstown stop, Ruth Ann avoided looking out the window to the platform. When boarding in Dickens, she checked the cars and sat in the most crowded one, which was only half full. Several people got off in Springstown, unfortunately. Only one got in her car.

Pepper Barnes.

He greeted her with a simple, "Ruth Ann," when he stretched to stow his carpetbag in the rack above the bench seat across from her.

After securing the bag, he dropped into the seat, leaned forward, and loosened his coat from being pinned against the seat.

"We need to go over things before Forbis Kanitobe boards at Tushkahomma," he said, as if their public telegraph exchange never took place.

Ruth Ann said nothing. The train jolted and pulled away from the depot.

Pepper stopped fidgeting and looked at her. "Are you going to act like a fickle female every time you don't like something I say? If so, you aren't going to do me or your brother any good."

Ruth Ann pressed her lips tight.

Pepper frowned. "You're doing it."

Ruth Ann sighed. "We need to make peace. I won't pout when you are rude and you will treat me decently, especially when we're in public."

"Fair enough. Now, this is how things are lined up."

As he talked about who would join them for the trip, including a man named Forbis Kanitobe and his wife, Pepper became more animated than Ruth Ann had seen him in a long while. He was convinced the Nationals would successfully dismantle the Dawes Commission once Jefferson Gardner was elected chief. It was only a matter of time before things settled down in the Choctaw Nation and they had full control of governing themselves again.

When Pepper came to this part, Ruth Ann knew his mind was on how he would be one of those governing. Folks said he was destined for politics. His father sent him to college and he graduated this year before most young men his age. He was as sharp as an ax blade, some said.

Still, people didn't trust Pepper to always be straight with them or to put others before himself. They did know he would fight to the death for what he believed in. And right then, he believed in sovereignty for the Choctaw people, making him popular enough for politics, even at his young age.

One thing Pepper didn't know was about Ruth Ann's own connection to the President of the United States. Ruth Ann needed to keep that to herself for the time being, or Pepper would never let her have a moment's peace until she got him an appointment with Grover Cleveland.

"In D.C., we're staying at Roseland House," he went on. "It's no ordinary boarding house. It's one of the finest homes in D.C. that hosts guests from around the world. Senator Newman of Georgia will be there, and I heard his two daughters are there for their summer vacation. They're about your age, so you should be able to make friends with them easy enough."

"You sound like that belongs on my list of responsibilities."

"Gaining Newman's support is at the top of my agenda for this trip," Pepper said. "He can introduce me to the most powerful men in the country, and could become a voice for the Choctaw people on the floor of Congress. And he's an old friend of my father's. They grew up together."

That didn't reassure Ruth Ann.

Pepper continued, "If we can convince Newman to become sympathetic to our people retaining our national sovereignty, he can help in booting Senator Dawes out of Indian Territory. The closer we get to Newman and his family, the better."

That sounded dangerously close to compromises and manipulation. Ruth Ann decided to try a new tactic to gain a measure of control with Pepper. "How is your sister?"

"She's fine. At Roseland's, there will also be—"

"She wasn't well when I was there. Has she recovered completely?"

"Completely."

Ruth Ann smiled. "Good. Now what were you saying?"

Pepper acknowledged her moment with a cocked eyebrow. "At Roseland's is also a Choctaw full-blood lawyer named Benjamin Nakishi. He's an anomaly, graduated Harvard and is one of the best lawyers in D.C., best our tribe could ever hope to have. He's also top of the agenda. We have to convince him to return home and fight for our people before we lose our sovereignty forever. Jefferson Gardner and I need him once Gardner is elected as chief and we Nationals get the nation on track again."

Ruth Ann straightened when Pepper mentioned the word "lawyer" and tried to pay close attention to Pepper's explanation, surprised to learn there was such an accomplished Choctaw lawyer in D.C. Her attention faded when Pepper brought it back to his politics.

Then he said, "You have the best chance of convincing him."

Ruth Ann blinked, realizing she missed part of what Pepper said. "Why is that?"

He spoke painfully slow. "I'll…say it…again."

"Don't use that patient tone with me, Pepper Barnes."

"Then stop trying my patience. Half the time you're mad at me is because you're not paying attention when I say something friendly to you."

"I'm listening now."

He nodded. "Like I said, you're a model of the good that comes from our people, and will show Nakishi we are still worth fighting for."

As the train chugged northward, Pepper continued filling her in on the plans. The United States midterm elections were coming, and Pepper wanted to take advantage of that, especially with Senator Newman. There was no better place to learn how to play politics than D.C.

At the Tushkahomma stop, Pepper stood to greet a man and woman entering their car. He introduced them to Ruth Ann as Mr. and Mrs. Forbis Kanitobe, then re-seated himself—right beside Ruth Ann.

Forbis Kanitobe seemed to watch her closely. Was he wondering if she was a full-blood or mixed like Pepper?

At Skullyville, they stood to stretch and greet the rest of the delegation joining them. The four women now in the group sat together, while the men split into two groups of four.

The conglomeration leaving Choctaw Nation in the Indian Territory for the United States of America and its capitol, Washington, D.C., was conjoined.

While the women talked of homemaking and children, Ruth Ann mulled over the conversation with Pepper and the part about the Choctaw lawyer that was *not* Tecumseh Shoemaker. She might not need to depend on Pepper to get Philip home after all, with his back room deals and threats or whatever he had in mind.

If this Benjamin Nakishi really was the best lawyer, she knew exactly why she wanted to convince him to return to the Choctaw Nation.

CHAPTER 9

The Baltimore and Potomac Railroad Station in Washington, D.C. was nothing like the train station in Chicago. Oh, it was the same in that there were more people about than Ruth Ann could comprehend, so exiting the Pullman Sleeper Car was a similar experience. But the atmosphere was charged with historical tension and a sense of awe.

Ruth Ann had arrived in the capitol of the United States.

They would be in D.C. through the 4th of July, which Ruth Ann couldn't help feeling a tingle of excitement over. Her family normally celebrated her peoples' part in founding the United States with fireworks and food at Uncle Preston's but what would it be like to do it in the nation's capitol? Chief Pushmataha took part in the War of 1812, earning him his request to be buried in the Congressional Cemetery with full military honors.

The extraordinary dome of the station soared fifty-five feet in the air, according to the guidebook Ruth Ann found on the train. It was Victorian Gothic of pressed red brick and belt courses of Ohio freestone. In the lower level they entered were waiting rooms, baggage rooms, and ticket offices.

The delegation of Choctaws gathered close and waited for the porters to offload their steamer trunks and suitcases. Ruth Ann excused herself from the other ladies to step up to one of the office windows marked *telegraph*.

When the operator acknowledged her, she turned over her brief message and coins to send it home. It was incredible to think of how much faster her words would arrive than she could herself. The modern world she lived in was so unlike her ancestors, who had been in this city before her.

Their luggage was loaded onto a cart and Ruth Ann watched it pulled away. She followed the delegation through the crowd and outside to see the row of shiny black buggies with matched horses and also the less attractive cabs lining the street outside the station. She halted and gazed in wonder.

Magnolia trees and their creamy white blooms lined the streets. A block down, she caught sight of the Center Market with its huge American flag and black chimney high above the largest fresh grocery market in the country. Hundreds of vendors were set up in the booths to supply the growing urban population.

What left her awestruck, though, was her first look at the distinctive neoclassical style of the United States Capitol Building up the hill from the station with the botanical garden sitting by it. It was like a scene from the White City at the Chicago World's Fair, only this building was real and permanent.

"Ruth Ann!"

She jerked her gaze around to see Pepper waving from next to one of the carriages, and realized the rest of the group had already boarded in three. Pepper held the door to an open carriage as she approached.

"Hurry up, these carriages were rented for us," he said. "There'll be time to gawk later."

As Ruth Ann allowed Pepper to hand her into the carriage, she was struck by the fact that the carriages had been arranged for them.

When the route took them past the Smithsonian Institution's Castle, the Agriculture Department, and the tallest structure of its kind in the world, the Washington Monument, she wondered if this was the quickest route or if they were already being courted and cajoled by whatever politician sent them the fancy carriages instead of ordinary cabs.

It reminded her of stories the Grandmother told of Choctaw chiefs who were well treated, overly so at times, when they went to negotiations at the nation's capitol. There were valuable resources in the Choctaw Nation.

That wasn't her only worry. Pepper sat too close to her in the carriage, with Forbis Kanitobe and his wife across from them. It seemed to her that Forbis was more interested in watching Pepper and Ruth Ann than he was in the magnificent sights on the glorious early summer day.

When they passed President's Park and then the President's House on Pennsylvania Avenue, she wished they could take photographs. But she didn't have the courage before she left Dickens to ask Matthew about bringing his camera, and he didn't offer it.

Several blocks later, Pepper motioned to the fine homes lining the narrow street in the neighborhood they entered. He spoke in a gentlemanly tone to Ruth Ann and the Kanitobes.

"This is Georgetown, where Roseland House is. There are ample restaurants within walking distance, along with shops and parks. We should be comfortable here."

Forbis folded his arms across his chest and stared at Pepper. "We aren't here to be comfortable."

Ruth Ann ignored the tension between them as she took in the street lined with shops and well-dressed couples. The road was crowded with traffic, as were the sidewalks.

The three carriages with the Choctaw delegation wound to a stop in front of a five story mansion. Ruth Ann held her awe in check. After all, she had stayed in one of the finest homes in

Chicago during the World's Fair and saw marvelous sights there. But she couldn't help being impressed by this fine house. A sign in the trimmed yard read *Roseland House*. This was her new home for the next four weeks.

Pepper was attentive to Ruth Ann as they disembarked the carriage, making sure her skirt didn't get caught in the door. He was taking his promise to be nice, seriously. He even carried her valise along with his, leaving Ruth Ann's hands-free to itch for her tablet.

As soon as they were up the steps and inside the grand foyer, she tucked herself in a corner and withdrew the tablet and pencil from her reticule and jotted notes of her first impressions, including her people's connections to the city for the past hundred-plus years.

She heard a voice, thick with a foreign accent, greeting the delegation. Ruth Ann was barely able to finish her notes as the lady swept around them.

"Welcome, welcome to you all. I am Mrs. Gertrud Schmitt, hostess of Roseland; or as some call me, the mother hen of the roost."

Everyone chuckled politely as the lady directed four footmen and five maids that scattered with the delegation's luggage and hats. At the same time, she gave the house guidelines for the new guests.

"While breakfast and the noon meal are informal, dinner is at seven sharp and you are expected to let us know if you will attend since many of you have meetings and appointments outside the home in the evenings. Curfew is at 10p.m. If you will be out later, please alert us beforehand, and the footman can let you in through the kitchen door. With your arrival, we are filled to capacity! But please, do not hesitate to let me or the staff know how we can make your stay here pleasant."

Mrs. Schmitt turned the quiet group over to the household staff, who led them in pairs up the grand staircase. Ruth Ann was relieved when she and Pepper parted ways at the top. He was led to the east wing where the single men stayed. The married couples were taken to the south wing and Ruth Ann followed a maid carrying her bag to the west wing where single ladies stayed. She learned from the maid that she was sharing a suite with three others.

She followed the maid into a large sitting room. Two doors to the right were open, revealing bedrooms with two double size beds each. The maid led her to the one on the left where Ruth Ann saw her steamer trunk was already deposited.

Knowing the routine from her time in Chicago, she allowed the maid to unpack her things while she freshened in the washroom. She had just finished when the door to the sitting room opened to the sound of giggles.

The maid had left, and Ruth Ann hoped for a few moments of privacy to gather herself before interacting with anyone. But she put on a pleasant smile and stepped through the bedroom door to greet the three young ladies who entered the sitting room, unaware of her presence. Ruth Ann cleared her throat, hoping not to startle them, but was unsuccessful.

A youthful blonde teenage girl turned and gasped, her fingers going to her lips. The other two young women, who appeared slightly older, maintained their composure.

Had they ever met an Indian? Ruth Ann would try to make a good first impression, using the social graces she'd learned the past few years. "I am Ruth Ann Teller of Dickens, Indian Territory. I hope you were expecting me?"

The older blonde stepped forward, her facial features matching the younger ones. Shoulders square, she offered her hand to shake. Ruth Ann returned it.

"I'm Virginia Lee Newman. This is my friend, Agatha Green." She gestured to the petite red head. "We are sharing the bedroom next to yours."

She turned to the youngest girl, who smiled tentatively. "This is my sister, Georgia Pearl. You must excuse her behavior, she's high strung. You'll be sharing the bedroom with her."

Ruth Ann repeated their names to solidify them. "It's nice to meet you, Miss Virginia Lee, Miss Agatha, and Miss Georgia Pearl. I hope we have an opportunity to get to know one another during my stay here."

As soon as the words were out, her mind finally caught up with the familiar surname. *Newman.*

These were the daughters of the senator Pepper wanted her to get close to. She was glad she hadn't made the connection first. She wasn't in the habit of greeting people kindly with the intent of manipulating them.

Virginia Lee unpinned her hat and hung it by the door. She turned back to Ruth Ann. "I understand you're a newspaper reporter. That's admirable, and so progressive for someone from the west."

"I've never really thought of myself as progressive."

There was a strange gleam in Virginia Lee's eyes. "I have a feeling we have a lot to teach one another."

Ruth Ann had the same feeling, which left her uneasy.

CHAPTER 10

That evening, Ruth Ann stood behind the folding screen to change into one of her new evening dresses, a muted pink satin trimmed with lace. With its leg-o-mutton sleeves and flared skirt in an inverted tulip shaped bell, it was enough to make a statement that she wasn't simply a hick from Indian Territory.

She bought it ready-made at a store in Paris, Texas, the week before the trip, along with several other pieces that Beulah helped her select to be reserved but fashionable. She gave into purchasing a bicycle riding outfit, too.

Georgia Pearl lost her bashfulness with Ruth Ann as they prepared for dinner that evening. From the washroom, Georgia Pearl chattered about how much fun Ruth Ann was going to have during her time in D.C., promising to show her all the gardens, monuments, and museums.

Ruth Ann started to interrupt her, let her know that she was there for business, not pleasure. But she didn't want to be rude. Besides, Georgia Pearl's fifteen years of age left Ruth Ann to doubt the young lady could go many places on her own. The girl was looking forward to her debutante year of sixteen when young beaus could really begin courting her.

Georgia Pearl's giggles reminded Ruth Ann of how youthful days sounded. Ruth Ann halted, adjusting the lace she had added to the swoop neckline to make it modest. Her mind went to her family back home, most especially Philip and how she had not once embraced him. He was Lazarus back from the dead, and untouchable for the moment.

This young lady had not known these kinds of pain. Georgia Pearl would face them someday and realize life was far beyond gardens and beaus. What was on the other side, Ruth Ann was still struggling to comprehend.

Ruth Ann moved to the vanity to put on her high heeled white slippers trimmed with matching pink bows. She was grateful Beulah had talked her into the extraordinary wardrobe. Mr. Nakishi, the future lawyer for Philip, was staying at Roseland House and she would meet him at dinner. She wasn't in complete agreement with Pepper, but if the Choctaw delegation impressed him enough—if *she* impressed him enough—he might think it a worthwhile cause to return to Indian Territory.

Georgia Pearl came out of the washroom with a dramatic sigh. "I read in a magazine once that ladies needed to be cautious when a young man proposes. She may feel faint, breathless, and overheated. The writer warned it might simply be that her corset is too tight. I made a vow that I would never accept a proposal until I had a chance to loosen my corset."

Ruth Ann smiled as she stood, checking the balance of the new heels. She glanced up at Georgia Pearl, the picture of a true Gibson girl, all decked out in voluminous hair, held with a shell comb and ringlets framing her face.

Ruth Ann was genuine when she said, "I'm glad you're prepared. I'm sure you'll face many proposals in the near future."

Georgia Pearl intertwined her fingers, stretching her arms straight out. "Oh, I wish I was already a debutante! We would have such fun." She hesitated. "You aren't too old to be courted, are you?"

Ruth Ann laughed, and they exited the bedroom to find the sitting room empty. The open door of the other bedroom told them Virginia Lee and Agatha had already left. Georgia Pearl gave another dramatic sigh.

"My sister and Agatha are supposed to join us at dinner this evening, but they have functions and meetings at all hours. Never mind them, let's get you introduced to all the eligible men staying at Roseland!"

Ruth Ann rolled her eyes. The last thing she needed were young men vying for her affections. She wore a loosened corset in that department.

But when they came to the top of the stairs where the three wings met and there stood Pepper Barnes, she still blushed. He was gussied up in a suit and tie, hands folded like a gentleman.

"Good evening, Ruth Ann. You look just fine."

She held back the snappy response that she wanted to give, asking why he felt the need to say she passed his inspection. But they had made a truce on the train, and she'd respect that as long as he did.

"You as well, Pepper."

"Hello, Mr. Barnes," Georgia Pearl sounded breathless. "You remember me, Georgia Pearl?"

Pepper bowed slightly at her. "Younger daughter of Senator Newman of…Georgia?"

He seemed to force out the polite words at how the names matched. Ruth Ann smiled to herself, wondering if Pepper thought the girl was silly, but needed to be nice to her because of her father's political position.

Pepper offered Ruth Ann his arm. She hesitated and then accepted it, while reaching behind her to hook her free hand in Georgia Pearl's arm to bring her along.

Georgia Pearl took no coaxing as they went down the wide

stairs. "Mr. Barnes, you must share all the news about your territory. It's causing quite a stir in my father's circles, and I know he will be most interested in hearing about you. About the territory, that is."

They arrived in the half-full dining room a few minutes before seven. Gertrude Schmitt was right when she said many of her guests took their meals out, and Ruth Ann suspected she might be doing the same in the coming evenings. But for now, it was nice to dine in the place they were staying for their time in D.C. and achieve a settled feeling.

No one was seated yet and Georgia Pearl took great delight introducing the new comers to long-time guests. Ruth Ann searched the unfamiliar faces for a man who was full-blood Indian—the lawyer she wanted to convince to take Philip's case. But no one outside their own party fit the bill.

The first introduction was to Georgia Pearl's father, Senator Newman. His mannerism was that of a true southern gentleman, but given his association with the Barnes family, Ruth Ann was inclined to give him a wide berth. Especially with Pepper's sugarcoated words to the senator of how progressive Indian Territory was becoming. They also met a man with a charming British accent, and a few other associates of the senator's.

Gertrude Schmitt rang a small hand bell, calling them to take their seats at the table. Virginia Lee and Agatha Green made a quiet appearance, coming in through the kitchen door.

To Ruth Ann's amazement, Pepper pulled out a chair for her, behaving like a perfect gentleman.

Once everyone was seated and grace said, chatter around the table started, mainly with questions directed at the Choctaw delegation. But a disturbance at the doorway caught Ruth Ann's attention.

She looked over her shoulder to spot a red-haired man hanging his derby hat on the hook outside the door and coming into the room without pausing his long stride. "Well, good evening all!"

Senator Newman gestured at the middle-aged man. "This is Joseph Griffin. Don't let his Irish charm fool you, he's as American as the grandson of an immigrant can be."

Joseph Griffin greeted those around the table but zeroed in on Ruth Ann. "And who might this astonishing young lady be?"

Ruth Ann smiled, detecting only a hint of an Irish accent.

Senator Newman answered, "Joseph, you will be most interested in getting to know this young lady from Indian Territory. You two have something unique in common."

"A pleasure to meet you, Mr. Griffin," Ruth Ann said. "I'm Ruth Ann Teller, one of the reporters and publishers of the *Choctaw Tribune* newspaper."

"Delighted!" Joseph plopped into a seat across from her. "This is stupendous. I heard a reporter was descending on Roseland but I had no idea she was so beautiful."

Ruth Ann tried to handle the compliment graciously. "Thank you, Mr. Griffin." She diverted her attention by glancing at Pepper to introduce him, only to see him twirling his steak knife, lips pressed tight. His amiable attitude had vanished.

Thankfully, Forbis Kanitobe engaged Senator Newman in a conversation about the Dawes Commission, drawing Pepper's attention to that.

Ruth Ann took the opportunity to talk to Joseph Griffin. "Senator Newman said we have something in common, Mr. Griffin. What would that be?"

He grinned as he buttered his roll. "Please, no Mr. Griffin, not 'til I'm old and decrepit which won't be long given the way my bones creak every frost, though I'm not quite to forty. But as long as I can hold a pencil, I'll be in the field and be called Joseph by charming young women, the likes of yourself."

He winked, and Ruth Ann should have been embarrassed by

his boldness but she felt no threat from Joseph Griffin as he continued, "I'm a reporter for the Associated Press."

Ruth Ann couldn't help the grin on her face. He laughed. "I can see that you and I shall have splendid times together in the coming weeks, swapping trade secrets and war stories."

He rightly judged that she was thrilled to be sitting across the table from an AP reporter. Wait until Matthew heard about this!

Her heart jolted at the thought, and she wondered if Matthew would care.

But she wouldn't let that spoil the moment. "That is thrilling, Mister, that is, Joseph. I am anxious to hear about your work and learn more about the AP. I know it only by reputation."

"Well, we shall fix that and we will get your newspaper subscribed to boot."

Over the conversation about the Dawes Commission and reaching Ruth Ann at the far end of the table, Virginia Lee's voice cast a question at her. "Miss Teller, do you know of our own Choctaw here at Roseland?"

Gertrude Schmitt entered the conversation. "Benjamin Nakishi is a fine man. We treasure having him at Roseland, although it's so scarce we see him."

Pepper turned to their hostess. "I thought he would be at dinner tonight. When will he be back?"

Gertrude Schmitt started to answer, but Virginia Lee came in from down the table again. "Since he no longer lives with Judge Eldridge, his mentor, he stays at Roseland when he's in the city."

Georgia Pearl added in a stage whisper that all could hear, "But he's so consumed by work since his heartbreak, we hardly see him around here."

Pepper frowned. "Heartbreak?"

Ruth Ann could tell from the look on Pepper's face that he was less concerned with the man's personal feelings as he was about how those might affect him returning to Indian Territory to fight for the Choctaw people.

Georgia Pearl went on in a normal tone. "We really shouldn't talk about it, but he was engaged to the judge's daughter for simply years, before she broke it off and went to New York, or Europe, or...somewhere. It was a heartbreaking scandal."

Gertrude Schmitt cleared her throat loudly. "You made an excellent point, Miss Newman. Someone's personal feelings are not appropriate for dinnertime conversations. If you wish to speak of Benjamin, you can talk about how well respected and admired he is in professional and social circles throughout the city."

Joseph Griffin added, "He's one of the smartest lawyers in the city, and has never lost a case. But he's on his most challenging one now, the first Supreme Court case he's argued."

Pepper, still sounding agitated, asked, "If he's hardly ever here, where does he spend his off time?"

Senator Newman answered, "He scarcely has any free time, but he's known to visit the Congressional Cemetery after he leaves his office, which is often quite late. He likes to visit the graves of some Choctaws there. Former chiefs, I believe?"

At this, Forbis stood, laying his napkin by his plate. Everyone stilled, allowing his low words to come through clearly.

"Chief Pushmataha and Chief Peter Pitchlynn's graves in this city remind it that the great Choctaw Nation has always been a proud and strong people, to have our leaders buried in the capitol of this nation."

Senator Newman nodded. "Of course."

As Forbis retook his seat, Ruth Ann noticed the senator's expression wasn't entirely congenial. But that disappeared, and he led the conversation once again, away from Choctaws and into the general world of politics. He engaged Joseph in telling stories about his travels in Cuba and the unrest there.

When dessert arrived, Ruth Ann was overcome with sudden fatigue. After two days on the train, she was exhausted and ready for a full night's sleep in a real bed. She hoped Georgia Pearl was not one to stay up late or she might hear Ruth Ann's undignified snore as soon as her head hit the pillow.

But it was Georgia Pearl who was asleep long before Ruth Ann. She informed Ruth Ann that it was critical for a lady to get at least ten hours of sleep without fail every night, or she risked the horror of dark circles under her eyes, completely unacceptable. No girl with dark circles under her eyes ever got a fine beau such as Pepper Barnes. Georgia Pearl's eyes twinkled when she said that.

The younger girl wore a velvet eye mask and was soon sound asleep. But Ruth Ann found herself staring out the window of the bedroom that faced the back lawn of Roseland House. A flower garden shown in the moonlight, quiet and peaceful like the country. Deceptively so. Ruth Ann was not in the country anymore.

When Georgia Pearl's breathing evened into sound sleep, Ruth Ann moved quietly to the secretary desk. She lowered the lid, letting it rest on the hinges with ample room for letter writing. Fortunately, the desk was stocked with pencils and stationary.

Ruth Ann seated herself and withdrew writing material. She needed to get started on one of the things she was supposed to do —get subscribers and good stories for the *Choctaw Tribune*.

But how did one address a note to the First Lady of the United States?

Dear Mrs. Cleveland,

I hope you remember me. I am Ruth Ann Teller from the Choctaw Tribune newspaper in Indian Territory. We met after your presentation at the Chicago World's Fair this past fall. At the time, you extended an invitation for me to visit you if I were ever in D.C.

I am currently in the city with a delegation from my tribe, and would be honored at the opportunity to see you once again. If this is possible, please address a reply to me at Roseland House in Georgetown.

I look forward to the possibility of seeing you again.

Sincerely,
Ruth Ann Teller

Ruth Ann chewed the end of the pencil, a nervous habit Matthew disliked because it ruined his pencils, but the taste of wood and lead helped her think.

Was she formal enough in addressing the First Lady? Too formal? She felt ridiculous expecting the First Lady to remember her, and it was even more ludicrous to think she'd extend an invitation to a young woman from backwoods Indian Territory. But if Ruth Ann could gain an invitation, how marvelous that would be among the stories that she sent home.

Home.

Ruth Ann stuffed the letter in an envelope and used the private address from the card the First Lady had given her in Chicago to address it.

Next, she wrote to her mother about the train trip and how pleasant everyone was at Roseland. She described the house, the guests, the dinner that evening.

In the back of her mind, Ruth Ann wondered what she could possibly write to Matthew.

By the time she finished her thoughts to her mother, nothing had come to her, so she simply tagged the letter with, *please tell Matthew I said hello.*

CHAPTER 11

Matthew sat at his desk, his new typewriter buried under a pile of newspapers. He would master the beast eventually, but for now, his mind worked too fast for typing out words one letter at a time. He was already two pages into writing an article about a new trial that Tecumseh Shoemaker was prosecuting.

The defendant was a Progressive accused of murdering a Nationalist. The men had been drunk and arguing the day before, and both threatened to kill the other. Whether the final result was a fair fight or murder, was in the hands of the Choctaw courts—and Tecumseh. In a "letter to the editor" that Matthew decided against printing, an irate Choctaw accused the courts of being ruled by political influence rather than law.

Matthew had attended the first day of the trial and could not shake his thoughts from it. He set his pencil down and leaned back, observing what he had written. The article was far too long to justify a case that was only beginning. There were so many new stories to run.

He was alone in the shop, fighting off feelings of guilt that his mother would have dinner with only Peter to keep her company.

On evenings when his cousin was back home at the ranch, Matthew needed to make sure he was home for meals. He wouldn't leave his mother alone, not ever again.

Matthew shoved the article aside. He had enough of analyzing Tecumseh's tactics and courtroom maneuvers. The man was a protégé who was defeating anyone who did not align with his ideologies for the Choctaw people.

This was the man his brother was going to face in trial.

The Teller family was not ready for what lay ahead, and they could not get ready if they weren't even talking.

Matthew pulled a sheet of paper from his messy pile. It had a few pencil marks on it, the cleanest thing he had. He'd go to Bates tomorrow and get more stationary, but this letter could not wait. Ruth Ann had sent a telegram that she'd arrived in D.C. She and Matthew needed to clear the air between them.

He missed her so much.

CHAPTER 12

Ruth Ann awoke to thin streams of sunlight coming through the curtain. She bolted upright. How could she have slept past daylight? This was a big day, her first full one in D.C.

She quietly took her clothes to the washroom to avoid disturbing Georgia Pearl's beauty sleep. She did her hair up in an attractive, yet comfortable bun for the day. She wanted to look her best because there was no telling who they might meet, but it was also going to be a long day.

After her experience at the Chicago World's Fair, she knew sensible shoes were far more important than fashionable. Her older boots were polished and her full skirt mostly covered them. They'd get around on foot or by electric streetcar and Herdic cabs as she'd read the public hacks were called.

In the bedroom again where Georgia Pearl snored softly, Ruth Ann left the room quietly with addressed letters in hand. Virginia Lee and Agatha Green's door was still closed. Considering they left the house after dinner, Ruth Ann wasn't surprised they were still asleep.

The halls were empty as well as the staircase when Ruth

Ann descended. She dropped her letters in the mailbox in the foyer and took note of the telephone on the wall by the door leading into the parlor. The black receiver was cool to the touch, sleek and shiny. Communicating by telegraph was enough of a marvel. Imagine hearing someone's actual voice over a wire!

Ruth Ann turned from there and headed straight across to the dining room where she found the sideboard ladened with breakfast foods. Scrambled eggs, bacon, muffins, fresh fruit, coffee, and tea greeted her. The rest of the Choctaw delegation was seated at the table, but no other guests from Roseland. Was she early or late?

The Choctaws greeted her as Ruth Ann brought a blueberry muffin and a glass of freshly squeezed orange juice to the table while her people continued discussing plans for the day. Senator Newman had invited them to join him at the U.S. Capitol where he would introduce them to congressmen that were interested in discussing the Dawes Commission.

Finishing breakfast, the delegation moved into the foyer to retrieve hats from the footman. Ruth Ann pinned her hat using the foyer mirror, meeting Pepper's eyes as he stood next to her, adjusting his derby hat.

She broke eye contact, hoping to head off any persnickety comments from either of them. She had neglected her Bible reading that morning, and prayed now for wisdom on this, her first full day in D.C. with Pepper Barnes.

Outside Roseland, carriages waited to carry the delegation to the capitol. Ruth Ann allowed Pepper to hand her in, thankful they weren't seated with Forbis Kanitobe and his wife. The man watched everyone as if determining who were traitors of their people and who he deemed trustworthy. Ruth Ann and Pepper were the only mixed bloods in the delegation.

On the ride, Ruth Ann kept her tablet and pencil in her lap, scribbling descriptions of the places they passed while traveling up Pennsylvania Avenue. All the while, she listened to Pepper talking with the two men in their carriage.

As they passed the President's House, Pepper said, "They never honored the Treaty of Dancing Rabbit Creek that stipulated we would have a representative on the floor of Congress, but there are ways we must fight for that representation."

Ruth Ann glanced out the right side of the open carriage to take in the National Mall with its tree-lined walking paths and benches. It gave her a chance to note the expression on the faces of the two Choctaw delegates seated across from her. They nodded at Pepper, but seemed more interested in the sights than conversation.

Ruth Ann recognized Pepper's agitated sigh. He had been to the city before and held absolutely no interest in the tremendous amount of history they rolled through on the climb to the nation's capitol building with the Statue of Freedom perched on top.

Ruth Ann realized the logic of calling this area Capitol Hill. The magnificent white dome overlooked the city from its position atop the hill. There were dozens of walkers and bicycle riders along the way, and she could see their strain as they made it to the top.

The carriages halted in a circle drive at the visitor's entrance in a line of vehicles with people alighting for tours.

As the Choctaw delegation disembarked, Senator Newman's clerk met them and said the man would receive them in his office.

They entered from the East Front, through the center doors under the main stairs. They passed through the Crypt, up the stairs and into the Great Rotunda on the principal floor.

Again, Ruth Ann regretted her lack of a camera. She tucked away her tablet, pencil, and gloves in her reticule, giving in to the temptation to brush her fingertips on the sandstone walls.

The interior dome, soaring 180 feet overhead, showed the

"Apotheosis of Washington" mural painted by Brumidi. There were rumors the artist fell to his death while painting the dome. Matthew would shake his head at the erroneous reporting.

Pepper came around beside her, and she rolled her eyes when he offered his arm. She reluctantly took it as they left the Rotunda. The clerk was in no hurry, and Ruth Ann suspected this route was intended to impress the Choctaw delegation. As far as she could tell, it was working.

They crossed another circular room and their guide paused in the marbled hall long enough to point out the Old Senate Chamber on their right that now served as the U.S. Supreme Court. The doors were closed, but Ruth Ann's heart jittered.

Benjamin Nakishi, a Choctaw lawyer, was arguing a case inside there, perhaps this very minute.

They moved down the long, gilded hallway that ended at the north end of the capitol where the Senate Chamber was located, in use since the 1850s when the new wings were added. The clerk explained that the need for office space among senators was a constant battle, but that Senator Newman had secured one of the sought-after west terrace rooms for his own.

The Library of Congress occupied much of the west front, he explained, but the collection of brittle old books and maps would soon be moved to the new building currently under construction, and the senate would have the coveted space. Ruth Ann was dying to visit the library, but she doubted that was on the agenda today.

They entered the third door on the right where Senator Newman greeted them and promised a personal tour of the capitol. He wasted no time in taking them door-to-door of the other offices where the Choctaws were not only received with smiles but gifts. The senator's clerk helped with managing the lavish baskets loaded with wine and whiskey bottles. One even had champagne. It was ironic, considering alcohol was illegal in the Choctaw Nation.

Ruth Ann felt herself ready to join in Pepper's annoyance. As they met politician after politician, none seemed genuinely interested in discussing the business they had come for. They were more concerned with flattering the Choctaw delegation. But these were only their first encounters. They could all get down to business later, so she tried not to judge either her people or the politicians too harshly.

The greatest amazement of the morning came when Senator Newman made special arrangements for them to tour the dome of the Great Rotunda. A narrow staircase, barely visible from the Rotunda floor, wound up to a little balcony at the very top of the dome. Ruth Ann almost stayed on the principal floor, but after riding the Ferris Wheel at the Chicago World's Fair, how could she pass on this opportunity?

She regretted it though, when the world slipped out from beneath her and she had to rely heavily on Pepper to keep from falling to the bottom.

They were invited to a luncheon in the Congressional Members' Dining Room, which they readily accepted after three hours of walking the capitol. The Choctaws were the guests of honor among scores of congressmen and foreign delegates.

They were seated at the table with guests of another senator—British officials who were stationed in India. Those men took great delight in meeting "American" Indians.

Ruth Ann listened to the conversations, though they did nothing to serve her primary purpose nor give her much for an article in the *Choctaw Tribune* beyond a side column. Like her time in Chicago, there was a lot of pomp and circumstance but not much meat for a story, not the kind Matthew nor she expected for their daily newspaper.

But she would be patient and consider this day as set up for real stories in the coming weeks. For now, she would be satisfied with back page material, interesting reading for the folks back home about the city and its historical aura.

After the luncheon that featured the chef's signature dish of terrapin stew, Ruth Ann expected Senator Newman to take them back to his office for a serious conversation about the Dawes Commission. But after the jostling of leaving the luncheon, Ruth Ann found herself outside in the hallway with no one but a frowning Pepper Barnes.

Ruth Ann glanced around at the dispersing crowd, everyone seeming to know where they were going. She asked Pepper, "Where is Mr. Kanitobe? Senator Newman?"

Pepper started down the hall. "They've received invitations to other frills and dressings this afternoon that I have no intention of wasting time on."

Ruth Ann hurried to catch up to him. He continued talking like he'd expected her to come along. "The senate is going back in session so there's no one we can speak with right now."

"So where exactly are we going?"

"Just follow me."

Ruth Ann halted. "The only one I follow without question is Christ."

Pepper whipped around to face her, eyebrows raised. "What's religion got to do with this?"

A few people glanced their way, but Ruth Ann remained still. "You tell me, Pepper Barnes."

A few more glances. Pepper noticed and lowered his voice.

"I know you Tellers are a religious bunch, but God helps those who help themselves. Your family has always done that, which is why I threw my hat in the ring to help your brothers. If you want to credit God for that in the end, that's your business. I'm here to save our people."

Pepper's irreverence caught Ruth Ann off guard, but she held his gaze steady. "You talk like you don't believe in God at all."

"I believe in Pepper Barnes. He's never let me down."

Pepper turned and began walking away. Ruth Ann joined him as she asked, "Has God ever let you down?"

Pepper said nothing. Ruth Ann decided to leave it be. She didn't want to get into a discussion about how maybe God let her family down when her daddy was killed and Philip fled from them in shame.

~

Georgia Pearl was gone for the evening, leaving Ruth Ann in the bedroom alone. She sat at the secretary desk, staring at her notes from the day, but unable to come up with a lead for an article. Or any words.

She and Pepper had reconnected with the rest of the Choctaw delegation, Senator Newman, and other politicians for an eight o'clock dinner that went even later with drinking. Ruth Ann finally asked Pepper to take her back to Roseland House.

To her surprise, he consented. He wasn't among those drinking. Ruth Ann hadn't realized until that time that Pepper was a teetotaler, but she was grateful for it. She could hardly handle a sober Pepper.

He was preoccupied with his own thoughts on the way back and didn't engage in conversation other than briefly telling her what they would do the next day.

Ruth Ann tapped her pencil tip to put some marks on the blank page, then scratched out a paragraph about the Choctaw delegation's experience at the capitol building, and what it was like to sit in the observation gallery while congress was in session, which was how she spent most of the afternoon.

She finished the article—still without a good lead—and pulled open a drawer to search for more envelopes. What she found inside was a map. When she opened it, she saw it was a small map of D.C., more detailed than the one in her travel book. Ruth Ann breathed a sigh of relief, deciding to keep this in her reticule. If she got separated from the others, she could navigate the city.

She turned up the gas lamp to study sections in D.C. besides

Georgetown. There were Washington Heights and Columbia Heights to the northeast. Between them to the west was the Zoological Park.

Observing the route the delegation was taken on from the Baltimore and Potomac Railroad Station around the National Mall, Ruth Ann saw they could have come straight down Pennsylvania Avenue. She didn't regret it. There was so much to see.

As her eyes wandered down Pennsylvania Avenue beyond the capitol, she noted the Congressional Cemetery next to the Eastern Branch of the Potomac River. One of her musts in D.C. was to visit the graves of the two Choctaw chiefs buried there.

She folded the map and tucked it in her reticule. She shouldn't need it tomorrow. She and Pepper Barnes were going straight to the Supreme Court at the Capitol Building for the final showdown in the case that Benjamin Nakishi was defending. That was a moment she did not want to miss.

But she recalled what Georgia Pearl said about Mr. Nakishi's broken engagement, and reminded herself to be compassionate toward the man while she worked out a way to talk to him about taking Philip's case.

CHAPTER 13

Ruth Ann slept past dawn again but took extra time in arranging her hair to accommodate her straw boater hat wrapped with a navy blue ribbon. She dressed in a matching navy blue suit—a skirt and jacket worn over a white shirtwaist—and slipped quietly out of the room. Georgia Pearl was still asleep.

During their late night conversation, the girl gushed about how she spent her day with friends picnicking on the Potomac River, and how Ruth Ann should stick with her if she wanted to have fun in D.C.

Ruth Ann dropped the somewhat finished article in the mailbox in the foyer, knowing Matthew could add the lead. The dining room was empty. Again, she wondered if she was late or early. The amount of food on the sideboard and perfectly set table told her it was the latter.

She ate alone, perusing one of the daily newspapers. She hadn't had the opportunity to read the Washington papers since arriving. The men always had their noses in them.

Ruth Ann just finished eating when she heard someone clomping down the main staircase. She hoped Mr. Nakishi would come in for breakfast. It was hard to believe she had been staying at the same house for two days and not gotten even a glimpse of the distinguished man.

But she could see into the foyer that it was Pepper. He dropped envelopes into the mailbox and when he turned around, he beckoned to her. She gathered her reticule and joined him in the foyer. He looked like he had a lot on his mind, so neither bothered with morning greetings as they went out the front door of Roseland.

A Herdic cab waited for them, apparently one Pepper arranged. It carried them briskly through the streets just beginning to come alive with life. Ruth Ann decided she may as well adjust to the city schedule of staying up later and sleeping in.

The Capitol Building felt more intimidating today without the delegation surrounding her. It looked as if it could swallow the two Choctaws whole and no one would know what happened to them. But Ruth Ann took heart in knowing there was another Choctaw inside, not in the least danger of that. Benjamin Nakishi was arguing before the Supreme Court even now.

Pepper and Ruth Ann entered on the principal floor, went through the Great Rotunda, and into the hall leading to the Senate Chambers. Partway down the hall was the Old Senate Chambers, now the Supreme Court of the United States.

Pepper knew his way around the Capitol Building and they were soon inside one of the visitors' galleries overlooking the courtroom. The semicircular two-story room was bedecked in crimson and gold throughout the marble columned and wrought iron room, all in neoclassical style.

The gallery was crowded. Ruth Ann read a snippet in the morning's paper about the case. The outcome was looking favorable for the petitioner, a farmer from Iowa claiming an income tax law violated the Constitution because it was a "direct taxation scheme not apportioned among the states." The farmer was backed by his state's senator, who believed the tax wasn't in proportion to their representation in Congress. Benjamin Nakishi represented the petitioner.

Ruth Ann settled in her seat, tablet in her lap as she took in the layout of the Supreme Court below. White quills lay on the counsel tables as a long standing tradition.

At one of the counsel tables, she noted a tall, stout man with his back to her, standing half bent over the table as he made notes.

Ruth Ann nudged Pepper, nodding the man's way. "Is that Mr. Nakishi?"

Pepper muttered, "Hold still."

Ruth Ann could hardly help fidgeting with her hands, thinking about the intensity she felt in the Tobucksy County Courthouse when Tecumseh questioned her and her family. Nelson Cobb just sat there, making notes about another case.

The all-rise call sounded, and Ruth Ann took a deep breath as she stood. The nine black-robed Justices entered and took their seats at the head of the room. Everyone retook their seats. The Chief Justice banged the gavel and called the court to order.

Ruth Ann didn't take her eyes off the petitioner's table. The tall man, Benjamin Nakishi, sat there quietly beside his client, who leaned over once to ask something and received a nod. The case was important to the Iowa farmer, but did he realize the importance for the lawyer next to him, the one who had yet to lose a case?

This had been Mr. Nakishi's first time to present oral arguments in the Supreme Court. Ruth Ann wished she could have watched him, but even now, his poise at the table before the black-robed justices was admirable. He was calm and focused, as though his client's case was the only thing on his mind.

Both parties stood for the Chief Justice to announce the outcome. They ruled in favor of the petitioner.

A cheer erupted from proponents of the case seated in the

observation gallery. Ruth Ann exhaled and clapped along with several others.

They were quickly reprimanded, though, by the justice banging his gavel and giving a centuries-old warning look to the visitors. No impropriety would be tolerated in this courtroom.

Mr. Nakishi shook his client's hand heartily, grinning. They turned to look up in the gallery still rumbling with excitement.

As Benjamin Nakishi's face turned her way, Ruth Ann caught her breath. He was younger than she thought he would be. Older than Matthew, but not by too many years. His face was full and kind, a joyful smile lighting his deep brown eyes.

Those eyes met Ruth Ann's, and she froze. Her heart thundered like never before in her life.

This was the one.

The certainty of it came to her like a prophetic vision of old. This was the man God would use to save her brother and her family.

~

"Come on." Pepper pulled Ruth Ann out of the visitors' gallery, forcing a tunnel for them to pass through despite the crowd. "We need to find Nakishi."

"Looks like everyone's plan," Ruth Ann murmured as she scanned the layers of people between them and where the lawyer was heading down the narrow spiral staircase leading down to the first floor.

What chance did she stand of convincing him to come back to the Choctaw Nation after this Supreme Court victory?

But the warmth she felt from his gaze, even from a distance, held her heart. He was the one. She'd find a way to convince him.

Pepper buffaloed his way through the crowd of men as he led Ruth Ann to the staircase and hurried down them. Ruth Ann caught a glimpse of Benjamin Nakishi near the doors because he stood a head taller than most of the other men. But he wasn't looking their way. He was in three conversations at once, it seemed. Though Pepper tried, they weren't able to reach him before his party exited the building.

With another group blocking the door, Pepper yanked Ruth Ann around to go out through one of the other doors. She held on to his arm as they trotted down the East Front steps. A couple of times, she lost her balance and was afraid she'd make them both tumble head over heels down the steps.

At the bottom, Pepper took up a jog and Ruth Ann let go. There was no way she could keep up in her skirt and high-heeled, buttoned-up boots.

By the time she caught up, Pepper was standing by the drive, hands on his hips as carriages rolled away.

Ruth Ann halted beside him and took a deep breath. "Guess we'll have to meet Mr. Nakishi when he returns to Roseland House."

Pepper frowned and turned to look at her. The way his eyes went over her face told her it was the first time he had actually noticed her all morning.

"I have another appointment and you should get back to Roseland and rest, freshen up," he said. "You look too worn out to meet Nakishi."

Ruth Ann bristled. He sounded like Matthew, sending her home after a rushed attempt to get the newspaper out on time. "Pepper Barnes, you will not send me away like a child—and there is nothing wrong with the way I look."

"I stand by what I said."

Pepper strode away from the Capitol Building, and Ruth Ann had no desire to follow him. Worse, he was right, in part. She was exhausted after going from dawn till late in the night since they arrived in D.C., and she hadn't recovered from the train trip.

Ruth Ann engaged a cab to take her back to the house, conscious of how slow this mode of transportation was compared to the bicycle riders out the window. The streets were heavy with traffic and she sat in one jam for nearly an hour before it finally loosened enough to get through. If only she had learned to ride a bicycle! She would have complete freedom to go about the city.

The cab dropped her off at Roseland and she was surprised to find something in her box in the mail closet. A letter from Matthew.

She took it up to her room. The suite was empty, so she changed into a robe, closed the drapes, and fluffed up the pillows on her bed before climbing in.

The letter from Matthew was postmarked two days before. Ruth Ann stared at it, tracing the familiar handwriting. She was well acquainted with it after setting type on hundreds of articles in English and Choctaw in the past two years. Trying to decipher his handwriting was one of her hardest challenges when she started working with him at the newspaper. But he was patient with her, and she eventually became an asset instead of a nuisance. That led to her running the newspaper on her own a short time ago, and launching the daily.

Ruth Ann and her brother had grown closer than she imagined they would as adults. When Matthew left for college, she thought they'd drift apart, both of them marrying, raising families, celebrating holidays together on Uncle Preston's ranch. Once her children came, he would step into his traditional responsibility in helping raise them.

But the *Choctaw Tribune* and its mission bonded them in a closeness she never dreamed they'd experience. They'd gone through life and death and now a rebirth neither of them knew how to handle.

She turned the envelope over, wondering what Matthew wanted to say that he hadn't before she left. She slowly slit the envelope with the letter opener from the nightstand and withdrew the single page.

Dear Ruth Ann,

I have just come from watching Tecumseh Shoemaker prosecute a Choctaw man at the Tobucksy County Courthouse. The only chance our family has of surviving this ordeal is if we band together.

This is not a time for us to quarrel. We must love and serve one another through this time or we will come out more broken than when we lost Philip the first time.

Please write me soon. We have to work out whatever is between us.

Your brother,
Matthew

Typical Matt—hit a problem head on, strong and sure. It was also how he reacted when he didn't know what the actual problem or solution was. The last line in his letter told her that.

He didn't know why there was a block between them, he just wanted to fix it. And he addressed her by her full name, which he'd done a lot lately. Maybe he would from now on.

She laid the letter aside, deciding to use the remainder of the afternoon to rest and catch up on writing before meeting Benjamin Nakishi.

Ruth Ann tossed and turned awhile, unable to nap. She kept thinking of the lawyer and how his smile made his deep brown eyes melt. She wondered how she could ever look into those eyes and tell him what Philip had done to their people, and how she wanted the man to bring her brother home unscathed so she could forgive him.

CHAPTER 14

When Benjamin Nakishi didn't appear at dinner that evening, Ruth Ann regretted not taking her meal in the room. She grew irritated with Pepper, who was in a lousy mood over how his meetings turned out. With the rest of the delegation out on the town, she endured his mood alone. He made no objection when she excused herself early.

The next morning, Ruth Ann's headache abated. She needed to finish writing an article and maybe a letter to Matthew, if she could figure out what to say.

She rang the servant's bell—a foreign feeling—and requested breakfast from the maid. She didn't plan on going anywhere that Saturday morning, since her only option was spending it with Pepper. Georgia Pearl had stayed the night at a friend's.

After breakfast, Ruth Ann remained on the fluffed pillows to write. She was terribly lazy, enjoying the luxuries of the fine home to its fullest, but she told herself it was for the best. She couldn't help her family if she lost her senses from exhaustion and wound up hitting Pepper Barnes before the trip ended.

Caught up in writing, Ruth Ann barely noticed the sound of

the outer door to the suite opening, admitting the voices of Agatha Green and Virginia Lee Newman.

Shaking out the cramp in her hand, Ruth Ann rose and put on a robe to enter the suite where the two young women sat on the sofa, changing their boots.

Virginia Lee looked up and cocked an eyebrow at Ruth Ann.

"I would think a professional business woman should be up before noon."

Ruth Ann had hoped the conversation would start off on a better note. These girls had a great many connections in the city, so she ignored the remark and asked, "What are you ladies doing today?"

Virginia Lee finished lacing her boot and stood. "We're off to..."

She glanced at Agatha, who grinned and nodded. "Do invite her."

Virginia Lee smiled sweetly at Ruth Ann, eliminating any trust she might have in the senator's daughter. "Why, Miss Teller, you should go with us. There's a gathering taking place at Garfield Park and we would love to have you. It will be the news event of the week, I assure you, and give you a chance to get away from all those men in your party."

Ruth Ann didn't agree with her sentiment entirely, but there was one particular young man she would like to stay away from today. She could not accomplish what she had come to D.C. for if she was always tied to Pepper Barnes.

"How should I dress?"

Ruth Ann changed into the most sporting outfit she had—a white shirtwaist and rose colored skirt hemmed as high as she dared— that she brought for bicycle riding, and went downstairs to find Agatha and Virginia Lee finishing lunch in the dining room.

Agatha handed Ruth Ann a wrapped sandwich. "You can eat it later," she said as they went into the foyer for their hats, scarves, and gloves. Ruth Ann tucked the sandwich in her reticule.

But they didn't go out the front door. Ruth Ann followed them through the kitchen and out a side door, where she discovered a small area in the fenced backyard of Roseland.

There, racks held a dozen bicycles. Most were like Lance Fuller's, designed for men, but a handful were with the lower bar to accommodate skirts.

Agatha and Virginia Lee tied their straw boaters hats on with their scarves while they went straight to the bicycles and pulled two off the rack. Ruth Ann's heart leapt into her throat. Virginia Lee paused when she realized Ruth Ann was frozen in place.

She rolled her eyes. "You're scared to ride a bicycle in public, aren't you?"

Ruth Ann shook her head. She wasn't afraid exactly. She just wasn't capable of doing it. But maybe Lance's instruction had somehow sunk into her muscles and they would perform at will.

Ruth Ann tied her straw boater securely with her chiffon scarf and moved to take a bicycle off the rack. She followed the two young women as they pushed the bicycles out the side gate and onto the front street. They mounted up—Ruth Ann very carefully—and the girls took off in front of her. She gave a push, trying to imitate their actions, but the bicycle wobbled wildly and she quickly put both feet on the paved road. She awkwardly walked the bicycle while still seated, waddling like a duck.

Agatha glanced over her shoulder and laughed. Virginia Lee turned her bike in a smooth arc on the empty neighborhood street and peddled back to Ruth Ann. She halted next to her.

"Do you honestly not know how to ride a bicycle?" Virginia Lee asked. "It's a necessity for any freethinking, independent young woman in today's world."

"I've been trying to learn." *Two whole times now.*

Virginia Lee rolled her eyes. "If you want to be something

other than a man's arm ornament, you need to learn to take care of yourself. Look at you. You're a female reporter and deserve an equal place among men. But do you have it? Women can do anything a man can do, only better, and we can use that to make them subservient. Not only do we have superior intelligence, we can wield our feminine powers when needed."

She lowered her eyelids and batted her lashes to demonstrate. Then she popped her eyes open and the look on her face was unlike anything Ruth Ann wanted to replicate.

Virginia Lee said, "I've seen how possessive Pepper Barnes is, lording over you. But you can gain power over him and keep him under control until you achieve what you want. But never let him get you off on a carriage ride alone. Intelligent, professional young women should never marry. You have too much to offer the world to end up barefoot in a dirt floor kitchen, pregnant with more children than your body can handle."

Ruth Ann had known this young woman was outspoken, but this was shocking. She stood up from the bicycle, legs still awkwardly astride it. "While I do not believe a woman's place is only in the kitchen, nor do I believe it is in lording over men. A woman's place is wherever God puts her."

Virginia Lee cocked her head with a condescending smile. "Well, at least you are capable of thinking for yourself. Somewhat. We can work with that, if a man doesn't crush it out of you first."

Ahead of them on the cross street, Agatha Green waved down a Herdic cab, which turned and headed their way. Virginia Lee motioned at it. "We will meet you at Garfield Park. You can practice riding the bicycle there."

Ruth Ann reluctantly agreed. She was ready to call off the entire excursion, but she couldn't accomplish anything sitting around Roseland House, and she wasn't ready to venture out on her own.

The driver hooked the bicycle to the back of the cab while

Ruth Ann got inside the closed two wheel vehicle. She ate her sandwich as they went along at a painfully slow pace along Pennsylvania Avenue because of traffic. Virginia Lee and Agatha disappeared from sight, far in advance. Whatever the gathering was might be over by the time Ruth Ann got there, but at least she could enjoy the sights along the way. She opened the city map to follow along with where they were.

They cut through the National Mall on 4th St. S.W. before turning onto Virginia Avenue, which ran along the railroad tracks. They pulled over at the Delaware Avenue intersection and the driver disembarked, telling her through the open window, "This is as close as we can get to Garfield Park today, ma'am."

He unhooked her bicycle while Ruth Ann refolded the map. She got out and paid him, then took the beastly contraption to walk it along the road he indicated to the park.

The tree-lined avenue was empty of horse and buggy traffic. It was too crowded with women and bicycles and signs that read: *VOTES FOR WOMEN.*

A small gathering? There were hundreds of women! Ruth Ann would never find Virginia Lee and Agatha.

One middle-aged woman marched up to her and pinned a red, white, and blue ribboned button near the collar of Ruth Ann's shirtwaist. Ruth Ann looked down, straining to read the words. They echoed the signs.

She didn't know what to think of it as she navigated to the center of the park where New Jersey Avenue ran through it.

The road was clear as a dozen women rode their bicycles in circles there. Ruth Ann was shocked.

These women were in their shirtwaists and *bloomers*! Not even puffed knickerbockers like some of the women. Their actual bloomers.

Ruth Ann's cheeks heated, and she instinctively looked around to see if there were any men present. There weren't, but there were three little boys hiding under a bush on the other side of the park, gawking.

She turned her attention back to the riders and realized they were riding in a pattern. Almost like a cavalry drill. Three of the young women broke off and went to form a center circle as they turned and went opposite of the wider outer circle. They passed one another by a hair's breath and the circles straightened. Then most of the riders paused, watching two young women as they began riding toward one another. One was Virginia Lee Newman.

As Ruth Ann watched, jaw dropped, the senator's daughter took her feet off the pedals and raised them to a cross legged position in front of her seat. The second bloomer clad girl lifted her hands from the handlebars. They passed one another closely before re-engaging fully with their bicycles. The women around Ruth Ann called out encouragement.

Virginia Lee spotted Ruth Ann and navigated toward her, hands off her handles as she guided the bicycle with her legs and body motion. She came to a smooth stop in front of Ruth Ann, her face aglow.

"Now do you understand how free women should be?"

Ruth Ann couldn't answer. She desperately wanted Virginia Lee to put her skirt back on, wherever it was.

A shrill whistle sounded from the other side of the park and the gaiety of the women turn to shouts of anger. Virginia Lee swiveled half around to glare toward where the whistles continued to shriek.

She said behind her to Ruth Ann, "Now you are about to see us exhibit our rights as women to protest men's oppression."

Ruth Ann gripped her bicycle handles tight. "Are those policemen?"

"They'll say we're causing a disturbance and are indecent. The only thing indecent about this is their presence."

Virginia Lee pushed off with her bicycle and began riding toward the line of police officers entering the park.

Ruth Ann took a step back, pulling the bicycle with her. She watched in horror as some of the women whacked the officers with their signs. The police focused on the women in bloomers, ordering them to dress or be arrested. When they refused, some of the officers began handcuffing the women.

Ruth Ann kept backing until her bicycle tires and her feet were in the grass under a tree. She was alone in the area as the women who weren't pushing toward the officers were fleeing down New Jersey Avenue in their bloomers. Some were being pursued.

Ruth Ann quickly popped the front wheel of the bicycle up and turned it completely around. She lowered it back down and pushed it out of the park as quickly as she could. She thought of abandoning it but since it belonged to Roseland House, she felt obligated to take care of it.

All the while, horrible images were going through her mind of Pepper Barnes coming to bail her out of jail.

Ruth Ann came to a grassy gully which she ran the bicycle into. She followed it down and away from the park. It was wet at the bottom of the gully and she almost got stuck as mud sucked on her boots and splattered her skirt. She released the bicycle with one hand to yank the ribboned button off her shirtwaist and paused to stuff it in her reticule swinging from the bicycle handle.

She reemerged on a street with no police officers or women in bloomers and breathed a sigh of relief. She pushed the bicycle calmly along the street as if she weren't fleeing arrest.

CHAPTER 15

Several blocks later, Ruth Ann felt it was safe enough to stop by the side of a building to get her bearings. She had fled in the opposite direction of Roseland, but she did not want to go back there until things calmed down.

What to do? She glanced up at the street signs nearest her. Georgia Avenue.

She furrowed her brows, wondering why the name held a ring of significance in her mind beyond her roommate's name. Leaning her bicycle against the building, she opened her reticule and withdrew the map. She opened it to a section she had marked.

The Congressional Cemetery.

She was only four blocks from it.

And thine ears shall hear a word behind thee, saying, This is the way, walk ye in it.

Looking beyond the map, she stared at her mud-splattered skirt and boots. Her chiffon scarf had come loose and a clump of hair fell over her shoulder. Her bun was coming apart. Ruth Ann removed her hat and pulled out the rest of the pins.

This was a sort of freedom she wanted to feel when she

visited the graves of chiefs of her people. Now was as good a time as any.

Ruth Ann pushed the bicycle the four blocks up Georgia Avenue, letting the cool breeze blow her hair where it willed.

She reached the point where there was almost no traffic and the buildings ended to her right. A high wrought-iron fence lined a grassy area that Ruth Ann could not see the end of. Grand headstones and monuments, along with crypts, filled the space as far as she could see.

Ruth Ann instinctively slowed her pace when she came alongside the wrought-iron fence. She followed it to a double gate that stood open with an empty guardhouse keeping watch.

Inhaling, she wondered if she was emotionally and spiritually prepared to visit these graves of the two Choctaw chiefs, especially Pushmataha's. She wondered if she was prepared to visit a grave at all. The last one had been her daddy's.

Ruth Ann left the bicycle in a rack inside the gate and walked along the brick road that led through the cemetery. She didn't know where the chiefs' graves were and it could take her hours to find them, but she was in no hurry. This was the kind of moment the Grandmother had trained her for.

Ruth Ann observed the markers along the way and ventured off the road to the left, stepping respectfully through the headstones. She noted when her walk became a climb, and she glanced up the hill before her.

At the top, next to a square monument, was a tall Indian man.

Ruth Ann put her hand over her stomach to calm the sudden flutters there. She hadn't expected to have such a reaction on seeing what had to be the monument of one of the chiefs.

Why else would Benjamin Nakishi be standing before it, head bowed?

Ruth Ann looked again at her muddy skirt, her loose hair falling over her shoulders. This was not the first impression she wanted to make on the lawyer who was going to save her brother and her family. She needed to leave.

But when she looked up, she realized Benjamin Nakishi had raised his head. He saw her.

Ruth Ann's cheeks flushed, once again caught by his gentle smile from a distance. There was no avoiding making his acquaintance. It would be more embarrassing if she fled and encountered him later at Roseland House.

Gathering in the courage of her ancestors, Ruth Ann strode up the hill to meet the Choctaw lawyer.

Benjamin Nakishi stood there, unmoving, hands folded in front of him, watching her as she came up. He wasn't scrutinizing, but he did seem to actually see her. That brought a sense of self-consciousness, yet also validation. She tried to manage a smile that matched his as she greeted him.

"Hello. I'm Ruth Ann Teller from Dickens, Indian Territory."

He offered his hand to shake. "Benjamin Nakishi-Dunn, currently of Washington D.C."

Ruth Ann took his hand and a lightning bolt went through her body. His hand wrapped hers in a firm, sure grip like her daddy's. It felt secure there, and Ruth Ann hated it only lasted a moment.

He released her hand and said, "You were in the viewers' gallery today with a young man, weren't you?"

Ruth Ann's cheeks flamed hot. "I wasn't with him. Well, I was, in the sense that we are traveling together with the Choctaw delegation. We're staying at Roseland House. I'm not actually with the delegation, I'm a newspaper reporter and I'm here to cover stories and things."

Ruth Ann hated how she stumbled on her words. But if Benjamin Nakishi noticed her awkwardness, he responded by kindly ignoring it.

He nodded at the monument, partially to her back. "Have you been to his grave before, Miss Teller?"

Ruth Ann turned and gasped lightly.

PUSH-MA-TA-HA
A
CHOCTAW CHIEF
LIES HERE.
THIS MONUMENT TO HIS MEMORY
IS ERECTED BY HIS BROTHER CHIEFS
WHO WERE ASSOCIATED WITH HIM
IN A
DELEGATION
FROM THEIR NATION,
IN THE YEAR 1824, TO THE
GENERAL GOVERNMENT
OF THE
UNITED STATES

By the time she finished reading the inscription, Ruth Ann was crying.

Chief Pushmataha—leader of her people before they were removed from their homelands. Hero of the War of 1812. Betrayed by his friend, Andrew Jackson. Still, the president expressed on Pushmataha's passing that he was the greatest and the bravest Indian he had ever known. He honored the chief's wishes to be buried with full military honors in the Congressional Cemetery. John Randolph of Roanoke pronounced a eulogy for him in the Senate regarding Pushmataha's wisdom, eloquence, and friendship.

Something touched Ruth Ann's hand and she realize Benjamin Nakishi was draping a handkerchief over it. She pressed the cloth against her eyes, taking a cleansing breath.

"Yakoke."

Benjamin released a deep sigh. "Pim anumpa haklo ka achuk-ma." *It is good to hear our language.*

Ruth Ann dabbed her eyes. She wondered how long it been since Benjamin Nakishi had spoken in Choctaw.

This moment was sacred in many ways.

He spoke softly. "Come. There's more."

Ruth Ann followed Benjamin Nakishi as he showed her the other three sides.

PUSH-MA-TA-HA WAS A WARRIOR
OF GREAT DISTINCTION
HE WAS WISE IN COUNCIL —
ELOQUENT IN AN EXTRAORDINARY
DEGREE, AND ON ALL OCCASIONS
& UNDER ALL CIRCUMSTANCES
THE WHITE MAN'S FRIEND

HE DIED IN WASHINGTON,
ON THE 24TH OF DECEMBER, 1824,
OF THE CROUP, IN THE
60TH YEAR OF HIS AGE.

AMONG HIS LAST WORDS
WERE THIS FOLLOWING :
'WHEN I AM GONE LET THE BIG GUNS
BE FIRED OVER ME.'
HE SAID THAT HIS DEATH
WOULD BE LIKE THE FALLING
OF A GREAT TREE
IN THE FOREST
WHEN THE WINDS WERE STILL.

They ended at the front again and stood quietly. Memory of digging her fingers through the grass of her father's grave, of rubbing the spit-splattered dirt on her cheeks, of wailing for a loved one as her people had done for centuries, made Ruth Ann bow her head and be still.

When the time was right, Ruth Ann shifted her feet and Benjamin Nakishi said, "Perhaps you would like to see Chief Peter Pitchlynn's the next time?"

Ruth Ann nodded. This experience was enough for today.

They departed the chief's grave and soon regained the brick road. At the entrance to the cemetery, Ruth Ann's thoughts were so scattered, she was grateful Benjamin Nakishi took the lead.

"Did you come here by bicycle?" He nodded at the rack.

Ruth Ann allowed herself an airy laugh, relieving some of the tension and grief. "It came here with me. I'm afraid I don't ride very well."

Benjamin smiled and pulled the bicycle off the rack. "May I escort you back to Roseland House, or do you have other plans?"

Ruth Ann wanted to say that her only plans were indeed to go back to the house, change her muddy clothes, and have a good cry. "That would be fine, thank you."

They walked along in comfortable silence. There was much they could talk about—the Choctaw Nation, Indian Territory, outlaws, D.C. politicians, the Supreme Court victory that morning. Philip's trial. But words didn't seem right in that moment.

Benjamin Nakishi and Ruth Ann Teller were walking with the thoughts of their ancestors—the past of their people, not the present nor the future. That would come.

This was the kind of moment the Grandmother had trained Ruth Ann for. Perhaps Benjamin Nakishi had the same kind of grandmother.

CHAPTER 16

Della lit a second lamp by her sewing table. Normally the light of a single lamp was enough for her to cut fabric by, but not tonight. Her eyes had aged in the past month since the moments they rested on her oldest son and then her first grandchild.

She held the taffeta flat with one hand while making a careful cut with sharpened scissors. She already ruined three yards of fabric by cutting in the wrong place. The fabric could be reused for another project, but it was an uncommon error.

The cool touch of the tightly woven fabric with its shimmering gold and black sidelined her thoughts to her daughter and the ballgown they had packed. Ruth Ann had purchased it at a store in Paris, Texas, because Della hadn't had time to make her one. She had not seen her daughter in the dress, but she knew it would be modest and fitting. Perhaps Ruth Ann would meet someone special while wearing it.

Della's hand jerked, causing a tiny tear in the fabric. She sighed and finished the cut, then took up the part with the tear and sat in her rocking chair to stitch it to prevent unraveling.

She had hoped her daughter would meet someone there in

the Choctaw Nation, close to the family, as Della had done with her beloved Jim. Philip was so far away, her grandchild even further. Could she bear her daughter departing the Indian Territory?

Della's eyes blurred from the richness of the fabric and she rested it with her hands in her lap while she looked at the far wall where a girl's dress hung. It was a soft yellow, still in good condition after many years. When she was a little girl, Ruth Ann was only allowed to wear it when they went to church on good weather days. She'd outgrown it in her fifth year.

Della saved it for Ruth Ann's own little girl someday, but wasn't certain why she took it from the trunk in the attic bedroom today and hung it in her sewing room. It had something to do with thoughts of her daughter gone so long, and wondering if she could make enough adjustments for the dress to fit Philip's daughter. Now, though, the innocence of it took her back to a time she wore a similar yellow dress at sixteen years old one special night...

It was a deep, dark night, the warmth of May weather coaxing young Della onto the porch past midnight to work on stitching a new shirt for her brother, Preston Frazier. They had not heard from him since the surrender at Appomattox on April 9, 1865. It was now early May and still no word from Preston. Her brother's wife, Liza, and toddler had kept her company on the ranch along with her mother, who often sat on this porch, keeping watch on the road for when her son came home.

The three women took turns on that porch every hour of the day and night. Her mother during the morning, Liza in the afternoon, and Della much of the night. She relished the sounds of the night, the ones on the ranch that her brother was building. They were alive tonight with reminders of God's promise that they were not alone.

When they learned the war had ended, Della began stitching her brother a new shirt to welcome him home. They expected him within days, perhaps a week. Other Choctaw soldiers returned home to their families, but none had word of Preston Frazier.

The dog barked, and Della looked up to see two dark figures coming at a slow pace down the road toward the log cabin. She turned down her sewing lamp and let her eyes adjust to the moonlight. One of the men leaned heavy on the other, and even though his steps were uneven, she knew the form and figure of her brother.

Della slowly put the shirt aside and stood. Then all of her energy came in a rush and she cried out, "He is home!"

Della went down the porch steps and ran down the road to her brother. He straightened and tried to stand on his own two feet. Della flung her arms around his neck, ignoring the other man whose arm she captured in her hug as she inhaled the musty scent of the dirty gray wool uniform, and of her brother. They'd not been ones for open affection, but after not seeing him since his leave two years before, she could not help the tight grip she held him in.

She didn't let go until the sobbing sounds of Liza told her it was time to surrender her brother to his wife and the toddler he'd not met, and their mother.

Della stepped back as the other two women and baby embraced Preston. She glanced at the young man who had supported her injured brother on the road home.

A sudden shyness overcame her when she realized he was watching her, his soft brown eyes not as hollowed as many of the Choctaw boys returning from war. She folded her hands and nodded at Preston, who couldn't stop kissing his wife.

"Yakoke, thank you for bringing him home."

The young man smiled. "Frazier saved my life. And with how he talked about his womenfolk, I sure didn't wanna pass up meeting them. But you ain't how he described his baby sister. I expected pigtails, not a pretty Choctaw lady."

Della flushed at his boldness but returned his smile. "I am Della."

"James Teller. Most folks call me Jim."

The memory of his grin faded and the yellow dress hanging on the wall cleared. Della shook her shoulders. She needed to finish this taffeta dress in two days, and it would take all of her focus.

But she did not regret falling back into the scene of another night twenty-nine years ago when she looked into the eyes of the man she knew she'd marry someday.

Della laid the taffeta aside for another moment and pulled out a bolt of yellow cloth she purchased at Bates' General Store yesterday. She didn't know why she had then. She did now.

There was time enough to make a yellow dress for Ruth Ann to welcome her when she returned home.

CHAPTER 17

On Sunday morning, Ruth Ann spent time in the sitting room of the girls' suite, reading. She had ample time to read her Bible before church, and to see if Virginia Lee and Agatha were going to get up early enough.

She wanted to apologize for leaving Garfield Park so abruptly, though she wasn't sure she owed them an apology considering what they'd gotten her into. But she did want to make sure they were all right after the scuffle.

The bedroom door was closed and Ruth Ann wasn't certain they were in there. She shuddered to think that they might be in jail.

After her scripture reading, Ruth Ann's mind returned to the Congressional Cemetery, a memory that warmed her to her toes. Benjamin Nakishi was a consummate gentleman, a kind soul that belonged among their people back in Indian Territory.

She recalled their greetings, and something tickled her thoughts. He said his name was Nakishi-*Dunn*? Pepper never mentioned he had two last names. She would ask Mr. Nakishi about it sometime, when he was ready for conversation.

When Benjamin Nakishi had parked her bicycle in the rack at

Roseland yesterday, he excused himself to go straight to his room. No doubt he knew the demands that Pepper Barnes and others in the Choctaw delegation would make on him.

Ruth Ann had spent time in the parlor Saturday afternoon, waiting for Pepper to return to ask him about church, but he never appeared. Ruth Ann finally gave up and took dinner at the house with Joseph Griffin. He invited her to attend the historic Georgetown Presbyterian Church, and she accepted.

With Georgia Pearl barely starting to awake that Sunday morning, Ruth Ann dressed and went down to the dining room. Pepper was in there, reading the newspaper. He glanced up when she walked in, then returned to the paper. She fixed a plate from the sideboard and sat across from him. When he made no attempt at conversation, she decided to tease him.

"I hope your Saturday went well, Pepper. I was nearly arrested in a riot at Garfield Park, but don't worry, the Choctaw reputation is intact since I escaped unrecognized. Oh, and by the way, I met Benjamin Nakishi-Dunn at the cemetery. He's a pleasant man."

She smothered a giggle when Pepper snapped the paper down, a corner splashing into his coffee.

"You had a meeting without me?" he said sharply.

Ruth Ann took her time spreading orange marmalade over an English muffin. "Calm down, sir. It was entirely by chance that we ran into one another at Chief Pushmataha's grave."

She sobered, recalling the emotional moment. "It was quite an experience."

Pepper did not look impressed. "I hope you didn't say anything about getting involved in that ruckus."

Ruth Ann took a delicate bite of the English muffin. "Well, I did say…"

She left it hanging as she slowly chewed the muffin and Pepper snapped the paper up again, sprinkling his sleeve with coffee. He didn't seem to mind, knowing his coat would cover it. Ruth Ann giggled.

"Now, Mr. Barnes, there's no need to get in a tizzy. Mr. Nakishi and I got along well. But why didn't you tell me his last name is Nakishi-Dunn?"

Pepper turned the page on the newspaper covering his face. "Leave the 'Dunn' part out of your articles, all right?"

Pepper was not playing the game. Ruth Ann frowned but decided not to press him.

High-pitched singing came from the grand staircase and into the dining room. Georgia Pearl swept in as though she were entering her debutante reception. Her dress and silk scarf were a little too frilly for church in Ruth Ann's opinion, but this was the big city after all.

"Good morning Miss Teller, good morning Mr. Barnes."

She picked up a muffin with two fingers and settled in a chair next to Pepper, right at his elbow. "I understand we are going with Mr. Griffin to the Georgetown Presbyterian Church this morning. Would you accompany—"

Clatter from the stairs sounded again, this time emitting Joseph Griffin, who gave an even more boisterous morning greeting. He swooped in on Ruth Ann. "I'm running late as usual, my dear, but are you ready?"

Pepper stood. "I was planning to—"

Joseph Griffin interrupted, "Of course you can come along, Mr. Barnes. No need to ask!"

Pepper's face reddened with annoyance. Georgia Pearl latched onto his arm while Joseph Griffin pulled out Ruth Ann's chair and escorted her to the foyer where they took up their hats for the short walk to the church on P Street.

Ruth Ann didn't know Joseph Griffin well, but she preferred his accompaniment to Pepper's.

Joseph Griffin led the way, with Pepper and Georgia Pearl trailing behind, the young woman thoroughly enjoying the chance to pretend she had a beau. She did seem attracted to Pepper, which wasn't surprising. He was a handsome young man, except when he was scowling. Like now.

As Ruth Ann enjoyed Joseph Griffin's explanation about the Georgetown Presbyterian Church history, she couldn't help wondering where Benjamin Nakishi went to church. She wished she had asked him before they parted yesterday.

Once inside the church, Ruth Ann had difficulty focusing on the service. Established in 1780, the church was filled with history, and she found her mind wandering to the founding of the country.

After the service, Joseph Griffin offered to show them Washington Heights to the northeast of Georgetown, suggesting they take lunch at a quaint café there. He added, "We may have a chance to meet a man who frequents the café, especially lunch on Sundays. He hails from Indian Territory as well, Cherokee country, I believe. I'll introduce you."

Pepper detangled himself from Georgia Pearl. "I'm going back to the house. I have correspondence to finish before business on Monday."

Pepper turned away and Georgia Pearl followed him, saying she wanted to write letters as well.

Ruth Ann and Joseph Griffin headed for Washington Heights. She asked him what it was like, being an AP reporter, adding, "It must be fascinating to travel the world and see different cultures and write about them."

Joseph sighed dramatically. "Well, my dear, it's not all fun and games. The first AP reporter to be killed on the job, Mark Kellogg, was at the Battle of the Little Big Horn. What a massacre."

He paused and smacked his forehead. "I apologize. I'm sure your people have a different view of that battle than most folks."

Ruth Ann kept her attention on the crossroad ahead. "It's all right, Mr. Griffin." She steered the conversation back around. "Tell me what the AP office in New York is like."

"I'll do better than that, I'll take you there someday. There are hundreds of telegraph operators in our office alone. I'm sure you'll be properly impressed."

Ruth Ann couldn't imagine so many operators and sounders in the same room! The clacking, yet the excitement. "And some telegrams come from overseas?"

"Absolutely. We're getting coverage even now of the Sino-Japanese War. But not all reporters are after facts, as I'm sure you've experienced in this business. Remember the saying, 'A lie can travel halfway around the world while the truth is still putting its boots on.'"

Ruth Ann laughed. Matthew would like that saying.

Joseph pointed to a café with a red awning covered outside seating area. "Here we are."

He opened the door to the café for her. They entered, and he nodded toward the back corner. "Ah, I see the man I was referring to is here. He's involved in discussions about the Dawes Commission and Indian land, but I don't have details on it. I don't believe there's much of a story there as far as he's concerned."

Ruth Ann halted and stared in shock at the pudgy man in the back corner. "I think there's a story there for me."

In discussion with a senator she'd met at the capitol was the former mayor of Dickens, Indian Territory. One of the men who tried to have Matthew killed.

Thaddeus Warren.

CHAPTER 18

When Monday morning came, Ruth Ann wasn't ready for an entire week in D.C. The evening before, Pepper gave her a hastily-written itinerary with bold underlines on the times and places where she was to meet him. He had the agenda packed from sunrise to well beyond sunset.

After seeing Thaddeus Warren talking with a senator in the café, Ruth Ann hadn't felt at peace. She and Joseph made a hasty exit from the cafe, and Ruth Ann explained who the man from Indian Territory really was. What was he up to? Joseph promised to see what he could find out.

With that fraying on her nerves and her work barely started, Ruth Ann didn't know how she was going to meet Pepper's expectations along with Matthew's. Not to mention her own, which included finding a way to keep the promise she made at her daddy's grave.

She needed to talk to Benjamin Nakishi about Philip's case, but she was afraid he would turn it down automatically. Why would an accomplished city lawyer walk away from a plethora of opportunities, money, and prestige to come back and help a Choctaw accused of hurting his people?

But Ruth Ann had to find a way, and the only way she knew was showing that her family was worth helping. That could take time, and Ruth Ann was aware that half a week of her time in D.C. was already gone.

Ruth Ann took breakfast in her room so she could pen a letter to Matthew while she ate. Whatever lay ahead, Matthew was right, as usual. They needed to work out what was between them in order to save their family. They couldn't do that if she didn't write to him, something she needed to bring herself to do now before she met Pepper.

She worded the letter carefully, deciding not to mention that she'd seen Thaddeus Warren in D.C. yet. She would find out more about him before sounding an alarm and sending the former mayor back into hiding.

Ruth Ann signed the letter, but it felt incomplete. She set it aside and checked her pocket watch. She rushed through dressing and going downstairs.

Pepper was all business and spent the cab ride explaining the importance of the meeting to her.

It was a long, dull morning at the Indian bureau with three of the Choctaw delegates, including Forbis Kanitobe. But Ruth Ann was grateful to see the Choctaw delegates ready to get back to business after a weekend of flittering around the city.

When the meeting ended, Pepper didn't go with Ruth Ann back to Roseland to eat because he had a men's business meeting for lunch.

Once again, she wished she had a bicycle to navigate the city instead of taking a cab. She opted instead to try the electric streetcar.

It was a smooth ride, but she had to walk a mile from the closest stop to the boarding house. Still, she didn't mind the walk, especially on the fresh summer day. But there were many miles to cover in the city, and she needed a quicker way of getting around.

She went through the backyard of Roseland to gaze at the bicycles before entering through the kitchen door to inform them she would be eating lunch there.

Mrs. Schmitt rushed to her in surprise. "Miss Teller, I tried to catch you at the bureau by telephone. This came for you Saturday but the maid on duty misplaced it. I'm so sorry." She handed Ruth Ann a small square envelope with a letterhead from the President's House.

Ruth Ann quickly opened it and pulled out a pristinely written note—a cordial invitation for a luncheon on the President's House lawn hosted by the First Lady on Monday.

Today.

Ruth Ann clutched her throat. "Oh dear. Dear, dear." Could she possibly make it in time?

"Don't I need an escort?"

Mrs. Schmitt rushed out the kitchen door and returned a few minutes later with a surprised Joseph Griffin in tow. "Mr. Griffin has nothing to occupy him and I'm certain he would love to escort you to the President's House. Wouldn't you, Joseph?"

Joseph Griffin looked between the two women and chuckled. "Why, only if you twist my arm hard enough."

Ruth Ann breathed a sigh of relief, but then looked down at her drab clothes. Completely inappropriate attire for a summer luncheon on the President's House lawn!

Mrs. Schmitt grabbed Ruth Ann by the arm and pulled her through the kitchen. "Come, we'll have you ready to dine with the First Lady in no time!"

Joseph Griffin called after them, "I'll have a carriage ready at the front in fifteen minutes."

Exactly fifteen minutes later, Joseph Griffin handed Ruth Ann into a Roseland House open carriage and they sped away. Ruth

Ann held onto her large garden hat, trimmed in bunches of lace and silk rosettes. She quickly added another pin to the hat to secure it to her hair. Hopefully she wouldn't be a sloppy mess when she greeted the First Lady!

Joseph chuckled from the seat opposite her. "Don't worry, my dear, you look as fashionable yet more charming than any young lady in D.C. It's a wonder some man hasn't put a ring on your finger yet."

Ruth Ann blushed. "Never mind that. Who can I expect to see at this luncheon?"

"Brace yourself. You'll be in the company of wives of the most influential men in the world. All the usual fluff and hubbub of congressmen's wives and their daughters, along with the wives of dignitaries from foreign countries. This is an opportunity to show them how civilized Indian Territory is, and don't forget to drop your newspaper's card liberally. These ladies collect those things like tickets at a fair and turn them in to their husbands, who decide how they might benefit from the offerings. Be sure they know how to subscribe to your newspaper and..." He winked. "Be prepared for their shock at how bold you are. I'm sure your little taste of the feminist movement at Garfield Park prepared you for facing these ladies."

Ruth Ann flushed deeper. She didn't bother asking how Joseph Griffin knew she'd been at the park. He reminded her of Matthew, always two steps ahead and everything figured out before she even got there.

Joseph reached into his coat pocket and withdrew a tiny contraption. "I noticed you don't have a cameraman handy, so why don't you borrow my folding pocket Kodak? You'll regret not taking pictures on your trip."

Ruth Ann eagerly accepted it. "Thank you!"

Joseph showed her how to pull the lens in and out, and explained how the flash-light worked to take pictures indoors. She couldn't wait to take her first photograph.

Ruth Ann started to ask Joseph what he planned to do after he accompanied her to the gate, but her tongue froze as she stared ahead. He turned in his seat. "You haven't seen the President's House this close, have you? Some people call it the White House. Seems a rather plain name to me."

There was certainly nothing plain about the President's House. When Ruth Ann was in Chicago for the World's Fair, she never dreamed she would see buildings so grand in her life. But the thing about the White City was it was all a facade, abandoned when the fair ended.

But this was a real White City, encompassed in the enormous house before her, a house that her people had visited throughout the past century. She could scarcely wrap her mind around the history as the carriage pulled into a circle drive and halted.

Joseph helped Ruth Ann disembark and assured her he would be back to pick her up in a few hours.

She showed her invitation to the guard at the iron gate and was admitted. The lawn was filled with ladies strolling about, carrying glasses of pink lemonade or seated at round wicker tables with tea cakes and sandwiches. They offered her smiles upon eye contact, but Ruth Ann sensed their distance. They may have thought she was from another country with her dark skin. Perhaps Italy, or India. An Indian. Ruth Ann suppressed a giggle.

"Are you Ruth Ann Teller, miss?"

Ruth Ann turned, surprised to hear her name. A girl in a starched black uniform with a spotless white apron beckoned toward a table across the lawn. "Mrs. Griswould invited you to join her at their table."

Ruth Ann followed the maid. She recalled meeting Senator Griswould on her first visit to the Capitol Building. She needed to greet the hostess, but so far, she hadn't seen the First Lady in the crowd of two hundred.

As she approached the indicated table, Ruth Ann took note of women, likely spouses of senators from the south that she met on her first rounds through the capitol with Senator Newman. While those men did have votes and influence, Ruth Ann hoped to spend time meeting people from other areas and even foreign visitors.

Wouldn't Matthew be shocked if she landed an international subscriber? Ruth Ann's mind spun with excitement, but practicality kicked in. How much did it cost to send a newspaper overseas?

No time to dwell on that. Before her was a table full of potential in her own backyard.

The women greeted her pleasantly as Ruth Ann seated herself in one of the white wicker chairs while a maid offered refreshments. Ruth Ann was politely asked questions about Indian Territory, though they stayed off the topic of Indians themselves.

To these ladies, the territory was simply the last frontier, a wilderness to be pioneered that started with the Oklahoma Land Rush of 1889. Ruth Ann thought of the business cards in her reticule and wondered if she would have the gumption to offer them around.

Halfway through her club sandwich and lemonade, Ruth Ann heard a familiar voice.

"Well, here is our brave friend from the Indian Territory."

Ruth Ann grimaced as Virginia Lee came up to the table and took a note of the southern scowls on the faces of the other women. Though Virginia Lee was one of them, she hadn't made a good impression. They probably knew of the scandal at Garfield Park and previous antics by the progressive—and aggressive—young woman.

Virginia Lee spoke to Ruth Ann. "Given your heritage, I wouldn't have thought you'd be one to run from a little excitement."

Mrs. Griswould lifted her chin. "Miss Newman, your behavior at the park was hardly a little excitement. You should know your place."

Virginia Lee ignored her, continuing to target Ruth Ann. "Could you not even take a carriage ride here without being looked after by a man? For a professional woman who should know her power over men, you certainly do not exhibit it."

As she thought of a certain young man in her life, Pepper Barnes, Ruth Ann couldn't stop herself from retorting, "I have no desire to become domineering like them. I don't want to become the oppressor."

Everyone looked shocked by her words, including Virginia Lee, and Ruth Ann knew it was time to move to another table. She rose and opened her reticule to pull out business cards for the *Choctaw Tribune*.

She laid a stack in the middle of the table. "Please feel free to take my business card. It's for the newspaper my brother *and* I publish in the Choctaw Nation."

Ruth Ann moved toward another side of the lawn as though she had somewhere specific to go. She nearly bumped into Frances Clara Cleveland's back.

The First Lady turned and smiled at Ruth Ann. "Why, hello Miss Teller, welcome to the White House. I'm so glad you came to visit me."

Despite having met the First Lady at the World's Fair and even interviewing her for a story, Ruth Ann was afraid her tongue would freeze.

But she relaxed her shoulders and replied, "I truly appreciated the invitation. It was kind of you to remember me from our meeting in Chicago."

Knowing this was the kind of opportunity Matthew wouldn't dare allow to slip by, Ruth Ann asked, "Would you mind if I stayed close to you for the luncheon? I'd like to take note of the special guests attending."

The First Lady laughed lightly, her warmth relaxing Ruth Ann even more.

"I am quite used to reporters being under my elbow, but not female ones. This is refreshing."

Relieved, Ruth Ann pulled out her tablet and pencil as Mrs. Cleveland introduced her to a lady who had been chatting with her before Ruth Ann entered the conversation.

After explaining Ruth Ann was from a newspaper in Indian Territory, Mrs. Cleveland said, "This is Mrs. Moore. Her husband is Senator Edwin Moore of Iowa. Actually, you may have heard that one of our premier lawyers, Benjamin Nakishi-Dunn, worked with Congressman Moore in a recent case at the Supreme Court."

Ruth Ann's heart skittered. "That's fascinating, Mrs. Moore." She scribbled gibberish on her tablet. "What was your husband's impression of how Mr. Nakishi handled the case?"

Mrs. Moore was stiff in a confident way. "We know Mr. Nakishi-Dunn to be a sharp, exemplary man and would trust any case to him, whether personal or when liberty is at stake. He was mentored by Judge Harrison Eldridge who recommended him to us. No one knows lawyers better than the judge. I understand Mr. Nakishi-Dunn grew up in your part of the country, though."

Ruth Ann knew little about Benjamin Nakishi's growing-up years. She settled with a simple nod as the lady opened her reticule and withdrew a card. "Do subscribe my husband to your newspaper. He is interested in what happens in your territory and we need a reliable source. I will read the newspaper as well, and will correspond with questions. Would it be satisfactory if I wrote to you directly?"

Ruth Ann accepted the card, her heart doing a flip with joy. Her first D.C. subscriber! Well, besides the First Lady. She had already subscribed at the World's Fair.

"Certainly," Ruth Ann said. "Here is my card. Simply address your correspondence to Ruth Ann Teller and I will respond promptly to any questions you have."

"Splendid."

If you only knew. Ruth Ann held back her grin and followed the First Lady to the next set of conversations.

They visited a table that held National Women's Association members who had great interest in Indian affairs. Ruth Ann wound up answering more questions than she asked, but her mission for the day was accomplished when they all enthusiastically subscribed to the *Choctaw Tribune*. Plus, they cordially allowed her to take a photograph of the table. It might well end up in the newspaper next to their story.

Ruth Ann was invited to sit at the front table with the First Lady and wives of foreign dignitaries, including one from India, who was British.

While a guest speaker from the National Women's Association spoke, Ruth Ann took notes. Her mind processed the power the newspaper had. If it wasn't for the *Choctaw Tribune*, she wouldn't be on this trip, meeting these influential people and knowing that they trusted the words she wrote. She could sway them any which way.

What Matthew always said about there not being "anything more powerful than the press except God Almighty" was startlingly true in that moment. The clarity of it struck Ruth Ann and frightened her.

Was she qualified to handle that power? Was it possible to use it to bring her brother Philip home, and would it be right to do so?

There, on the President's House lawn, were women who could help his cause, even the First Lady whose husband could extend a pardon to her brother, overruling the Choctaw justice system. It could be similar to when George Sloan obtained a stay of execution from Fort Smith for his father, Silas Sloan.

But those things chipped away at their sovereignty still more. Ruth Ann pushed the idea far away, although she couldn't help thinking of how Pepper told her that this was how politics were handled, how laws were made, how nations were changed. It was how she could bring her brother home.

But that was Pepper's way, not Ruth Ann's. And there she was, without him, and still making a success of her trip and her place as a woman.

She didn't need to be on a man's arm nor become an oppressor to prove her worth.

CHAPTER 19

On the way back to Roseland, Joseph Griffin took Ruth Ann to a telegraph office to help her subscribe the *Choctaw Tribune* to the AP so it could begin receiving stories from around the world. She took Joseph Griffin's caution to heart that some of the stories were hyperbole, but it was an access point to things a real newspaper should know.

Joseph and Ruth Ann were talking about world events when they entered the front door of Roseland. As Joseph hung his hat in the foyer, his jovial expression changed to a grimace. He nodded toward the open door leading into the parlor.

"I believe someone is waiting to speak with you."

Ruth Ann turned, hands still in the air as she removed the last pin from her hat. She caught Pepper's stare from where he stood next to the empty fireplace, arms crossed.

Joseph Griffin mumbled an excuse and quietly disappeared up the staircase, leaving Ruth Ann to face Pepper. She didn't mind. Pepper was not her trail boss on this trip.

She entered the parlor, head high. That proved to be a mistake. Her foot caught on the corner of the area rug that was turned up and she stumbled, nearly falling as her other foot caught in her skirt. She couldn't think of a more undignified way to enter a room, but there was only Pepper to witness it. She straightened her skirt and moved forward to greet Pepper.

"I hope your business meeting with the men went well," she said. "I had a pleasant afternoon with a group of ladies."

"On the President's House lawn without me!"

Ruth Ann was taken aback at Pepper's vehemence. Well, it was understandable for him to be upset at such a missed opportunity, but she wasn't going to let him take it out on her.

"Pepper, it happened to be a ladies' luncheon. There were no men there, so it wouldn't have been appropriate for you to be there. Besides, I'm not obliged to take you on every social call."

"Social call?" Pepper dropped his arms to his sides and took a step toward her, leaving only a short stride between them. "You had the ear of the wife of the United States president, and didn't think to include me? I thought you were here to help our people."

Ruth Ann swallowed, hard. That wasn't truly why she was there. "I'm trying, Pepper. But while we're on that note, you may as well know I'm going to ask Benjamin Nakishi to take my brother's case—since you won't tell me straight out what your plan is. Mr. Nakishi is the only one who has a chance against Tecumseh Shoemaker."

The tension in Pepper's face relaxed, his expression showing mild shock, but he recovered quickly and ran both hands through his hair, gaze turning to the ceiling as if to hold his temper with her.

"We do not need Nakishi getting mixed up with an internal conflict among our people, especially not a criminal case like your brother's." Pepper dropped his hands and looked at her again, his expression a mix of frustration and understanding. "I told you I'm going to take care of things with Philip. Would you just trust me?"

Ruth Ann tightened her arms to keep from slapping Pepper.

"And just how do you plan on taking care of things? Tell me now."

Pepper took another step closer, and she caught her breath at his nearness. He had the comforting scent of home, but she didn't trust it.

He lowered his voice, gentled it. "I've always admired your ability to think for yourself. But you don't need to do that this time. I'm going to take care of everything, including you, if you'll just let me."

Ruth Ann swallowed. The only thing she knew was that she needed to get away from Pepper Barnes. Now.

She turned, mindful of the offensive rug, and hurried from the room and up the stairs. No footsteps pursued her.

Dear Matthew,

I've written and rewritten this letter many times and have settled on bluntness. You were right, sort of. Pepper Barnes is not to be trusted, yet I cannot help but feel you were part of pushing me into this ridiculous alliance with him.

I agree we need to work out what is between you and me in order to set our family back to rights. The only way is to be perfectly honest. I will begin by saying you pushed me away when I needed you. And you knew about Philip for days, or longer, and did not tell me, even when I found you in McAlester.

I feel the trust between us is broken, and I do not know how to fix it. I hope you do.

Your sister,
Ruth Ann

Sounds coming from the dining room alerted Ruth Ann that it was fuller than usual as she dropped her letters in the foyer mailbox. Ruth Ann hadn't used the whole roll of film Joseph gave her, so she would develop and send the pictures later. Hopefully, they came out.

Georgia Pearl had gone out with Virginia Lee and Agatha to visit friends at the university in Wesley Heights, leaving the suite quiet for the day. Ruth Ann spent the afternoon writing an article about her luncheon with the First Lady, the Supreme Court case victory, and a description of Chief Pushmataha's resting place in the Congressional Cemetery.

When she penned the article about the Supreme Court case, she hesitated, thinking about Pepper's demand that she not include "Dunn" when writing about Benjamin Nakishi. But why? Pepper expected her to obey blindly, but she told herself that wasn't why she ultimately decided to use his full name. That was how the man introduced himself and how she would report it.

She slipped the personal letter to Matthew in the mailbox last, addressed to their home so no one at the newspaper would see it.

When Ruth Ann entered the dining room, she saw the center of the attention was Benjamin Nakishi.

Senator Newman, Joseph Griffin, and other guests at Roseland, along with their host, Mrs. Schmitt, circled close to the lawyer. A few of the Choctaw delegates were in the room, including Forbis Kanitobe and Pepper, but they stood aloof by the other wall, as though waiting for general excitement over the Supreme Court case victory to die down. Ruth Ann hesitated in the doorway, unsure if she should join the Choctaw delegates or the party around the Choctaw lawyer.

Mrs. Schmidt caught her eye and waved her over. Benjamin Nakishi turned and greeted Ruth Ann with a smile.

"Good evening, Miss Teller."

Ruth Ann returned his smile shyly, wondering at the depth of his voice. In the open space of the cemetery, she hadn't noticed it. Nor how his smile was one that could win over even Judge Kendrick—if only she could get Benjamin Nakishi inside the Tobucksy County Courthouse for Philip's trial. Neither Judge Kendrick nor Tecumseh Shoemaker would buffalo her again, not with Benjamin Nakishi there.

Joseph nodded at the lawyer. "Ruth Ann, I was just offering my congratulations for that monumental win, and you know us catty reporters. We want to know what's next on Mr. Nakishi's agenda before he's even had a chance to get back to his office."

The others laughed lightly, but Ruth Ann caught Benjamin looking into her eyes, conveying a message. When his eyes went over to the Choctaws briefly, she understood. He knew what they would want of him, and he would face that first.

She didn't know why he communicated that to her, but it made her warm and uneasy at the same time. What would he think if he knew she had selfish motives for wanting to spend time with him?

A bell jingled from the kitchen, and Mrs. Schmitt invited everyone to the table. Ruth Ann was surprised yet pleased when

Benjamin Nakishi pulled out a chair for her despite, or maybe because of, Pepper still being frustrated with her. But Pepper concealed it, even where he sat directly across from her.

As he took the seat beside her, Benjamin Nakishi said, "I understand you visited the First Lady today, Miss Teller. Have you heard how she may be related to Chief Peter Pitchlynn?"

Ruth Ann nodded, grateful the first topic of the dinner was Choctaw-related since the delegates were taking seats close around them.

"She mentioned it when I interviewed her at the Chicago World's Fair," Ruth Ann said. "When I returned home, I looked up the passage in Charles Dickens' *American Notes* to read the description again of him meeting Peter Pitchlynn on a river boat. Our people have had extraordinary impact on this country, and still do."

She smiled to let Benjamin Nakishi know she was congratulating him on his Supreme Court case in her own way.

Seated close to him, she felt what a tremendous presence he was in the room. No wonder Pepper wanted him in the Choctaw Nation, fighting for their people.

Yet Benjamin Nakishi didn't make her feel small. There was a meekness about him that she admired.

"Now that you're done with this case for the whites, what are your plans?" Pepper asked.

Ruth Ann frowned at Pepper. He was too blunt if he really wanted to get into politics, but that served him well most times, feeding his ego, unfortunately.

Benjamin answered, "I have a policy to not look at any other cases until I've taken a rest. It's something my mentor taught me."

From the head of the table, Mrs. Schmidt asked, "Benjamin, would you say grace for us this evening?"

Head bowed and eyes closed made Ruth Ann feel as though she were in a dream world, listening to the gentle cadence of Benjamin Nakishi's words.

"Father, thank You for each person seated here. Thank You for my Choctaw relatives who are here. I pray for everyone's safety and for this food to be blessed to the nourishment of our bodies. In Jesus' name. Amen."

Ruth Ann whispered, "amen." She added a prayer in her heart that God would bring Benjamin Nakishi home with her.

Conversation restarted as the servants brought out steaming dishes. One of the maids stretched between Ruth Ann and Mrs. Kanitobe. Ruth Ann leaned away to allow more room, and her arm brushed Benjamin's coat. It held the scent of a summer breeze, and Ruth Ann reluctantly straightened after the dish was on the table.

Benjamin held another dish for Ruth Ann to scoop from while he directed a question at the other Choctaws. "I would like to take you all on a tour tomorrow if you don't have prior commitments. There are a great deal of books and papers at the Library of Congress and the archives in the Capitol Building basement that pertain to our people. There is a particular piece I made arrangements to see. Would you all please join me for the day?"

Ruth Ann quickly responded. "That is generous of you to take the time, Mr. Nakishi. I would love to see the library."

She slid a sideways glance at Pepper. He should be happy at the chance for them to get close to Benjamin Nakishi. But there was the hint of a storm in Pepper's eyes. She wasn't sure why, other than he was still annoyed with her for going off to the President's House without him.

But he wasn't the one who spoke next. Forbis Kanitobe, who had hardly said a word since their arrival in D.C., stared at Benjamin Nakishi. He said roughly, "You have been away from your people too long."

Ruth Ann wished she could say something to counter the abrupt remark, but she had no words. Neither did Benjamin. He quietly filled his plate.

Surprisingly, it was Pepper who saved the day. Sort of.

"Annie and I will join you," he said, using her nickname in front of everyone, just like Matthew did. But it sounded different, more as if he was establishing their relationship as closer than it was. Ironically, she was closer to Pepper than anyone in the room.

"In addition to fighting for our sovereignty and the future of our people, I want to know everything about Choctaws that there is in D.C.," Pepper added. "Anything to help us win the fight back home."

There it was—Pepper's first hint about Benjamin joining that fight. From the look on the lawyer's face, he knew it.

Ruth Ann turned the conversation to the history of Choctaws visiting D.C. and asked what sort of papers were in the capitol basement.

But her mind fretted about how Pepper might offend Benjamin Nakishi and ruin her chance to convince the best lawyer in the country to defend her brother in a Choctaw court back home.

CHAPTER 21

The Choctaw delegation entered the Capitol Building together. It was the first time Ruth Ann had seen all of her traveling companions in one place since they arrived in D.C. Everyone, herself included, was always off sightseeing or being hosted at private functions around the city. It was good to group up, especially under the guidance of Benjamin Nakishi, who led them to the north wing where the Congressional Library was housed. He explained that the new building for the Library of Congress would be completed in a few years.

Ruth Ann stepped to the side to allow the others to pass while she took photographs in the Great Rotunda and the marbled halls with Joseph Griffin's pocket Kodak. She had offered to return his camera, but he insisted she keep it for the remainder of her trip.

When they entered the library's long reading room, the Choctaws spoke in hushed tones as they moved about the room, not disturbing the researchers there. Before they arrived, Benjamin explained how he spent a great deal of time researching, and also relied on research assistants for major cases.

Ruth Ann could see why. The library work tables overflowed

with books. She gazed up at the two floors visible in the open ceiling that showed yet more rows of books and rooms dedicated to librarians in various sections, like the map room. Benjamin showed them how to search the index cards for books that contained Choctaw matters for when they wanted to come back.

After exploring the long room, Benjamin led them out to the second floor and asked a librarian he knew to show them the first book ever mass printed—the Gutenberg Bible. How Ruth Ann wished Matthew were there to see where the printing industry began!

Benjamin encouraged the group to stay close, but that proved impossible when they exited the library. The Choctaws were stopped by curious visitors, especially foreign ones, and by acquaintances. Conversations started in the middle of the hallway, and others in their party wandered off to explore the Capitol Building grounds or went back into the library to look up books.

By the time the entourage made its way back to the Rotunda and the spiral staircase leading to the first floor, only Ruth Ann, Pepper, and Mr. and Mrs. Kanitobe remained with Benjamin.

He assessed their party and said, "We'll eat as planned in the Congressional Members' Dining Room, but if the others don't join us soon, we will need to move on. I have a very special appointment for us to keep."

Going through the dining room, they took a table outside on the flagstone terrace encased with tall hedges. After they were seated, Ruth Ann felt the awkward silence settling heavy with Forbis Kanitobe remaining cold toward Benjamin. Pepper was intent on the menu.

Thankfully, a waiter entertained them while they ordered. Then Benjamin picked up outlining what lay ahead in the basement and the long list of records kept before their people were removed from their homeland in Mississippi. He explained how most of the United States' documents were stored in basements, attics, and libraries throughout the city with little care for preservation. But Benjamin did know where to locate vital paperwork for their people.

Pepper asked questions about specific documents, then declared he would return to D.C. and spend several months collecting material their people needed to retain sovereignty as a nation.

It was after this declaration that a crackly voice boomed, "Well, if it isn't my friend, Benny!"

A man approached their table, hands deep in his pockets that seemed to reach to his knees, a coat a size too large, and too warm for the mild day. Because of his short stature, the man was able to bump shoulders with the seated Benjamin, who greeted him.

"Hello, Ed. Allow me to introduce some friends."

Ed gave Ruth Ann an extra wide grin when she was introduced. A worn fedora perched on his head, and several days of growth sporadically covered his chin and neck.

The man removed his hat. "Good to meet you folks and don't hesitate one minute to tell ol' Ed what you need. I know every nook and cranny of this city and can squeeze you through any you've got mind to."

While Pepper and Forbis were unamused, Ruth Ann replied, "Thank you, Mister..." She glanced at Benjamin, who filled in, "Ernie. Ed Ernie."

"But folks just call me Ed, little lady. I reckon you folks are off to see those Indian treaties?"

A jolt went through Ruth Ann like she experienced at Pushmataha's grave. She looked to Benjamin.

He grimaced, but smiled amiably. "Well, that was going to be a surprise, but I take it from the looks on their faces, they are surprised."

Mrs. Kanitobe breathed, "We will see the treaties our people signed with America?"

Even Pepper looked astonished. It likely never occurred to him to ask where the old treaties were kept. Who knew when the last time was that their people saw them? Perhaps not since Chief Peter Pitchlynn, and even longer before then.

Benjamin nodded in answer to Mrs. Kanitobe's question. "Senator Newman assisted in making the arrangements. He understands what this will mean to us. I haven't seen them myself, but I've always wanted to."

Benjamin motioned for Ed to join them at the table, but Ed waved him off, grinning sheepishly. "I'm 'fraid I left my wallet in my other trousers."

Benjamin shook his head with a smile. He reached into the inner pocket of his coat and withdrew a thin leather wallet. He took some bills and placed them in Ed's outstretched hand.

"Thank you, sir. I'll put this on your account."

With a final grin, Ed Earnie left them as their food arrived.

Benjamin explained, "Ed does investigation work for me. This city does have many nooks and crannies he can squeeze into."

Ruth Ann lifted her roast beef sandwich, though suddenly lost her appetite. She credited it to being anxious and excited about seeing the treaties, but she also felt uneasy at Benjamin's offhanded explanation.

Did he use that man to conduct shady work during court cases? Was that why Benjamin Nakishi was so good at what he did? Perhaps she'd been too quick in her trust, and in her desire to get close to him.

CHAPTER 22

A sapling thin woman inserted a large brass key into the lock of the door to the room and turned it. The clicking of the tumblers resounded in the silence of the present and the past. To Ruth Ann, it was as though they were unlocking a portal to their people's history.

The group was in the bowels of the Capitol Building in a section where thousands of the young nation's documents were kept. They entered the small room and stepped up to a high table as directed. Ruth Ann was sandwiched between Benjamin Nakishi and Pepper Barnes as they waited for the woman to return from the rows of shelves that held boxes secured with thick red string. The woman explained that the first acts of Congress were stored in this place, along with Indian treaties.

She returned and placed a box on the table. She untied the red string, letting it fall away as she lifted the lid on the wide, flat box.

As it had been the first moment at Pushmataha's headstone, Ruth Ann caught her breath and tears sprang to her eyes.

Treaty of Dancing Rabbit Creek.

Signed September 27, 1830.

Most of her people back home would never have this

opportunity to stand shoulder to shoulder with four other Choctaws, viewing the final treaty that ceded their homelands in Mississippi for land in the new Indian Territory. This treaty led to the disastrous forced removal of Ruth Ann's people across a trail of tears that many perished on, like her grandmother's parents.

She closed her eyes and let memories of the Grandmother's stories coat her memory of this moment. The grandmother survived that trail and later bore children, including Ruth Ann's mother, who bore three children. All of whom, as Ruth Ann recently learned, were still alive.

She opened her eyes and joined in silently reading each page of the 64-year-old document. On the final pages were the names of the chiefs who signed it with their marks, and the signature of the President of the United States at the time, Andrew Jackson.

The pages transported Ruth Ann to another time, another place, a mile marker in her people's history. How many mile markers lay ahead?

After several minutes, Pepper stepped away from the table. Ruth Ann glanced over at him and caught her breath to see his eyes red as if with tears. She suspected he read every word of the treaty, ready to take this as ammunition into their peoples' current battle.

Forbis Kanitobe and his wife, neither of whom had fully stepped up to the table, turned and went to stand by the door. From the brief glimpse Ruth Ann got of the man's face, she knew the moment affected him as deeply as it did her.

Benjamin shifted, and she felt a release from the moment. They both turned to join the others by the door. Ruth Ann realized she was gripping her hands together. She released them, her energy spent.

The Choctaws waited outside the room while the woman returned the document to its box and tied it once again with red string. Then she conducted them to the main entrance and bid them good day, not seeming to comprehend the significance of the visit.

When they exited into the June sunshine, Forbis said abruptly, "We are returning to the house now."

He and his wife started walking west. Though they were a good three miles from Roseland, Ruth Ann doubted they would hail a cab or take the streetcar. Her people were used to walking. They had walked over four hundred miles west to their new homeland. Perhaps the Kanitobes were reliving a piece of that history there in the nation's capitol.

Ruth Ann stood quietly, collecting her thoughts. Pepper, eyes clear now, stared off as though plotting the next thirty years of his life. Benjamin waited.

The moment was broken when a familiar figure wove through the foot traffic toward them and up the steps. Georgia Pearl regained her breath after the climb and set her sights on Pepper.

"Mr. Nakishi's assistant mentioned I could find you all here," she said. "I was supposed to be at a charity fundraiser this afternoon, but it was postponed, so I thought I would join you all. Perhaps we could rent bicycles and ride around the National Mall?"

After glancing at Ruth Ann, Benjamin answered, "That's a fine idea. I planned nothing else because I knew the Choctaw delegation had other business to take care of." He chuckled. "I was correct. This is all that's left."

Ruth Ann glanced up at him with a light laugh. "It seems so."

Then her brain made the connection with Georgia Pearl's words and her stomach dropped. "But as you know, bicycles and I have not made friends."

Georgia Pearl latched onto Pepper's arm, finally jolting him out of his thousand-mile stare. "That is no problem," she said, grinning. "We'll get tandem bicycles. I am good at riding and with

Mr. Barnes' strength, I'm sure we won't have any trouble. And I know Mr. Nakishi gets around often on a bicycle, don't you?"

Benjamin looked down at Ruth Ann and she felt more than the sun warming her cheeks. What if she embarrassed herself by attempting to ride a bicycle with the man who might be God's answer to her prayers?

But she swallowed and nodded. "I suppose we could give it a try."

CHAPTER 23

Ruth Ann gripped the handlebars of the tandem bicycle, feet planted on the ground behind the pedals. She had worn her rose-colored skirt with its high hem because she knew they faced a lot of walking that day. But she still did not feel prepared as Benjamin Nakishi stood beside the bicycle, holding it steady while he observed Pepper and Georgia Pearl mount theirs.

Ruth Ann wasn't sure Pepper knew how to ride. She only knew he didn't look happy with the arrangements. When they rented the two tandem bicycles, he tried to insist he be the one to ride with Ruth Ann.

Georgia Pearl put an end to that by saying they should pair up with an experienced rider each. Benjamin agreed. Once they were seated, Pepper waved for Benjamin to lead the way.

Benjamin glanced at Ruth Ann. She nodded hesitantly. She wasn't ready, but it was time to try. Benjamin mounted the bicycle by throwing his long leg forward over the center bar as though they were riding a horse and she was already behind the saddle.

He spoke over his shoulder. "Now, just put your feet on the pedals. When I push off, match my pace. I'll do the rest."

Ruth Ann swallowed and reluctantly lifted her feet to place them on the pedals, holding her breath, precariously balanced on the seat. Benjamin held the tandem bicycle firmly upright and pushed off, planting his feet on the pedals and getting them started. Ruth Ann tried to match his peddling speed, waiting to topple over.

But they didn't! She'd gone more than two feet on a bicycle, the brick road beneath them flying by.

Ruth Ann didn't look up as Benjamin turned them in a smooth arc. When they completed it, Ruth Ann finally breathed and glanced around him to see they were headed back toward Pepper and Georgia Pearl who were getting pushed off. They managed to stay upright, though wobbly, and turned the bicycle in a half circle to follow after Benjamin and Ruth Ann.

The feeling of the speed beneath and the wind catching her hair reminded Ruth Ann of being on her horse, Skyline, at a gallop on Uncle Preston's ranch, the only place she ever rode astride.

How thrilling to ride a bicycle!

Ruth Ann worked her legs more than she did when horseback riding, but she also experienced a sense of control and power over the contraption. It wasn't merely a mode of transportation —it was a vehicle to go wherever she wanted and however fast she wanted.

No wonder Virginia Lee said progressive young women should know how to ride bicycles. She understood why Lance Fuller got one despite the rough roads in Indian Territory.

"All right back there?" Benjamin asked.

Ruth Ann said, "Oh, yes. This is wonderful, thank you!"

Feeling more confident, Ruth Ann glanced around at the tree-lined street flashing by. They were headed downhill toward the Potomac River, traveling B Street NW, the same road where the

Baltimore and Potomac Railroad station was located. She hadn't seen much of the National Mall by cab, and thought she would make the trek around it on foot. But this was much easier.

She glanced back to see that Pepper and Georgia Pearl had fallen behind, but they were keeping pace. Ruth Ann faced forward again.

Benjamin had removed his coat and tied it to the handlebars before they started. His long sleeved white shirt showed he had a strong frame suited for athletics. According to one of the city papers, athletic leagues were rapidly gaining in popularity, especially football. Though not all the men were stout like Benjamin, Ruth Ann definitely saw an advantage in football for big men. But it seemed to her that the game was taken far too seriously, with leagues and college scholarships forming for it.

"There's the Washington Monument," he said.

Ruth Ann didn't need to strain to see the towering white obelisk rising before them. They peddled around it, much closer than she had gotten before. It was enormous.

"Can I get a photograph?" she asked. She hated to stop, but she was confident Benjamin could get them going again.

Benjamin slowed and braked. Ruth Ann pulled out the pocket camera from the case strapped over her shoulder and around her back. She angled the lens to capture the height of the monument from bottom to top.

They started off again, Pepper and Georgia Pearl coming alongside them. Georgia Pearl grinned at Ruth Ann, obviously enjoying the tandem ride with Pepper Barnes.

Ruth Ann smiled back, then turned her attention to focusing on the movement of the bicycle. She was beginning to feel at one with it, understanding its balance and rhythm. Perhaps she could ride one of the bicycles at Roseland soon.

Benjamin slowed their pace and turned the bicycle in an arc to circle around the large ponds at the end of the mall and head back up the other side. Ruth Ann spotted the Bureau of

Engraving and Printing. A definite stop for Matthew if he were there.

If only he were.

Ruth Ann pushed that thought from her mind. This was an afternoon to make good memories, not dwell on her family's turmoil.

At 12th Street, Benjamin turned off at a rack for bicycles. He braked and dismounted the same as he'd gotten on. He held the bicycle while Ruth Ann stepped off. Her legs were shaking, but she grinned up at him.

"Thank you, Mr. Nakishi! I thought I'd never be able to ride one of those without crashing."

There was a high pitch to her voice that she couldn't help. The ride was exhilarating, and Benjamin Nakishi was so progressive, living in this big city, having assistants and arguing cases in the Supreme Court.

But then her people, Choctaw Indians, had always been part of this country's history, both in founding it and driving it forward into the new century. She just wasn't sure where her people would be when the twentieth century came.

Benjamin pulled the bicycle into the rack and turned to Ruth Ann. "I'm glad you enjoyed it. But please, call me Benjamin. 'Mister' is too formal for us Choctaw folks."

Ruth Ann bit her lips to ward off a bashful smile. "All right. Please call me Ruth Ann."

Pepper and Georgia Pearl had lagged behind again but caught the turnoff and now skidded to a halt by the rack. Pepper kept the tandem balanced for Georgia Pearl to get off.

"A very fine place to stop, Mr. Nakishi!" she said, dismounting and clasping Pepper's arm before he had the bicycle in the rack. "I love this apothecary shop. Ruth Ann, have you had the new Hershey Chocolates?"

Pepper shook Georgia Pearl off to finish putting the bicycle on the rack. He had trouble getting it in. Benjamin went to help.

Georgia Pearl leaned over Ruth Ann and Benjamin's bicycle, one foot off the ground behind her as she whispered, "You look positively radiant, my friend. You best loosen your corset!"

Ruth Ann's cheeks burned as they all entered the shop. Benjamin treated them to a large box of Hershey Chocolates, saying they would need the extra energy for the return up the hill.

As she relished a piece of chocolate, Ruth Ann knew she hadn't felt such joy in her being in quite some time. Whether it was the extraordinary chocolates, the invigorating bicycle ride, or Benjamin Nakishi's kind brown eyes, she couldn't say.

It wouldn't hurt to follow Georgia Pearl's advice when they got back to Roseland.

CHAPTER 24

After they returned the bicycles to the rental stand late that afternoon, Georgia Pearl suggested they go back to Georgetown for dinner. She described an Italian restaurant with lots of music and fun that young people liked to frequent.

Ruth Ann wasn't sure about spending her evening frivolously, but when Benjamin mentioned there was a fine bookshop close to the restaurant that had poetry readings every evening, Ruth Ann consented. It would do them good to enjoy an evening without political pressures. And no time spent with Benjamin was frivolous.

Now that they were acquainted on a first name basis, she needed to find a way to begin testing the waters on convincing him to return to Indian Territory. She thought Pepper might have the same idea, but he wasn't acting very friendly toward Benjamin for some reason.

At the restaurant, Ruth Ann found that Georgia Pearl was right. It was frequented by young people and there was a group of musicians on a stage set in one corner. Conversation was nearly impossible with the music, whistles, and applause for songs Ruth Ann had never heard before. Georgia Pearl assured them this music was all the rage.

After walking and bicycling all day, Ruth Ann felt herself drifting into a sleepy state during the meal. Progress with Benjamin might have to come tomorrow.

Benjamin clicked open his pocket watch, bringing her back to the moment. "The poetry reading begins at 8p.m.," he said. "We should get started if we want to get a table. It normally fills up."

Georgia Pearl groaned dramatically. "Wouldn't we all prefer this lively beat?"

To Ruth Ann's surprise, Pepper stood. "I promised my father to look up a book he wanted. This bookstore of Nakishi's might have it."

Georgia Pearl readily consented.

Benjamin started to pay their tab, but Pepper beat him to it. Ruth Ann resisted rolling her eyes at the front Pepper put on.

The bookstore was only a few blocks away and, as Benjamin had cautioned, it was nearly full. Ruth Ann inhaled the scent of thousands of books in the narrow space, along with freshly brewed coffee. Chairs fanned out from the back corner, facing a small wooden platform. Four round tables sat behind the rows of chairs.

Ruth Ann and her party secured the last table, and they settled in, all except Pepper. He began perusing the shelves and didn't return, even when the reading began.

Was this Ruth Ann's opportunity to talk to Benjamin directly? How else could she bring up her brother's case with Pepper always hovering around?

But Benjamin's attention was on the reading. With the first lines Ruth Ann, too, found herself captivated by the woman who passionately shared her poem, a narrative on poverty stricken streets in New York City. Ruth Ann envisioned such areas that she saw in Chicago, along with stories Beulah Levitt told of her years living in New York as a Jewish Russian immigrant.

The cadence of the words made Ruth Ann's heart ache. She wished she could capture tragedy in such a stunning way. Matthew could if he would, but he insisted writing was for changing the world, not entertainment. Listening that evening, Ruth Ann wondered if writing could be both.

When the first reading ended, Georgia Pearl popped out of her seat and excused herself, going to find Pepper Barnes among the bookshelves. Benjamin, who had risen in respect to Georgia Pearl's exit, asked Ruth Ann if she could hold their table while he went to get a book himself.

Ruth Ann held back her sigh as he left. Another lost opportunity. If only Georgia Pearl had stayed. Ruth Ann was anxious to peruse the shelves too, especially when she watched Benjamin go up a wrought iron spiral staircase that she hadn't noticed before.

Glancing up, she realized there was a loft area with yet more shelves of books overlooking the lower half of the bookstore.

Ruth Ann brought her gaze back down in time to see Pepper Barnes approaching the table again. He halted across from her.

"I found my book," he said. "Let's go. We have a lot of work to do this week."

Ruth Ann straightened in her chair. "I'm not ready to leave. I want to look through the books, too. And besides, it's early. In case you haven't noticed, late evenings are part of the culture here, so I suggest we adjust and enjoy it."

Pepper bent over and placed his fists on the table in front of her. Ruth Ann raised her eyebrows at the intensity of his gaze so close to her.

"There is nothing in this city to enjoy, Annie," he said. "These politicians have ravaged our people for generations. And you agreed to come write stories about what the delegation is doing, not flitter around sightseeing with Nakishi."

Ruth Ann leaned back in her chair, as much to settle in deeper as to put a bit of distance between her and Pepper. "I thought one of your main objectives was to get close to

Benjamin Nakishi, to show him our people are worth coming home for?"

That stormy look edging Pepper's eyes came on with the full force of a tornado swirling in them. "I changed my mind. I'll take care of Nakishi, not you. Now let's go."

Pepper shoved away from the table and strode for the door. He halted at it and looked back. Ruth Ann didn't move. He glared at her until Georgia Pearl blocked his view as she came back to the table. She looked around, asking Ruth Ann, "Where's Mr. Barnes?"

Ruth Ann held her voice steady as she said, "He is returning to Roseland."

Georgia Pearl spun to look toward the door. Pepper was gone. "Oh! I'll go with him. You coming?"

Even as she said it, Georgia Pearl was off for the door. She looked back and gave Ruth Ann a mischievous grin as she left to catch up with Pepper.

Ruth Ann sat there, astonished at both Pepper's words and that he left them so rudely. She had ignored the agitation she felt from him when she rode the tandem bicycle with Benjamin instead of him.

Was he jealous? That didn't seem likely, but it didn't matter. Ruth Ann wasn't going to bend to his every whim. Besides, this was the opportunity she so wanted, to speak to Benjamin without interruption.

But there was one problem she didn't want to think about just yet.

Benjamin returned to the table, holding up a book. "This is from a local poet who did a reading a few months ago," he said. "She wrote a great deal about the natural wonders of the west from many visits out there. I thought you might enjoy a copy, Miss Ruth Ann."

She hesitantly accepted the gift, but there was nothing wrong with doing so that she knew of. She smiled. "Yakoke. I'm certain I will."

As he took a seat, Ruth Ann gathered her courage. "Mr. Nakishi—Benjamin—there's something I want to ask you about."

He settled and turned to her. "Of course."

She forged ahead, trying to disguise the anxiousness in her voice. "You seem very content in your work here in D.C." She halted. How could she say this without asking directly?

"Yes?" he prompted.

"I'm just curious if it's the location that makes you content, or the work itself?"

Benjamin nodded slowly, as though understanding what she meant. "I am content here, Miss Ruth Ann. It is where I feel God has me. I know the Choctaws would like to see me return to Indian Territory, but this is home for me now."

Ruth Ann swallowed. She dared not ask anymore, not yet, or risk having him refuse her personal request. He thought she was asking on behalf of the Choctaw delegation, and it was best to leave it at that.

Matthew taught her that if a story wasn't coming together, to try another angle. That was what she needed to find.

The bookshop quieted again as the poet took the platform once more. Benjamin glanced around. "Where are our companions?"

Ruth Ann sighed. "Like everyone else today, I'm afraid they drifted away. Georgia Pearl and Pepper left a few minutes ago to return to Roseland."

Benjamin quickly stood, looking toward the door with a frown.

Ruth Ann sighed. "I'm sorry Pepper left without even thanking you for giving us such monumental experiences."

Benjamin lifted his coat from the back of his chair, not meeting Ruth Ann's gaze. "I'll escort you back to Roseland right away."

Ruth Ann sighed and gathered her things, sad she was missing an opportunity to explore the bookstore. But they couldn't very well stay out that evening without a chaperone.

On the sidewalk, Ruth Ann accepted Benjamin's arm as they headed down P Street toward Roseland a few blocks away. Somehow, being on his arm felt different from Pepper's. She wasn't an ornament like Virginia Lee said. She felt valued. Even Benjamin's insistence that they return to the house was to protect her reputation. He was quite a fellow.

Could she possibly persuade such a man of integrity to return to the Choctaw Nation and defend her brother who was accused of hideous crimes? She needed that other angle.

There was one person in D.C. said to know Benjamin Nakishi better than anyone. There was nothing to stop Ruth Ann from paying Judge Harrison Eldridge a call tomorrow morning.

$\mathcal{A}$ note awaited Ruth Ann when she returned to Roseland with Benjamin Nakishi. It was from Pepper, directing her to be ready at 10a.m. for a private meeting with Senator Newman at the Capitol Building.

All well and good, but she had something to do before then.

Ruth Ann rose early the next morning, dressed quickly, and begged a muffin from the kitchen staff. She also wrangled the judge's address from one of the knowledgeable carriage drivers. She didn't ask him to take her, though. She wanted to be discreet.

Outside, Ruth Ann debated trying one of the bicycles, but she wasn't ready to ride on her own. She headed east and caught the streetcar to Dupont Circle. She got off and headed up 19th Street, finally arriving in front of a stately home, its narrow yard trimmed with a white picket fence. She was being rude by arriving unannounced, but she couldn't always follow the rules of etiquette. Her time in D.C. was ticking away.

She walked past the residence, turned around, and walked past it again, trying to observe if the household was awake. Smoke wafted from the kitchen chimney and the front drapes were drawn back. Someone was up.

Ruth Ann lifted the gate latch and entered the yard. It was manicured, but had an old, comfortable feel to it that said it wouldn't mind if not every blade of grass or flower petal was in place.

She mounted the steps and used the brass lion head knocker to rap. This was not the time for timidness. Her family's future hung in the balance.

The door creaked open and an elderly man dressed in a morning sweater, baggy trousers, and brown loafers stood there. He peered out, adjusting the spectacles on his sharp nose beneath his blue eyes.

"May I help you?" he asked.

"I'm Ruth Ann Teller of Dickens, Indian Territory, a newspaper reporter traveling with a Choctaw delegation. I have come to see Judge Eldridge about a mutual acquaintance, Benjamin Nakishi-Dunn."

It sounded as though she were introducing herself as a politician running for office. How ridiculous.

The man, likely the judge's butler, let an amused smile play on his lips.

"A female reporter from Indian Territory to see the judge? Well, you'd best come into his office then."

Ruth Ann followed the butler down the narrow hall with its high ceiling. The dark interior was far from the bright Roseland House mansion and other grand buildings Ruth Ann had visited, yet it felt cool and homey.

The man led her into a room at the end of the hall and indicated two leather wingback chairs positioned in front of a heavy oak desk. The office was large but pressed close with bookcases on all four walls, barely leaving room for the door where they entered.

Ruth Ann imagined if she were wealthy, this was the sort of office she'd have—one step away from a library.

She took a seat in one of the wingbacks. "Is the judge about yet?"

"Oh, he's a fairly early riser." The butler went to a stack of books by a chair near the fireplace and began re-shelving them. "What was it you wanted to see him about, again?"

"I, well, I'd rather speak to him directly."

"That serious, is it?"

He finished shelving the books and rubbed his chin. The sparkle in his eye gave him away, and Ruth Ann smiled, relaxing.

"You're Judge Eldridge, aren't you?"

The old man returned her smile. "You have good instincts, young lady. A fine thing for a reporter."

He took a pipe from his desk and stuffed it with tobacco, holding it where Ruth Ann could see a forest intricately carved into it—deer, pine trees, a river.

The judge examined the carved scene himself. "Young Ben gave me this pipe on my retirement a decade ago. He's like a son to me." He lit the pipe, inhaled, and sighed heavily. "Old men should never play matchmakers."

Ruth Ann shifted, uncomfortable at the statement. Was he referring to Benjamin's engagement to the judge's daughter? Former engagement, to be precise.

Ruth Ann decided not to respond. The judge seemed to have his thoughts arranged, and she was to listen, then ask questions to try and find the new angle she needed.

The judge settled into the wingback chair next to hers, a round table situated between the two.

"Ben is the finest young man I've ever known," he continued. "The kind of son I would have wished for."

Judge Eldridge settled deep in the chair, crossing one leg over the other. Ruth Ann had a feeling he'd sat there in conversation like this hundreds of times with Benjamin.

"But enough of my rambling for now," the judge said, shifting to look at Ruth Ann. "You are with that Choctaw delegation and I know your people would be very glad to see Benjamin return home and work for the tribe, especially with the opposition you're facing."

The judge paused and looked at Ruth Ann, giving her the opportunity to steer the conversation in that direction. If Pepper were there, he would jump at the opportunity in a heartbeat. Ruth Ann didn't know what to say. She did want Benjamin to return the same as Pepper did, but for a different reason. And she wasn't ready to share her family's story with the judge, no matter how comfortable she already felt in his presence.

She chose her words carefully. "Mr. Nakishi is originally from Indian Territory, isn't he? How did he come to be here?"

The judge had that amused smile again. Ruth Ann wasn't good at being clever. A straightforward approach was one she learned from Matthew. He didn't dance around an issue. That was, until he decided to hide the fact that Philip was still alive.

"I suppose I'll start at the beginning and give you some of Ben's life story," the judge said, drawing on his pipe. "At least from the time I've known him. The things before that, well, that's for him to tell.

"I had an old friend who owned one of the largest department store chains in the east. John was based in New York but came down to me in D.C. for legal advice. He often brought up his interest in the west and the first people of this land. He was fascinated with Indigenous people and their future. We had long discussions on whether they would be around in the next hundred years."

The judge paused and met Ruth Ann's eyes. She nodded for him to go on, though it was hard to hear of her people spoken of in third person. And the speculation that they might not be in the 20th century.

The judge went on. "John wanted to do something about it. He concocted a study of sorts, to prove that Indians were as intelligent as any white man. He decided to sponsor an essay competition for Indian boys across the country, offering scholarships for the top three entrants. I helped by contacting Indian boarding schools from Carlisle to Spencer Academy."

Ruth Ann waited during the pause while the judge drew on his pipe for a few puffs. She knew Spencer Academy was established by the Choctaw Nation in 1841, named for Secretary of War John C. Spencer. This was where Benjamin's story began.

The judge laid the back of his hand on his knee, smoke from the pipe drifting up. "We received over two hundred fine entries, but there was one that stood out head and shoulders above the rest. It painted such a captivating, thought-out future for the young man's people that I knew we found one of our recipients. John selected the other two, but my focus was on Benjamin, the Choctaw full-blood from Spencer. He was seventeen when we brought him and the other boys out for their first semester at an ivy league preparatory school. Ben didn't disappoint me. He had heart and grit, and I knew that boy could do anything he set his mind to. And without hurting others in the process."

The judge paused again, still. In that moment, he reminded Ruth Ann of the Grandmother. The story would be told in its own time and there was nothing she could do to hurry it.

The judge went on. "That spring, I invited Ben to take his break with me and my daughter, Nora, at our oceanfront home in Charleston. I wanted to get to know him better, to see if he could hold a conversation as well as he could a book. I found that he was not only intelligent in writing, but kind and gentle.

"One morning, I was up before sunrise and saw him by the neighbor's house on the beach. Their dog had gotten trapped under the porch. Unfortunately, the owner didn't realize what was happening and came out with a gun, threatening young Ben. I intervened, but the man wasn't convinced. He called Ben..."

To Ruth Ann's surprise, the judge's eyes teared up and his next words came out shaky. "...he called Ben a heathen savage, and that if he ever caught him on his property again, he'd shoot him."

Ruth Ann swallowed, the story striking her in the heart.

The judge shook himself. "I sued that man for a prior infringement on my property I hadn't pressed before and he paid a hefty fine, but I knew then the challenges Ben would face if he pursued the life I was pushing him toward. Yet he's faced down every single one of them."

The judge met Ruth Ann's eyes. "I don't normally tell people that part of the story but I think Ben's people should know that he understands what they still go through, even him as an ivy league scholar."

Ruth Ann nodded, not sure she trusted herself to speak but asked, "Has Benjamin returned to the Choctaw Nation since he first came here?"

The judge rose and tapped out the pipe in a tray on his desk. "There was no one for him to return to. But between me and you, I think it would do him a world of good to go home for a spell."

Ruth Ann's heart hammered at his words. This was exactly what she wanted to hear. Could she ask the judge to talk to Benjamin about going back with the Choctaw delegation? Any delay would make it too late for Philip's case.

"Don't get me wrong," the judge said. "Ben knows exactly who he is and what his purpose is but the boy needs a break. He's seen more in life than I had at thirty."

The judge leaned against his desk. "I think it'd be a fine thing for him to spend time with his people before he gets himself lost in this political jungle." The judge smiled. "And I suppose that's exactly what your people would like to see as well."

It's what I must see. Ruth Ann bit back the words. The delegation would be in D.C. for three more weeks. Was that enough time for her to convince Benjamin to make such a dramatic change in his life and career?

And thine ears shall hear a word behind thee, saying, This is the way, walk ye in it, when ye turn to the right hand, and when ye turn to the left.

Ruth Ann stood. "Thank you, sir, for sharing what you did. We do hope Benjamin will come back with us, but could you do me a tremendous service?"

"Anything within my power that's not unethical."

"Would you please not mention to anyone that I was here?"

The judge grinned. "I'll make a deal with you—your secrets will be as safe with me as mine are with you."

"Then they are safe."

CHAPTER 26

During the meeting with Senator Newman, in which Ruth Ann thanked the senator for his part in helping them see the treaties, she couldn't stop thinking about her conversation with Judge Eldridge. What had the judge meant about things that took place before he met Benjamin? Surely nothing terribly dark, especially for a boy who attended Spencer Academy.

Which brought up another question. What happened to his parents? Judge Eldridge said there was no one for Benjamin to go home to. Were they still alive, and how did that affect the kind of man and lawyer he had become?

Really, though, did whatever happen long ago in Indian Territory have any bearing on Benjamin Nakishi's ability to defend Philip against Tecumseh Shoemaker in the Tobucksy County Courthouse?

"Ruth Ann?"

She jolted, aware of Pepper and Senator Newman staring at her. Pepper said, "Ruth Ann, the senator asked you a question."

Ruth Ann straightened, aware that her pencil had dragged a lazy line across the blank page of her tablet. She realized how awful her neglect was. The *Choctaw Tribune* was counting on her for accurate stories. Her people faced a serious situation, and all she could think of was her family's trouble. Even getting up early after a late evening had caused her brain to be mush during this meeting.

"I apologize, Senator Newman," she said. "What was your question again?"

The senator was less annoyed than Pepper, but just as calculating. "I was asking about your brother's newspaper back in Indian Territory. Does it side with the Nationals or Progressives among the Choctaws?"

Ruth Ann glanced at Pepper, wondering why he hadn't indicated that the newspaper was unbiased. Furthermore, that it couldn't be used to a D.C. politician's advantage. That wouldn't happen as long as Matthew and she were the publishers.

She had picked up at the first part of the conversation that Senator Newman was at odds with Senator Dawes. An Indian newspaper gaining a foothold in the nation's capitol could influence larger newspapers through the AP.

Ruth Ann felt the power of the press pulsing inside her. She needed to learn to harness it like Mr. Tesla did electricity at the Chicago World's Fair. Words could light up the world.

The verse, *"In the beginning was the Word, and the Word was with God, and the Word was God,"* echoed in her heart, steadying it.

"The *Choctaw Tribune* reports all sides of a story, Senator Newman," she said. "We don't take political sides."

The senator nodded. He and Pepper went back to discussing the Dawes situation. Ruth Ann paid close attention to the conversation that wrapped up with Pepper asking for the senator's support in running Dawes out of Indian Territory.

"You make a convincing argument for the sovereignty of your people, young Barnes," Senator Newman said, his face unreadable. "I know how hard your father has fought for tribal sovereignty, and of his little war with the current chief. Let me make some appointments, and I will get back to you on it."

Ruth Ann closed her notebook after jotting down the lackluster conclusion. It sounded awfully politician-y to her. But they exited politely with Senator Newman assuring them he would see them at the Grand Opera House that evening for a reception being held for several tribes visiting D.C.

Outside the capitol building, Pepper wheeled on Ruth Ann.

"Annie, do you even realize how important this trip is to our people? To me?" He sighed, sweeping his hat off and thumping it against his leg. "Newman knows about the high-ranking subscribers you're getting here in D.C. He wants to know where the *Choctaw Tribune* stands, and you have to give men like him more assurance than your brother does with his unbiased hogwash. Everyone has to take a side in this fight for our people. You'd better make up your own mind about yours."

Ruth Ann didn't move, didn't respond. She had already made up her own mind, but she was tired of arguing with Pepper all the time. She'd rather be on a bicycle ride with Benjamin.

Pepper matched her silence as they boarded the waiting Roseland carriage. They returned to the house and Pepper went straight up the stairs, not yielding to the tempting aromas coming from the dining room.

Ruth Ann did and took lunch with Joseph Griffin. He asked if she would like to accompany him in "chasing ambulances" for breaking stories.

Ruth Ann started to decline. She was exhausted and needed a nap before the reception. But she was in D.C. and should squeeze out every opportunity. Joseph Griffin was a seasoned reporter, and she could learn things to make her a better one.

She spent the afternoon searching for stories around the city. They walked and caught the electric streetcar all day, and ended back at Roseland just in time to change and eat in the dining room. They met the other Choctaws in the foyer for the trip to the Grand Opera House reception. Pepper, recovered from their spat, offered to escort her. She accepted, exhausted.

The day had run away from Ruth Ann, abandoning her to the piles of writing and socializing she needed to do. She was thoroughly spent and not looking forward to being on her toes around Senator Newman and the rest of the politicians.

Amid the group departing Roseland, Ruth Ann's stomach dropped in disappointment to see that Benjamin Nakishi wasn't among them.

~

"Well, if it isn't the man about town." A representative from Oregon rigorously shook Pepper's hand as he and Ruth Ann entered the reception at the Grand Opera House.

The place was grand all right, and Ruth Ann hoped to have a chance to come back and actually see one of the theatrical plays held there in the auditorium. But for now, she would stay on top of the drama in a room filled with tribal representatives and politicians.

Though she hailed from Indian Territory, she had not met many from other tribes beyond the Five Civilized Tribes in her part of the world—Chickasaws, Cherokees, Seminole, Muskogee Creek, and Choctaws.

There was the feel of a dance in the room. Not one of pleasure, but of carefully rehearsed steps as those gathered discussed the futures of the first peoples of the United States.

The representative from Oregon trying to engage Pepper in a conversation reeked of flattery. Ruth Ann looked for a way to escape, but the man turned to her with a fake grin.

"You must be the little reporter from that newspaper in Indian Territory," he said. "Hugo's the town, isn't it?"

"Dickens." The word came out clipped, but Ruth Ann didn't care. She did not like the way the man looked at her as though she were a hapless female rather than a professional young woman.

The man snapped his fingers. "Ah, yes. Wrong author. Well, perhaps you should consider penning novels like those of Jane Austen, what with your own romantic intrigues going on here in D.C."

Ruth Ann stared at him. "I have no idea what you are talking about, sir."

She wished Pepper would step in, but he was looking about the room and picking out his next target to rub elbows with.

The representative spread his hands in innocence. "Why, you must have missed this evening's paper. Not that any names were used, but when the story described a fair Indian maiden and her two brave warriors in dress suits, I immediately knew, as I'm sure the author of the society column intended."

Ruth Ann's face burned, and she wished she had opted for a lighter outfit. Pepper didn't seem to have heard the man. He took Ruth Ann's elbow. "If you'll excuse us, I see someone waiting to speak with us."

She breathed out as Pepper guided them over to a new group discussion. But to her dismay, two of the young women looked at her and Pepper, whispering behind their hands. Giggling.

Ruth Ann excused herself and headed for the door. She needed to find a washroom to catch her breath and think. What gossip was in the newspaper about her?

She bumped into Senator Newman and Georgia Pearl at the doorway. Her roommate grabbed her hand and pulled her over to the wall, giggling like the other girls.

"Imagine, you've only been in D.C. a week and you're already in the society columns!" Georgia Pearl squealed.

"I've gathered that." Ruth Ann's voice came out as a squeak. "Could you please explain what is going on?"

Georgia Pearl let out a light gasp. "Didn't you read this evening's paper? "

"Apparently not the entire thing. I went through the headlines—"

Georgia Pearl yanked open her reticule. "Oh, I never bother with that boring stuff. You have to go straight to the back pages for the best reading. Here, I clipped this out to save in my scrap-book. I must study your techniques."

Ruth Ann hesitantly took the clipping that contained three horrible paragraphs:

Indian maiden finds herself courted by two civilized Indian braves. Though they dress in suits, will the old ways of fighting to the death over a lover come into play at an undisclosed, elegant boarding house in the city? And what goes on after the gas lamps go out at night?

With two out-of-towners encountering a local, integrated Indian brave, we can only guess what the coming days hold. Will the lifelong friend-ship between the Indian maiden and her escort survive the prestige of the tall Indian man whom she met at the grave of one of the chiefs of their tribe?

Only time will tell for this Indian love triangle.

The paper crinkled in Ruth Ann's sweaty grip. "How could they—who could have—?"

A heavy presence shadowed the clipping, and Ruth Ann glanced up to see Pepper towering over her. He spoke to Georgia Pearl without looking at the girl. "You'll excuse us. Now."

Georgia Pearl lost her humor and slipped away. Ruth Ann stared at the vacant spot, unable to process her mortification. Pepper had no trouble filling in the blanks.

"Indian braves fighting to the death over a lover?" Pepper's eyes were ablaze. "Why didn't that reporter friend of yours have us sending smoke signals and sharpening our scalping knives, too? If I catch you going out with Joseph Griffin again..."

Ruth Ann snapped to attention. "You're always quick to your accusations, Mr. Barnes."

"If I'm wrong, I'll apologize."

Ruth Ann knew he wouldn't. She'd never heard Pepper apologize for anything. "I will find out who did it and put a stop to it before it spreads any further," she said.

Pepper scoffed. "Ruth Ann, it went out to hundreds of papers across the country through the AP. Newspapers eat up anything to do with romanticizing the noble savage."

Ruth Ann felt the color drain from her face as realization sunk in that this column was sent out to all AP subscribers.

Including the *Choctaw Tribune*.

CHAPTER 27

Matthew lay awake, staring at the moon beam across the ceiling of the low roof of his bedroom. He and Peter built this lean-to last summer when the family needed the extra space with Peter staying often. It also allowed Della and Ruth Ann privacy in the loft bedroom the three previously shared.

But the lean-to felt big and empty along with the rest of the house. Peter was home on Uncle Preston's ranch and Ruth Ann was far, far away in D.C. That left Matthew alone in his lean-to and Della in her sewing room that she scarcely left these days.

There was no way to know what their family portrait would look like once the fractured pieces were pasted together. Would Philip come home to them? Perhaps he could stay at Uncle Preston's ranch, or share the lean-to with Matthew and Peter. That would be crowded, more than physically.

But Philip wasn't coming home, not soon. Maybe never. Not that he wouldn't be welcome. But with how the inquest went and the true guilt Philip carried, it was doubtful. He wouldn't come home, at least not for a very long time.

That wasn't what weighed heaviest on Matthew's mind as the stream of moonlight made its way across the ceiling in tiny increments. It was the telegram clutched in his right hand, the nasty gossip that had come over the wire from the AP Ruth Ann subscribed to—without even communicating to him about it first.

Not that he minded her initiative or disagreed with her decision. It was a good one. But if she was out there making life decisions…she was in such a vulnerable state with the emotional upheaval in their family.

Matthew knew the dangers of being away from home and vulnerable.

This was no time for romance, especially the kind that made it into D.C. gossip columns, if any of the newspapers actually printed it. Matthew would know once his *Washington Post* came in the next few days' mail.

People gossiping about their family was bad. But that didn't compare to the brotherly concern Matthew felt over his baby sister, so alone and defenseless in the big city, with two men pursuing her.

Who was the "tall Indian man" in the story? Matthew had to find out more about him. Maybe Lance Fuller knew something from his life in D.C.

The other Indian, Pepper Barnes, was another matter. Matthew knew him well enough not to trust him alone with his sister. Not only could he influence her writing, but her reputation was in jeopardy. Pepper could do a lot of damage in a short period of time.

When the telegram had arrived, Matthew was tempted to jump on the next train to D.C. and tear Pepper apart with his bare hands. But until Ruth Ann called for his help, or his mother sent him, Matthew had to stay on task there at home. He'd been away too long already.

He was beginning to understand the problems that caused.

Matthew rolled the telegram around in his hand, wadding it into a tight ball. He hadn't shown it to their mother yet. He would tell her in the morning and let her guide his next steps.

CHAPTER 28

*R*uth Ann sank onto her bed at Roseland, grateful she chose to return early from the reception. She intended to catch up on writing but instead changed, washed her face, and went straight to her bed. Perhaps if she managed a good night's sleep, she could wake early and get her writing done. Maybe in the morning, the embarrassment of the column wouldn't sting so much.

Had Benjamin Nakishi read it? How many others would easily see through the stereotypes and know that the "Indian love triangle" was about her, Pepper Barnes, and Benjamin Nakishi? Worst, had the column reached home through the AP by telegram to Matthew?

Ruth Ann squeezed her eyes shut. He would never print gossip in the *Choctaw Tribune*, but would he withhold it from their mother? Would anyone else at the office know? If Peter saw the AP telegram, she knew he would never spread harmful gossip.

Father, please forgive me for…

Ruth Ann didn't know what she had done to bring on the humiliation. Meeting Benjamin Nakishi in the cemetery had been completely unintentional, and Pepper escorting her was a natural thing for this trip. What could she have done differently? What should she do differently to avoid horrible rumors?

And thine ears shall hear a word behind thee, saying, This is the way, walk ye in it...

Father, thank you for your grace.

Ruth Ann had almost drifted to sleep when thumping in the sitting room announced that Georgia Pearl was back from the reception. After a week in Roseland House, Ruth Ann could tell when it was Georgia Pearl or Virginia Lee entering the suite.

Georgia Pearl slipped into the room and crept over to Ruth Ann's bed, peering at her in the dark.

Ruth Ann sighed. "I'm awake."

Georgia Pearl knelt beside the bed, eyes gleaming. "I know Pepper is an old friend of yours but that you can hardly stand him. I just wanted you to know that you're not the only one he has an eye on. I don't think Pepper is the type who will marry and settle down soon. He wants to enjoy the company of different ladies first. That makes him so exciting, doesn't it?"

Ruth Ann pushed herself up on one elbow, staring at her young friend. "Georgia Pearl, that is a hideous thing to say. There is nothing admirable about a man who goes from one love interest to another."

Georgia Pearl shrugged. "Then, you really don't mind if he does things like accompany me to the charity ball next week or..." She bit her lower lip, trying hard not to smile. "If he just pays extra attention to me, do you?"

"I advise you to be very, very cautious on anything to do with Pepper Barnes."

Georgia Pearl's voice was barely audible, sounding out of breath. "Don't tell my father or sister, but last night when Pepper and I left from the bookstore, when we got back to the house, I was just sure he was going to try to kiss me."

From the giggling yet hesitant way Georgia Pearl said it, Ruth

Ann decided to take her words in stride. Georgia Pearl desperately wanted to be older than she was and wanted Ruth Ann's validation.

Well, Ruth Ann had no experience in the kissing department and didn't intend to until she married. And it wasn't Pepper Barnes she was thinking of.

She didn't know if what Georgia Pearl said was true, but she was done with the conversation and the whole situation. She turned over to face the other way. "Good night, Georgia Pearl."

The room didn't quiet as Georgia Pearl moved about, getting ready for bed. Ruth Ann pretended to sleep but she couldn't stop thinking about what Georgia Pearl said. Ruth Ann was getting in deeper with Pepper and his drama than she wanted.

Matthew's warning came back to her, but there was no way out yet. Pepper promised to help with Philip's trial. If Ruth Ann failed to convince Benjamin Nakishi to return to Indian Territory, Pepper might be her only hope.

But Ruth Ann didn't want Georgia Pearl to be taken advantage of in any way. Ruth Ann knew how to handle Pepper. Georgia Pearl did not. She'd have to keep a closer eye on them.

CHAPTER 29

When Matthew told Della about the gossip column of the Indian love triangle in D.C., she frowned and asked Matthew probing questions, and how much—if any—of the column Matthew thought was true. He answered honestly, that the column was most likely nonsense. He added that Ruth Ann was a smart girl. But he refrained from advising his mother on what they should do.

He helped her wash the breakfast dishes, and when she said nothing else, Matthew headed out the door to the newspaper office. He did plan on leaving Dickens today. He just hadn't been sure if it would be to go to D.C. to rescue his sister, or his original plans to go up to Springstown and get a new horse.

Before he left, Matthew flipped through the envelopes at his desk from the morning's mail, in beat with the operation of the press by Caleb Gentry. Matthew halted at two envelopes with familiar handwriting from the many articles she'd written for the *Choctaw Tribune.*

Matthew tore open the thicker envelope from Ruth Ann and found articles about her excursions so far in D.C. There was a well written one about a luncheon with the First Lady. Impressive.

There was a more extensive article about a Choctaw lawyer, Benjamin Nakishi-Dunn, who won a major Supreme Court case that week. Matthew had heard of this lawyer, but he was still surprised at the man's achievement.

Then Matthew started with realization and read the story again. Was this the "tall Indian" the gossip column referred to?

Matthew added the articles to his publishing stack for that weekend's edition and opened the thinner envelope addressed directly to him. He pulled out the letter and read it, then reread it. Maybe he should go to D.C. after all.

The northbound train to Springstown whistled as it rolled in.

Matthew tucked the letter in his breast pocket over his heart, praying for the words to soak in there as he headed out to catch the train. He needed a new horse.

Robert Barnes met Matthew at the gate of the main paddock where well-bred quarter horses trotted, showing their fine conformation. Matthew had wired Barnes about his visit and went straight out to the horses when he arrived.

The time had come to replace Little Chief.

It wasn't only that Matthew needed a riding horse. He did. But he also needed a sure companion, one who didn't question his every word and motive. One who was slow to judge, quick to forgive, and had a heart bigger than Matthew could understand. That was the friend Little Chief, the quarter horse his father had given him, had become. Matthew hadn't known it until he used a bullet to end the suffering horse's life.

Barnes crossed his arms over the top rail next to Matthew, who did the same, his eyes going between a sorrel and a buck-skin. He didn't want another bay like Little Chief, the horse he'd lost during an ambush in the mountains north of Wilburton while hunting for his father's killers.

His sister was in danger now, too, which was the main reason Matthew kept his appointment to visit the Barnes'.

"Have you heard from your son lately?" Matthew intentionally avoided using Pepper's name. He wanted Robert Barnes to know he held the man responsible for his son's actions.

Barnes rubbed his chin. "He sends me a telegraph every few days."

Matthew knew this. Peter jotted down Pepper's messages, though they weren't for their station. Matthew read them, same as he would if he were operating the wire. He needed to keep a close eye on Pepper Barnes, even from a distance.

Matthew looked over at the older man, the toughest white man he knew. One he respected to a degree, despite his politics and brash ways. Barnes had paid for Jim Teller's headstone to express admiration for his friend.

"Does Pepper ever talk about my sister?" Matthew asked.

Robert Barnes shifted to face Matthew square on. Since Matthew started the *Choctaw Tribune*, the patriarch of the Barnes family treated Matthew like an equal, showing him more respect than he did the current chief of the Choctaw Nation.

"Your sister is a mighty fine young lady," Barnes said, low and firm. "She can take care of herself."

It wasn't the assurance Matthew sought. Barnes thought enough of Ruth Ann and his own son, that he wasn't fretting over their time together in D.C. It was no secret that Mr. and Mrs. Barnes would be proud to welcome Ruth Ann into their family.

But Matthew wanted to make sure Barnes understood his position. "She can, but she's still my sister, and she's a long way from home."

Barnes pointed toward the horses. "You don't want that sorrel or that buckskin. You don't want any of these horses, son."

Matthew lifted one eyebrow, not liking the change in subject. Barnes motioned toward the next paddock over.

"You want a stout Choctaw pony that can carry you a long way without stopping, and also take off at a run if you need him to. But you're needing more than a good mount, ain't you?"

Matthew held still. Robert Barnes picked out his pain well. Their conversation wasn't about Ruth Ann or Pepper or horses. Barnes understood the deeper issue clouding Matthew's vision, making it hard for him to reason out everything else.

Barnes turned and pointed to the foothills that bordered his ranch. "Choctaw horses have run wild up there for decades. Been repopulating since your people came across the long trail to this territory. There's a wild herd I manage up on Blackjack Mountain. One of them has your name on it. If you can catch it, you can keep it."

Matthew stared at the foothills of Blackjack Mountain.

He'd lost his treasured horse in the mountains. He'd lost his father and brother in the mountains. What did this mountain hold?

Matthew nodded. "I'll be back in a few days."

CHAPTER 30

Ruth Ann spent the next two days dodging Pepper. She stayed in her suite in the ladies' wing, which young men were forbidden to enter, resting and catching up on writing. She also loitered in the Roseland kitchen, getting to know the working class of the city to give her a more balanced view of her time there.

Gertrud Schmitt spoke with her about the "Indian love triangle" column and assured Ruth Ann that no one took such nonsense seriously. It made Ruth Ann feel a little better, and she hoped the embarrassing piece was soon forgotten.

She hadn't seen Benjamin Nakishi since it went out. She heard he was spending time with Judge Eldridge, reviewing the Supreme Court case he won. Ruth Ann also encountered Joseph Griffin. He told her he absolutely did not write the ridiculous column, but he would find out who did and have them flogged.

Hours spent in the large bed on a mountain of pillows were truly the best for Ruth Ann. She read, journaled, and felt her body and mind adjusting to this place in a way that would help her do well there. Even in talking with Benjamin about returning to Indian Territory.

Georgia Pearl said Ruth Ann looked much better after the two days. The dark circles under her eyes, a complete fright for any single young lady, finally faded, and Ruth Ann's skin was a fresh rose color, according to the fashion expert.

All in all, Ruth Ann did feel refreshed and ready for the dinner party at Roseland with Georgetown society people that Friday evening. As she and Georgia Pearl dressed in their room, she caught the younger girl observing her.

Ruth Ann cocked her head, mindful of the hot curling iron a maid brought up from the kitchen that Ruth Ann was using to add ringlets to her updo. "Something on your mind, Georgia Pearl?"

The girl sighed wistfully, folding her hands under her chin. "I can't believe that you aren't aware of how fascinated men are with Indian women. You are the perfect portrait of a dusky Indian maiden. Why don't you at least wear feathers in your hair? You would be all the rage in D.C."

Ruth Ann cringed and finished twisting a strand of hair around the hot iron. Beulah taught her how to use one, though Ruth Ann rarely had occasion to.

She unfurled the strand and checked her image in the mirror, all the ringlets in place. When she was in Chicago, society ladies thought she was Italian.

Ruth Ann wondered if people would ever fully understand that there were hundreds of distinct Indigenous people groups in the U.S. before Europeans arrived. Not all of them wore feather bonnets. Her people still had traditional dress they used for ceremony. But for a dinner party in D.C., Ruth Ann would dress for the occasion like everyone else.

She decided to let Georgia Pearl's question go unanswered as she headed for the door. "Are you ready?"

Georgia Pearl waved for her to go on. "I'll be down shortly."

Ruth Ann descended the grand staircase and entered the ballroom located on the main floor of Roseland. A grand piano sat in one corner where a group of young people gathered around it, playing and singing the same style as at the restaurant in Georgetown. Ruth Ann gravitated toward Mrs. Schmitt, offering to help the hostess.

The woman assured her that everything was under control, but there was an appreciative light in her eyes. "Thank you again, dear. But you will want to visit with the two gentlemen over in the alcove."

Ruth Ann didn't know what that meant. But at least she had a direction to go in that took her opposite of where Pepper Barnes stood in a knit of politicians and Forbis Kanitobe.

The alcove was dimmer than the main room and allowed privacy. The two men in it were Benjamin Nakishi and Judge Eldridge, who greeted her. The judge allowed Benjamin to introduce Ruth Ann without commenting about their previous encounter.

Ruth Ann avoided meeting Benjamin's eyes, and he seemed standoffish as well. Was it because of the awkward end to their day together when they left the bookstore, just the two of them? She preferred to think that. It was too soon to hope the gossip column had been forgotten.

Thankfully, Judge Eldridge filled the space by starting a new conversation. He addressed Ruth Ann. "I hope you have your calendar marked for this Monday evening. The charity ball for children is the grandest social event of the year."

Ruth Ann recalled Pepper having it on the agenda. Few people of influence missed it. She smiled at the judge. "I understand you are one of its founders?"

Judge Eldridge *tsked*. "Don't give an old man too much credit."

He glanced between Benjamin and Ruth Ann as though he were going to add something about the ball. Surely not anything about asking Ruth Ann who would accompany her. *No.* Not after that mortifying column!

But the judge's expression shifted, and he said, "Ben tells me you were able to view the original Choctaw treaties. What are your thoughts on the nation to nation negotiations that took place while your people were still in Mississippi?"

It was a heavy topic, but Ruth Ann appreciated the judge's willingness to broach it. "Some of our people are still there," she said.

She went on to articulate her family's story about the forced Removal, and the condition of the Mississippi Choctaws still in their homeland. They had not received their promised land and U.S. citizenship. There was talk of how the last of them might migrate to Indian Territory to get deeded land if the Dawes Commission went through.

Benjamin weighed in to say that there were descendants in Indian Territory and Mississippi still trying to win claims on their grandparents' and great grandparents' losses during the Removal. Ruth Ann noticed a lack of personal anecdotes to go with his comments, and she wondered again about his family.

He knew a great deal about the legal history of the tribe. Pepper would be upset at missing this conversation, but that was his own doing. He could join them at anytime.

Besides, the more he stayed away from Benjamin, the better chance Ruth Ann had of recruiting the lawyer for her personal cause, not Pepper for his.

A disturbance sounded at the ballroom entrance and Ruth Ann turned, expecting an announcement for dinner.

Instead, she found herself staring in shock at Georgia Pearl and two other young ladies entering the room with ecstatic grins. They wore their usual fluff and frills, but added something to their attire that made Ruth Ann recoil in disbelief.

The girls had braided eagle feathers in the ringlets of their hair, tossing them back-and-forth flamboyantly. People in the room gathered around the girls in delight.

A woman reached out and fingered one feather, damaging the fine piece. "Wherever did you get these luscious feathers?"

Georgia Pearl's grin broadened at the attention. "My father knows the curator at a museum. These are on loan."

Ruth Ann pressed her fingers over her lips, nauseated. Eagle feathers were sacred to so many tribes.

Judge Eldridge shifted. He looked pale, then his face reddened. He strode over to the young ladies, looking as though he were going to scold them. But he slowed and stopped, glancing around a moment. Ruth Ann could see his face paling again, perspiration on his forehead shining under the chandelier light. He sidestepped the enamored group and whispered something to their hostess before departing.

After the initial fanfare died down, Georgia Pearl made a beeline for Ruth Ann.

"I told you feathers would be all the rage!" she said. "I was going to ask if you wanted to wear them this evening, but since you weren't interested, I asked two of my other friends. I may have started a new trend in the city! Do you think Pepper will be impressed?"

Benjamin excused himself and left the room. The judge hadn't looked well and Benjamin was no doubt going to check on him. Ruth Ann was grateful he had an excuse to leave. She would be returning home soon, but he lived in that city. Ruth Ann was starting to feel like she'd been the cause of making that more difficult for him.

Ruth Ann looked over Georgia Pearl's shoulder, watching Pepper leave after Benjamin. "Very few things impress Pepper Barnes," she said quietly.

Virginia Lee and Agatha Green strolled over to them. Virginia Lee ignored the disappointed look on her sister's face about Pepper and spoke to Ruth Ann. "I don't suppose you would be interested in joining us for another rally, would you?"

Ruth Ann's mind swirled with the conflicts around and inside her. The gossip column and Pepper. Benjamin and the judge. Georgia Pearl and the eagle feathers. So much for the rest she'd gotten. It didn't prepare her to face all of this *and* Virginia Lee's mocking.

A voice barked from somewhere behind Ruth Ann.

"I wouldn't think you'd have much time for rallies with keeping the gossip columns supplied."

Virginia Lee jerked in surprise, and Ruth Ann stared at her. Then Ruth Ann turned to see Joseph Griffin coming to stand at her side. She faced Virginia Lee again. "Did you write that ghastly story about the Indian love triangle?"

When Virginia Lee tightened her lips, Joseph filled in. "I found out through an AP telegraph operator in New York. Friend of mine. I have a lot of those in the AP office, so I'm sure no such story will get through again, Miss Newman? In fact, I'm pretty sure an apology will show up before long."

Virginia Lee raised her chin. "Ruth Ann Teller is such a damsel in distress, isn't she? Always needing a man to rescue her. Well, she has certainly attracted enough of those here, good for her. She will need rescuing if she becomes an enemy to our cause. There is no middle ground." She glared at Ruth Ann. "You are either a feminist or a frail female. If the latter, why don't you just run along home to Indian Territory with one of your beaus? We have no need of your kind here."

Virginia Lee and Agatha Green exited, leaving Georgia Pearl to release a nervous giggle in their wake. "My sister takes herself and her causes too seriously."

Ruth Ann wanted to say that Georgia Pearl should take herself more seriously, stop being enamored with the romantic idea of Indians, and please, *please* remove those eagle feathers from her hair. But she bit her tongue and allowed Joseph Griffin to escort her to the dining room. Mrs. Schmitt had called that dinner was ready.

It was a long evening, but Ruth Ann stuck close to Joseph, certainly feeling like a damsel in distress. She didn't see Pepper or Benjamin or the judge for the rest of the evening.

CHAPTER 31

*R*uth Ann awoke the next morning and lay still awhile, praying. She felt her spirit calming about the feathers incident and thought through how to explain to Georgia Pearl how unkind her actions were.

When Ruth Ann stretched and tossed back the white comforter, she saw Georgia Pearl's bed empty. To her surprise, the younger girl came out of the washroom, dressed for the day with only her hair left to do.

Georgia Pearl clasped her hands together, grinning as she plopped beside Ruth Ann on the bed.

"You're awake, finally!" Georgia Pearl said. "I spoke with my father last night—or this morning I guess it was—and he is willing to support Pepper in whatever he has going on in Indian Territory. My father is impressed with how smart and polished Pepper is, and he doesn't think he looks enough like an Indian to cause a problem in our circles. I don't remember all the details but I know it's important to Pepper and I can't wait to tell him." She squealed on the last part. "I heard through the grapevine that he and Mr. Nakishi are meeting in the parlor this morning.

Please come with me. I need to present this in a way that leaves it open for Pepper to ask to escort me to the charity ball. It's the social event of the season!"

Georgia Pearl held up her clasped hands in a pleading gesture, her eyes twinkling with mischief.

Ruth Ann didn't know what to say. She needed to set Georgia Pearl straight on several things, but maybe it would be easier if they talked to Pepper first. Actually, Pepper would probably take care of setting Georgia Pearl straight. But Ruth Ann hated to see the young girl hurt.

Georgia Pearl went on, "Oh, and my father also hinted that your newspaper, the *Choctaw Tribune*, was influential in his decision. He's been impressed with the daily editions he received this week." Georgia Pearl's eyes glowed in admiration, and Ruth Ann didn't have the heart to scold her.

"I'll go with you to speak with Pepper."

A short time later, the two young women descended the staircase. Georgia Pearl beat Ruth Ann to the bottom and did a light skip as she headed across the wide hall. Ruth Ann heard voices coming from the parlor, including a deep one that belonged to Benjamin Nakishi.

Her heart sped up even as her feet slowed. She felt self conscious and wanted to enter the parlor properly.

Ruth Ann made it to the entrance in time to see Georgia Pearl skipping right toward the rug with its upturned corner.

Ruth Ann called, "Look out!"

Too late. Georgia Pearl's boot caught the corner of the rug and she yelped, tumbling to the floor. She tried to catch herself with the sofa table, but landed in an awkward heap beside it.

Ruth Ann rushed to her side, aware of Pepper on the other side of the sofa, rolling his eyes while Benjamin moved to help. He carefully pulled Georgia Pearl up as she danced around to keep from tripping on her skirt. Ruth Ann straightened the skirt from behind where it was twisted.

"Thank you, Mr. Nakishi, Ruth Ann." Georgia Pearl sighed and started to brush back her loose hair, then gasped at the blood streaming across the palm of her hand.

"Oh dear, it'll stain my dress!"

Benjamin reached into his pocket and unfurled a white handkerchief. Taking Georgia Pearl's hand in his large one, he pressed the handkerchief to the cut.

She sighed again, this time with a wistful tone as she touched the back of his dark hand. "You have such swarthy skin, Mr. Nakishi. No wonder white women hostages didn't always try to run away from their savage captors."

Ruth Ann stared in shock even as Georgia Pearl smiled at her with such innocent ignorance, batting her eyes knowingly. But she didn't know a thing.

Time froze Ruth Ann's mind and heart. The moment was like a hot iron touching her soul. She recalled stories of Chief Pushmataha in this very city, and the women cooing over him, romanticizing the noble savage they thought he was.

So much had happened to her people before and since then.

The moment shattered when Pepper slammed his coffee cup on the low tea table. Benjamin, his expression neutral, released Georgia Pearl's hand, the handkerchief still pressed in it. Ruth Ann couldn't breathe, tears clogging her throat at the pain in her heart and what must surely be in Benjamin's.

Pepper strode over to them, reaching into his pocket and withdrawing a folded knife. He flipped the knife open and halted in front of Georgia Pearl, holding out his other hand, palm up. Not taking his eyes off her, he swiped the sharp blade across his palm.

Georgia Pearl shrieked and jumped back. Ruth Ann glared at Pepper, but he responded by tossing the blood-smeared knife aside and grabbing Georgia Pearl's wrist. He held the two bleeding hands together, hers and his. Georgia Pearl whimpered, staring at the blood running together.

"Same blood," Pepper said, his fury barely contained. "We savages have always had mothers and fathers, just like you. We love, we hurt. Same as you. Our history and our culture aren't for your museums or dinner party amusements."

Tears streamed down Georgia Pearl's face. Benjamin gently pulled her hand away from Pepper and pressed his handkerchief against her cut again. She flinched and jerked back, gripping the handkerchief as she ran from the room.

Ruth Ann reached into her dress pocket and pulled out a handkerchief, fumbling it. Her shoulders heaved as though she were sobbing. She could hardly see for the tears welling in her eyes as she wrapped the handkerchief around Pepper's hand. "You're dripping blood everywhere."

"I don't care."

"I'll get you something from the kitchen for the pain," she whispered.

He was silent a moment, then said, "It doesn't hurt, Annie."

Ruth Ann caught her breath. "Yes...yes, it does." She looked over at Benjamin, who offered her an understanding smile. The tears really came then.

Pepper pulled his hand away. "You don't have to go all to pieces."

"Tears wash the windows of our soul," Benjamin said quietly.

"Who told you that nonsense?"

"A wise woman."

Ruth Ann let her tears out fully. It wasn't a hard sob, but a cleansing one, like Benjamin said. Thankfully, he had another handkerchief for her.

Pepper sighed, rubbing his bandaged hand. "I guess sometimes we get so caught up in today's fight, tomorrow's fight, we forget to grieve how much we've lost. How much we'll likely lose." He shrugged. "Yeah, it hurts."

Benjamin nodded. "Yes. But with time...with the right care..."

He lifted one side of the tied handkerchief on Pepper's hand. The bleeding had slowed.

"...it heals."

Ruth Ann took a shaky breath, drying the last of her tears, and looked in Benjamin's eyes again. But he was staring at the cut on Pepper's palm, and she had a feeling he was talking about something other than their peoples' suffering. Something deeply personal. And it was as if he were just realizing it.

Then his expression changed back to the one Ruth Ann was familiar with—calm, in control, professional yet personable. Benjamin went to where Pepper had tossed aside the knife and picked it up. He wiped the blood clean from the blade and snapped the knife closed. "I appreciate you speaking up. But you did not have to traumatize the girl."

He tossed the knife to Pepper, who caught it one handed. Pepper shrugged again. "Guess I won't be getting her father's vote or anyone else that he has influence with."

Ruth Ann wiped away the last of her tears, recovering her voice. "And that's what she was coming to tell you, Pepper Barnes. That you had his support. You've done it this time."

The three stood in silence. Then Pepper said, "Some things are more important for us to do in D.C. And back home."

He looked to Benjamin, who didn't falter under the demanding gaze that Pepper targeted him with. Pepper said, "Nakishi, if you would just come back to work for our people, you wouldn't have to deal with the likes of those girls."

Ruth Ann was tempted to second Pepper's opinion, but she didn't. Benjamin would face problems with race the same as her family did back home. She wanted him to return for different reasons.

Benjamin said quietly, "We all have our roles that God has appointed us to."

From the look on his face, he didn't seem to believe that

included returning to their people. But Ruth Ann prayed right then that Benjamin Nakishi's God-appointed role in life, in part, would be to help her family heal.

They needed more than time for that.

CHAPTER 32

In the Teller barn before dawn on Saturday morning, Matthew tightened the cinch of his saddle on Ruth Ann's Choctaw pony, Skyline. He figured if he was going to hunt up a herd of wild horses, this little mare was the one for the job.

"Hello the barn!" a voice called from the darkness outside.

Matthew guided the bit into Skyline's mouth as he called over his shoulder, "You're right on time."

He flipped Skyline's forelock clear of the headstall and turned to shake hands with his cousin-in-law, Daniel Garvin, who entered the barn, leading his own horse.

"I appreciate you coming," Matthew said.

Daniel shook his hand with a firm grip, more confident than usual. He was a good-looking young fellow, solid jawline outlined by his dark skin. "Glad to help."

Since the battle with deadly quicksand last Christmas on the Red River, Daniel seemed to have gained footing in the family he married into. He was finding his place on his father-in-law's ranch, Matthew's Uncle Preston. Of course, Daniel still seemed to appreciate getting off work from the ranch for a couple of days to help Matthew capture a horse on Blackjack Mountain.

They mounted up, Daniel on a quarter horse born on the ranch. The gray dawn gave them enough light to see the road that would take them past Springstown and to Blackjack Mountain.

They loped awhile, men and horses feeling the energy of a new day. Then they settled into a steady walk side by side, Matthew taking in the scent of dew covered grass and horseflesh.

A sharp corner of Ruth Ann's letter in his breast pocket poked him over the heart. Another letter was with it, one he scribbled a few words on each day, trying to find the right ones to send her. He hadn't found them yet.

Daniel breathed deep as well, then asked, "Why a wild mustang instead of another quarter horse?" He gave his own a pat with his gloved hand.

The simple question really stabbed Matthew. He thought of expounding on how their people had brought these horses across on the long walk, a walk his grandmother endured as a teenager and survived. Though Daniel was Choctaw, the young man was raised as an orphan at Spencer Academy. He didn't know his family history, didn't know the story of his ancestors who had made the long walk or if they had come later in the 1850s, or maybe after the War Between the States.

Talking about distant family history or their people would have been the easier route. But this morning was not about easy. Life was not about easy.

"Little Chief was a gift from my father on my 16th birthday."

From the quick look Daniel gave him, Matthew guessed this was new information. Daniel had never met Jim Teller, nor Philip. He'd come into the family when he married Preston's youngest daughter, Daisy, over a year ago.

Matthew trusted him enough to let some of his heart seep out. "I rode Little Chief for a neighbor rancher and won a race at a local fair. Daddy saw how I took to him and traded off his war carbine for him. That was also the day Daddy told me he thought of me as a man."

Daniel absently flipped his horse's mane back-and-forth. "Wish I could've known him."

"Me too."

Those two words sliced into Matthew. If only Philip hadn't…

Matthew halted his thoughts. He couldn't talk or think about the story Philip told him, the details of how their father had died. He stared ahead between Skyline's flicking ears as she listened to the conversation, perhaps feeling Matthew's thoughts. He was still dealing with the pain of Philip's betrayal, and he'd had a chance to really get up close with it. Ruth Ann hadn't yet.

No wonder she went off to D.C. with Pepper Barnes, trying to find a way to fix everything on her own. Maybe it was her way of dealing with the overwhelming emotions he didn't even know what to do with.

To Matthew's relief, Daniel changed the subject. "I want to ask for your advice on something, but I'd appreciate if you kept it in your confidence." He paused, then said, "I'm thinking about becoming a lawman."

Matthew shifted in his saddle to better face Daniel. This was big news. "What about your work on the ranch?"

Daniel shrugged, running the reins loosely through his hands. "You know I'm not much at ranch work. I need to do something that makes me stand on my own two feet. I used to clip out stories of Bass Reeves and Indian police when I was in school. I guess I always figured I'd be a lawman. Until I met Daisy." He smiled, face reddening in that bashful, newlywed way that hadn't faded yet.

While Matthew couldn't advise Daniel about women or marriage, he did know something about making a tough choice to pursue what he felt was his life's calling over the security of Uncle Preston's ranch. That calling had cost a lot. But Matthew wouldn't have done it different.

"If you really feel it's what the Creator has called you to do, then do it," Matthew said.

Daniel stared at Matthew, and rubbed his jaw. "Is it really that simple?"

"It is."

They settled in for a quiet ride up the mountain.

&

The sounds of summer in the forest on Blackjack Mountain lacked the frenzy of spring and nest building. In this season, creatures went quietly about their daily rituals, preparing for winter.

Matthew and Daniel sat in stillness on their horses, listening to the work going on around them. Matthew scanned the woods. Two hundred yards away, a patch of sun landed on brown and white hair in the brush. He pointed in that direction. Daniel nodded, and they nudged their horses down an embankment, rocky soil clattering beneath them.

One hundred yards closer, Matthew signaled for them to stop. He dismounted and pulled off the grain sack tied behind his saddle. He handed Skyline's reins to Daniel and moved several feet away from their own horses to spread the grain on the ground. He backed up next to Skyline and waited.

The summer forest sounds skittered away when a dozen horses suddenly emerged from the woods. Daniel whistled low, surprised. Apparently he hadn't spotted the herd in the woods until they came in the little clearing where Matthew had spread the grain.

The band of Choctaw horses didn't appear alarmed at the sight of humans. They encountered Robert Barnes on occasion and knew that contact with humans meant a treat. One thing about Robert Barnes, he had a good way with horses. Some of these were even saddle broke, but thrived on the mountain, so he let them roam at will.

Matthew stepped next to Daniel, where he sat on his horse. "Looks like all mares in this band and they foaled," Matthew said. "The blue roan is their stallion. I was leaning toward a stallion, but I can't take this one from his herd."

Matthew watched the mares and their foals, little broomstick tails flicking. The babies took far greater interest in the humans than the feed. One fawn-colored one pranced by, checking him out, then turned and pranced the other way, still looking at him.

Matthew wondered if he should come back when the foals were weaned and pick a stallion from them. But he needed a riding horse now, and this herd wouldn't provide it. He had to keep searching.

That thought sent a shiver of displeasure through him. It felt like when he had taken off for Krebs to search for his father and brother's killers, followed by the seemingly endless search to get the truth from Philip. In too many ways, his searching wasn't over.

The saddle creaked as Daniel turned the other way in it. "Hey, would you look at that?"

Daniel motioned to the woods east of them. A stunning, tri-colored stallion trotted into the opening then halted and warily eyed the humans. He flicked his ears, then meandered over to the feed as though he were being casual, but still keeping a sharp eye on the strangers. His one blue eye, at least. Matthew had gotten a good look at his face and saw the young stallion had one blue eye and one brown. He bore a white bald face and was streaked like a calico cat with orange, white, and black colorings.

"That's him," Matthew said. This was the horse that had his name on it, like Robert Barnes said.

The young stallion maneuvered to the other side of the mares who had taken their fill of the grain. Matthew watched, amused, as the young stallion cleverly nudged the mares and their babies back toward the woods. The older blue roan continued munching the grain, unaware that his herd of mares was being quietly stolen.

Matthew mounted Skyline, his movements causing the blue roan stallion to look up and then around. His head swiveled both directions, the whites of his eyes showing.

"Better hold on tight," Matthew told Daniel, getting a good grip on his own saddle horn.

The stallion's tail went up to match the elevation of his head as he took off at a fast trot along a game trail. Matthew and Daniel's horses jerked around to follow. Though they settled at a soft lope, they almost lost sight of the blue roan, whose purposeful strides carried him along. He picked up a gallop and bolted into a thick grove of trees. Matthew plunged Skyline in after him, then pulled her up as he watched the blue roan charge headlong into the side of the tri-colored stallion.

The roan hit the tri-colored in the side with a sickening thud. The tri-colored reared, whipped around, and nipped the blue roan in the flanks. But the blue roan was quick to turn and came up on his hind legs to lash out with his front hooves.

Once on Uncle Preston's ranch, Matthew witnessed two stallions get into an altercation. One struck the other in the head with his sharp hoof and killed it instantly.

Matthew withdrew his Winchester from its scabbard and aimed overhead. He fired off two shots, and the stallions broke apart. The blue roan trotted toward his mares, urging them away and up the mountain.

The tri-colored stood there, tail and ears flicking as he watched his attempt to steal the blue roan's herd melt from sight.

Matthew slid his rifle back into the scabbard and unhooked his lariat. He nodded for Daniel to move to the left and block the stallion if he wheeled about and away.

They had this horse cornered, just like Matthew finally did with Philip at the bottom of a mine shaft. He didn't know how to fix things with Annie, though. What was going on with her and Pepper? If only she'd listened to Matthew…

After Daniel got in position behind the distracted stallion, Matthew shook out the rope and swung it in an arc over his head. That caught the youngster's attention, but before he could move, Matthew sent the loop for his head, anticipating the stallion side-running.

The tri-colored did just that, but Matthew's loop fell across his back instead of his head. The young stallion took off from underneath it, racing into the woods and out of sight.

Daniel started to pursue him, but halted when he saw Matthew sitting still.

Matthew slowly wound his rope. Back on the ranch, he won every roping competition against his cousins. This was the first time he'd missed since he was a boy.

He leaned back in his saddle, trying to comprehend how he'd let his chosen stallion slip away. When Daniel re-joined him at his side, Matthew shook his head.

"I'm thinking about too much."

Daniel shrugged. "We'll track him down. But first, how about some food? We've been in the saddle for hours."

Matthew nodded and directed Skyline's head north. They were about a mile from Daniel Springs, a good place to stop and get his bearings. But that area brought up memories of when he and Ruth Ann stopped there and were threatened by three Choctaws over politics.

But he turned his mind back to missing the throw. That animal gave him senseless trouble same as Philip.

That thought made Matthew more determined than ever to catch and tame that tri-colored Choctaw horse.

When Daniel Springs came into view, Daniel joked, "Bet you didn't know they named this place after me."

"Hmm?"

Matthew looked over at his cousin, who was grinning. It faded. "What's on your mind, Matt? I've never seen you like this."

Matthew dismounted and went to the springs where he tossed aside his hat and plunged his head into the cool mineral water. He came up and shook his head vigorously, then ran splayed fingers through his hair and forward again, flinging the water droplets out of it.

Daniel imitated him, then opened their saddlebags for sandwiches Della made for them the night before. They sat on the log near the springs and Matthew accepted a sandwich. He didn't eat.

Philip. Ruth Ann. Mama. The Choctaw Tribune, *the tri-colored stallion.* Matthew was thinking about too much.

He rested his elbows on his knees. "My brother Philip is sitting in McAlester, waiting to be tried for his part in a robbery that took my father's life. He's up against the best lawyer in Indian Territory. My sister Ruth Ann is off in D.C. with Pepper Barnes and cutthroat politicians. She wrote me that things aren't right between us, but neither of us knows what it is. And there are rumors that she's being courted by a well-to-do Choctaw lawyer, Benjamin Nakishi-Dunn."

Daniel coughed, spitting out part of the bite he'd taken of his sandwich.

"Benjamin Dunn is in D.C.?"

Matthew's heart hammered at the look on Daniel's face, not sure if this was good or bad news. "You know him?"

"Sure do," Daniel said. "I didn't know he was a rich lawyer, though. Guess I should read your newspaper more." Daniel grinned sheepishly. "Ben was one of the older students when I was put in Spencer Academy. He graduated that year but he wrote to me for a while after leaving school. Guess he knew how scared I was, an orphan same as him, and that I might grow up in Spencer like he did. Best fellow I ever knew."

Matthew let out the breath he'd been holding, his body shaking with relief. "I hope he hasn't changed."

"Is he really courting Ruth Ann?" Daniel asked, still grinning.

"I don't know. I'm not there."

One thing Matthew did know. They were going to catch that tri-colored stallion today, and as soon as he got home, he had a letter to write. He and Annie needed to start talking through things and get them settled.

CHAPTER 33

"You go on to church without me; I—I'm not feeling well."

Georgia Pearl's voice cracked, like she had cried through the night instead of sleeping.

Ruth Ann hesitated by Georgia Pearl's bedside, wondering if she should offer to bring the girl's breakfast. She knew the dark circles under the girl's eyes weren't from sickness or fatigue.

After the incident in the parlor Saturday, Georgia Pearl successfully avoided Ruth Ann until Sunday morning.

Ruth Ann didn't know what to say now, so she quietly left Georgia Pearl and headed down to the dining room for breakfast. The room was empty, and she had a sinking feeling that everyone stayed out late last night, drinking at yet another reception the delegation attended. Ruth Ann left early, tired after the useless day at a garden party with Senator Newman.

She had to talk to Benjamin. Time would wave goodbye to her, same as she would Benjamin Nakishi at the Baltimore and Potomac Railroad Station if she didn't convince him to go home with her.

She ate, wondering if Joseph Griffin would appear, though

206

more hopefully Benjamin, to go with her to church. But no one arrived by the time she finished and entered the foyer for her wrap.

A harrumph came from the parlor, and she glanced down the hall to see Pepper coming toward her. She didn't know what to say other than, "Are you going to church this morning?"

"Why didn't you back me when I talked to Nakishi about returning to Indian Territory?"

"Because, as he said, God has a role He appointed each of us to, and I've met very few people who are as sure of their calling as Benjamin—unless it's my brother."

Pepper stared at her, fire in his eyes. "Oh, so it's 'Benjamin' now?"

Ruth Ann sighed. Surely he couldn't be jealous. Not Pepper Barnes. "Are you going to church with me or not?" she asked.

Pepper responded by turning his back and going up the stairs.

Ruth Ann walked to the Georgetown Presbyterian Church and barely stayed awake through the long service. Thoughts of how Pepper was at least partially right flittered in her mind. She should have seized the opportunity in the parlor yesterday morning to talk to Benjamin about returning to Indian Territory and representing her brother in the trial. Instead, Ruth Ann was a mess and Benjamin left shortly afterward, saying he needed to spend time with Judge Eldridge doing paperwork.

Ruth Ann wished she knew what church Benjamin attended and mentally kicked herself for not asking. She must find him after the service and take advantage of the slow pace of the day to speak with him.

Back at Roseland, Ruth Ann changed and enlisted the help of Mrs. Schmitt in getting ideas on where Benjamin might be.

The hostess counted Sundays in the calendar hanging on the wall by the enormous cookstove. "This being the second Sunday of the month, likely you will find him down at the orphanage on the wharf near the Navy Yard. He takes lunch with the children and gives gifts every month. Very fine young man, if I have not mentioned that before."

Mrs. Schmitt had a motherly smile that was hinting at something, but Ruth Ann quickly excused herself and exited through the side kitchen door.

There stood the rack of bicycles that belonged to the house. Ruth Ann hesitated. Would Benjamin be impressed if she rode a bicycle across town on her own? Would he see her as smart and capable and worthy of listening to?

Maybe. Maybe not. Either way, a bicycle was the best way to track him down in this city.

Ruth Ann double checked her map, then unhooked one of the ladies bicycles and rolled it out to the road. With a resolute nod, she mounted and pushed off before she thought about it too much. She found the pedals and pressed hard as the bicycle wobbled beneath her. She gasped, expecting to fall.

But she stayed upright! As soon as Ruth Ann got it into forward motion, it was just like riding the tandem bicycle with Benjamin. Though his sure form wasn't in front of her, he had instilled confidence in her to take the city herself by bicycle. This was the independence she needed on this trip.

Ruth Ann took the route to the Navy Yard that had the least number of turns—down Pennsylvania Avenue to New Jersey Avenue. Unfortunately, she had to go through Garfield Park, but it was quiet today.

The Navy Yard wasn't all that far from the Congressional Cemetery. She'd been hesitant to visit the wharf since Joseph told her there were rough fishermen who frequented there. But Mrs. Schmitt didn't seem concerned. And who would bother an Indian girl out for a bicycle ride on a Sunday afternoon?

The ride was invigorating. Both the fresh air and the physical exercise helped clear Ruth Ann's mind of the cobwebs that had formed after yesterday's incident with Georgia Pearl. Ruth Ann was determined to put the drama aside and firm up her resolve to ask Benjamin about her brother at the right moment. She would do it today.

The tangy scent of salt air and fish told her she was nearing the wharf. She turned down a wide road lined with empty fish carts and boats moored along the pier. There was little activity this Sunday, so she had no trouble slowing enough to read the building numbers until she came to the one Mrs. Schmitt gave her with a sign over it that read, *Byington Home for Orphans*.

Ruth Ann parked her bicycle in a rack next to another one by the building, legs unsteady as though she were getting off one of the boats at the wharf. Her legs steadied as she climbed the stairs, thinking through what reason she would give Benjamin for her unexpected appearance. Should she bring up Pepper's request and tie it into her own, or was it too soon?

She pulled the ringer by the door. A few minutes later, it opened to the smiling face of a young girl about Georgia Pearl's age. She wore a starched gray dress and white apron with a prim cap set atop her head.

"May I help you, miss?"

"I was told I might find Benjamin Nakishi here."

The girl motioned her in. "You must be part of the group of Choctaws visiting this month. He's telling stories about your people today and, oh, how the children love it. They love him."

Ruth Ann felt a twinge of something at the buttery words and glow on the young girl's face. But she ignored it as she followed her inside and down a dark hallway that opened into a sunroom filled with green plants and bright faces.

In the middle of the floor on the Venetian carpet, Benjamin Nakishi sat cross-legged, surrounded by boys and girls with chins propped up on their hands, listening to him. A little girl sat in his lap as he said, "And the turtle was sad because all of his bird friends were flying south for the winter…"

Benjamin halted his story at the sight of Ruth Ann and she was suddenly the center of attention, much to her dismay.

Benjamin cocked his head, smiled. "This is a surprise, Miss Ruth Ann." To the children, he said, "Miss Ruth Ann Teller is from the place where I grew up."

The children looked up at her, awed, and one blurted out, "Have you ever shot a deer?"

That set off a flurry of questions.

"Do you have a horse?"

"Do you have brothers and sisters?"

"Will you tell us a story about panthers?"

"Do you know how turtle got cracks on his back?"

Benjamin raised a hand for quiet. "Now, let's not pester Miss Teller. And as I recall Miss Rose saying, this is the last story. Maybe you could make room for Miss Ruth Ann and she can help tell it."

Two of the little boys scooted apart and Ruth Ann settled between them, tucking her feet under her skirts, trying not to look too directly at Benjamin across from her. She smiled at the boys. "I'm sure Mr. Benjamin tells the story of *luksi,* of turtle, better. Please continue."

The attention was off her again as Benjamin resumed the story, his deep voice echoing in her heart and taking her back to her own childhood.

"So turtle was sad and walked around in the woods, thinking. Then he had an idea. He told his little bird friend to find a big, strong stick. The next morning, when all the birds left, two of them would hold the stick in the claws between them and turtle would clamp on with his mouth and they could carry him south with them! He was so excited about his very clever plan." Benjamin held the room with his animated expressions.

For Ruth Ann, she was a child again, listening to her father tell the story over and over in their home. Only in those times, Philip, Matthew, and Ruth Ann traded out being the animal characters while he narrated. Matthew was more hesitant on the stage, but Philip never outgrew it, even in his early teens. Which brought her back to the present reality and the reason she was there. But the story wasn't over.

Benjamin shifted the little girl on his lap to spread his arms wide. "The birds found a stick the next morning and turtle grabbed on with his mouth. They flapped their wings and up, up, up they went. Turtle was flying! It was such a feat, and he was proud. Then three crows flew by. They cackled at one another…" Benjamin's voice took on the characters. "… 'What a clever idea! I wonder who thought of it?' And turtle was so proud that he opened his mouth and said, 'I did…'" Benjamin's voice faded the same as Daddy's at this part of the story. "And too late, turtle realized that he'd let go of the stick and down, down, down, he fell to the ground!"

The little girl covered her mouth and Benjamin shook his head. "And that's how turtle got cracks on his back. And it reminds us, 'pride goeth before destruction and a haughty spirit before a fall.'"

Ruth Ann found herself adding, just as her daddy did at the end of the scripture verse, "And sometimes, it's best to keep your mouth shut."

Benjamin laughed, making the children giggle, even though they wouldn't realize how important that was until they'd gotten older.

Benjamin had a hearty laugh and used it to finish with, "That was the last story. Time for you all to go with Miss Rose for your naps."

A chorus of groaning sounded, to which Benjamin chuckled. "You will look back on these treacherous naps as glorious times after you grow up."

Ruth Ann smiled at the children, giving the boys a caring pat on the head as they stood, saying their farewells. The young girl in uniform herded the children down the hallway and up the stairs.

Ruth Ann turned back, finding herself awkwardly sitting with

Benjamin on the floor. He stood first and helped her up. He pulled on his coat, looking at her expectantly.

Ruth Ann rushed through her words. "Mrs. Schmitt told me you come here some Sundays. I wanted to speak with you about something. But I didn't mean to disrupt your time with the children."

He shook his head as he picked up his derby hat from one of the tables that held a potted plant. "No disruption. The children enjoyed meeting you. And it's a pleasure to see you. Seems every time we're together, there are a host of people and demands and conversations. Perhaps a stroll on the wharf will give us a better chance to talk?"

Ruth Ann took a steady breath, suddenly realizing she'd stopped breathing when he had said something about them being together. They didn't have a chaperone, but the wharf was a public place and Benjamin was a well-respected man in the city.

"That would be lovely," she said.

Outside, Benjamin halted at the bottom of the steps by the bicycle rack. He gave Ruth Ann a sidelong grin. "Did you ride here?"

"I did." Ruth Ann tried to keep herself from feeling ridiculously pleased at his recognition of her accomplishment.

They left the bicycles behind to head down a long pier that stretched into the bay. Benjamin asked if Ruth Ann had eaten lunch, and when she said no, he squatted beside one of the boats that bobbed even with the pier. He negotiated two bowls of something called gumbo from the only vendor open. The man served the bowls right from his boat.

Benjamin directed Ruth Ann to a cluster of empty tables in the middle of the pier positioned for those dining from the boats.

After they blessed the food, Ruth Ann asked, "How long have you been visiting this orphanage?"

Benjamin rubbed his chin, gazing at the building, a calculating look on his face. "Since it was founded four years ago. I grew up admiring the work of Cyrus Byington among the Choctaws, especially in translating part of the Bible into our language. Seemed an appropriate name for this home."

Ruth Ann glanced over her shoulder at the building, then met his eyes. "You mean, you founded this orphanage?"

Benjamin flushed, and she knew it was from modesty. "Growing up an orphan is lonely when there's no family to visit," he said quietly. "Seems right to give back. I had a good upbringing at Spencer Academy."

He cleared his throat. "You said there was something you wanted to talk over?"

Ruth Ann stirred the gumbo, stalling. The liquid was red and loaded with shrimp and okra. She tried to think of the first thing to say to Benjamin.

She took a bite of the gumbo and froze. Her mouth lit up like she just swallowed a torch, her eyes watering with fresh onion intensity.

Benjamin shook out a handkerchief and handed it to her. "Eat the crackers, it'll help."

Ruth Ann coughed into the handkerchief and shoved three crackers into her mouth as inconspicuously as she could. It relieved the burn, and she caught her breath. She dabbed her eyes, trying to laugh.

"Well, that was a new experience," she said.

She lowered the handkerchief and was startled to see it stained with light red blotches. This was her handkerchief she'd used for Pepper's cut.

Benjamin winced. "Sorry. I was planning to have Mrs. Schmitt see about getting the stains all the way out before giving it back to you. I'm afraid I'm not very adept with a wash pan."

"That's all right. I thought Pepper still had it."

"I retrieved it from him. I don't feel it's appropriate for a man to keep a lady's handkerchief, which is why I cleaned and planned to return it today."

Ruth Ann folded the handkerchief carefully, smiling. "May as well leave it as is. We have quite a bit more time with Pepper before all of this is over."

They chuckled and Benjamin went to get Ruth Ann something more palatable from the boat vendor.

In their casual conversation that followed, she tried to find a way to bring up Philip, but talking about her brother's betrayal and her father's violent death was too heavy after the turtle story. Sometimes, it really was better to keep her mouth shut.

She enjoyed Benjamin's story of the time he'd been out on a fishing boat in a hurricane. She recalled Judge Eldridge's story of the first time Benjamin had been to the beach and the man who threatened to shoot him.

That incident apparently hadn't dampened Benjamin's enthusiasm for the ocean, and Ruth Ann had a sinking feeling this was yet another block that would keep him from returning to the Choctaw Nation.

But he must. No one else could defeat Tecumseh Shoemaker in court.

Besides, if he didn't come back to Indian Territory, would she ever see him again?

Benjamin and Ruth Ann rode their bicycles side by side on the way back to Roseland. After steadily climbing from the wharf and nearing the National Mall, Benjamin glanced over at her. "Take a breather?"

"Please."

Ruth Ann's limbs were tired from peddling the bicycle on her own and she wished they were riding tandem. But she did enjoy the freedom of riding single, too.

They slowed to a stop and Ruth Ann awkwardly took a few straddle-steps before getting her balance, but nothing too embarrassing. They dismounted and pushed their bicycles toward the Chestnut trees on the edge of the grassy lawn.

Shouts came from the center of the lawn, and Ruth Ann was surprised to see several young men running to-and-fro. For a moment, she was transported home to Indian Territory and a stickball game. "Little Brother of War" was sometimes used to settle disputes in place of a violent conflict.

But these boys had no sticks and the ball they threw was far larger than the small, woven balls used in the traditional game.

"Do you like football, Miss Ruth Ann?" Benjamin asked.

"Hardly."

She should have recognized the sport from the photographs in the cities' newspapers. She crinkled her nose. "I don't see the sense of having organized leagues, especially colleges and universities offering scholarships to play a game. It seems a bit silly."

One of the young men ran out past his defender, straight toward where Ruth Ann and Benjamin stood. The pigskin ball sailed high, far too high. Ruth Ann squealed and jerked back, pulling her bicycle in front of her as though the contraption might protect her from the incoming projectile.

Benjamin dropped his bicycle and, with his long arm extended from his six foot frame, he caught the ball and curled it under his arm. Spinning with the momentum, he turned and launched the pigskin at the receiver in the distance.

The young man caught it and called, "We were wondering when our star quarterback would show up! See you brought us a new player."

Benjamin turned back to Ruth Ann, grinning from the exertion.

She felt herself flush. "I didn't know you played. I must've sounded so rude!"

Benjamin put one hand on her bicycle handle, not leaning terribly close but enough for her to catch the teasing in his low voice. "You can make up for it by playing with us. We'll take it easy, no tackling."

Ruth Ann's eyes widened, and she opened her mouth with an automatic *no*. But she couldn't bring herself to decline. "Surely I'd just be a bother."

Benjamin was already pulling off his shoes, and motioned for her to do the same. "I'll bet you are a fierce player when you want to be."

Ruth Ann found those warm, Hershey chocolate eyes impossible to refuse. And she had played stickball as a child.

With a laugh, she unlaced her boots while Benjamin parked their bicycles under a tree.

Ruth Ann was amazed at how quick Benjamin was to shed his dress shoes, socks, and suit coat, and roll up the hems of his trousers. He transformed from a stylish, capitol city lawyer into an average man with a heart for orphan children and sports.

He had such a polished veneer, she wondered how many people ever got a glimpse of this side of Benjamin Nakishi.

She tossed her boots aside and trotted alongside him. In her bicycle riding skirt, she could run fairly easy. This was one reason why progressive young ladies like Virginia Lee wanted to enjoy modern freedoms afforded young women. While Ruth Ann could never imagine running around in bloomers—good heavens!—the feel of green grass cool on her bare feet was exhilarating. It was as if she were back home in Indian Territory on Uncle Preston's ranch.

The faces of the young men lit up when they realized she was really going to jump into the fray. They gave up their traditional game filled with roughhousing and tackling in lieu of throwing passes and chasing each other up and down the field.

When Benjamin got ahold of the ball, he waved for Ruth Ann to take a run. She did and found one of the young men chasing after her to try to block the pass.

She glanced back to see Benjamin flick his hand to the left.

She stopped short and spun away from the defender to run in the opposite direction from him.

Benjamin had already launched the ball, and it landed right in her arms so perfectly she knew it was Benjamin's skill, not her own.

The game went on for an hour. Ruth Ann was giddy with her hair all undone and feet dusty, and she was sure her face was streaked with sweat lines, but it didn't matter. She had a grand time with the boys. Maybe this sport wasn't so silly after all.

Benjamin and Ruth Ann parted from the players. One of them told Benjamin he could show up only if he brought the pretty Indian girl with him again.

Back at their bicycles, Ruth Ann grinned at Benjamin as they put their shoes on. "Thank you for wrangling me into that. My brother is quite a stickball player but he wouldn't have gotten me on a public field like that."

Benjamin held her bicycle upright for her as she straddled it. "Your brother, Matthew, isn't it?" he asked. "Who does the *Choctaw Tribune* newspaper with you?"

Ruth Ann hesitated while Benjamin turned away to get his own bicycle. She hadn't spoken much of her family with him and now she wondered if this was the perfect time to bring up her other brother, Philip. When would she ever feel more bold and brash than after playing a game of football on the National Mall?

"Yes, Matthew is my brother who owns the newspaper," she said slowly. "I do have another brother that I wanted to..."

She halted. Benjamin was looking behind her, a frown replacing his grin. She glanced over her shoulder to see Joseph Griffin pedaling on a bicycle toward them.

When Ruth Ann caught sight of Joseph's face, she understood Benjamin's expression. Something had happened.

Joseph came to a stop beside them and nodded a greeting at Ruth Ann before addressing Benjamin. "We tried to telephone you at the orphanage, but you'd already left."

"What has happened?" Benjamin's voice was low and Ruth Ann had a sickening feeling he knew.

There was always that sense, that foreboding, that knowing when great tragedy had already struck and your world was changed forever. Like that day for her on Uncle Preston's ranch when the news of her daddy and brother's death came.

Joseph dismounted and stood beside his bicycle, taking off his hat.

"I'm sorry to be the one to tell you this, but Judge Eldridge passed away."

CHAPTER 34

On Monday evening, Ruth Ann let Georgia Pearl sweep out of their room ahead of her, her billow of the sky blue skirt with lace and sequins barely clearing the doorway. The younger girl was in better spirits this evening, but still subdued. She made no comments about wearing eagle feathers. Hopefully, no one would follow her prior fashion statement at the charity ball this evening.

Ruth Ann followed in the gold silk ball gown that Mrs. Schmitt loaned her. She'd packed two perfectly fine dresses for evenings, but after seeing photographs in the Washington papers of formal galas, Ruth Ann knew she didn't possess anything suitable.

The dress she wore was more grand than anything she owned, and the maid went so far as to work a gold and pearl tiara into her updo. But getting in the gown proved an extraordinary challenge. It took the maid and Mrs. Schmitt's help to tighten Ruth Ann's undergarments enough for the form fitting bodice. Ruth Ann was sure she wasn't overweight, but that experience had her questioning if she was eating too much on this trip.

Nothing to worry about tonight. She wouldn't be able to eat a bite trussed up like she was. Besides, she was too nervous, dressed so grandly.

Would Benjamin Nakishi be at the charity ball?

After Joseph Griffin delivered the news of Judge Eldridge's sudden passing yesterday, Benjamin excused himself to ride his bicycle to the judge's home. Ruth Ann scarcely had a chance to offer her sympathies. There were no words for those moments, nothing she could do to ease the devastation on his face. The judge had been a father to him. Did Benjamin have anyone to give him comfort right now?

There was no reason to expect Benjamin to attend the charity ball, even though Judge Eldridge was one of its founders. She'd heard he was the largest donor and that it wouldn't take place each year if not for him.

Still, Benjamin was in shock and grief. The last place he needed to be was in a room full of people that lacked the most important person in his life.

Ruth Ann and Georgia Pearl went down the grand staircase together. They found a smattering of Roseland House guests that had not departed for the grand ball yet, including Pepper and Joseph Griffin. Mrs. Schmitt had assured everyone that the house carriages would go between the ball and Roseland throughout the evening to transport guests.

Pepper came straight for Ruth Ann. To her embarrassment, he gave her an openly appraising look, like he might examine a filly at a horse auction.

He was dressed in a tailcoat, white tie, black trousers, polished shoes, and even wore white gloves. Ruth Ann had to admit that he was one of the handsomest young men she knew. Not as handsome as Matthew, but it helped on this evening that Pepper offered a pleasant smile, even if it wasn't fully genuine. She assumed it had more to do with the rumor that the president and First Lady would be at the charity ball than the gold dress that complimented Ruth Ann's dark skin.

Pepper offered his arm to her. "You look lovely this evening, my dear."

Ruth Ann cautiously accepted Pepper's arm, not at all happy with the term of endearment. Joseph Griffin let out in unabashed whistle.

"If you two ladies aren't going to be the grandest at the gala tonight."

Joseph offered Georgia Pearl his arm, which she accepted with a humble smile. The two couples exited Roseland and boarded a carriage that just returned. The horses were decked out with purple plumes on their headstalls and bells on their harnesses. The soft leather of the seats smelled of lemon wax in the warm evening air.

During the ride, Ruth Ann chatted with Joseph Griffin about the day's news and the potential guests of honor at the ball. None spoke about Benjamin Nakishi, though Ruth Ann wanted to.

They arrived at the estate of a prominent D.C. family, the carriage circling the drive and stopping in front of the wide porch steps of the three-story mansion. Light, music, and subdued laughter drifted from the open doors and windows.

Pepper assisted Ruth Ann from the carriage. He even covered her gloved hand with his, as though making sure she couldn't escape. She frowned, resenting his possessiveness. But she'd go along with it for now.

They entered the burgundy carpeted hall lit with electric sconces and handed their wraps and tickets to the footman. Another footman directed them through the foyer and into the Willowbrook Ballroom.

The ceiling rose a remarkable twenty-five feet in the air with crystal chandeliers lighting the marble floored room. A full orchestra sat in one corner, playing softly in the background, and Ruth Ann was taken aback at the number of guests there. Hundreds!

But her eyes roamed the faces for a one tall Indian man. A

foolish hope. Even if Benjamin did come, she couldn't possibly talk to him about Philip there, the day after the judge's passing. When would enough time have passed for grief to talk business? She should know, but she didn't. She only knew she didn't have much time left to do it.

Pepper guided Ruth Ann to a nearby circle that contained Senator Newman, while Georgia Pearl and Joseph Griffin drifted away. Senator Newman greeted them and introduced them to the circle. Ruth Ann barely got any acknowledgment. She was simply an ornament on Pepper Barnes' arm tonight.

Appropriate to that thought, Virginia Lee made an appearance, unescorted. The circle greeted her, then Senator Newman continued a previous line of conversation with, "We will see what the other party does. It's doubtful the committee will come to an agreement and nothing will get settled as usual."

The people in the circle laughed. Virginia Lee took a sip from her punch glass, then stared straight at her father. She said, "If you spent more time on the floor of the senate and less trying to make backroom deals like typical politicians, women would have the right to vote already."

The ladies in the circle gasped as though shocked, which Ruth Ann thought was ridiculous. She wasn't surprised by Virginia Lee's bold statement.

Nor was Senator Newman. He chuckled and addressed his audience. "Most people are afraid to tell me exactly what they think. My daughter isn't one of them."

The orchestra struck a high note and light applause broke out as people began clearing off the ballroom floor for dancing.

In the crowd pressing toward Ruth Ann were Mr. and Mrs. Kanitobe. Though wearing their finest, they looked out of place among the tuxedoes and ballgowns.

Ruth Ann was surprised to find Forbis Kanitobe staring intently at her. Actually, it seemed as though he was staring at her and Pepper. As in, them together.

Ruth Ann tried to pry her hand loose from Pepper's arm. He did loosen it as he turned toward her. "May I have the privilege of the first dance, Ruth Ann?"

She stared up at him, not sure why she felt caught off guard. Perhaps it was because of dance parties at the Barnes' place throughout her young adult years when Pepper never once asked her to dance. That was back when she secretly wished he would.

People in the territory gossiped that she and Pepper Barnes were destined to marry someday. But as they grew through their teen years, Ruth Ann saw the likelihood of that drifting away. She wasn't sorry.

Now, as he offered his hand, she froze. But it seemed rude to refuse the invitation, and she finally allowed him to lead her onto the dance floor among the other waltzing couples.

She wasn't an experienced dancer, but Pepper was good and managed to keep them from embarrassment. She was grateful for the corset and gown that separated her from Pepper's hand on her waist.

As they danced, she couldn't look him in the face and opted instead to take in the swirl of faces as they moved around the ballroom floor.

A familiar face caught her eye, and she stumbled, but Pepper kept them moving.

"What is it?" he asked.

"I just saw someone I know, a man from Indian Territory."

"A *man*?"

"Oh, Pepper."

He tightened his grip on her waist. "Don't forget I'm the one who bought your very expensive ticket for this evening."

They finished the dance in silence, and when it was over, Ruth Ann had lost track of Thaddeus Warren. Did he see her, too? Would he recognize her if he did, dressed up as she was?

Pepper tugged on Ruth Ann's bare arm. "There's the First

Lady. Now's your chance to strike up a conversation. I'll come in a few minutes for an introduction. I'm going to find Kanitobe."

Without waiting for agreement, Pepper disappeared into the crowd. Ruth Ann spotted the First Lady surrounded as usual by an entourage. She recognized ladies from the luncheon at the President's House, though this time they were accompanied by their husbands. She didn't see President Cleveland and wondered if he was there.

Ruth Ann had no intention of fluffing up Pepper Barnes with the First Lady, but why not offer greetings at this social event?

Ruth Ann joined the entourage but three layers back from the First Lady. As Ruth Ann waited for an opening, she caught snippets of the conversation. The topic was Judge Eldridge.

"It was so sudden, none of us expected it."

"I heard it was his heart."

"I don't believe he was seen in public much the past few years."

"I suppose the one who was closest to him was the Indian lawyer."

Ruth Ann sidestepped around the circle, trying to find an opening to better hear the conversation. Then she wished she hadn't.

"That Indian is smart as a whip. The judge was wise to mentor him. Why, if not for his dark skin, he would be like one of us. The other young Indian in town has about the right shade. If only we could merge his skin with our lawyer's mind, we would have the perfect Indian."

A smatter of laughter went around the interior circle. Ruth Ann could feel heat flaming on her own dark skin. She caught sight of the First Lady, who wasn't smiling as her soft eyes took in the faces around her. She locked gazes with Ruth Ann.

The First Lady looked as if she were about to acknowledge Ruth Ann. There wasn't a worse thing in that moment Ruth Ann could imagine.

"May I have this dance?"

The quiet, deep voice was for her ears only, and Ruth Ann turned to find Benjamin Nakishi offering his arm to her.

She quickly took it, breaking away from the circle before she was pointed out. Ruth Ann wondered if he had been privy to the conversation. She sincerely hoped not.

As they moved to the dance floor, Ruth Ann didn't feel over-dressed. Benjamin wore a custom-fitted black tail coat, white bow tie, and red silk pocket square, scoring top position as the most handsome and well dressed man in the room.

Before she realized it, they were on the dance floor, Benjamin's hand lightly on her well-secured waist, her right hand nestled safely in his gloved one. She found it hard to look into his eyes, and not just because of his height.

Benjamin moved them about the dance floor. He wasn't as skilled a dancer as Pepper, but Ruth Ann relaxed more.

"You look lovely this evening, Miss Ruth Ann."

Same words as Pepper. Yet how different they felt.

Benjamin was a full decade older than her, but had still seemed young and tender. That was covered over with grief, aging him beyond the star quarterback she caught a football from on the National Mall the day before.

"Yakoke. I...wasn't sure you would be here," Ruth Ann said quietly. "I'm so sorry again for your loss."

"Judge Eldridge was a fine Christian man," Benjamin said, his voice soft, hoarse. "He is with our Lord Jesus Christ now and we will be reunited someday."

"Maybe he will meet my father in Heaven." The words slipped out before Ruth Ann gave them proper thought. She swallowed down her tears, feeling true compassion for Benjamin's loss. Daring to lift her eyes, she saw Benjamin's gentle smile.

"I hope so, Miss Ruth Ann. I would like to hear more about your father sometime."

The dance ended and Benjamin guided Ruth Ann from the

floor as he said, "I've only come for a brief time this evening. Judge Eldridge was deeply involved in this charity ball and it felt right to see that his memory was retained in it."

"I wish you could stay longer." Again, words she didn't mean to say came out, but she didn't want to draw these back. Benjamin glanced down at her, holding her gaze carefully in his.

"I do as well. But there is a great deal to do in settling the judge's affairs and planning...the funeral."

Now Ruth Ann did regret her selfishness. She hadn't realized Benjamin would be the one making the judge's funeral arrangements.

What about the judge's daughter? Had she learned of her father's death yet? With a sick feeling, Ruth Ann realized the young woman would make an appearance before long.

Nora Eldridge. Benjamin's ex-fiancé.

Still gazing at one another, neither Ruth Ann nor Benjamin were braced when Pepper suddenly appeared close beside them. Ruth Ann frowned at his glare. Pepper cleared his throat, his temper simmering beneath an overly polite exterior.

"Ruth Ann, dear, I've been looking for you. You weren't where I left you."

Ruth Ann realized that Forbis Kanitobe was with Pepper. Pepper probably promised him an introduction to the president's wife, and Ruth Ann failed to deliver.

With Benjamin's grief still palpable in her heart, she didn't have the strength to banter with Pepper. She didn't release Benjamin's arm. She had no desire for Pepper to claim her whole evening.

"Pepper, you may not have heard yet that Benjamin's mentor, Judge Eldridge, passed yesterday."

"I heard."

He gave Benjamin a nod. Benjamin returned it. That was that. Ruth Ann sighed. Men.

Forbis Kanitobe didn't have sympathy to offer Benjamin. He

looked him straight in the eyes and said, "He made a white man of you."

Ruth Ann stared at Forbis Kanitobe, shocked. His look was stern as he added, "You are an apple—red on the outside and white on the inside."

Benjamin said nothing, but a look passed between him and Pepper that Ruth Ann understood. Benjamin would face race problems even among his own people in Indian Territory. How harder had Forbis just made it to convince Benjamin to return long enough to represent Philip at his trial?

"There you all are." Georgia Pearl latched onto Ruth Ann's free arm. Forbis snorted and walked away.

Georgia Pearl slipped her hand into Ruth Ann's as though trying to draw strength from her. Ruth Ann had none to give.

Georgia Pearl looked between Benjamin and Pepper. "I really wanted to talk to the three of you. I've been trying to find the courage all evening to confess how terribly rude and ignorant I am. I just don't know what to say."

Pepper crossed his arms. "Obviously."

Her face reddened, and she squeezed Ruth Ann's hand. "I'm trying to apologize."

"Fine," Pepper said. "Let us know when you're done trying and decide to do it."

Georgia Pearl's eyes watered. She released Ruth Ann's hand and turned away, but Benjamin said, "I accept your apology, Miss Newman."

Georgia Pearl turned back, sniffing. "I am so truly sorry, to all of you."

Ruth Ann reached out to take Georgia Pearl's hand. She gave her a reassuring squeeze and tiny smile. Georgia Pearl returned it, but Pepper broke the conciliatory mood.

"Now that that's all settled, what were you saying about your father's support the other day? I'd say you owe us something after your hideous display."

Ruth Ann interjected, "You owe Georgia Pearl an apology for how abrasive you were. There were better ways to handle what happened."

Pepper matched her stare, and she knew he never would say he was sorry. But once, just *once*, Ruth Ann wanted to hear Pepper Barnes apologize for something.

Benjamin diverted the tension when he said, "If you will excuse me." He released Ruth Ann from his arm. Hollow air rushed in the gap between them and her disappointment showed, but she quickly masked it as he finished, "I'll take my leave of the evening."

Pepper barely bid him goodnight, his attention on Georgia Pearl, who looked lost. Benjamin bowed away, but held Ruth Ann's gaze for a fleeting moment.

The grief was in his eyes again and she understood the cliffs and gullies and dry gulches his heart was going through. She offered him an understanding smile, but her heart ached with the honest question, *Will you come back to Indian Territory for my family?*

For me?

CHAPTER 35

Ruth Ann was incredibly sleepy by the time she let Pepper hand her into the enclosed Roseland carriage. They were among the last to leave the Willowbrook Ballroom, staying until they finally had a chance to greet the First Lady.

The president never made an appearance. Ruth Ann credited that as being the reason Pepper seemed preoccupied as they got into the carriage. He sat beside her as a footman closed the door.

The carriage jolted in the motion, which brought Ruth Ann awake again. Several guests from Roseland were departing late, and she wondered why the driver didn't wait for more to fill the carriage before heading back.

It wasn't important. She leaned her forehead against the glass window, letting it cool her from the heat of the ballroom on the summer evening. It was nearly midnight, and there was so much to do yet in the nation's capitol during this trip.

Should she confront Thaddeus Warren? But what would she say? What would Benjamin think of all the trouble her family attracted with alarming regularity? Between Matthew and the *Choctaw Tribune* and now Philip and outlaws, there was no reason

229

for a fine man with a spotless reputation to get involved with them.

Ruth Ann sighed and opened her eyes, gazing out the window. She was startled to see they were passing the Washington Monument. They were headed south instead of west toward Roseland.

"I think the driver took a wrong turn," she said.

When Pepper didn't respond, Ruth Ann looked over at him. He was staring at the empty seat across from them, his expression impossible to read.

She straightened in her seat, an odd feeling in the pit of her stomach. "Pepper Barnes, what are you up to?"

The carriage halted. Pepper opened the door and jumped out. He turned back to offer his hand to help her down. The cool air from the Potomac River was refreshing, but Ruth Ann had absolutely no intention of taking a midnight stroll along its banks.

"You tell the driver to take us to Roseland House immediately," she said.

Pepper sighed, long and deep. There was nothing malicious in his voice, just a genuine seriousness when he said, "There's something I need to talk to you about. Something Forbis Kanitobe told me about your brother."

He didn't need to say which brother. Still, Ruth Ann hesitated. Did she dare follow Pepper? What could be so secretive that he wanted to talk like this?

"We cannot be out unchaperoned," she said.

"The driver is right here. Now come on, it's important. Please."

Ruth Ann had known Pepper their entire lives. Though she didn't trust him, she did. There were certain times and certain ways, but she did.

She shifted and allowed Pepper to assist her down from the carriage.

They walked down to the tidal basin, a popular place during

the day where people fed ducks. The basin was alive with sounds of nature's nighttime gaiety, far from the pretense of the ballrooms where most everyone had an agenda.

Ruth Ann was anxious to hear what Forbis Kanitobe knew about Philip, but she was too tired to wrangle Pepper into telling her sooner than he wanted to. He didn't seem in a hurry, hands deep in his trouser pockets as he stared across the Potomac River. A snap of cool air blew into her face and she was grateful for the light wrap over her ball gown.

They stood awhile before Pepper went to the river bank, squatted and rifled through the grass. He raised and looked her directly in her eyes as he tossed a pebble at her feet.

Ruth Ann caught her breath. It was as though cold water from the Potomac River was seeping through her slippers and stockings, chilling her from head to toe.

In one old Choctaw tradition, when a young man courted a girl, he tossed a pebble at her feet in a nonverbal proposal.

A proposal of marriage.

If she accepted, she tossed the pebble back.

Ruth Ann didn't move.

Pepper sighed. "Will you marry me?"

He said it as almost as though speaking to a child who couldn't grasp her lesson.

Ruth Ann wasn't a child, but a girlish giggle bubbled out of her.

"Be serious, Pepper Barnes. I...how could you..."

He took a long step toward her, closing off the gap between them. She forgot to breathe.

"Ruth Ann Teller, you are the most intelligent, and beautiful, woman in Indian Territory," he said, the tone of his voice striking her heart. He believed what he was saying. And he wasn't finished. "You're the kind of woman I need at my side to see that our people, our nation goes into the new century right. We make a strong team every time we partner up. Like a match set of horses."

Ruth Ann gulped. "I'm no horse, Pepper Barnes."

"No. You sure aren't." He tipped his face closer to kiss her.

Ruth Ann whipped an open palm across Pepper's face, slapping him hard. Her hand stung, and her body trembled to the tips of her toes. This was the part of Pepper she didn't trust.

His face jerked to one side from the slap, but he didn't move away. He turned back slowly, jaw twitching. "All right, Annie. You want truth so bad, well, here it is. You need me, Ruth Ann Teller, to save your brother's life."

Ruth Ann swallowed hard as he towered over her. But she wasn't going to back down. "I don't need you for anything, Pepper Barnes."

Pepper's eyes darkened. "If you think that fine Benjamin Nakishi is sweet enough on you to travel all the way to the Choctaw Nation and defend Philip in court, you're wrong. He's not the man for you. And besides, he wouldn't even win, not against Tecumseh Shoemaker."

Ruth Ann wasn't about to give any hint of how Pepper's word's hit their mark. She lifted her chin. "Are you going to tell me what Forbis Kanitobe said about my brother or not?"

Pepper finally took a step back, giving them breathing room. But his gaze intensified, and Ruth Ann held her breath.

This was another one of those moments. Whatever the news was, she would never be the same.

Pepper flipped his tailcoat back and put his hands on his hips. "Tecumseh plans to seek the death penalty for Philip."

Ruth Ann's knees weakened, and she collapsed on the ground. She landed in a heap, the skirt of her gold ball gown spread across the deep grass by the river. A sob came up her throat and Ruth Ann covered her mouth, a vision of her daddy's tombstone fresh in her mind—and Philip's beside it.

She dropped her hand and ripped a handful of grass from the

earth. She twisted it, willing it to wring out the pain in her heart, longing to smear her face with mud again.

Pepper squatted eye level in front of her, but she couldn't make out his face for the blur of her tears.

"Did you really think Tecumseh would be satisfied with a few lashes on Philip's back?" Pepper said in that terrible tone of truth. "To him, traitors in the Choctaw Nation get executed. He wants Philip dead. *Dead*, Annie. All over again. Only this time, your family will have to watch."

CHAPTER 36

When Ruth Ann sensed a presence hovering over her, she knew something wasn't right.

She pried her eyes open from a deep sleep to realize it wasn't the presence that was wrong. It was the fact that she was sleeping on the sofa in the sitting room of the girls' suite, still clothed in her gold ball gown.

She squinted against the grain in her eyes to see Georgia Pearl squatted next to the sofa, face showing her concern.

Ruth Ann moistened her lips and mumbled, "I got in a little late last night and didn't want to wake you."

It was hardly an explanation, but she wasn't going to talk about Pepper's ridiculous proposal on the bank of the Potomac River, nor was she going to tell how she returned to the suite, crying. That was why she slept on the sofa, to be free to cry throughout the night after Pepper's announcement about her brother.

"Can I bring you anything?" Georgia Pearl asked.

Her sincerity nearly undid Ruth Ann again, but she held fast to her emotions and whispered, "No."

Once Georgia Pearl left the room for breakfast, Ruth Ann got up and went into the bedroom, tripping once on the ball gown.

A long soak in the clawfoot tub helped wash away the pain and humiliation of last night enough for Ruth Ann to think through what she must do. Her quest was no longer about bringing Philip home. It was about saving his life, and Benjamin Nakishi was the only person in the world who could defeat Tecumseh in court.

She would not turn to Pepper for help. He made it clear that marrying him would achieve whatever he was trying to do, but he was crazy to think she would.

Her next move was so clear, Ruth Ann didn't waste time contemplating. The situation had turned into a life or death one, and she had to ask Benjamin now. If he declined, she was back to Pepper. Or one more option that came to mind again after seeing the First Lady at the ball. But she wouldn't contemplate that until she had Benjamin's answer.

Downstairs, she found Mrs. Schmitt in the kitchen. The whole boarding house was quiet and there was no sign of Pepper. He and Ruth Ann were supposed to go to some meeting or another, but apparently he'd left without Ruth Ann. Fine with her.

Mrs. Schmitt told her that Benjamin Nakishi left early that morning for his country estate eight miles south of the city, near Alexandria.

Ruth Ann's heart sank at the news. How could she have forgotten Benjamin was in the midst of deep grief, and just barge in on him?

But it couldn't be helped if she wanted to save her mother from the deepest grief of her life.

After getting directions, Ruth Ann debated renting a carriage, but eight miles in the countryside by bicycle sounded like the thing she needed. It would give her time to process the fear for her brother's life and to think of how to present that to Benjamin.

Ruth Ann, dressed in her riding skirt, began the journey out to Alexandria, finding the ride as challenging as she expected. But she began mastering new techniques on the bicycle, such as gaining speeds far greater than she was comfortable with, to make a hill possible. She even raised from her seat for extra pushing power up one hill and stole glances at the Potomac River when it came into view.

She was actually surprised how quickly she reached the crossroad that Mrs. Schmitt directed her to, about an hour of peddling later. She turned right and headed down a tree-lined dirt road that ended at an open gate with a white cottage set back among green shrubbery and pink blossoms.

Benjamin's country home.

She peddled up the driveway and nodded at an older man tending a garden to the side of the house. He looked surprised to see her, but waved. She parked in front of the house and dismounted as the door opened.

Benjamin stepped onto the porch in stocking feet, casual white shirt, and gray trousers, a cluster of papers in one hand. She'd never seen him dressed so informally, except when they played football.

The moment reminded her of when she met Judge Eldridge. The two men knew how to balance giving off a stately air with being real people. Behind the scenes, Benjamin Nakishi was like any ordinary man. Surely he would understand her plea.

"Miss Ruth Ann," he greeted her. "I wasn't expecting you."

After Pepper's escapade and the terrifying news about her brother, Ruth Ann didn't feel embarrassed about her lack of social graces. "I apologize for coming unannounced, but there is something I really must speak with you about."

He hesitated, then laid the papers on a small table beside the door. "Of course. We can sit in the garden."

Benjamin led her around the side of the house and motioned to a wrought-iron table and chair set that looked as though it wasn't used often. They were just out of earshot of the elderly gardener as they sat.

Ruth Ann took a moment to observe her surroundings, including the lattice arbor covered with rose bushes over them. It was a shady spot where the breeze could get at them. Rows of flowers and shrubs extended beyond the back of the house.

Benjamin shifted in the silence. He was waiting for her to state why she'd invaded his privacy just two days after his mentor passed. That was probably why he was there, to be alone to work on paperwork and funeral arrangements.

For all her time of riding out to the estate, Ruth Ann really didn't have a good way to start the conversation. She diverted for a minute. "You must have a great deal of paperwork to do. I really am sorry to show up unannounced."

Benjamin's fingers roamed the edge of the table, picking at peeling paint on the wrought iron. "Everything is almost in order for Judge Eldridge, but back at my office in D.C., I have a stack of case requests awaiting my decision on which I will accept next. But I'm contemplating taking a three-month sabbatical after the funeral."

This was definitely a bad time to ask Benjamin about traveling to Indian Territory. Even if he decided to take the case, they would be in D.C. a few more weeks, until the delegation left for home. But she couldn't help feeling she was in the right place. Perhaps because…

She blurted, "Will the judge's daughter be returning for the funeral?"

As soon as she spoke, Ruth Ann wished the words back. She wanted to stall on explaining why she was there, but she couldn't have picked a worse thing to say.

Benjamin rigorously rubbed the flakes, dislodging more of the peeling paint. Ruth Ann gripped her hands in her lap under the table. "I'm sorry, that was very rude."

"Actually, I'm glad you brought it up," Benjamin said. "I wanted to talk to someone, but in this world, we only talk about personal affairs behind people's backs. Bringing up your own is taboo. Not like back home when another Indian will tell you exactly what he's thinking."

He smiled and looked out across the garden. "I suspect you've heard the gossip, but I would like for you to know the whole truth before she gets here. I was engaged to Nora for two years, and it wasn't until that incident with Georgia Pearl at Roseland that I realized how much it did hurt. Nora jilted me because I'm an Indian."

Ruth Ann put two fingers to her lips to hold in the gasp that escaped anyway.

Benjamin went on, still looking at the garden. "That wasn't the whole issue, but it was the bottom line in the end. We knew there wasn't love going into the relationship, but I believed it would grow with time. Her father had already made me a part of the family, and when suitors for Nora didn't come, when her peers began having their second child, it seemed to the three of us that Nora and I were to marry. I thought her wanting to put off the wedding so long was for me to become more established in my career, and to finish what would be our home here."

Benjamin gestured to the cottage. Ruth Ann noticed that the back sported window frames covered with canvas and a few glass windows leaning against the side. A half fulfilled dream, yet with nothing left of it.

"I thought of selling this place but it's still a retreat for me." He absently rubbed the spot where he had flicked away the paint, keeping his eyes down. "Please don't misunderstand. Nora isn't prejudiced against Indians, but it wasn't something she felt she could handle in public. In the note she left with the judge before going to New York, she expressed how she didn't believe she was strong enough to be the wife I needed."

Ruth Ann remained quiet and still. She didn't know what to say but then, she didn't expect Benjamin wanted her to say anything. She could feel the depth of his words and that was enough for the moment.

He continued. "She knew I eventually wanted to move back to the Choctaw Nation. She didn't want to live in a wilderness."

Benjamin finally raised his gaze to give Ruth Ann a knowing smile. She struggled to return it, heart stopping at his words. She measured her own carefully. "You intend to move back to the Choctaw Nation?"

Benjamin shifted forward and shook his head. "I know what you're thinking. Pepper Barnes wants me to work for the Choctaw Nation but I will not return to Indian Territory until I retire. I have my reasons."

Ruth Ann found her own spot of peeling paint to pick, heart sinking. "I see."

"Now, you said there was something urgent you peddled all this way to talk with me about?" There was a teasing note in his voice, like when they were playing football. It was nice to hear, and Ruth Ann could tell he was gratified she'd made such an effort to see him instead of waiting for him to return to D.C.

He wouldn't be when he learned her reason.

Ruth Ann hesitated no more. Either she was going to talk Benjamin Nakishi into saving Philip or not. She looked him directly in the eyes and said, "My brother is in trouble."

Benjamin frowned, the tease gone from his eyes. "Sounds serious. Is it his newspaper?"

"No." She swallowed. "Not Matthew. My oldest brother, Philip. He is facing serious criminal charges for robbery and… there was a killing involved."

Benjamin leaned back in his chair and steepled his fingers under his chin, gaze on the glassless windows. "So that's why."

Ruth Ann rubbed her hands together furiously beneath the table, trying to calm herself, trying to understand his demeanor. He didn't seem upset or angry.

Disappointed. That was the word.

Ruth Ann had wounded him. She used their time together to get close to him only so she could ask for his help. How foolish and selfish she was!

But she couldn't hide her desperation as she said, "Would you come back to the Choctaw Nation, long enough to—"

"I cannot."

Ruth Ann wasn't sure which crushed her spirit more. Benjamin declining the case so quickly—or that she just destroyed their blossoming friendship. He would never trust her again.

"I wish you had asked sooner, Miss Teller," Benjamin said, dropping his hands to his lap. "The answer is simple. I do not take criminal cases."

Ruth Ann wished she had asked sooner as well, before his heart had gotten involved. And hers.

Benjamin insisted on accompanying Ruth Ann back to D.C. They rode side-by-side on the road, but didn't speak. The trip added to Ruth Ann's guilt, knowing she was taking him away from the funeral arrangements.

She'd been nothing but an imposition to Benjamin Nakishi and now, he believed the reason for her friendship was that she wanted to get him to take her brother's case.

It broke Ruth Ann's heart to admit that was exactly what she had done.

Ruth Ann walked in the side door of Roseland alone. Someone put a sandwich in her hands, but she doubted she would eat until supper.

Then she realized a telegram and letter lay on top of the sandwich, and was vaguely aware of Mrs. Schmitt saying how they both came for Ruth Ann that morning.

Ruth Ann thanked the hostess and went through the kitchen and dining room, down the long hallway and into the conservatory. It was empty and Ruth Ann found a bench placed amongst the ferns.

She should have gone to her room instead of sitting in a garden that reminded her of Benjamin's home, but she didn't have the strength to climb the stairs. Her limbs were shaking from fatigue and sadness.

She laid the sandwich aside and picked up the envelope. It was written in Matthew's hand. She should read the telegram first, the most current news, but she couldn't let go of the envelope. Was there a lifeline in it?

Dear Annie,

I'm sorry. I guess that's all I can say to try and mend our trust. At least, start with those words. Maybe if I keep going, more will come.

I wish I could have told you everything before you left. Being in the coal mining towns was tough. Remember how I looked like I'd been blown up when you found me in McAlester? I was in an explosion in one of the mines in Krebs. (Don't tell Mama).

But there were good people there. You saw the young lady with me in McAlester. She was kind and feisty and helped me through (Reminded me of you sometimes). I found later she'd been seeing a man named Toby who was said to look a whole lot like me. I was all set to come home when I met Toby. I found out it was really Philip.

There's a lot more I could write, but I need to tell the story in person. This is one time written words just aren't working.

Matt

Ruth Ann sniffed and nodded. Matthew was finally understanding. Now if only she could. He went through more than he would ever say, and she offered him no compassion before she left.

She tucked the letter in her dress pocket, planning to read it again to take in the frightening parts more fully, and unfolded the telegram, expecting it to be from Matthew.

But it was from Beulah Levitt. The bold words stood out on the page:

Caution, my friend. Lawyer accused of murder as teenager. The Dickens Herald reported. Check Washington papers tomorrow. Use great caution.

The cryptic message was meant as a letter, one that wouldn't cost a fortune. Its meaning was clear to Ruth Ann as she read it again, eyes growing wider, the fleeting warmth of Matthew's letter leaving her.

Beulah was talking about Benjamin Nakishi being involved in a murder.

CHAPTER 37

$\mathcal{R}$uth Ann rose early that Wednesday morning, up before anyone except staff. In the foyer, she leaned forward on her toes, looking out one window, awaiting delivery of the morning papers.

The footman received them and promptly let Ruth Ann have her pick. She thanked him, taking one newspaper outside. Seating herself in a rocker at the end of the porch, she used the morning's light to scan headlines. She halted at the one on page 3 that read:

D.C. Indian Lawyer Committed Murder

A reliable source in Indian Territory revealed a stunning accusation against an Indian lawyer practicing in D.C. The lawyer, Benjamin Nakishi-Dunn, who recently won a victory in his first Supreme Court case, is said to have taken part in committing murder while a teenage orphan in Indian Territory. The victim was a white man. It is unclear if Dunn paid for his crime or if he was released on grounds of being a citizen in the Choctaw Nation.

Ruth Ann read the article only once, heart hammering. She didn't want to imprint the words in her mind. Who knew if the scant story was accurate at all? If Christopher Maxwell and the *Dickens Herald* was involved, there were plenty of reasons to doubt. But Beulah did send that telegram. What more did she know? Surely a letter was on its way now with the facts.

Did Matthew dig up anything, too? Why didn't he send her a telegram?

"The early bird certainly got the worm this morning."

Ruth Ann couldn't look up despite Joseph Griffin's jovial tone. He sat in the chair next to her, leaning over her shoulder to read.

A few seconds later, he exclaimed, "Hogwash!"

Ruth Ann jumped at his outburst. Joseph snatched the newspaper from her, saying, "I guess this is why I'm in the business, to send corrected stories through the AP lines."

Ruth Ann stared at the porch rail, wishing she were on the back porch of Uncle Preston's house on the ranch. Somewhere her heart, mind, and body weren't being trampled by the world at every turn.

Joseph patted her hand. "Don't you worry, my dear. Benjamin Nakishi-Dunn is one of the finest men in the city. No one will pay attention to this rubbish."

Ruth Ann couldn't respond. Joseph didn't know about the telegram Beulah had sent about Benjamin. He didn't know that Ruth Ann's own brother was involved in the death of their father. He didn't know that Philip had been hiding, living a lie for six years and ripping their family apart.

Her own brother betrayed her. How could she trust anyone closer than that? Did she even know Benjamin Nakishi-Dunn?

And thine ears shall hear a word behind thee...

The front door banged open and Pepper barreled out, a newspaper rolled in a death grip.

"Take off." His sharp words were directed at Joseph.

Joseph put one hand on his hip, still seated, and shot back, "Not if you intend to use that tone with Miss Teller."

Ruth Ann murmured, "It's all right, Joseph. I'll see you at breakfast."

Joseph reluctantly stood and intentionally bumped into Pepper's shoulder as he passed.

The front door had scarcely closed behind him before Pepper growled at Ruth Ann, "So it's *Joseph*? And *Benjamin*? How many men are you on first name basis with in this city?"

Ruth Ann didn't have the strength to shoot back that Pepper was the only young man she didn't want to be on a first name basis with. There was little she could give this day, and it was only beginning.

Pepper cut the air in front of her nose with the newspaper. "This is why I did not want you using Nakishi's full name. From Indian Territory to Fort Smith to Leavenworth, Kansas, the name of 'Dunn' is associated with Benjamin's father and the murder he was convicted of. If people back home didn't know Benjamin Nakishi was his son, he could have helped the Nationals run Dawes out and establish our sovereignty to where no government could try to take it again. But no. You had to go and put his whole name, just to spite me."

Ruth Ann rubbed her temple, feeling hot already in the morning sun. She didn't understand Pepper's political ambitions and what he was trying to do in the tribe, other than gain power at a young age.

But he did know exactly what he wanted in life and he'd made at least one part of it clear. That was more than Ruth Ann could say for any other man in her life, including her brothers.

Pepper dropped into the chair vacated by Joseph. "My proposal still stands."

He paused, then his voice took on that earnest tone. "I know you went out to Nakishi's yesterday. Why do you keep going to him for help instead of me?"

A tear escaped Ruth Ann's eye and rolled down her cheek.

Pepper leaned close as he said, almost tenderly, "Look, I saved Matthew's life once. Let me save Philip."

ear Matthew,

I have enclosed articles highlighting recent events. I am also including a short column about Thaddeus Warren, whom I saw in D.C. He is in some sort of dealings with Indian land in our territory. I haven't found out what yet.

Ruth Ann leaned back in the chair at the secretary desk in her room, rubbing her grainy eyes. Georgia Pearl was fast asleep, so Ruth Ann kept the lamp low. The small clock on the top level of the desk showed 1 a.m.

Ruth Ann hadn't written all the articles she was promising Matthew in this letter. She thought that writing the letter first would make the articles easier. But how could she talk through the past few days in a letter to Matthew, and how could she respond to the revelations in his letter? If only he were there with her!

She had little chance of bringing Benjamin Nakishi back to Indian Territory, and now she was fairly certain she didn't want to. Pepper was right. Benjamin's reputation, and therefore usefulness, with the Choctaws—and to her—was ruined.

She couldn't face how heartbreaking that was. She must stay focused on how else she could save Philip from the justice of the Choctaw Lighthorsemen if Judge Kendrick sentenced him to death.

Tears seeped out as Ruth Ann remembered the execution of Silas Sloan, found guilty of killing those in his rival political party. She watched that man executed. She could not possibly do the same with her brother.

A sob rose in her throat, and she covered her mouth to hold it in. She had cried enough tears since Pepper told her the news. She couldn't spend time or energy on it anymore. She had to find a way through this.

Was Pepper that way? What did he have planned to save Philip the way he kept promising he would?

Oh, God, what am I supposed to do? How is it that everything I've done has made everything worse?

A tear dripped on her letter to Matthew. She wadded the paper and tossed it in the wastebasket next to the desk, along with a half dozen false starts on articles.

She knew what her writing troubles were, in part. Pepper Barnes.

She could not imagine accepting his proposal of marriage to save her brother's life, but there was something else he wanted from the beginning but hadn't asked for directly—favorable articles slanted toward him and his Nationalist politics. With being there among a Nationals delegation, Ruth Ann could easily provide those.

It would only cost her integrity and the integrity of the *Choctaw Tribune*.

But if it saved Philip's life, was it worth the high price?

Dear Matt,

I didn't know you went through so much. You didn't tell me. But then, I never gave you a fair chance to, did I?

But the worst is yet to come. I received disturbing news this week about Philip's trial. Tecumseh Shoemaker intends to seek the death penalty.

Those were the ugliest words Ruth Ann had ever written and she wanted to wad up that letter as well.

Yet somehow, seeing it in ink released her mind from the horror of it. Not that it wasn't still terrifying, but sending these words off to Matthew would give her the strength to face whatever lay ahead.

She wasn't in this fight alone.

Ruth Ann laid the letter aside to finish later and pulled a fresh stack of paper in front of her. She was ready to write the articles the way they needed to be written—the way they always were for the *Choctaw Tribune*, with all sides of the truth, not any one man or woman's truth.

CHAPTER 39

Matthew leaned heavily on his crossed arms on an outside rail of the high round pen he, Daniel, and Peter had built behind the Teller home before the second journey to Blackjack Mountain. Matthew went with the intention of bringing back a Choctaw stallion, though this was hardly the time to undertake a monumental project.

But if not now, when? So he had gone and come back with his tri-colored stallion, the one with his name on it. Robert Barnes even confirmed it, saying the stallion was partially broke, but that he kept running off to the mountains. If anyone could finish breaking him, Barnes believed Matthew could.

The railing of the pen was taller than Matthew, ensuring that his new horse wouldn't injure himself trying to jump the fence. As it was, the young tri-colored stallion trotted around inside, ears, head, and tail high.

He charged at Matthew, then braked hard and snorted as they came face-to-face with the log fence between them. Matthew felt the heat of the stallion's frustration as he snorted and pawed the ground.

Trapped. Just like Philip at the bottom of the mineshaft when he finally confessed the whole truth of what happened on that dark day in the Winding Stair Mountains.

Being trapped in the bottom of the mineshaft was what it had taken to finally break Philip. It broke Matthew, too. Was Ruth Ann being broken now?

His puny letter to her fell short in so many ways. He needed to go to her, and soon. He needed to protect her from whatever was going on with Pepper Barnes and Benjamin Nakishi-Dunn and anyone else in the nation's capitol who threatened to break her heart.

Daniel came out of the barn near where the round pen sat, carrying the length of rope Matthew sent him for. His cousin-in-law arrived before dawn to lend a hand with the first day of training. Matthew needed him for much more than that.

Daniel held up the coiled rope. "This the one you wanted?"

Matthew looked past it and into Daniel's eyes. "The *Dickens Herald* ran a story saying that Benjamin Nakishi-Dunn committed murder as a teenager. I need you to tell me everything you know about him."

Daniel lowered the coiled rope, his expression shifting from shock to sadness. He shook his head. "You might want to sit down. It's a long, hard story."

CHAPTER 40

A soft knock sounded at the front door of Roseland House. Ruth Ann had slept in after the long night of writing and just dropped her letters and articles off in the foyer when the quiet tapping caught her attention.

The footman would come shortly to answer it, although it was so soft Ruth Ann wondered if he would hear it. She opened the door, but immediately regretted it.

There stood a tall, slender woman dressed in a navy blue traveling suit with a deep blue felt hat. A matching veil covered her face, but it didn't hide the sharp nose and ocean blue eyes that matched the late Judge Eldridge.

This was Nora.

The woman's voice was so low, Ruth Ann had trouble making out her words.

"I understand Mr. Dunn is staying here."

Ruth Ann took a step back, physically and in her heart. "Come in."

As the young woman moved past her, Ruth Ann struggled with what to say next. If this were her own home, she'd know. If Nora wasn't the ex-fiancé who jilted Benjamin, she would know.

Mercifully, a maid entered and offered to take Nora's hat and wrap. The young woman declined and said, "Is Mr. Dunn in?"

"I believe he is at your father's home today, Miss Eldridge," the maid said. "Would you like one of our carriages to take you over?"

No! The tiny word screamed inside Ruth Ann, though she would not allow herself to think why.

"Thank you, but no," Nora said. "I have a rented carriage waiting."

As the maid let Nora back out, it occurred to Ruth Ann that she had not done the most basic human thing on meeting Nora. She hadn't offered condolences.

Ruth Ann knew what it was like to bury a father.

Judge Eldridge's funeral was held Friday morning, a bright and beautiful summer day hardly fitting for the circle of black around the graveside in the Congressional Cemetery. Judge Eldridge was being granted his request to be buried among some of the greatest men in the country.

Ruth Ann stayed close to Mrs. Schmitt and Joseph Griffin among the two hundred gathered for the service. She felt more comfortable with the German immigrant woman and newspaper reporter than other acquaintances, like Senator Newman and his daughters.

During the minister's short sermon, Ruth Ann suddenly wondered why she was there. Yet while she had only seen Judge Eldridge a few times, she felt a kinship with him.

Or maybe her need to be there had to do with the man who stood a head taller than everyone, and the woman at his side who nearly matched his height.

Ruth Ann blinked and look down. Mrs. Schmitt put a hand on

her arm, giving it a squeeze. Ruth Ann had a terrible suspicion that the older woman knew what was distressing her.

Benjamin gave the judge's eulogy, his voice deep and steady. But after having listened to it attentively the past few weeks, Ruth Ann detected the cracks grief put in it.

After prayer, the line of mourners filed past Benjamin and Nora, the judge's only family at the funeral. Ruth Ann joined the line with Mrs. Schmitt, dreading the moment of offering her condolences, especially when the man ahead of her asked Benjamin and Nora if the two intended to live at the judge's house after they married.

Ruth Ann coughed into her handkerchief but thankfully didn't draw attention. The man moved on, and Ruth Ann let Mrs. Schmitt go in front of her to give Benjamin a strong hug and kiss on his cheek. He bent low to accommodate the short woman, whispering something in her ear.

Mrs. Schmitt shifted to Nora, but Ruth Ann couldn't move when Benjamin turned toward her. His eyes didn't portray anything except grief.

Ruth Ann inclined her head at him. "I'm so sorry." Between her selfishness and the article about the murder, there was so much between them. So much she was sorry for.

She moved to take Nora Eldridge's hand in hers.

"I only knew your father a brief time, but he was very kind," Ruth Ann said.

Nora nodded, her neck stiff and eyes watery beneath the black veil. Ruth Ann recognized the tight pull of her lips. Judge Eldridge had died too soon.

Impulsively, Ruth Ann leaned forward to wrap her arms around the woman in a light hug. She whispered, "It's all right to be angry. Just don't stay there. God knows."

Nora's arms went around her for a quick squeeze, and the two parted with an understanding deeper than most could share.

"*Ruth Ann.*"

"Ruth Ann!"

Before she reached the bottom of the grand staircase on Saturday morning, Ruth Ann's name was called from two directions.

She swiveled her gaze between Pepper, who stood near the front door, hat in hand, and Georgia Pearl, who was at the top of the grand staircase, calling down to her. Georgia Pearl was in her robe and Ruth Ann hadn't even known she was awake when she slipped out of the room for breakfast.

Ruth Ann started with looking to Pepper, who frowned. "We have an outing planned with Mr. and Mrs. Kanitobe," he said, sounding like it was as important as a meeting with the president himself. "You didn't forget, did you?"

Ruth Ann settled her hand on the staircase railing, fairly certain Pepper neglected to mention the outing before. But then, her mind was mush from late-night article writing and the judge's funeral. Not to mention Nora Eldridge's arrival.

She looked up the stairs at Georgia Pearl who was scurrying down them, ignoring Pepper.

"Ruth Ann, my friend, I really need to talk to you. Please?"

Ruth Ann's stomach growled. She wasn't leaving the house without breakfast, and she also found herself wanting to yield to her young friend.

To Pepper, Ruth Ann said, "I'll be ready after breakfast."

"I'm leaving now."

"Then have a good day."

Pepper stuffed his derby hat down on his head and left.

Georgia Pearl sighed. "There's no pleasing him, is there?"

A half a dozen responses leapt to Ruth Ann's mind, but she bit her tongue on them as she headed for the dining room. "What did you want to speak to me about?" she asked.

Georgia Pearl snagged Ruth Ann's elbow before they entered the dining room, voices alerting them that other guests were taking breakfast.

"Not in there," Georgia Pearl whispered. "Somewhere private."

Ruth Ann put a hand over her stomach, it growling at the delicious smells coming from the dining room. But she turned to allow Georgia Pearl to lead them past the grand staircase and down the long hallway to a door on the right. Ruth Ann had enjoyed a few visits to that particular room, but her intense schedule didn't allow for much leisure.

They entered the library with its twelve foot high recessed ceiling. Bookcases stretched to the top and around all four walls like Judge Eldridge's office. The room held a strong book and candle scent. A cup of lemon tea would make it perfect.

There was a comfortable sitting area in the middle of the room with two sofas and arm chairs. Georgia Pearl led the way to the burgundy velvet sofa and grasped Ruth Ann's hand in hers as soon as they were seated.

"How I've wanted to speak with you for a week," Georgia Pearl said, her wistful tone taking on a mature note. "I still feel so awful for what I did, and I want to make it up to you."

"That's not necessary."

"Oh, but it is." Georgia Pearl squeezed Ruth Ann's hands tighter. "And I've come up with the way to do it. After his gallant behavior at the ball, it was so clear to me. You and Mr. Nakishi belong with one another. I cannot stand by and watch it ruined."

Ruth Ann pulled her hands from Georgia Pearl's, knowing her palms would turn clammy.

Georgia Pearl rushed on. "I spoke with my father last night, asking how long the judge's daughter will be in town. Of course, I didn't tell him why. But he let me know that the reading of the will was shortly after the funeral service yesterday because Nora is scheduled to depart for Europe the first part of next week. She has a wedding to prepare for. She's engaged to a gentleman she met in England last summer."

Georgia Pearl's eyes twinkled with the old mischievousness Ruth Ann had first learned about her.

"That isn't the best part," Georgia Pearl continued. "The judge left half his estate to Nora, and the other half to Benjamin, including his home. Do you know what that means, Ruth Ann? Benjamin inherited one of the most grand old homes in Washington, plus a small fortune, and with his recent win at the Supreme Court, my father said he is the most eligible bachelor in the city!"

Georgia Pearl's eyes dimmed, and she said quietly, "I may as well say, my father added that Mr. Nakishi was the most eligible, if not for his race."

She grabbed Ruth Ann's hand again, insistently. "That's when I knew! Ruth Ann, you two would be wealthy, and the most happy, envied couple in Washington."

Ruth Ann left her hand in Georgia Pearl's this time, her gaze roving to one of the high bookcases, wishing she could escape in their pages. Georgia Pearl could not possibly understand how devastating the news was to Ruth Ann.

With having a permanent home and rich clients in D.C., there was not a chance of convincing Benjamin Nakishi to return to backwoods Indian Territory. The last thread of hope for that was cut with Georgia Pearl's enthusiastic revelation.

It was time for Ruth Ann to set her sights on the next best chance at saving Philip's life, the option that seemed most impossible: A pardon from the President of the United States.

~

Ruth Ann almost made it to the dining room this time. Georgia Pearl departed up the stairs to dress for the day, but halted and rushed back down.

"Oh! One more thing," Georgia Pearl said. "I'm reading a novel that a friend loaned me. It's written about Chickasaws. Are you familiar with them? Anyway, I'm almost finished and would love for you to read it and tell me if it is at all accurate. I truly want to know more about your people."

Ruth Ann nodded her consent, the thought jumping to mind that one of the best ways for Georgia Pearl to learn about her people was to read the *Choctaw Tribune*. Perhaps Ruth Ann would gift her a personal subscription.

The dining room was empty, but the food bar was still laden with pastries and hot coffee. Ruth Ann fixed a plate and seated herself. The footman appeared then, a telegram on a silver tray extended to her.

"This just came for you, miss."

Ruth Ann accepted the message and flipped it open, wondering if it was another fire alarm from Beulah.

It wasn't. This was from Lance Fuller.

Ruth Ann. Aunt took morning train to D.C. Heard news about Thaddeus there. Has gun. I cannot come. Please help.

CHAPTER 42

The heat of the day hadn't dissipated even though it was nearly suppertime on Sunday evening when Matthew rode Skyline through a creek, letting her splash cool water on them both. The papers he carried were safely tucked in his saddlebags, although Matthew wouldn't mind if one in particular drowned in the creek.

He was headed to McAlester by way of Krebs. After a brief hello to his coal mining friends, he planned to stay overnight at a hotel in McAlester. He wanted to be present at the sentencing for the trial Tecumseh Shoemaker was prosecuting.

Matthew had followed the trial closely, mostly by telegraph. He had not planned to attend the sentencing. But after his mother went to Uncle Preston's to look after Daisy and Daniel's baby, who had chickenpox, and receiving Ruth Ann's letter on Saturday, Matthew made the last-minute decision to ride up to McAlester.

Ruth Ann's letter shook him to the core. He should have suspected Tecumseh Shoemaker would want to see his brother shot for what he did. But saving Philip's life after thinking he was dead and then fighting side-by-side with him to capture outlaws, battling for his brother's life in a courtroom hadn't crossed Matthew's mind.

But that was why Tecumseh pressed so hard on the Teller family during the inquest. He wanted to prove prior animosity in the family and that Jim Teller's death in the robbery was intentional. That Philip planned it that way. Tecumseh really suspected that, and he likely wasn't the only one.

After the sentencing tomorrow morning, Matthew needed to meet with Nelson Cobb, even though he knew the man was no match for Tecumseh in court. No lawyer was.

Matthew stopped in for dinner and a brief visit with Raphael and Ricco Bianchi, their wives, and Cadenza. They asked after his brother, but Matthew had little to say, and they respected that.

It was well after dark when Matthew made it into McAlester. After boarding Skyline at the livery, he checked into a hotel.

In the privacy of his room, Matthew began reviewing the work he brought with him that would normally be done Monday morning, like editing articles.

Ruth Ann included ones with her letter that he hadn't read yet, too disturbed by the letter. While he honed in on the second paragraph about the death penalty, he went back to the first one.

I didn't know you went through so much. You didn't tell me. But then, I never gave you a fair chance to, did I?

There was no reason for her to blame herself for that. Matthew was at fault for so many things the past few months. He left her alone to run the *Choctaw Tribune* and she raised it to a level Matthew didn't bother dreaming about yet. Did he even thank her for that before the news of Philip's betrayal ripped them apart? He couldn't remember.

He only knew he was right in that they needed to work out things between them. Letters fell short. Or did they? There were things he said in his letter he couldn't face to face. She wrote things she didn't say before. Maybe this was the best way for them.

Still, she was spending a great deal of time with Pepper Barnes and if that man had his way, he would use the *Choctaw Tribune* to influence their people politically. He was likely pressuring Ruth Ann for that.

But after reading the articles, Matthew knew he didn't need to worry. Ruth Ann's articles weren't the best she'd done—he recognized the signs of fatigue-influenced writing—but they were filled with factual details and a hint of beauty. Ruth Ann was doing well.

Matthew made minor edits to the articles then stuffed them back in his saddlebag, thinking about the one with the former mayor of Dickens being in D.C. Thaddeus Warren would be arrested if he set foot back in Indian Territory, hence the reason the man skipped town on a mule. Now he was in D.C. and Matthew had intended to print it in the *Choctaw Tribune*. He mentioned it to his employees, but he should have kept it a secret.

It didn't take long for the news to spread through town about the location of the former mayor. By Sunday morning, Mrs. Warren got wind of it and disappeared.

Lance Fuller and Peter tracked her through the telegraph operators up the line to discover she was headed north to St. Louis to catch a transfer train to Washington D.C. She knew her way to the city where she lived before the Warrens came west to Indian Territory.

All the Jessop children had chickenpox, including Amarillo's baby. Lance couldn't leave them. That left caring hands short to chase after the armed and grieved Mrs. Warren.

Lance had sent Ruth Ann a telegram. That was all they could do, but Matthew doubted Mrs. Warren would do the former mayor much harm if she found him. Not that he didn't deserve whatever he got.

Matthew still struggled against the memories and pain of

getting shot as part of Thaddeus Warren's scheme. But Matthew didn't want to hold on to bitterness in life, and truly hoped his sister found Mrs. Warren soon.

He pulled out Ruth Ann's crumpled letter he had crushed in his hand after reading it the first time. The part of the letter that Matthew wanted to drown in the creek was the single sentence that could seal Philip's, and their family's, future.

Matthew thought he had regained control of his emotions, especially after the tiring ride to McAlester. But he crushed the letter in one hand again and pressed it against his forehead.

"Please, God. Don't have brought him back into our lives only for him to be torn out again."

CHAPTER 43

"May God have mercy on your soul." Judge Kendrick banged the gavel, and the courtroom erupted in chatter.

Matthew sat at the back of the tiny courthouse, staring straight ahead at the defendant and his family, who stood stoically after the pronouncement of death.

Matthew's gaze followed Tecumseh Shoemaker as the lawyer spoke with his assistant, who made notes. Not being able to read or write didn't hinder Tecumseh's deadly capabilities.

His assistant finished and began filing papers in a brown briefcase. Tecumseh straightened and turned. He locked gazes with Matthew, their first eye contact since the inquest when Tecumseh put the entire Teller family on trial.

His calculating eyes transmitted to Matthew that he intended to do it again, and to gain another death sentence victory.

And there was nothing Matthew could do to stop him.

Matthew dug his heels into Skyline's sides, pushing her up the mountain road he had avoided traveling for years. When news arrived of his father and brother's deaths, he had gone straight home from college and barely made it to Uncle Preston's ranch in time for the funeral.

Right after, he wanted to ride up to the place of the crime and do everything he could to find out exactly what happened. But he needed to take care of his mother and sister.

It wasn't long before resistance built against him ever going.

At first, it was taking care of his family. Then work at the ranch, then the *Dickens Herald*, and starting his own newspaper. All along, Matthew knew those were excuses not to face going to the spot where his daddy took his last breath.

It was time.

Matthew approached the site from the opposite direction that his daddy and Philip traveled that day when they came from Skullyville.

Matthew had wanted to retrace their steps, to know what the road ahead looked like when the Holder gang ambushed them. But coming from the opposite direction let Matthew see the overlook where his father always stopped.

Matthew made plenty of those trips with his father throughout his teen years and knew his father had planned to stop at the outlook that day and talk over life with Chihowa.

His father hadn't reached the spot that day.

Matthew passed it slowly, staring at the outlook as long as he could, turning in the saddle to keep it in sight a few moments longer. Then he faced forward again. His destination was two miles ahead.

And there it was, coming up faster than Matthew expected. Though he had prepared for it, he could never truly be prepared.

The Holder gang attacked from this direction. Dan Holder shot their father and Philip struggled to save him but ended up falling off the wagon as it lurched close to the precipice. Philip miraculously got hold of a bush at the edge of the drop, and Lester Cotton threw him a rope to pull him back to safety.

That gave no warmth toward Cotton in Matthew's heart as he pulled Skyline to a halt near the precipice that Philip described. Matthew dismounted and tied the mare to a tree branch before walking over the ground once stained with his father's blood.

He knelt on one knee in the red dirt road and ran his hand over the surface. He collected a handful of pebbly clay and gripped it in a fist.

Matthew went to the edge of the precipice, staring at the beauty of the mountains, still lush with summer green. Fresh and alive.

He flung the red clay into the abyss.

"Why!" he shouted.

Matthew's chest heaved, and he doubled over, pressing his fists into his eyes, weeping as he never had before.

CHAPTER 44

Though the wives of Della's nephews were able to care for their children as chickenpox swept through the area, Della felt the urge to help her niece, Daisy, care for her six-month-old baby.

Only when Della arrived at the little cabin by the lake where Daniel and Daisy Garvin had made their nest, did she understand the urge. The couple hadn't come to church because of the sickness, but when Della arrived, she found it wasn't only the baby not well.

Daniel let her in with a small smile as he accepted the basket of freshly baked bread. "Yakoke, Aunt Della. Come on in, Daisy will be happy to see you. Where's Matthew?"

"He is traveling."

Della had answered this question before, bringing to mind when Matthew left them for his arduous journey to find out what happened six years ago. He uncovered it, reviving and devastating the family all at once.

Della entered the bedroom of the two-room cabin to find Daisy propped on pillows, her face pale despite her Choctaw blood. Her eyes widened.

"Oh, Aunt Della. It's good to have you here." She began crying, and a coughing fit followed.

Della carefully lifted the baby from Daisy's limp arms as he wailed. She swayed with the baby, feeling the heat of a fever in his scab-covered body.

Daniel went to his wife, slipping an arm under her and offering a cup of water for her to sip. She then laid her head heavy on his shoulder, eyes closed.

"Aunt Della, I've been so exhausted these past few months," Daisy murmured. "Will you help me?"

"That is why I am here."

The dark circles under Daisy's eyes and listlessness of her breathing concerned Della more than the scabs over the baby's body. Daisy needed rest the most right now.

With the baby still crying, Della carried him out into the sunshine. He quieted, though Della didn't trust it. He puckered his lips, chin quivering. Another wail was coming. She knew that because Philip did the same thing when he was a baby…

Della gazed down into the face of her first-born son as the pain seeped from her body. The two day and night struggle of agony and tears, blood and laughter, until at last, her 18-year-old body released its first child. The pain of birth was a sweet pain, much like the verse her mother read over her during the long labor.

A woman when she is in travail hath sorrow, because her hour is come: but as soon as she is delivered of the child, she remembereth no more the anguish, for joy that a man is born into the world.

Della cradled the bright red baby, wondering what kind of mother she would be and praying she and Jim could raise their son into a fine Choctaw man.

The newborn puckered his lips, chin quivering, then wailed.

· · ·

Della cradled her niece's first-born son as he let out a tremendous wail. She held him close, allowing their heartbeats to thump as one like she had with Philip after his birth.

CHAPTER 45

"Excuse me, have you seen an older woman about my height with brown hair and..." Ruth Ann didn't finish.

The woman she had interrupted at the chaotic train depot looked at her as though she were crazy. Perhaps Ruth Ann was, thinking she could find Mrs. Warren, whose description fit hundreds in the city.

Ruth Ann mumbled, "Never mind," and turned away. She was there to meet the first trains from the west, all too aware that there would be several that day. She could not possibly meet them all. Could she? Ruth Ann recalled how Mrs. Warren stepped in to comfort Della in her deep grief over Philip.

Ruth Ann had to find her.

It had been two days since Mrs. Warren hopped onto a train to D.C. If she didn't dillydally, it was possible that she would arrive today. But what if she had stopped at friends or family along the way? What if she got lost? What if she changed her mind entirely and went right back home? If that were the case, Ruth Ann would get a telegram from Lance.

After his first telegram alerting her, Ruth Ann wondered why Lance didn't come after his aunt himself. She sent a telegram to

Peter, asking for details, and found out chickenpox was going through the children in Dickens. There was no one to come after the poor woman who had been abandoned by her husband.

Ruth Ann knew of women who shot their husbands for less than the humiliation Thaddeus Warren left Mrs. Warren in, but Ruth Ann couldn't believe that she would do something like that. Still, it was possible, and Ruth Ann needed to do all she could to save the woman, whatever her intentions.

A train whistled, the second one coming in from the west so far that morning. Ruth Ann stood on her toes, trying to see around a heavyset man as the train pulled in with so many cars she knew it was highly possible she could miss Mrs. Warren no matter how fast she perused the disembarking passengers. But Mrs. Warren never spoke in a quiet voice, so she would draw attention if she were on the train.

The quicker Ruth Ann found her, turned her around, and sent her home, the better. Ruth Ann had tried to build a semblance of a good reputation in D.C. She wasn't being entirely successful, and getting involved in the sticky Warren situation could make it worse.

Ruth Ann had a note tucked in her reticule to send to the First Lady, requesting a meeting where she intended to ask Mrs. Cleveland to speak to her husband about a presidential pardon for Philip. As far as Ruth Ann knew, the president could pardon her brother, but it would take stepping on toes to do it. That didn't matter, if it kept Philip alive.

But Ruth Ann couldn't send the note until she had Mrs. Warren out of D.C.

The train jerked to a stop and passengers disembarked. Porters shoved luggage carts to-and-fro. Ruth Ann skimmed through the crowd as rapidly as she could, checking every woman's face, especially those with extravagant hats.

When the hubbub cleared, Ruth Ann was certain Mrs. Warren

was not among the passengers. There were four more trains that could possibly carry her.

It was going to be a long day. But Ruth Ann didn't know what else to do. She wanted to stay away from Pepper and avoid encountering Benjamin. He said he wouldn't help her, and after the murder accusation, how could she want him to?

Yet she did, despite the pain of death and betrayal stinging her heart from Philip.

Lord, what am I supposed to do? I can't win this battle for my brother alone.

CHAPTER 46

Matthew allowed the young Choctaw stallion to circle him in the corral for the hundredth time. Maybe two hundred times. He wasn't sure, but he knew the only way to bond with this animal was to let him wear himself out first.

Matthew flipped the end of the rope toward the stallion when the horse slowed to inspect the barnyard through the fencing. The rope touched the horse's brown hocks, and he skittered around Matthew again, staying close to the rails in the round pen. He refused to look at Matthew.

The sooner this horse quit fighting, the sooner they could get to work. Stallions were too often self-interested and could be ruined if the trainer didn't know how to handle them. Matthew had never trained a stallion, but Uncle Preston was a master horseman, and Matthew once watched him work a wild stallion down into a gentle riding horse.

This tri-colored was different, though. He was stubborn and arrogant. Just like Philip, and Matthew was losing patience.

Matthew started to flick the rope again, but he caught sight of movement outside the corral. His mother was out of the house for the early morning coolness and now stood by the pen, watching the two young males face off.

Della had come home last night after two days at the ranch, but she and Matthew hadn't spoken much. His tears shed on the mountain relieved part of his pain, but it left him ragged and near angry. He had spent so much energy trying to find the outlaws, only to find his brother alive and among them, in a sense.

Now Philip faced death again. Matthew hadn't told his mother that, knowing it would cause her inconsolable grief. He would find a way to save Philip first.

Matthew went opposite of the stallion and climbed the eight-foot fence. He spoke as he swung his leg over the top rail.

"Good morning, Mama. Did you sleep well? How's everyone at the ranch?"

He dropped to the ground, turned to face her, and immediately knew his rudimentary questions would go unanswered. His mother had come with her own.

She held a newspaper in one hand and Matthew recognized it was the *Dickens Herald*. Furthermore, he knew it was from last week, the edition that contained the condemning story about Benjamin Nakishi-Dunn.

His mother had been preoccupied with a sewing job when the article came out and Matthew hadn't brought the edition home. He knew she was concerned about Ruth Ann, and the other gossip column about the Indian love triangle supposedly happening out in D.C. Those were tormenting for a mother's heart.

Matthew took the paper from her. It was opened to the story about Benjamin Nakishi and murder.

"Mama…"

He halted. Someone was shouting from the front of the house.

Through the open back door of the kitchen, Matthew could see the front door swung open and his cousin Peter barreling through the house. He called for them and made a beeline for the back door. He shot out and opened his mouth for another unnecessary holler.

Matthew patted the air with his hands, indicating his cousin needed to quiet down. The tri-colored stallion reared and pawed the air in the pen, disturbed by the emotional charges in the air. Matthew was disturbed by them, too.

Peter skidded to a stop with a quick glance at the corral. He lowered his voice and said, "You need to get to the office right away. Someone here to see you."

"I told you I would be in later today."

Peter shook his head. "No good. He's catching the north-bound train in twenty minutes. He wants to see you now."

"Who is this all-important 'he?'"

"Tecumseh Shoemaker."

As he crossed Main Street in Dickens at a rapid walk, Matthew could see through the large picture windows of the newspaper shop. Tecumseh Shoemaker waited inside.

The bell over the door jingled when Matthew entered, Peter on his heels, though his cousin dodged off to the right and entered the telegraph office lien-to.

Matthew halted inside the door. Tecumseh pivoted to face him, arms folded.

"He lied."

Tecumseh's voice echoed across the distance between them, causing Caleb Gentry to halt from operating the printing press. Beulah Levitt poked her head through the back store-room door where she was teaching a violin lesson.

Tecumseh's authoritative courtroom voice had everyone's attention. Exactly what Matthew did not want, but there was no place for a private conversation around here.

Matthew motioned toward his desk, indicating a chair for Tecumseh. But the man didn't sit. He waited until Matthew was closer and they stood by the desk, facing off. Matthew mimicked Tecumseh and folded his arms across his chest, staring at the Choctaw full-blood lawyer—the man who was trying to have his brother executed.

Matthew tightened his arms, restraining himself from striking out. Tecumseh Shoemaker was in his domain now.

"Who lied?" Matthew asked.

"That man from the other newspaper," Tecumseh spat the words.

This was not new information. Christopher Maxwell at the *Dickens Herald* was always lying. But what interested Tecumseh about it? The *Herald* hadn't even bothered to report on the lawyer's latest case.

"What did he lie about?" Matthew asked.

"Nakishi is a good man."

Matthew slowly sat on the corner of his desk. This was not the conversation he'd braced for. "You know Benjamin Nakishi-Dunn?"

"I was there the day he was born. The day the killing happened. The day he was sent off to Spencer. He didn't do nothing to nobody ever. I want you to tell everyone the truth in your newspaper."

Matthew loosened his arms and reached for a piece of paper on his cluttered desk, rifling through a pile to find a pencil. His heart thumped as he thought of his sister.

He didn't know why Tecumseh was coming to him. This man was trying to have his brother executed. But if he had information that would help his sister, Matthew was willing to listen.

Maybe both Matthew Teller and Tecumseh Shoemaker just wanted the same thing—truth and justice. Sometimes, there was more than one version of that.

Matthew sat still, holding his pad and pencil ready. "Let's start with you giving me the whole story of what really happened."

CHAPTER 47

Matthew kicked Peter out of the telegraph office so he could contemplate the message he wanted to send Ruth Ann. There was much to say, and he planned to say it through an article sent to the AP. But for now, he needed to get word to Ruth Ann.

He couldn't write a letter-length telegram and he wasn't sure what he could say in short that she would understand.

The sibling understanding they always shared was damaged, that much he knew. But maybe, somehow, through being apart yet working together, they could learn the language again.

Matthew settled on two words and sent them in Morse code. Two simple words that could not be misconstrued or twisted. Two words that would reach Ruth Ann and, if they were still speaking the same language, she would understand.

When she got home, he'd tell her about his suspicions that Christopher Maxwell knew of the crime connected to the Dunn name and ran the erroneous story to damage an innocent Choctaw's reputation. The publisher knew about the Indian love triangle article in the AP, and could have made the connection with Benjamin Nakishi-Dunn and Ruth Ann.

Any jab Maxwell could make at the *Choctaw Tribune*, he would.

The bell over the door jingled. For a moment, Matthew wondered if Tecumseh was returning with something else to add to his stunning story about Benjamin Nakishi's past. But it wasn't.

With his back to the door, he heard Peter chirp, "Aunt Della, you going off on a trip?"

Matthew rose and turned. Della was in the lien-to door, staring at him. It only took a heartbeat for Matthew to take in the fact that she wore her traveling hat, wrap, and was carrying a carpetbag.

Matthew motioned her into the tiny telegraph office and turned the single chair around so that she could sit. His mother had sat so little in his life, always cooking or in the garden or at her sewing table. The only time she really sat was in the evening in her rocking chair, either Bible or sewing project in hand.

To his surprise, she did sit, putting the carpetbag on the floor beside her. Matthew guessed it had what she needed to take a trip to Washington, D.C. She was still thinking about those two articles.

He leaned against the shelf of the outside window of the telegraph office and propped his hands on it behind him.

"I wasn't sure exactly what to tell you about him earlier, but now I do," Matthew said. "You can rest your mind easy, Mama. Benjamin Nakishi is a good man."

From the way Della's shoulders went slack, Matthew knew she trusted her son completely. It was undeserved after the way he'd held back telling her and Ruth Ann about Philip. But his mother respected his judgement. That was enough for now, another piece of healing, but not the whole.

He stared at the telegraph sounder, having an odd wish it would start clacking, giving him something to do, work to keep his hands busy as he'd done the past six years to deal with his grief.

He was preoccupied enough with the silent sounder that he didn't realize his mother's closeness until she covered his hand with hers. He looked down into her eyes, so rich with love for her son, a supernatural love that could only come from the Creator.

She spoke softly. "It is not that stallion or your brother who needs to surrender."

Matthew swallowed a dry cry he couldn't let out. She continued, "You are all you have control over. Surrender that control to the Master."

Matthew turned his hand over to clasp hers, but he couldn't speak.

He hath shewed thee, O man, what is good; and what doth the LORD require of thee, but to do justly, and to love mercy, and to walk humbly with thy God?

His mother wasn't finished. "Losing someone is like falling off a runaway horse. You hit hard, you are blinded by pain, all you see are black swirls. But with time, you open your eyes. The pain is there but you can see again. That is what loss is like, hitting the ground hard. Then days, maybe years later, though the pain is still there, you see the world again."

Matthew choked. "It's like that. It's just like that."

Della held him close as they cried.

CHAPTER 48

"Telegram for Ruth Ann Teller!"

Ruth Ann waved at the porter who worked his way toward her in the depot.

This was her second day of searching for Mrs. Warren, but who would have known she was at the depot? Ruth Ann hadn't been sure that morning if she should go after the first long, hot day there in her fruitless effort to catch Mrs. Warren. But it felt right, and someone else knew that.

The porter skirted a trunk and handed her a folded telegram. She tipped him and opened it to find a short message.

Trust Ben.—Matt

A sob rose in Ruth Ann's throat. Whatever Matthew had found about Benjamin Nakishi, he was certain of it. He knew she would be there at the depot, and that told her it was where she was supposed to be.

Thank you, Lord.

Ruth Ann went to one of the windows where a telegraph operator was receiving a message. She took a card and pencil from the shelf and scribbled a reply. When the telegraph operator looked up, she handed him the note and coins. She stayed to listen to the familiar clacking as the operator transmitted her words to Dickens.

I trust you.—Annie.

Matthew would know what she meant.

Ruth Ann remained at the depot through the afternoon and into the evening. She would miss dinner at Roseland but the last train was at 7:30p.m. and she was determined to see her mission through.

When that last train came and went, Ruth Ann exited into the summer evening, taking in the fresh, cooler air of the wide walkway in front of the depot. She moved slowly, observing the line of cabs and private carriages taking passengers from the last train. She wished she had come by bicycle instead of a streetcar. She'd rather ride back to Roseland, although she doubted her legs would push her up and down the hills on the way there.

"Miss Teller."

Ruth Ann halted, absorbing the deep voice from behind her that flowed through the marrow of her bones and strengthened them.

Benjamin Nakishi came up beside her and removed his hat as he addressed her. "Are you returning to Roseland now?"

Ruth Ann nodded, unable to speak from fatigue and seeing him after the stretch of absence, and so many other things she couldn't wrap her mind around.

"I have one of the Roseland carriages secured at the corner," he said. "Would you care to return in it?"

Ruth Ann finally found words. "Yes, please."

Once the carriage was underway, Benjamin, seated across from her, said, "I'd hoped to catch you at the depot. I was seeing Nora Eldridge off on the evening train."

Ruth Ann chewed her lower lip, afraid of saying the wrong thing. Fortunately, Benjamin wasn't finished.

"I spoke with Joseph Griffin at dinner yesterday evening and he shared about your current situation with your friend and Thaddeus Warren here in D.C."

Oh no. No! Ruth Ann held her dismay in check. This was exactly her fear of getting involved with the Warrens. The scandal was already galloping through the gossip grapevines and now threatened her connection with Benjamin just when she was thinking of how to approach him about her brother's case again. There must be a way to convince him, despite him refusing criminal cases.

"Please don't be distressed," he said.

Ruth Ann realized she was staring at Benjamin's coat buttons. She raised her gaze to see his words were delivered with a slight smile.

"Mrs. Warren is blessed to have a loyal friend like you," he said.

Ruth Ann opened her mouth, wondering how she could explain the complex relationship of the woman she'd known at first as a pompous, prejudiced politician's wife to the endearing grandmother-like figure to the Jessop children.

That was a story for another time and Ruth Ann closed her mouth, allowing Benjamin to go on.

"After Joseph told me what Thaddeus Warren did in the Choctaw Nation, I began an investigation into his dealings in D.C.," he said. "I have a feeling they are not in the best interest of our people. I would like to offer my services in helping your friend."

No. Oh no!

Why Benjamin would offer to help in the situation, Ruth Ann had no idea, but she needed him for Philip's case. Not this!

"That's very kind of you, but I could never impose in that way."

Benjamin leaned forward and rested his elbows on his knees, clasping his hands before him as he stared at them. "I need to make restitution for tainting your reputation here in D.C."

Ruth Ann's eyes widened. "What do you mean?"

Benjamin didn't look up. "I scarcely read newspapers when I'm working on a case, and avoid them for a while afterwards. My assistant clips out anything that might be pertinent to cases and files them. Apparently, Judge Eldridge did the same. I didn't know that until I was going through his desk this weekend, sorting papers to send off with Nora—Miss Eldridge. I found a stack he saved on my recent Supreme Court case...and an embarrassing article about an Indian love triangle."

Ruth Ann stifled her gasp before it escaped her lips. Benjamin had not even known about the column!

"Oh, I'm so sorry about that," she said. "It was entirely my fault. As was the terrible story about..."

Ruth Ann caught herself, suddenly wondering if Benjamin had seen the other article about murder.

He nodded, his mood going from humble to solemn. "I saw the story about the murder case that happened in Indian Territory. Fortunately, Joseph Griffin ran a rebuttal that saved my reputation from severe damage here in D.C. Perhaps there's a newspaper in the Choctaw Nation that would do the same." He smiled, then looked into her eyes. "But that story wasn't your fault."

"It was, in a sense," she confessed. "I sent a story back home, using your full last name, and it got the *Dickens Herald* interested. I guess Christopher Maxwell knew something about it already. Anyway, Pepper told me not to use the Dunn part of your name."

Benjamin leaned back in the carriage seat, chuckling. "I'm grateful you don't do everything Pepper Barnes tells you to."

Ruth Ann's smile was strained. She wasn't comfortable talking about Pepper Barnes with Benjamin Nakishi, especially since he was a part of the supposed triangle.

Benjamin looked her straight in the eye and said, "The story of the murder was misreported in almost every way. I was only five years old when the killing happened. But I don't wish to relive what did happen, if you'll forgive me?"

Ruth Ann desperately wanted to know the entire story, but she respected the bounds Benjamin placed. Matthew told her to trust him, so it was likely he had the full story already. She said, "The *Choctaw Tribune* will rebut the story." She sighed. "Here I've only been in D.C. a short time and caused two indiscreet stories involving you. I'm very sorry."

"They aren't important." Benjamin took up his derby hat and began fiddling with the brim. Nervous gestures weren't a part of who she knew him to be.

He went on. "At least, that one is not the only reason I want to help you find your friend. Perhaps you will allow me to not share the other reason yet?"

The carriage halted in front of Roseland and Ruth Ann responded, "Of course."

In her mind, she added, *Please, if you feel you owe me anything, help my brother. What can I do to convince you?*

CHAPTER 49

A tapping on the bedroom door woke Ruth Ann early the next morning. She stayed up late writing articles and wasn't surprised she slept past dawn. Gray light streaked the room to show that Georgia Pearl was still sound asleep.

Ruth Ann climbed out of bed, grabbing her robe on the end and swinging it on. She cracked the door open to see the upstairs maid patiently waiting.

"Sorry to disturb you, miss, but Mr. Nakishi is on the telephone for you. He said it's urgent."

"Thank you."

As Ruth Ann quietly closed the door, she contemplated getting dressed or going on out to the telephone downstairs in the foyer. But even in this early morning, she risked someone seeing her in her robe.

Ruth Ann pulled on a simple gingham dress that she wore around the suite when relaxing or writing, and quietly made her way out and down to the foyer.

It was empty except the footman who stood holding the telephone receiver out to her. The telephone was attached to the wall near the coat rack that Ruth Ann passed every day, but she never imagined actually using the modern piece of technology.

She hesitantly took the receiver from the footman who guided her in placing the earpiece and motioning for her to stand closer to the receiver before he left to give her privacy.

Ruth Ann held the earpiece tight and got close to the receiver, tempted to raise her voice to be heard through the lines. But she'd watched others use the telephone, and they spoke normally. She didn't want to wake the household.

Did one greet someone on the telephone the same as if they were in person?

"Hello?" Ruth Ann sounded timid, how she must have over the wires when she sent her first telegram. She'd tackled new technology before and a telephone call didn't require Morse code training.

She cleared her throat from the lingering morning hoarseness. "Hello, this is Ruth Ann Teller."

"Good morning, Miss Ruth Ann."

Because of the early hour, the timbre of Benjamin's voice was deeper than she'd ever heard it. Or perhaps because he hadn't slept much after dropping her off at Roseland to have the carriage take him back to the judge's house where he was staying.

Actually, it was Benjamin's home now. She shivered at the strange displeasure that brought on.

"I have news," he said. "It seems Mrs. Warren took an alternate route to see friends in North Carolina, and entered Washington on a northbound train yesterday afternoon."

Ruth Ann sighed in frustration at the two days she'd wasted greeting all the wrong trains. "Do you know where she is now?"

"I believe so. She telegraphed friends in the city to pick her up. I can take you to their home this morning."

"Oh."

Ruth Ann wasn't sure why she was suddenly filled with hesitation. Matthew told her to trust Benjamin. Maybe her feelings had less to do with trusting him as trusting herself.

But if he was able to track Mrs. Warren down so quickly, what he could do for Philip's case! Benjamin would prove her brother was innocent and she could forgive him and bring him home like she promised her daddy. Perhaps if she told Benjamin of the death sentence hanging over her brother…

But she didn't want her friendship with Benjamin to be solely about saving Philip. That was how she wounded him before.

"There's more, Miss Ruth Ann."

"Oh?"

The line was silent and Ruth Ann wondered if Benjamin had hung up. But there was the sound of his breathing. It was as though he was close, about to whisper in her ear.

She lifted the earpiece away slightly and steadied her own breathing. What concerned her most was that she wasn't even wearing a corset.

Benjamin's breathing finally turned into words. "I discovered through another source that Mrs. Warren's sister, Agnes York, arrived last night. Thaddeus Warren contacted her saying that his wife is threatening to kill him. The sister is looking to have Mrs. Warren committed to an insane asylum."

After her telephone call with Benjamin, Ruth Ann was in a daze when she entered the dining room. Both the nearness of his voice and his startling news about Mrs. Warren's sister left her off-balance.

He would be there soon to pick her up, and had cautioned her to eat a hearty breakfast because it could be a long day. That direction gave Ruth Ann enough sense to go straight to the dining room. She barely had enough time to eat and dress for the day before Benjamin arrived.

Joseph Griffin was having breakfast, reading a newspaper while sipping coffee. He rose in greeting.

"I see my colleague from the Indian Territory is up and at 'em this morning," he said. "I guess we'll have to fight over who gets the worm."

He grinned, showing he would be delighted to have her along for whatever adventure he had that day. But he quickly lost his jovial expression at Ruth Ann's quiet demeanor.

He joined her at the sideboard to claim a blueberry muffin while Ruth Ann fixed her plate. She told him what Benjamin had discovered about Mrs. Warren.

Joseph shook his head in pity as they sat at the table. "Poor woman. From what I've learned about Thaddeus Warren, it would drive anyone crazy. But I'm sure you'll find her in time. You have the right man at your side for the job. Really, any job."

Ruth Ann dug into her breakfast and they lapsed into silence awhile. Partway through, she had her words formed enough to say, "There is another task I truly hope Benjamin will help me with. It's in defending someone who is very close to me, someone who's been accused of an awful crime and faces a death sentence if found guilty, which is…possible."

It was the first time Ruth Ann had spoken the words out loud. She nearly choked on tears, but pushed forward. She had Joseph's full attention. "Do you think there is any possible way to convince Benjamin to return to Indian Territory and take the case?"

Joseph polished off his muffin and turned in his chair to better face her as he said, "I'm afraid Benjamin only does civil cases, not criminal ones."

Benjamin had said that, too, but there was something else in Joseph's eyes. She urged, "Please, speak your mind. I need to know."

Joseph broke eye contact. "It sounds like there's a lot stacked against your friend," he said slowly. "Benjamin has quite the reputation because he has never lost a case. But aside from his extraordinary talent, one of the reasons for that is he doesn't take a case unless he is certain he will win."

Ruth Ann couldn't take another bite of her breakfast.

CHAPTER 50

Georgia Pearl was still asleep when Ruth Ann slipped back into the room and changed, doing her hair in a tight bun. It would be a long day and she had a serious task ahead of her, both in finding Mrs. Warren and in asking Benjamin to take Philip's case again.

After what Joseph told her, though, that was a fruitless effort. There was little chance Philip's case could be won, so even if Benjamin took criminal cases, he wouldn't touch this deadly one.

Ruth Ann had just finished when a hard knock sounded at the sitting room door. She heard the bedroom door next to hers open, and she assumed either Virginia Lee or Agatha Green would answer their door.

It was an awfully hard knock for the upstairs maid. Perhaps it was urgent. Benjamin had probably arrived for Ruth Ann, so she grabbed her hat and reticule and went out the bedroom door.

She jerked to a halt when she saw Pepper Barnes standing in the middle of the girls' suite, asking Virginia Lee, "Which one is Ruth Ann's room?"

Ruth Ann sputtered, "You can't be in here!"

"Can and am."

Virginia Lee smirked and stepped back, watching. Pepper crossed his arms at Ruth Ann. "Since you seem bent on avoiding me, this was the only thing to do."

"I've been trying to find Mrs. Warren. She needs my help desperately."

"I heard she came to kill her husband."

Pepper was irritatingly casual about the situation. Ruth Ann shot back, "I must find her before she does something awful."

"I'd give her the bullets. Now, can we get back to what we came to D.C. for?"

Ruth Ann held her anger in check as she used the mirror on the wall between the two bedroom doors to pin on her hat. She could see Pepper in the reflection and Virginia Lee, who seemed to be enjoying the exchange.

Pepper said, "Senator Newman invited me to a private dinner with Forbis Kanitobe and influential congressmen. I want you to go as my fiancé, whether you're ready to accept my proposal or not."

Ruth Ann jabbed the hat pin into her scalp, but she didn't care if it drew blood. Pepper was pushing beyond her limits.

"I will do no such thing," she said.

Pepper gave Virginia Lee a look, and the young woman responded with a mocking gasp. She left, only partially closing her bedroom door. Ruth Ann knew she still listened.

Ruth Ann turned away from the mirror, her swinging reticule almost catching Pepper in the midsection. He'd moved up behind her and lowered his voice.

"Listen to me for once," he said, his mint freshened breath in her face. "I just learned that Jefferson Gardner's nomination got fouled up, and he's now running as a Progressive. There's nothing I can do politically to help your brother unless you agree to marry me. Conservatives like Forbis Kanitobe don't like seeing a young man running around loose when he's in charge of serious business."

Ruth Ann balled her hand into a fist, ever so close to hitting Pepper. "How dare you try to use me that way!"

"You need this as much as I do," Pepper said. "Do you think you would have even gotten to D.C. without a man to back you? Besides, you need the protection for your reputation. Virginia Lee told me…"

The storm clouds normally in his eyes spread to the rest of his face. He moved a half a step closer. "She said how intimate you and Nakishi's relationship has gotten, you going out to his home in the country to stay the night."

Ruth Ann took a step back, bumping into the table beneath the mirror, mouth dry. "I did no such thing!"

Pepper ran his tongue over his teeth with a smack. "You think I don't know that, Annie? But if you don't stop running around with Nakishi when we're supposed to be getting engaged, you'll damage my chances with Kanitobe, and you better believe that man has some influence back home."

Ruth Ann gripped the table's edge with both hands, trying to comprehend what Pepper was saying.

He didn't give her time to. "Know this, Annie: Benjamin Nakishi will not take your brother's case. It's too similar to his father's, and Benjamin already lost that case to Tecumseh Shoemaker."

Ruth Ann gulped. "What do you know about it? What about Benjamin's father? I thought he was an orphan."

Pepper ran both hands over his face, scrubbing it with a harsh sigh. "See? You don't know what I know, and you just need to trust me. I told you not to use Nakishi's full name because his father, Dunn, was convicted of murder and is still in prison. But as long as people back home didn't make that connection, Nakishi could have been useful to me in the legal battle for our sovereignty."

He put his hands behind his neck as if to keep from shaking her. "There is so much more at stake than your brother. But I can take care of everything if you'll only let me, and that starts with marrying me and settling down back home for the fights ahead." He dropped his hands and stared at her, dead serious.

Ruth Ann's lips quivered, confusion weakening her mind. Fear gripped her heart.

Pepper lifted one hand and brushed the back of it against Ruth Ann's cheek.

"Don't you understand, Annie? Benjamin couldn't help you, even if he wanted. I'm the only one who can."

Benjamin was waiting for Ruth Ann at the side door of Roseland, holding up a tandem bicycle. She closed the door behind her, but didn't move beyond the stoop.

She couldn't go with Benjamin, and therefore could not find Mrs. Warren. She could not do any good in D.C. for the *Choctaw Tribune* with Pepper hovering over her. She could do nothing to convince Benjamin to take her brother's case, and there was no reason to try.

Sometimes the world out there was too big for someone like her.

Benjamin studied her face, then placed the tandem bicycle on the rack and came towards her. She instinctively took a step back, and he halted.

"Are you all right, Miss Ruth Ann?"

Ruth Ann slowly shook her head and forced the humiliating words out. "I cannot go with you. Virginia Lee Newman is spreading vicious gossip about us."

Benjamin put a hand on the corner post supporting the stoop, leaning on it. "I've been informed that she made another attempt to run a derogatory column through the AP. I am taking care of it so she will not try that again."

He was so serious and confident, Ruth Ann felt her heart stutter. What sort of power did this man wield behind the scenes? It seemed there was nothing he couldn't do. How could she trust that?

But just as quickly, the two words from Matthew's telegram leapt to her mind.

Trust Ben.

Ruth Ann swallowed. "Then we better get going. I feel there isn't much time."

Benjamin pulled the tandem bicycle out again and let her mount first. She felt as though she were moving through quicksand on the Red River, it dragging her down.

Through the fog of her mind, she heard Benjamin say, "Match my pace. I'll do the rest."

CHAPTER 51

Their first stop was at a home in Washington Heights where Benjamin had tracked Mrs. Warren. The lady of the house, Mrs. Pierce, confirmed that Mrs. Warren stayed with them the night before, but left that morning and didn't say where she was going.

Ruth Ann and Benjamin departed the home with no leads, but he still seemed to know where to go. They peddled up Florida Avenue and he slowed to a stop beside a two wheel street sweeper drawn by a Clydesdale.

The man perched atop the single seat was Ed Ernie. He pulled the horse to a stop with a grin.

"I see you're out with your pretty lady friend, Mr. Benjamin."

Benjamin held the bicycle upright with one foot firmly planted. "Ed, the Pierces had a visitor yesterday evening, the woman I asked you about. Do you know which way she went?"

Ed Ernie didn't hesitate. "She hailed a cab and told him to take her to Tudor Place. And I found that information about her husband that you wanted. Passed it on to your friend at the Department of the Treasury like you asked." He leaned down from the seat and handed Benjamin a piece of paper.

Benjamin accepted it, read it quickly, and nodded. "Thanks. Please put it on my tab."

Ruth Ann was prepared when he pushed off and they began peddling. Ed Earnie grinned as she passed, and she returned a small smile of gratitude.

They retraced their path back to Georgetown, coming in on P Street, then north on 31st. It was hard to believe Mrs. Warren was only blocks from Roseland.

They peddled uphill, Ruth Ann feeling the strain in her legs and wishing she were horseback. But Benjamin got them up the hill and turned left to enter the vine-wrapped gate that stood open.

He guided them around the boxwood ellipse that was as wide as the five-part home with its two-story central block. Low hyphen buildings connected to two-story wings. Clad in stucco and coated in golden lime wash, the home was a model of Federal-period architecture.

Its construction was finished around 1816, if Ruth Ann recalled the description from her guide book correctly. A legacy from President George Washington's estate helped build the home and ornamental gardens, cradling the family of Martha Washington's granddaughter for 78 years.

Benjamin halted and dismounted. He held the bicycle while Ruth Ann did the same.

"Do you know the family of Tudor Place?" she asked.

"Only by reputation," he said. "The elderly owner now lives alone with her servants. I'm not surprised Mrs. Warren is acquainted with her."

Benjamin propped the bicycle near the porch and led the way up the steps. A knock brought a maid to the door. The maid, a plump woman in her 50s, gave them a second look.

Ruth Ann and Benjamin were an oddity there in D.C., dressed like city folks but as dark skinned as any Indian on the plains.

Benjamin removed his hat, his coal black hair trimmed and

styled despite his season of grief over the judge's death. And Ruth Ann's disruptions in his life.

Benjamin handed the maid his calling card. "We are here to see Mrs. Susan Warren. I understand she came to visit today."

The maid had positioned the door so that only her face showed. She stretched out a hand to take the card.

"Wait here," she said. "I will check with the mistress of the house."

The door shut and Ruth Ann glanced at Benjamin to see there was no emotion in his eyes. She wondered how often he was made to wait on a porch until he was confirmed as a reputable citizen.

Actually, Ruth Ann wasn't sure Benjamin was a citizen of the United States. She wasn't, at least not yet. If Senator Dawes had his way, U.S. citizenship for Choctaws would come with land allotments, ending tribal sovereignty.

After several minutes, the door opened to reveal an elderly gentleman in a butler's uniform. He beckoned them inside, apologizing for them being left on the porch, and led them through the central reception hall. At the other end, the temple portico with floor to ceiling windows jutted into the hall.

Maple pocket doors partially blocked the view of the formal drawing room. The old gentleman led them instead to the parlor.

Ruth Ann felt the moment of stepping over the threshold and into history. The room was filled with memorabilia dispersed after Martha Washington's passing, along with items collected by the family. Decades worth of lives had lived there, seeing honest struggles, triumph, and love.

But Ruth Ann's attention was drawn to Mrs. Warren's hat, piled with the colorful feathers she was prone to wearing. Her elaborate hats made her stand out back in Dickens and even here in the parlor where one normally removed their hats.

Mrs. Warren sat in a light green armchair, her back to Ruth Ann as she calmly sipped tea with the matron of the house.

The woman rose and spoke to Mrs. Warren. "Susan, dear, I believe these young people are here to see you. Perhaps natives of the land where you live?"

Mrs. Warren deposited her tea cup on the table and turned as she stood. She gasped. "Why, Ruth Ann Teller! What in heaven's name are you doing here?"

Isn't that my line? Ruth Ann thought as she braced herself.

Mrs. Warren hurried around the chair, tripping on one corner and stumbling into Ruth Ann's arms with a generous hug. Ruth Ann returned it, holding tight to this strange little piece of home, not at all regretting the time she spent searching for the woman.

She pulled back and helped Mrs. Warren steady herself, her hat lopsided from the rushed embrace.

"It's good to see you, Mrs. Warren. I would like to introduce you to—"

Mrs. Warren slapped her own cheeks with both hands. "Don't tell me. This is your beau! How do you do? I'm one of Ruth Ann's dearest friends."

Ruth Ann's cheeks flamed as Mrs. Warren offered her hand to Benjamin. He took it and bowed. "I'm Benjamin Nakishi-Dunn. It's a pleasure to finally meet you, Mrs. Warren."

Mrs. Warren's hand flew to her cheek again. "Oh my, have you been looking for me?"

Ruth Ann rubbed her temple. "Mrs. Warren, Lance telegraphed me that you were coming to D.C. He is so worried about you. I think you should come back to Roseland House with me until I return to Indian Territory."

Mrs. Warren looked confused, but then she laughed. "That would be perfectly delightful, my dear. I will show you all the wonderful things there are to see in this city, but we must first start with Tudor Place. Have you been out on the magnificent grounds yet?"

"We really should be going," Ruth Ann said.

Mrs. Warren sighed, almost a gasp, her face paling. Ruth Ann reached out to touch her arm. "Are you unwell?"

Mrs. Warren chuckled, some of the color coming back to her face. "Britannia and I are both well enough for old ladies."

In the background, the matron said, "Speak for yourself, Susan."

Mrs. Warren patted Ruth Ann's hand. "You must meet Britannia Peter Kennon. She's older than this house!"

Mrs. Warren turned to make the introduction, but snapped her attention to an engraving of a uniformed man hanging on the wall near the mantel. "Ruth Ann, didn't one of your chiefs fight in the war of 1812? Do you suppose he met Marquis de Lafayette? Or do I have the wars confused?"

"General Lafayette was a Revolutionary War hero." Benjamin moved to study the image of the American hero. "Pushmataha met him in D.C., before the chief's death in 1824."

"My, my, what a small world," Mrs. Kennon sighed, her voice crackling with age. "I met General Lafayette, too, when he returned to America in 1824. I was a little girl, but I remember when he presented this likeness to my mother. I can see the grand old man now as he entered this very parlor; his genial manner and dignified appearance made an impression on my mind which time cannot efface."

Mrs. Warren swayed and gripped Ruth Ann's hand. "Oh my. I am tired, my dear. If it's all right with you, I believe I will rest before we go to Roseland House. I could use a refreshing bath in this heat."

The interior of the house was cooler than the rapidly warming day, but Ruth Ann agreed. Mrs. Warren didn't look well.

She left with the maid for one of the second-floor guest rooms. Mrs. Kennon said she would also like to lie down and that the couple was free to roam the house and the grounds.

Ruth Ann and Benjamin retraced their steps out the front

door and around the boxwood ellipse, taking the butler's advice to walk the Crossbasket Castle sundial to the rose arbor near the lily pool. Ruth Ann caressed one of the roses and caught a petal that drifted off.

She wanted to ask about the information Benjamin received on Thaddeus Warren, but there was time for that later. There were other things on her mind. Namely, saving Philip.

She barely looked at Benjamin as she said quietly, "Yakoke. Thank you for helping me find Mrs. Warren."

Benjamin nodded, coat flipped back and thumbs resting in his pant pockets as he stared down the slope to the dell filled with white oaks, magnolias, shrubs, and dogwoods that went to the fence of the property. The breeze carried up the scent of the magnolia blooms.

Ruth Ann rubbed the velvety rose petal with her thumb. "I've been nothing but trouble to you since I arrived."

They had talked about the two scandalous stories, but Ruth Ann was thinking of how she'd purposely tried to get close to Benjamin for selfish reasons, and how she'd disrupted his grief over the judge and seeing his ex-fiancé.

"You've been no trouble, Miss Ruth Ann."

A distraction then? Ruth Ann wasn't sure how she felt about that, but there might not be a chance in the future when she'd have an opportunity to say what she had to say.

"My mind has been consumed with my brother Philip." She hated how the words choked her. "Then, the night of the charity ball, I learned that the prosecuting attorney intends to seek the death penalty against him. It could very well happen." She swallowed, forcing through the last of the words. "The prosecutor, Tecumseh Shoemaker, has never lost a case."

Ruth Ann wasn't sure which jolted her more—saying the terrible words out loud or Benjamin's reaction.

He dropped his hands and turned to look directly at her. She bit her lower lip, studying the concentration and pain on his face.

"Tecumseh Shoemaker?" he said, his voice going high.

Ruth Ann took a deep breath, ready to spill everything about the lawyer and how he had attempted to set the Tellers against one another, and had succeeded at terrifying her on the witness stand.

But up the path behind them, Ruth Ann spotted the maid rushing toward them. The older woman called out, "Mrs. Kennon needs to see you right away. Mrs. Warren has disappeared."

~

Ruth Ann peddled as fast as she could, trying to match Benjamin's pace as they flew up and down the hills of D.C. She wasn't afraid, though. Benjamin's strength and skill would keep them on the road.

They'd gone back inside Tudor Place to discover Mrs. Warren had slipped out and hailed a cab. Mrs. Kennon gave Ruth Ann a note that read, *After arduous debate with myself, I have decided the time has come. I must do what I came to do. Forgive me for leaving so abruptly.*

Ruth Ann trusted Benjamin to keep them from crashing, and also to take them to Mrs. Warren. He had kept track of Thaddeus Warren's movements, working to uncover if he was still connected with any dealings in the Choctaw Nation. Where they found that man, Mrs. Warren would be.

They arrived at the Smithsonian Institution Building, constructed of Seneca red sandstone in Norman Revival style. That earned its nickname of the *Castle*.

Ruth Ann was off the bicycle as fast as Benjamin. He racked it before taking her arm to help steady her as they hurried up the front steps.

Inside, a crowd was gathered in one corner of the Victorian-adorned room, a poster announcing an unveiling ceremony for a donated painting.

The crowd was quiet and Benjamin led Ruth Ann around the edge to where they could see Thaddeus Warren standing next to an easel covered with a black cloth, face red with embarrassment and anger. Mrs. Warren stood before him, her back to Ruth Ann and Benjamin.

But it was never hard to hear Mrs. Warren. "And so, Thaddeus, among those heathen savages as you once called my dear friends in Indian Territory, I've learned that forgiveness is the true fountain of youth. Bitterness, for me, was taking the poison and expecting you to die. But I no longer wish death for either of us. Isn't that a fine thing?"

Ruth Ann hesitated at the back of the crowd, relief seeping into her bones at the proclamation. The memory of finding Mrs. Warren after the woman had taken an entire bottle of laudanum was suddenly fresh for Ruth Ann, but there was something more in this moment.

Why couldn't forgiveness just happen? Why did one so hurt as Mrs. Warren—as Ruth Ann—have to make the decision in her heart to do it? It wasn't something Ruth Ann was ready to face. Unlike Mrs. Warren, her own journey was not over.

In the silence of the scene as everyone waited, not knowing what to do, Mrs. Warren said, "Well, Thaddeus, now that I've gotten that off my chest, I can say that I honestly forgive you." Her laughter echoed through the room. "I didn't expect to feel this free!"

Thaddeus Warren's face reddened more, eyes flashing with fire as he took a step toward her. But he halted. Benjamin had moved to Mrs. Warren's side, his stature overshadowing the former mayor of Dickens.

Ruth Ann made her feet move to stand at Mrs. Warren's other side. The woman turned and locked Ruth Ann in a tight side hug, not at all surprised to see her there.

"Dear Ruth Ann, it's a good day to be alive, isn't it?" Mrs.

Warren said. "I'm finally free. Come, let's go out and touch the sunshine!"

Before they could move though, a disturbance at the back of the crowd made the people part and Ruth Ann stared at the three men in white coats who pushed their way through. A woman came up at the rear, her resemblance to Mrs. Warren unmistakable.

Susan Warren lifted her chin, her eyes defiant. "Agnes. I didn't expect to see you for quite some time after our last correspondence."

Mrs. Warren's sister spoke in a dignified yet harsh voice. "You won't see me for quite some time after today."

The men in white coats took Mrs. Warren by the arms, nudging Ruth Ann aside. Ruth Ann was ready to kick shins on those three white-coated men from the insane asylum, but Benjamin stepped in front of her and spoke to Mrs. Warren.

"Don't worry, I will take care of things. We will have you to Roseland House by morning."

While Agnes huffed, Mrs. Warren patted Benjamin's cheek—barely able to reach it—then went along peaceably with the men.

The organizer of the unveiling cleared his throat nervously and said, "Well, I'm sure none of us expected that excitement, but we will now proceed with the ceremony for this antique portrait donated to the Smithsonian by Mr. Thaddeus Warren."

Benjamin addressed the organizer. "Sir, you may want to hold on taking photographs with Thaddeus Warren." Benjamin held up the slip of paper he'd gotten from Ed Earnie. "He will find himself in jail shortly for tax evasion. All his assets are frozen by now, so I hope any pledges he made to the museum have already been processed."

CHAPTER 52

Ruth Ann peddled a bicycle from Roseland House to the Congressional Cemetery, not needing to look at her map of D.C. even once.

After Mrs. Warren was delivered safe and sound to Roseland that morning, Ruth Ann's heart should have been light as she rode through the sprinkles of sunshine on the tree-lined road. Thaddeus Warren was in jail at last, though not for the crimes he committed in Indian Territory, including attempting to have Matthew killed.

But Warren's life and reputation were in ruin, derailing anything he may have wanted to do regarding land in Indian Territory. Benjamin said Warren hadn't done anything illegal in that regard, yet, but that sometimes the way to stop someone was by coming through a back door. That was what he'd done in alerting the Department of the Treasury and facilitating Warren's arrest.

But Ruth Ann's heart was still heavy with both the thoughts of her family and how she had betrayed Benjamin's trust. He had little reason to trust her, yet he helped take care of the Warren situation. Because he was still her friend? What was his other reason that he hadn't wanted to reveal yet?

Maybe he would today. He sent a message to Roseland, asking Ruth Ann to meet him in the Congressional Cemetery.

What if he planned to end their friendship before she could ask him again about taking her brother's case? No matter what feelings were jumbled inside her, her brother's life and her family's future were at stake. She couldn't let that go.

And thine ears shall hear a word behind thee, saying, This is the way, walk ye in it.

Ruth Ann parked the bicycle at the cemetery gate. She stepped off the brick road and headed up the grassy hillside filled with purple coneflowers in bloom.

The breeze pulled at her skirt and hair. Raising her head, she saw a tall Indian man standing next to the grave of Chief Pushmataha.

Benjamin held her gaze all the way up as she quietly joined him.

After a time of silence, Benjamin said, "Virginia Lee Newman won't cause any more problems. I've done work for Senator Newman and he is keen on protecting my reputation. He sent Miss Newman and her friend, Agatha Green, home to Georgia yesterday."

Ruth Ann closed her eyes in relief. "Yakoke."

How she did value Benjamin's friendship! He had the kind of power and connections Pepper wanted, but Benjamin earned them without shortcuts.

Still, there were questions Ruth Ann longed to ask. "When I was traveling to D.C. with Pepper Barnes, he told me your name was Benjamin Nakishi. He was upset when I included 'Dunn' in a newspaper article for the *Choctaw Tribune*."

She looked up to gauge Benjamin's reaction, and was surprised to see a sad smile.

"There's an irony to that," he said, his deep voice giving her a feeling of home that she couldn't explain. "Nakishi was my grandfather's name. I added it as an adult to better connect with fellow full-bloods. They often don't feel comfortable talking to me like they do this other full-blood lawyer, and at that time in my life, it was important that they did. But it all came to nothing in the end."

Ruth Ann swallowed. "The other lawyer. Tecumseh Shoemaker?"

Benjamin looked at Ruth Ann a long while before he said, "It was the greatest battle of my life, one that we could not both win. Our fathers were convicted of the same murder."

Ruth Ann fought to maintain Benjamin's steady gaze. She trusted him despite what the newspaper had said, not only because her brother told her to, but because he'd proven the kind of man he was.

Benjamin lowered his large frame to sit in the shade of Pushmataha's headstone. Ruth Ann joined him, relishing the feel of the cool grass beneath her hand as Benjamin shared his story.

"Tecumseh and his father were at our place that day," he began, his voice not as steady as when he told the children at the orphanage the story of how turtle got cracks on his back. "Tecumseh and I were in the woods, hunting with our rabbit sticks. He was a teenager, and I was five years old. He liked to push me around even then."

Benjamin smiled a little, then grew solemn. "We heard a shot fired. And a scream. When we ran back, both my father and his were standing over the body of a white man. My father is not a murderer, but he wouldn't tell me what happened. I always suspected it was self-defense. The trial took place at Fort Smith because the man killed was white, and both our fathers were convicted of murder. As full-bloods, both accepted the verdict without question.

"They were sent to Leavenworth. My mother had passed when I was a baby and, with no close relatives, I was sent to

Spencer Academy. Tecumseh later became a lawyer, determined to get his father free. He proved his father's innocence by portraying my father as the murderer. His father went free."

Benjamin paused, looking as though he were reading the words on Pushmataha's headstone before continuing. "I became a lawyer for the same reason as Tecumseh. That's how we came to face off in court. We knew one of our fathers had to bear the guilt of the killing. We were right. My father is still in Leavenworth."

Ruth Ann's chin quivered at the heartbreaking story. She'd known what it was to have her father ripped away when she still needed him.

She dug her fingers in the grass and dirt of the Congressional Cemetery, wanting to rip out a handful and smear them over her face, mourning both her father and Benjamin's.

"I'm so sorry."

Benjamin met her eyes as though realizing he had shared the entire story aloud. Then his peaceful smile returned. "It was hard, but God used that tribulation for good. It was at Spencer that I found Christ, and the words of Scripture became like the beat of my heart."

Ruth Ann struggled to hold back her tears. "I've only thought of myself since meeting you, wanting to find a way to convince you to take my brother's case. I didn't know you'd be who you are."

Benjamin laid one arm across his propped up knee and shook his head. "I am not the one to take your brother's case. I don't stand a chance against Tecumseh in court."

He gestured toward the headstone. "I don't want to die in D.C. like the chiefs buried here, but I cannot return to Indian Territory, not yet. I'm not ready to face what lies back there. I hope this is something you can forgive me for."

"I understand."

With those two words, Ruth Ann's heavy heart shattered like a dropped pottery bowl on a stone. She clung to the thought that her pain was because her best chance of saving her brother was gone, but it was more than that.

She released the grass, sitting up straighter. Her hand came up with a purple coneflower and she held tight to it.

Benjamin rubbed his mouth, then shifted to face her. "Ruth Ann, would you do me the honor of allowing me to escort you to the nation's Fourth of July festivities next week?"

Ruth Ann held her hands still in her lap, staring at the purple coneflower. It was better for her and Benjamin to say goodbye now and go back to living in the two worlds they belonged in—he in Washington, D.C., her in the Choctaw Nation.

But when she opened her mouth, the words that came out were, "Yes, you may."

She would deal with the consequences of her heart later.

CHAPTER 53

Ruth Ann barely made it to the stairs at Roseland, intending to freshen up before the noon meal, when a rough voice stopped her.

"I want to talk to you, Ruth Ann Teller."

The last thing she wanted was to engage with Pepper Barnes. But without Benjamin's help and the chance of a presidential pardon simply ridiculous, Pepper was perhaps her only way to save Philip's life.

Ruth Ann turned to see Pepper standing in the parlor door with a rolled up newspaper, tapping it against one palm. Her legs were tired from the bicycle ride this morning, but she yielded and started past him, intending to take a seat in one of the armchairs.

But before she reached the chair, Pepper grasped her arm and pulled her back around to face him.

She gasped. "Pepper Barnes, what is wrong with you?"

He held the newspaper under her nose. "That Warren woman landed on the front page, complete with a photograph of her and men from the asylum, and you standing right in the middle of things. That woman and her husband wreaked enough havoc in the Choctaw Nation, and you had to get involved with them in D.C. First you ruined things with Nakishi, and now this."

Ruth Ann jerked her arm out of his grip. "I suppose you missed the favorable article that Joseph Griffin released about Senator Newman and several congressmen endorsing Benjamin, putting him back into excellent standing. Not to mention the news that Thaddeus Warren was arrested for tax evasion in the midst of his latest scheme to swindle Indians out of our land."

Pepper unfurled the paper and held it too close to her face. But she could see it was the gossip section.

"I suppose *you* missed the piece in yesterday's paper about how you and I are engaged," he said. "I guess I should thank your friend Griffin for helping you make up your mind. He even sent this back home. I got a telegram from your brother this morning."

Ruth Ann couldn't help giggling. It was either that or kick Pepper in the shin. "What did Matthew say?"

"None of your business."

"What is my business is knowing that Virginia Lee was spreading the gossip to newspapers, not Joseph," she said. "Benjamin took care of her better than you could have."

Ruth Ann regretted the words at the immediate shift in Pepper's demeanor. She'd insulted him before, but this was the first time she directly compared him to another man. She might as well push on.

"You were right about one thing," she said, voice even and determined. "Benjamin will not be taking Philip's case, which leaves me to ask you exactly what your plan is. No games, Pepper —tell me straight out how you're going to guarantee my brother's life."

Pepper drilled her with his brown eyes, daring her to look away. She didn't.

He growled, "I have my ways and influence with men like Kanitobe if you'll cooperate. If all else fails, money talks."

Ruth Ann swayed. Bribery. Had she expected anything better from Pepper?

Anger rose up in her. She didn't know who she should be most furious with.

Philip, for getting their family into the whole situation.

Dan Holder and Lester Cotton for being outlaws and dragging Philip into it.

Cub Wassom for threatening her family and shooting Matthew.

Tecumseh Shoemaker for believing Philip was a traitor and wanting to have him executed.

Pepper for his schemes and the way he'd tried to take advantage of her vulnerability.

Sometimes the world out there was too big for someone like her.

Pepper took a step closer. He was always too close. "Is Nakishi courting you? That was not my intention when I told you I wanted you to convince him to return to Indian Territory. I want whatever is between you to stop."

Ruth Ann's anger boiled over, hot words flying from her lips. "Benjamin Nakishi-Dunn is my friend, which is more than I can say for you, Pepper Barnes."

That terrible look flashed in his eyes. She'd known him enough years to know when he was truly angry.

He clenched his fists, and she wondered if he would hit her like he would have Matthew. But instead, he hit her in the heart.

"Not a friend? I helped load your father's body in a wagon!"

Ruth Ann coughed on the bile in her throat, moving back and landing in a side chair, hand over her mouth.

Pepper Barnes had seen Ruth Ann's family through more hard times than most anyone not blood related to them. Yes, he had been part of the search party that returned her father to Uncle Preston's ranch. He saved her and Matthew on the road outside of Finley. He helped save Beulah and the Jessops from Cub Wassom.

But how could he be so terrible, speaking coldly about that day in the mountains when the search party found her daddy? What had Pepper seen? The blood, bones…Ruth Ann gagged.

"I'm done with treating you like you have good sense," Pepper said, standing over her. "You're to blame for my work in D.C. and the work of the entire Choctaw delegation failing! Most have already gone home. I should have too, after I had to attend that dinner party alone, when I was supposed to be with my fiancé, seated with Forbis Kanitobe and his wife." His chest heaved. "You've ruined everything!"

Pepper flung the newspaper at her feet and turned away. He kicked over an end table with its crystal water pitcher and glasses, the pieces hitting the floor with a crash.

Ruth Ann sobbed.

CHAPTER 54

Ruth Ann's final week in D.C. passed more quickly than she thought it would. Pepper moved out of Roseland, opting to stay in the Willard Hotel located near the President's House. It was a tremendous relief to have both him and Virginia Lee out of the boarding house.

Ruth Ann telegraphed Lance and assured him that his aunt was well, and the news that his uncle was in jail, which came as no surprise. She wrote a longer letter with details, especially about Lance's pistol and how Mrs. Warren said she would never enter a city with as many crooks in D.C. without one.

Keeping track of Mrs. Warren actually turned out far more beneficial than Ruth Ann would have guessed. Mrs. Warren, free from her sister thanks to Benjamin threatening a lawsuit, enjoyed many connections in the city, and she was more than happy to share them. Ruth Ann met dozens more wives of politicians, all of whom subscribed to the *Choctaw Tribune* after Mrs. Warren's enthusiastic endorsement.

Ruth Ann tucked the profit away for the remainder of her trip that would not be funded by Pepper. She would send him money to repay her train tickets and boarding as soon as she returned home.

She also saw all the sights she could ever dream of in the nation's capitol, giving her more content for the *Choctaw Tribune*. She wrote an extra story for Joseph on her perspective as a Choctaw visiting the capitol, and how momentous it was to visit the graves of the two Choctaw chiefs there. She included some history of her people for the general population of D.C., and plugged the *Choctaw Tribune*. Based on a telegram she received from Peter, it yielded dozens of subscription requests.

Ruth Ann purchased souvenirs and postcards for family and friends back home and dashed off notes to them. Though in D.C. four weeks, she had found herself so occupied she didn't take care of basic tourism things that many people did on a trip. She took extra time with Matthew's postcard that featured the Capitol Building, telling him he needed to make his own journey there and see the Choctaw treaties.

She needed to write him a letter about what they should do next for Philip after she failed with the two men she thought could save her brother. But that conversation would wait until she returned home and talked it over with Matthew face-to-face. Hopefully they would be able to do that now.

After considerable hesitation, Ruth Ann mailed off her note to the First Lady. Not even Mrs. Warren was acquainted with her. It was the highest connection Ruth Ann held on this trip, and she had made it solely on her own. So much for Pepper's theory that she needed him to do anything.

But she didn't hold a grudge against him, at least not entirely. Pepper was who he was, and she didn't imagine him ever changing.

She didn't give him much thought after their argument. Her mind was preoccupied with the movements of Benjamin Nakishi, and anticipating their outing on Wednesday, July 4.

Benjamin wasn't around much, spending time at his country

home. Ruth Ann missed him. She didn't know how she would say goodbye when the time came. But her people didn't have a word for goodbye in their language, only *chi pisa la chike. I will see you again.*

Ruth Ann decided to spend funds from the new subscribers—her first real salary with the *Choctaw Tribune*—to go shopping with Georgia Pearl the day before the Fourth of July celebration. She let Georgia Pearl talk her into purchasing a stunning white and pink striped taffeta dress with short, puffed sleeves. They picked out a white boater hat trimmed with pink ribbon to go with it.

This was a special occasion and Ruth Ann could wear the dress and hat again if the First Lady extended the invitation Ruth Ann hoped for.

Done up with Gibson Girl curls around their faces and Ruth Ann in the new peppermint dress, the young ladies were ready and waiting on the porch the morning of the 4th of July.

Ruth Ann hid her smile at Georgia Pearl's giddiness over her first beau as he came up the walkway. He was a gangly, spectacle wearing young man in a pinstripe suit with freckles on his nose. They'd met at the private dinner party Ruth Ann missed, and Georgia Pearl had talked about him nonstop since. The younger girl's eyes were bright and cheeks rosy as he approached, carrying a bouquet of roses practically as big as him.

Ruth Ann leaned over and breathed into Georgia Pearl's ear, "You'd best loosen your corset, young lady."

Georgia Pearl giggled and whispered back, "Speak for yourself, my friend."

Ruth Ann understood why, suddenly unable to breathe. Arriving in an open carriage behind the boy, was Benjamin Nakishi-Dunn.

Before the carriage halted, Benjamin hopped off without using the steps, reminding Ruth Ann of the day they'd played football on the National Mall lawn. Athletic and quick.

Today, Benjamin was dressed in a stylish summer suit and derby hat which spoke of his city lifestyle. But the warm, raised-in-Indian Territory expression on his dark face captured her heart. She could deny that no longer, corset or not.

Georgia Pearl accepted the lavish bouquet from her beau and bid Ruth Ann a hasty "have a good time," before leaving. Ruth Ann couldn't break away from Benjamin's gaze as he came up the porch and extended a bouquet of purple coneflowers to her.

"I thought these from the cemetery were appropriate after my visit there this morning," he said, his voice steady and ready to carry her through the day. "Had serious thinking and praying to do."

Ruth Ann took the bouquet with a trembling smile. "Yakoke."

She accepted his arm, and he led her down the steps and handed her into the carriage.

As the carriage pulled them away from Roseland and toward the festival, Ruth Ann couldn't help asking, "What serious thoughts occupied your mind on this splendid day?"

Benjamin shifted in the seat to better face her. "I've been thinking of Pepper Barnes's departure from Roseland House. I don't need to know the details, but since the other Choctaws, except Forbis Kanitobe and his wife, have already gone home, I'm concerned about your traveling back to Indian Territory alone." He paused long, then said, "I would be honored to escort you safely there."

It was a good thing Ruth Ann was sitting down. Her heart flipped one way, then another. She breathed out, "But...are you certain? You said you did not want to return for a long time."

Benjamin shrugged, but Ruth Ann knew he had weighed the decision carefully. "I thought I would take a look at your brother's case, as well. But please don't get your hopes up. I cannot represent him for reasons you are aware of, but perhaps I could offer advice to the lawyer you've obtained. Maybe together, we can achieve a milder sentence." He paused. "You may have a steeper hill to climb with Mr. Barnes in the mix. I understand the Barnes family have a great deal of influence in Choctaw courts."

Ruth Ann's mouth went dry. She considered Pepper an unhelpful friend in the situation, not a devoted enemy. What had she done!

She pressed her fingertips to her forehead. "How could I have made things worse when I was trying so hard to fix it all? I never intended to push Pepper to fight against us." She dropped her hand. "I believe he will grow into a bitter man with the path he's on. Why is it that struggles and hardships drive some people away from God and others to Him?"

Benjamin let silence work between them before answering, "The same sun that softens the wax hardens the clay. God is unchanging. We are the ones who respond differently."

Ruth Ann looked up into Benjamin's eyes, not caring to hide her deep admiration for him.

How opposite Pepper Barnes and Benjamin Nakishi were. Pepper had many opportunities from birth with his well-to-do family, compared to the orphan raised in a boarding school, his father in prison for murder.

If only she could combine the two men—Benjamin's character with Pepper's dedication to the Choctaw Nation.

Looking at the street ahead lined with red, white, and blue streamers, Ruth Ann said softly, "I'm grateful you responded to the sun the way you did."

The rest of the day was like a dream for Ruth Ann. Knowing Benjamin was coming back to Indian Territory as she had longed for him to do ever since Pepper first spoke his name, let her not think about when their goodbye would eventually come. Who was she to say what God's plans were for her or for Benjamin? She would live life one moment at a time.

She enjoyed every bit of eating watermelon and also cake slathered with white icing, orchestra music next to the Washington Monument, an impromptu football game that Benjamin joined, then meeting with Senator Newman, Georgia Pearl, and her beau for a display of fireworks over the Potomac that evening. In the background, the orchestra played the Star-Spangled Banner.

Ruth Ann lay on a blanket spread on the green grass between Benjamin and Georgia Pearl as they watched the display. She thought of Francis Scott Key, the man held prisoner on a ship with the bombs bursting in air, giving proof through the night that the flag was still there.

The flag.

That flag was as much the Choctaw peoples' as any. From Pushmataha onward, her people had never fought against the Americans, opting instead to fight alongside them in more than one war.

Our flag.

Ruth Ann might not be a U.S. citizen, but in that moment, watching the brilliant flashes explode in the night sky, she felt as American as ever in her life.

Maybe living in this city wasn't an impossible thought.

CHAPTER 55

Like most of the guests at Roseland, Ruth Ann slept late after the Fourth of July celebration. Then she and Georgia Pearl spent another half hour sitting cross-legged on their beds as they talked about the fun of the day before.

Georgia Pearl gave Ruth Ann the novel she'd read about Chickasaws and insisted Ruth Ann write her a letter about its inaccuracies. The younger girl teared up at the thought of saying farewell the next day, but Ruth Ann taught her how to say *chi pisa la chike*. They would see one another again.

When they finally made their way to the dining room for brunch, Ruth Ann received a letter from the footman.

"Just came for you, ma'am."

Ruth Ann halted outside the dining room, taking note of the astonishing return address.

Next to her, Georgia Pearl squealed. "Well, open it!"

Ruth Ann did and found not a standard invitation but one written by the First Lady herself.

My dear Ruth Ann,

My husband has enjoyed reading your newspaper, the Choctaw Tribune, *and the article you wrote for the* Washington Times *about your impression of the nation's capitol. He appreciates that your reporting doesn't villainize anyone for the sake of political or personal gain. It is refreshing.*

We would consider it an honor if you joined us for tea this afternoon at 2:15p.m. in the Yellow Oval Room. President Cleveland would like to meet you.

Sincerely,

Frances Clara Cleveland
First Lady of the United States of America

Ruth Ann could have fainted. Georgia Pearl shook her arm vigorously.

"I'll get stationary and you can write your immediate acceptance!" Georgia Pearl nearly shouted.

Ruth Ann might need to dictate her reply. She would hardly be able to hold a pencil with how her hands trembled.

The prospect of meeting the President of the United States was thrilling, but she was also terrified of saying the wrong things. She had the opportunity she prayed for—to meet the president face-to-face and ask him to pardon her brother before the Choctaw judicial system sentenced him to death.

Was this her last opportunity to save Philip?

When Ruth Ann stepped into the Grand Foyer of the President's House, she was overwhelmed with the wonder of the people who had entered the State Floor in that century—leaders of this nation and of her nation. Men who had done great good and great harm, both lasting generations.

She shook away the feeling and focused on following the agent taking her to meet the current President of the United States.

Her peppermint taffeta dress sounded loud in her ears, despite the voices in the large entrance hall. Louis Comfort Tiffany's ornate stained glass screen sparkled in the natural light coming from the huge windows on the north wall, illuminating the patterns of American eagles, and a shield with stripes, stars, and the initials "U.S." on the glass.

The President's House bustled with activity, but Ruth Ann took note of the men in black suits who watched every twitch of the eye. It made her stand straighter and clutch her reticule, with its faithful tablet and pencil tucked inside, more tightly to her.

She thought about the First Lady's invitation again and was ever so grateful for her decision to remain true to the integrity of the *Choctaw Tribune*, not slanting articles in Pepper's favor. That was part of the broken link with him, but it now forged a new, stronger one for Philip.

The agent paused at the bottom of the stairs leading to the second floor to allow three men who were coming down in flamboyant discussion. Ruth Ann recognized two of the men from Congress that she met, but she kept tucked close behind the agent so they wouldn't see her. She didn't want to be interrupted and miss her small window of time with the president.

The man she didn't recognize spoke loudly over his shoulder in response to another's question. "The intelligent Indians and intermarried whites throughout the territory are gobbling up the resources, and the uneducated class are left with nothing. We must push this commission through, for the Indians' own good."

The man behind him cut the air with one hand emphatically. "If you want to die on that hill, Dawes, you'll do it without my help. Those Indians will never capitulate."

Ruth Ann pressed against the wall to steady herself, mouth agape as she stared at the passing men. More specifically, Senator Henry Dawes.

She couldn't help feeling the waves of shock that went through her at seeing the face of the man who was trying to strip the sovereignty of the Choctaw Nation by individual land allotments.

Everything hit her at once—her reporter instincts for a story, and her personal feelings. She could take both of those and rush up to him, demand he answer her questions. But she couldn't. She could not control her emotions enough to conduct an unbiased and civil interview.

The opportunity passed as the agent led her up the stairs. Ruth Ann struggled mightily to regain control of her emotions. Her peoples' sovereignty was so threatened by that man.

With terrible realization, Ruth Ann knew she was on the threshold of disregarding that sovereignty herself. Asking the President of the United States to pardon her brother would put another rip in it. Who knew if it wouldn't be the last one to destroy her people entirely?

Two men in black guarded the door to the Yellow Oval Room. The agent opened the door for Ruth Ann's first glimpse at the President of the United States, Grover Cleveland.

Ruth Ann needed to make her decision before she crossed the threshold. It took her an eternity.

For a moment, she was standing over the treaties at the Capitol Building again, absorbing their significance and how often those words had been trampled in the past century and would be in the coming one.

She knew the right thing.

As she stepped into the room, Ruth Ann felt as though she just pulled the trigger to end her brother's life.

"If you've got any clever tricks up your sleeve, now would be the time to use them." Philip hefted his end of the log onto the corner of the split-rail fence. He grinned, but Matthew could see the grimness behind it and his lighthearted words.

The log landed in the notches with a thump when Matthew dropped his end in place where they were building the fence for a Choctaw farmer near Skullyville.

Philip told Matthew he had stayed often on this farm over the past six years. He did odd and end jobs between Skullyville and Fort Smith, searching for an opportunity to trap Dan Holder. He lived with Kat Russell for a time, but she kicked him out.

Ranch and farm work came the most natural for Philip. Then there were the coal mines in McAlester that he worked to get close to Al Percy, his best chance at Holder.

Now Philip was chopping wood, working fields, building fences, and hauling water for a plate of beans and a shabby corner of a shed while he awaited trial. There was no reason he couldn't have done his waiting in Dickens or on Uncle Preston's ranch, but Philip refused to go home. Matthew supposed his brother couldn't stand the thought of settling back into the family only to be ripped away—for good, this time.

Matthew didn't respond to his brother's quip, still not able to form his thoughts into words. Not this time. He hadn't seen Philip since the inquest and now he had come with the news that his brother was facing execution by the Choctaw Lighthorsemen.

Matthew had hoped to ride his new stallion up to the farm after disembarking from the train at Skullyville, giving him time to think in quiet. He'd finally settled on a name for the stallion —*Falama*, the Choctaw word for resilience. In the past week, he and the stallion had reached a truce, bonded even during a few rides. Falama was stubborn but, like Philip, finally ready to surrender. So was Matthew.

Who knew catching and training a Choctaw horse from the mountains would be God's way of starting to heal Matthew's heart? Robert Barnes was an odd character for God to use, but the Lord did move in mysterious ways.

Still, Falama's stubborn streak was running high that day, so Matthew left him behind.

Philip dragged another notched log to the corner of the fence, then he and Matthew lifted it at the same time.

Philip grinned. "We work good together."

They rolled the log onto the fence, but the notches weren't lined up and the log rolled off the other side.

Philip chuckled. "Sometimes."

He put both hands on the fence, staring at the failed attempt to get the last section in place. "I could always run off before the Lighthorse shoot me."

Matthew leaned against the fence, crossing his arms and looking at his brother. Growing up, Philip took life too lightly for Matthew's liking, always joking, even making Matthew laugh when he really wanted to shake him. Now, Matthew understood. Philip's humor was his way of dealing with the harder parts of life.

That only went so far, though, and Philip was nearly at the end.

Philip glanced at Matthew, still a half grin on his face. He pushed away from the fence. "Back in the old days, if a Choctaw ran out on his sentence, his closest male relative had to take his place. You'd be stubborn enough to do that."

He vaulted the fence. Matthew did the same. They picked up the log and settled it in place. The scent of fresh cut cedar made Matthew wish for home at the ranch, and simpler days.

Philip said quietly, "I've put enough shame on our family. It would be worth my life not to add more."

Matthew gripped the rail. The threat of death hanging over them was too real. The anticipation of it, the terror.

Philip went on. "You know, you can make a lot of excuses for yourself, letting your life tumble down a mine shaft. Trouble is, you don't realize what a deep hole you're in 'til you hit bottom. I thought I hit it when I was left stuck in that mine. But that wasn't bottom. This is."

All Philip's attempts at humor were gone. Matthew couldn't do this, couldn't be there. He was ready to run out on Philip, to leave and forget he ever had a brother.

But when Philip looked him in the eyes, there was fear there that he hadn't had, not even when he was preparing to face down Dan Holder and Lester Cotton. He wet his lips. "I wish God would just save me."

Matthew squeezed his eyes shut, swallowed, and opened them with what he hoped was a brave smile. "He already has, my brother."

Philip sniffed and rubbed his forehead. "Yeah, I believe that. But…would you promise to do two things for me…after?"

Matthew straightened, fire coming back into his heart. It was a hopeless one with the downpour of rain that was coming, but a fire for the moment. "We aren't giving up."

Philip shook his head. "I know, but promise me."

Matthew nodded. There were very few things he wouldn't promise his brother right then.

Philip stared out at the planted fields. Would he be alive for the harvest? Matthew couldn't think about that.

"Take care of my little girl," Philip finally said, his tone sad. "She needs to know who she is, the good family she comes from, not just what her daddy did. Her name…her name is *Nita*. My little Choctaw bear." Philip coughed, his eyes red and watery. "And the other thing…please don't tell anyone what a coward I am."

Matthew wrapped his arms around his brother's shoulders, wanting to squeeze life into him. If only he could.

CHAPTER 57

The rocking train and green mountains of Tennessee were a comfort to Ruth Ann as she gave her eyes a break from reading to look out the window. The sun was setting, gold and crimson bathing the landscape in brilliant colors and creating a glowing mist in the hills.

Washington, D.C., with its glamour and drama, was far behind Ruth Ann. She would be home tomorrow.

While it was good to be going home, Ruth Ann also dreaded it. Unless a miracle happened, she'd have to tell her brother Philip goodbye. It was something she couldn't bring herself to imagine.

Ruth Ann looked up as Benjamin settled on the seat across from her again, handing her a tin cup that smelled of tea. She inhaled the mint aroma. "Yakoke. I hope you didn't run into Pepper again."

Benjamin adjusted the tail of his coat, holding his own mug steady to keep from spilling it. "All is well."

The way he said it left Ruth Ann to wonder if he had taken a verbal blow for her. She took a sip of the mint tea. Since they'd left D.C. early that morning, she tried to avoid the forward cars where Pepper was also traveling home. Forbis Kanitobe and his wife were somewhere in the middle cars, Benjamin and Ruth Ann at the very back on the full train. Mrs. Warren opted to remain in D.C. for an extended stay at Tudor Place.

After traveling to D.C. with the entire delegation, it seemed odd to return with only one other Choctaw. But it was the only Choctaw on this train Ruth Ann wanted to be around.

Benjamin and Ruth Ann had carried on pleasant conversations during the ride, but over the past few hours, he grew quiet. Ruth Ann wondered how long it had been since he traveled this way, and what he anticipated when he got to Indian Territory.

Were there old friends he would visit? Enemies—besides Tecumseh Shoemaker—that he wanted to avoid?

He had told Ruth Ann he would stay a week, then he needed to return to D.C. He'd selected his next case and his assistant was already doing preliminary work on it. Ruth Ann caught wind that Benjamin's next step was to start his own law firm in D.C. She didn't want to think about that gossip.

When the quiet continued, Ruth Ann returned to the novel Georgia Pearl gave her. She was almost at the end, keeping in mind her friend's request that Ruth Ann pick it apart for inaccuracies.

Surprisingly, there wasn't anything alarming. In fact, the novel was refreshing in that it contained no stereotypes of Indians in savage or barbaric behavior, as though Indians only knew how to live as animals.

The story portrayed a Chickasaw family living on the Blue River, and dealing with the challenges that came their way— man-made and natural disasters, prejudices—and surviving to come out stronger on the other side. It was gentle in places, tear-filled in others, then laugh out loud funny.

Ruth Ann was anxious to write a letter to share her thoughts with Georgia Pearl on the book that was a healing salve for Ruth Ann and the prejudices she'd faced.

There were other letters to write, including to Joseph Griffin, who promised to send her insider stories on anything that related to her people in D.C. She appreciated having a newspaper colleague with ties to the AP and who valued honest reporting.

Half an hour later, as the conductor lit gas lamps in the car, Ruth Ann set the book aside with a satisfied smile. The last page didn't disappoint, and she looked forward to starting that letter to Georgia Pearl.

But Benjamin caught her eye. He was watching her.

"How was your book?" he asked.

"Well done. You can read it next if you like."

Benjamin hesitated. "I've been thinking about your brother's case. You told me about visiting the president and first lady, and I wanted to ask if you've considered enlisting the president's help for Philip?"

Ruth Ann stared at her hands. "I did think about it. But I can't jeopardize our people's sovereignty. His judgement is in the hands of the Choctaw courts."

Benjamin leaned back in his seat and Ruth Ann glanced up to see something in his eyes she couldn't place. Then it was gone, and he asked, "I know it's hard to speak about, but there's one piece of the case I need the details of."

Ruth Ann steeled herself for the conversation. She remembered the flashes of horrible images Pepper brought to mind when he talked about loading her father's body in a wagon. But she would share anything that might keep Philip alive.

"What were Lester Cotton and Cub Wassom blackmailing Philip with?" Benjamin asked.

Ruth Ann turned to look out the window into the darkness too quickly, her face going scarlet. That was one piece she intentionally left out of the story and desperately hoped Benjamin wouldn't ask. It was mortifying to talk about.

Matthew had sent Ruth Ann a letter during her last days in D.C. It contained details of the blackmailing per what Philip told him. He ended with saying he truly believed Philip did what he did to protect his family from the Dan Holder gang, especially Cub Wassom. It didn't turn out that way, scarring the family for life instead.

But Benjamin would find it all out sooner or later. Still, Ruth Ann couldn't meet his eyes.

"There…" her voice caught, and she cleared her throat before starting again. "There was a young lady he was seeing in Fort Smith when he made freight runs with my father. I remember my daddy getting on to Philip about anything to do with her. I didn't understand back then, but I do now. That is, I know what my daddy was warning him about and what came of it because Philip didn't listen."

She bit her lower lip, then pushed on. "The young lady became…she was with child and demanded Philip leave his family and marry her. Lester Cotton knew Philip would do most anything to keep his family from finding out and tried to talk him into the robbery. When Philip refused, Cub Wassom threatened him and his family."

Ruth Ann closed her eyes against the flashing countryside of hills and cliffs in the rapidly falling darkness. Life was going too fast. She hadn't slowed down enough to really contemplate Philip's decisions and how Matthew was right. In his own foolish way, Philip had tried to protect his family after endangering them with his poor choices.

Cub Wassom proved what a vicious soul he was when he tried to murder Matthew on that road to Finley, right beside Ruth Ann. He would have killed them both if it hadn't been for Pepper Barnes.

Why did those two young men, Philip and Pepper, make so many bad decisions, yet she still owed them her life?

She opened her eyes and found Benjamin still watching her, a gentle expression on his face. "You don't need to be ashamed,

Miss Ruth Ann. Your brother made his choices and you are making yours. He is blessed to have you as a sister."

Ruth Ann smiled a little, thinking of how she had two brothers, a mother, and a father most of her life. Benjamin grew up without siblings, essentially an orphan in a boarding school with his father in prison. Of all the people who would be understanding toward her family's situation, this man was it.

Her thoughts were drifting farther than she wanted to allow them to, so she steered the conversation to something she was curious about. "You said there were two reasons you wanted to help me with the Warrens. One was because Thaddeus Warren had shady dealings going on with our people. May I ask what the other one was?"

She was sure his face flushed, something unusual for his level demeanor. His lips parted. How would she describe his smile? Innocent guilt?

He rubbed his hands together. "Miss Ruth Ann, I must confess as a lawyer, I am tactical in my decisions. When I learned of the situation you were in, I thought it was a good opportunity to... well, spend time with you and see if you were what I judged you to be when we first met."

Ruth Ann bit her lower lip to keep anything silly from bubbling out.

Benjamin met her eyes, his Hershey brown ones making her lose her senses for a moment, but his voice grounded her again.

"I was right," he said. "I've come to know you as an unselfish individual who puts others, and your people, before yourself. You helped your friend at your own expense of time, energy, and reputation. And when you had an opportunity to speak to the President of the United States about intervening for your brother, you made a choice for your peoples' past, present, and future. That took courage."

Ruth Ann's mind scrambled for the right thing to say. Did she dare voice her deep admiration for him? But there was more than admiration in her heart, and that frightened her. The nation's capitol had its appeal, but she didn't want to wait to return to Indian Territory when she was old.

She settled for safe. "Benjamin, do you think there could be a chance for Philip? I mean, if he's a traitor to our people and justice is truly served…he'll be executed." Ruth Ann swallowed. It wasn't a safe question, but it was all she had. She didn't cry. That would come again soon.

Benjamin leaned forward, propping his elbows on his knees. He was being an ordinary man, the one Ruth Ann needed in the moment. The godly, gentle, strong Choctaw man of the Congressional Cemetery and football field.

No. She couldn't let her thoughts drift that way.

Benjamin met her eyes and spoke slow, soft. "Miss Ruth Ann, I don't have an answer for that. Our people are facing complete loss of sovereignty as a nation. While we can, and should, fight the wrongs and injustices in the world, I know this—God is sovereign and He will bring ultimate justice for all of mankind."

He straightened. "I know you are very hurt by what your brother did to your family. You've lost so much. But it's by Chihowa's power through forgiveness that you can heal from it all."

Ruth Ann closed her eyes, her heart awash with more emotions than ever in her life. She needed to be home, needed to talk to Matthew, to be held by her mother. But her daddy was right—*God knows.*

Ruth Ann opened her eyes. "I am trying—"

She didn't finish. A screech pierced the evening air, catching everyone's attention in the full passenger car.

Ruth Ann froze, staring out the window at the train engine making the curve ahead of their car, its headlamp poking a hole in the darkness.

Only the engine wasn't making the curve. It was going over the side of a cliff.

CHAPTER 58

*R*uth Ann screamed as she gripped the windowsill. The passenger car surged forward, lurching around on the tracks. She lost sight of the disaster ahead, faintly aware of Benjamin leaping to his feet.

He grabbed a blanket from the overhead rack and threw it over her head. In the sudden blackness under the blanket, Ruth Ann felt him wrap her tight in his arms and swing her to the floor, then rolled her under the seat. He pressed close and Ruth Ann sensed every muscle in his body braced.

The passengers in the car were screaming, and the conductor shouted once before Ruth Ann felt the car rock. It seemed to go faster and there was a strange absence of clacking wheels on rails.

Then the car tilted and Ruth Ann instinctively braced her feet against the wall as time hung suspended before splitting in two as the car slammed on its side, glass and wood shattering.

The impact would have crushed Ruth Ann, but Benjamin took the brunt as he held her tight between the floor and underside of the seat. She heard him gasp, but she couldn't see anything for the blanket still over her head.

The passenger car slid on its side a short distance before everything stopped.

All was quiet. Ruth Ann experienced a floating feeling as though she were wrapped in one of the Grandmother's quilts, all tucked in and ready for bed.

Was she dying?

Wailing told her she was still in the physical world. So did Benjamin's form as he loosened his grip and yanked the blanket away from her face.

"Are you all right, Ruth Ann?"

Ruth Ann suddenly began breathing so hard colorful spots sprinkled her vision, pain shooting through more points in her body than she could track.

"Shhh, it's all right," he said, his voice close like on the telephone. "We're alive. Breathe slow."

Ruth Ann looked up to see Benjamin's pained face over her. She took several slow breaths, realizing she was gripping his forearm. "Are you all right?" she asked.

Benjamin blinked, and his expression changed. He sniffed. "We need to get out of the car. Now."

Ruth Ann couldn't see much from under the seat, but enough beyond his shoulder to realize the passenger car was filling with smoke.

The passengers' screams intensified and Benjamin jerked partly out from under the seat, twisting and standing awkwardly on the wall of the car.

Ruth Ann looked down, wincing at the pain in her neck, to see why his left leg wasn't moving. Her head went light when she saw his leg was impaled on metal from the broken seat.

Benjamin yanked his leg free, causing a spurt of blood. Ruth Ann screamed and gripped the front of his coat to try and steady him.

Benjamin put one hand on the sideways floor, glass crunching beneath his feet on the wall of the car. He reached out for her with his free hand.

"Come, Ruth Ann, we must…hurry."

She moved, breathless from the pain in her body. But she pressed close to Benjamin, who wrapped one arm around her waist. She coughed on the increasing smoke and looked for an escape in the sideways car. The conductor knelt on the arm of one of the seats, directing people away from spreading flames of fire and through a window above him. He pointed at Ruth Ann and Benjamin.

"You two go out the window up there! The door here is blocked."

He motioned to a chain forming to get people out a broken window several rows down from Ruth Ann. Before she could think of how she was going to climb around the rows of seats, luggage racks, and debris in a full skirt, Benjamin lifted and swung her over the first obstacle. He vaulted over on his good leg and rapidly repeated the process until they were at the end of the car.

Two men were by the window above, one of them standing on a seat and the other laying on the outside of the car and helping pull people up and through.

Smoke filled the car, heat intensifying from the fire devouring anything flammable, soaked with gas from the lamps.

Ruth Ann and Benjamin were the last ones to reach the window. The man quickly lifted her up to where the other dragged her out.

"Go to the side!" he shouted, even though he was right by her ear.

Ruth Ann started to crawl away, but looked back to make sure Benjamin got out. It seemed an eternity before his head appeared in the smoke and orange glow of the fire that was spreading through the car.

Benjamin shoved on his hands to pull himself up through the

window. But his elbows gave way, and he slipped back. The man on the side of the car held on and helped pull him out. The last man was right behind him, and the four of them scrambled for the edge. They climbed down the underbelly of the car.

The two men rushed off to where their families were, leaving Ruth Ann to let Benjamin lean on her as they struggled away from the fire on the sloped ground, the terrain hard to follow in the dark lit only by fires. She looked around to see hundreds of people and the ten passenger cars scattered over the mountainside. The train engine was nowhere in sight.

Pepper had been in the forward cars, the ones that would have suffered the greatest calamity. Had he survived?

Benjamin gasped, his full weight pressing on Ruth Ann. She stumbled to the ground, blinding pain shooting through her shoulder. She struggled out from beneath Benjamin as he rolled onto his back, breathing hard.

Ruth Ann screamed, "Help! Someone, please help!"

Her cry was lost among the hundreds of others. Everyone needed help.

There was no one to help.

Please, God, please, was all Ruth Ann could pray as she gripped the lapels of Benjamin's coat, her eyes blurred with tears. She'd seen men die in her lifetime, had watched her brother Matthew bleed on a roadside in Indian Territory. She could not watch this good man die right in front of her.

Ruth Ann undid her waist belt, crying in frustration when her left shoulder refused to work. Her cousin William had dislocated his shoulder once, and she knew she wouldn't be able to use it until it was set. But there wasn't time for that.

She scooted down to Benjamin's leg and slipped the belt underneath it, above the deep gash. She looped a knot but when she went to tighten it, her shoulder screamed and so did she. Blackness and nausea washed over her, but she couldn't halt, not until she stopped the blood flowing from Benjamin's leg. She used her knee to hold one side of the knot while she cinched it with her other hand.

Benjamin tried to sit up. "Ruth Ann..." He fell back, eyes closed.

Ruth Ann started ripping at the torn sleeves of her shirtwaist. She needed to pack the wound, stop the bleeding.

Benjamin Nakishi-Dunn was not going to die on a mountainside like her daddy.

"Move."

A gruff voice sounded beside her and even gruffer hands pushed her away. Ruth Ann struggled to her knees and wiped her tears to see Forbis Kanitobe withdrawing a red bandana from his pocket. He stuffed it into the wound, then tied it securely with his own belt.

Ruth Ann breathed, "Your wife?"

"She fine."

Forbis half crawled over Benjamin to his other side. He pulled one eyelid open and then the other. He nodded, satisfied at whatever he saw. "He a tough Choctaw. He make it."

Ruth Ann swallowed the taste of ashes and crawled back to Benjamin's side. She brushed his sweat dampened hair away from his eyes and pressed her forehead to his.

"Yakoke, Forbis Kanitobe."

Forbis muttered, "He a good Choctaw."

Ruth Ann looked up at him, thinking of how Forbis Kanitobe had once accused Benjamin of being an apple—red on the outside and white on the inside.

Sometimes you had to get in a train wreck with someone to realize truths about them.

"So are you, Mr. Kanitobe."

CHAPTER 59

Matthew pressed the floorboard of the passenger car with his boot heel, willing the train to do something. It had stopped 50 miles short of Memphis, Tennessee, jammed up with several trains delayed by the wreck down the line. The survivors of the wreck were taken to a hospital in Memphis.

He was so close, yet stuck. When the news had come and he confirmed the wrecked train was the one Ruth Ann was traveling home on, Matthew rushed home with the news. Daniel was at the box house visiting Della and volunteered to go with them to Memphis. Matthew left Peter to monitor news on the telegraph, waiting to see if Ruth Ann sent word that she was all right.

Matthew jumped to his feet on the stock-still train and paced the length of the passenger car. It was mostly empty since the news spread about the train wreck the night before. The wreck was caused by a jack, used to level rails, left on the tracks.

Thirty-two dead. The number burned in Matthew's mind as he sat down hard by his mother on the static train. She squeezed his hand, her own hot and sweating.

Matthew whispered, "She's all right, Mama. She's all right."

But he had to prove it, prove it like it was a story he was chasing down facts for. He needed them now.

Matthew bolted to his feet again. In the rush to get to the train depot, he had made a split decision to load Daniel's quarter horse and Falama onto the train in case they needed them.

"Daniel, take care of my mama," Matthew said. "I'm riding on down the line."

Della looked up at him sharply. Daniel pressed his lips tight. "That's a long ride, Matt. They'll have the way clear and us getting there before you can make it by horseback."

"I can't just sit here. I'll send a telegram as soon as I find out…" Matthew couldn't say it all. He was already losing his brother. Heaven help him, he wasn't going to lose his sister.

Daniel nodded. "Well, if anyone can beat a train, it's a stubborn Choctaw like you."

Matthew ran down the aisle of the passenger car and out the door into the assault of muggy summer heat. He leaped off the steps and hit the ground in the middle of the farm fields where the train had stopped.

He sprinted to the livestock car. The livestock worker had the animals out to graze on the grass growing by the tracks.

Matthew looked between Daniel's well-broke horse and the Choctaw stallion. Falama was green. Did Matthew really trust him?

He'd chosen to trust Philip when they faced off with Dan Holder. But it was only as a team that they survived. Matthew knew in his spirit it was the same with this stallion. He would give Falama trust but keep things under control.

He quickly saddled the tri-colored stallion and mounted. Falama pranced, but heeded Matthew's urging into a quick warm-up, then they galloped past car after car of the stuck trains.

Matthew let Falama have his head to set a fast yet sustainable pace. Choctaw horses were renowned for their endurance over other breeds. Time to put that legend, and his trust, to the test.

CHAPTER 60

*T*hrough the haze of sleep, Ruth Ann sensed a presence next to her. It was the second afternoon since the train wreck and she hadn't had visitors at the hospital. But there was one now disturbing her nap.

Benjamin?

Her eyes popped open. She rolled her head to see Pepper Barnes seated at her bedside.

A bandage was wrapped around his head, his right arm in a sling. Ruth Ann breathed a quiet prayer of thanks.

"Pepper. You're alive."

"So they tell me." Pepper's voice was scratchy, but not gruff. There was something different about him, something beyond surviving a train wreck. Something beyond the fact that he was looking at her civilly.

Ruth Ann swallowed to clear away the dryness in her throat. "They said nearly everyone in the front cars were killed."

He reached for a glass of water on the stand beside her hospital bed. "I guess I'm what you call a miracle."

He held the glass to her lips, and she managed to take a sip as some of it spilled onto the sheets. At least he was trying to be kind.

Pepper downed the rest of the water in one gulp, then spoke fast. "Something peculiar happened to me this morning. After coming through the wreck with just a few scratches, I figured I'd better give thanks to the good Lord above and all that. He helped me when I couldn't help myself. Anyway, I went into the hospital chapel and there was a crowd of black folks in there, singing and shouting, raising all kinds of ruckus in the service. I started backing out, but one fella put his arm around me and pushed me down into a pew and started preaching at me. I didn't know what was going on, but before the service was over, I was walking down that aisle, bawling like a baby."

Ruth Ann stared in wonder at Pepper, a smile spreading over her face.

He scowled. "Don't think I'm going to get like your Mr. Perfect Benjamin Nakishi-Dunn, but I did come to apologize."

Ruth Ann subdued her smile, but the wonder didn't leave her. Never in her life had she heard Pepper Barnes apologize for anything.

He looked her straight in the eyes. "I have a confession to make." He paused. "Actually, there are several I could make, but we'll just do a few. I'm the one who put the engagement announcement in the paper, same as how I started the gossip awhile back that I was courting you when I was really seeing a girl who lived on the Red River."

Ruth Ann narrowed her eyes. "*You* started those rumors?" The old flair of their constant bickering rose in her. She had to tamp it down.

He rested his free hand in his sling, shifting in his chair like he'd never get comfortable. He met her eyes again. "Annie, I'm sorry for everything, going back years, I guess. Will you forgive me for that and for how I treated you in D.C.?"

Ruth Ann couldn't stay agitated. She'd thought Pepper Barnes was one person who would never change. My, had she been wrong! He acted like a new man, and she wanted to encourage him.

"I forgive you, Pepper."

He let out his breath in one gush and pulled his hand out to rake his fingers through his hair. "Whew, I'm glad that's over with."

Ruth Ann laughed, feeling light. The air was finally clear between her and Pepper. So clear, she was seeing him in a brand new light, the new light in his life that was shining out, one she felt an urge to nurture.

The thought jolted her, and she searched his handsome features for more signs of true change. They were there, and her heart fluttered with joy. But was it only relief she felt? What if she had been in love with Pepper Barnes for years but denied it because of his character?

That was as far as her thoughts wandered before he said, "Annie, there's one more thing. I'm willing to court you properly. That seems like the honorable, or at least right, thing to do."

Ruth Ann closed her eyes. She knew her answer. She knew where the true feelings of her heart lay and who she belonged with for life.

"You did do the right thing in asking, Pepper Barnes."

He sighed. "There are few times in my life I can say that about."

Before supper, Ruth Ann shuffled to a window in one of the waiting rooms that showcased a sun-bathed garden outside the hospital. It was the first time she'd gotten out of bed on her own, and her body felt better for it. Her shoulder was still painful, but with the dislocation set and her arm in a sling, there was no reason for her to remain in bed. She'd even managed to change into a morning dress a nurse gave her for when she left the hospital.

Ruth Ann had sent a wire off to her family the afternoon after the wreck, and Peter assured her he would get the message down the line where Matthew and her mother were trying to reach her. From news floating around the hospital, Ruth Ann knew the railroad lines were clogged.

It might be awhile before her family arrived. She was anxious to be with them, wanted them to hold her and love her and make her feel that all was well, even with Philip.

Halting footsteps sounded behind Ruth Ann in the empty room, long and slow. She turned to see Benjamin making his way toward her on a cane.

She swallowed hard and took in his face for the first time since they'd been transported in separate ambulances for the hospital in Memphis. The nurses said he was not up for receiving visitors. No matter how much she pestered them, even before coming to this waiting room, they wouldn't tell her which ward he was in, only that he was recovering as well as could be expected.

Now there he was, dressed in pajamas with a lightweight robe wrapped around him. Nothing like the stately suit he'd worn in the Supreme Court when she saw him for the first time. But he had the same gentle smile for her.

Ruth Ann's eyes watered, and she prayed for the courage to tell him what she must.

His smile disappeared, and he hobbled closer. "Are you all right, Ruth Ann?"

Those were the first words he'd said to her after the wreck, even with metal stuck in his leg. He had offered to accompany her to Indian Territory and help with her brother's case. He had been gentle and kind from the first day they'd met.

She nodded. "I'm well. And you? I've heard you're one tough Choctaw."

Benjamin reached out and took her good hand lightly in his. "Sometimes."

His hand was warm and fit hers well. "I've spent so much time thinking while I've been laid up," he said. "I wasn't at the cemetery but it was still with me, and reminded me of how I don't want to die in D.C. Yet, I nearly died in a train wreck. Our lives are terribly short." He intertwined his fingers with hers. "It made me realize God never intended for me to wait until I was nearly on my deathbed to go home. It's time to face that now…with you beside me, I hope."

Ruth Ann gazed up at him, his height overwhelming her as she stood in the shadow of his peace.

She nodded. "It's what I've been praying for all afternoon."

Benjamin's eyes reddened, and he stroked the back of her hand with his thumb. He shifted the cane to his other hand and offered her his arm. "Come, let's go out and touch the sunshine."

She took his arm, relishing the opportunity to support him. He didn't really need it. But he wanted it.

That meant more.

They had scarcely cleared the doorway into the garden when Ruth Ann spotted a figure bounding up the gravel path toward them. She bit her lip, letting the tears flow down her cheeks. She released Benjamin's arm and stepped forward.

Matthew skidded to a halt in front of her, his face streaked with two day's worth of sweat, dirt, and stubble. And he needed a haircut, as always.

Ruth Ann had never seen a dearer sight.

Matthew sucked in a deep breath. "Annie, I didn't know if you…"

She nodded, and her brother took her in a fierce hug, holding her tenderly.

They understood one another without words.

$\mathcal{R}$uth Ann squeezed her mother's hand on one side, Matthew's on the other as she sat between them at the Tobucksy County Courthouse. Ruth Ann wore a yellow dress Della made for her while she was gone. It was wrapped around Ruth Ann just like her mother's arms, and she was very, very thankful to be in it.

They were waiting for Philip's sentencing by Judge Kendrick. It was late September and the long anticipated trial had finally taken place. Philip had been found guilty.

Guilty.

In front of her, Philip sat quietly next to Benjamin. His former attorney, Nelson Cobb, had ditched the case when Matthew announced that Benjamin would be assisting. Cobb had no desire to work with a big shot city lawyer and left the case solely to Benjamin.

Ruth Ann couldn't say she was sorry. Benjamin had handled the case with expertise and wisdom, including calling Pepper Barnes to the stand as a character witness during the sentencing phase.

Pepper testified how that, although he shared rowdy times

with Philip in the past, he knew the young man never had intentions of harming his family or the Choctaw people. Pepper's reputation was helped by his conversion, and Forbis Kanitobe endorsing him as a representative for the National's party.

Pepper sat behind the Teller family now with his lady friend, Jenny Crocket, the white girl from the Red River he'd been in love with since his teens. He meant his offer to court Ruth Ann as honorable, but they were both relieved when she said no.

"All rise."

Ruth Ann joined her family in standing as Judge Kendrick re-entered the small courtroom from his chambers. Tecumseh Shoemaker had been as tough in court as they expected during the trial, painting Philip as a traitor to the Choctaw people, and the judge was no friend of the Tellers.

It was life or death moment for Philip Teller.

Judge Kendrick took his seat and Ruth Ann could read nothing of his expression as she sat with everyone once again. Philip and Benjamin remained standing for the sentencing.

Judge Kendrick stared them down a long time before speaking.

"Philip Teller, you have been found guilty of betraying the Choctaw people by aiding the Holder gang in stealing annuity money and special funds from the chief. Though the money was recovered and the charge of participating in your father's killing was dropped, everyone in this courtroom knows he would be alive had you not sold out your people."

Ruth Ann closed her eyes. For the first time, she accepted the full truth of what her brother had done, the pain he caused them.

In that same moment, she forgave him. She kept her promise to her daddy.

Judge Kendrick stated in a ringing voice, "Taking into consideration all the testimonies and recommendations, I hereby sentence you to ten years hard labor."

Ruth Ann's air gushed out, and she wrapped her arms around

her mother. Matthew wrapped his arms around both of them as they cried, both in grief and joy. They stood to include Philip, whose downcast eyes betrayed no emotion except shock. Della hugged him, cradling his head like a baby. When she released him, Ruth Ann pinned his face between her hands.

"I love you," she whispered. "You are my brother. Nothing on earth will ever change that."

Philip put his hands on top of hers and held tight, letting his tears go unchecked. "I love you, too, baby sister."

The courtroom emptied in a few minutes, but Matthew, Ruth Ann, and Della waited for Benjamin and Philip to finish speaking with the judge. Tecumseh was still at his table, dictating notes to his assistant.

Matthew nodded toward Tecumseh and said quietly to Ruth Ann, "He's the reason I told you to trust Benjamin Nakishi. Proverbs says that when a man's ways please the Lord, He makes even his enemies to be at peace with him."

Ruth Ann smiled, her heart light with joy. Benjamin had no trouble winning over her family in the few months he'd been in Indian Territory. He set up a law office in McAlester and began establishing a list of clients, all while juggling correspondence to retain part of his practice in D.C., and preparing to move back to the Choctaw Nation for good.

But he spent most of his time in Dickens, working on Philip's case and taking many dinners at the Teller home and Uncle Preston's ranch. He didn't seem to have any regrets, not even in the fact that he'd lost the first case in his career.

When Benjamin and Philip finished speaking with the judge, they headed for the family. But Benjamin halted and turned. He went to Tecumseh Shoemaker and offered his hand to shake.

Tecumseh met his eyes, and the two stared at one another a good while before Tecumseh returned the handshake with a solid nod.

Benjamin joined the Teller family, still in his courtroom

lawyer mode. He said, "We spoke to Judge Kendrick about allowing Philip the old tribal tradition of taking care of one last piece of business before his sentence is carried out. That's normally for a death sentence but that was before prison sentencing for our people. In any case, the judge approved. I might add that he extended leniency in the sentencing thanks in no small part to that letter the First Lady sent Ruth Ann for Chief Jefferson Gardner."

Philip chuckled, draping an arm around Ruth Ann. "Seems my life was saved by your tea party with the American president's wife."

Ruth Ann jabbed him lightly with her elbow, but she allowed herself to soak in that victory from her trip. The First Lady had learned of her brother's situation through Joseph Griffin and asked the president to write a letter to the newly elected Chief Jefferson Gardner, requesting leniency.

Judge Kendrick, politician to the core, had not mentioned the letter publicly but understood the weight of it. Ruth Ann feared at first that it would cause more problems, but Benjamin assured her it did not threaten tribal sovereignty for one nation to advise another.

It had helped save Philip's life, along with having the best lawyer in Indian Territory.

~

Outlaws Sentenced to Hang for Robbery and Murder of Choctaw Citizen

By Matthew Teller

The federal court in Little Rock, Arkansas, found Dan Holder and Lester Cotton guilty of the robbery and murder of Jim Teller, a Choctaw citizen. Jim Teller was carrying a freight shipment along with annuity payments when he and his son were ambushed in the Winding Stair Mountains. The son, Philip Teller, was found culpable in the robbery but not the killing of his father. He was sentenced to ten years in prison.

Eldest Barnes Son to Wed

By Ruth Ann Teller

The engagement of Pepper Barnes and Jenny Crocket was announced during a community dance at the Barnes' mansion last week. The staff at the Choctaw Tribune wishes them all the best.

There was a light breeze coming over the lake on Uncle Preston's ranch. It climbed the hill to whistle in Ruth Ann's ears as she knelt by the grave of her father.

But she wasn't alone today.

Della, Matthew, and Philip knelt beside her, releasing their grief. The Grandmother and all of Uncle Preston's family were there, along with Benjamin and the Barnes. A close friend of Jim Teller's, Robert Barnes was the only white man present.

It was highly unusual for whites to attend a Choctaw *yaya*, a cry. Most people thought Choctaws no longer had them because they were never seen. They didn't realize it was a closely guarded cultural practice.

When the time was right, when that phase of grieving ended, Ruth Ann rose with her family to find Benjamin at her side.

Benjamin nodded at them. He met Uncle Preston's eyes, the man who was responsible for Ruth Ann's upbringing like her father.

Benjamin's voice came through deep, confident. "If you will allow, I have something to ask and it feels right to do it here at Ruth Ann's father's grave, and before Philip leaves."

Ruth Ann held her breath, staring into the face of the man she loved.

Benjamin looked between her brothers and mother, then held Uncle Preston's gaze when he asked, "May I have permission to court Ruth Ann?"

She took in the expressions on her family's faces—the approval in her mother's eyes, Matthew's pressing look, the surprise on Philip's face.

Uncle Preston saved the day. Sort of. "No one is good enough for our Annie," he said, drawing out the words. "But I reckon you're as good as we'll ever get. You have our blessing."

Ruth Ann took Benjamin's offered arm. She let that gentle smile and Hershey brown eyes consume her heart for good.

They had faced down death together. They would face life as one.

I want to start this section with sharing about the book cover itself, and the background photo that is of an actual Choctaw Nation treaty. The signatures in this rare photograph are of the three Great Medal Mingoes (Mikos in Choctaw) on the Mount Dexter treaty, dated November 16, 1805. This was one of the treaties signed by Chief Pushmataha (Pooshamataha). During my NMAI trip to Washington, D.C., my mother (Lynda Kay Sawyer) and me were allowed a rare viewing of some of our tribe's treaties that are preserved in the National Archives vault alongside the first Acts of Congress. Her photograph, "Great Medal Mingoes," is available as a fine art print. (ChoctawSpirit.com)

As with most of my historical fiction works, the incidences portrayed in this novel draw a great deal from actual happenings of the time period. That said, I want to mention a couple of specific items:

The Choctaw Progressives party was commonly referred to by their adversaries as "Bald Eagles" (possibly in reference to Green McCurtain, a rotund and balding mixed-blood, and a leading Progressive politician). I drew the term "polecats" from

Choctaw Kisses, Bullets, and Blood by Vance Trimble, but have been unable to verify the source of the term.

If you live in or are well familiar with D.C., you may have gotten wildly confused at the street names in this book. The answer to that is, several names changed over the years. For example, Georgia Avenue is now named Potomac Avenue that runs in front of the Congressional Cemetery. I based my directions and street names on a map from the time period.

Three Choctaw men inspired two of the characters in *Sovereign Justice*:

Charles McGilberry

This is one of the young men I've greatly admired for years. When I learned of his story through his granddaughter's book, *Touch by Greatness* (Carolee and S. Wayne Maxwell), I knew I wanted to do something to share a part of Charles' life with my readers. My first effort was through *Anumpa Warrior: Choctaw Code Talkers of World War I*, where I included actual quotes and letters of Charles' through my fictional character. This time, though, it's more nuanced, drawing from his life as a whole.

He is reflected in the character of Benjamin Nakishi-Dunn. Though Charles McGilberry wasn't a Choctaw lawyer in Washington, D.C., he did attend an Ivy League Preparatory school after winning an essay contest for American Indian boys. There are several layers to his story that are reflected in *Sovereign Justice*.

To be clear, Benjamin is not a direct historical representation of Charles, but rather he exhibits the gentle strength of a young man who endured much in his early life. Charles witnessed God take the ashes of life and turn them into something remarkably beautiful. That was what I wanted to capture through Benjamin's character.

James McDonald

While Charles McGilberry came after the time period of this

story, James McDonald (1801 - 1831) was considerably earlier. So early, he is credited as the first American Indian lawyer. James inspired much of the history I used of Choctaws in law, laying foundations for what Choctaws accomplished throughout the 19th century. I've found some documents mentioning Choctaw lawyers who practiced before the Supreme Court as well, like James Standley.

Josiah Gardner

Last but by no means least, is a character who comes from the actual timeframe of *Sovereign Justice*: Josiah Gardner. Though he could neither read nor write, Josiah won numerous court cases as a lawyer. Most of his cases took place at the Choctaw-run Tobucksy County Courthouse in McAlester.

Tecumseh Shoemaker draws from Josiah's life, including how Choctaw full-blood Indians told him their entire stories when they would hold back from others. Again, Tecumseh is not a direct representation of Josiah Gardner.

The dialogue of Senator Dawes in this book are not exact quotes, but offers the general sentiments he expressed in other sources.

Matthew and Daniel's adventure on Blackjack Mountain came from my personal experience with preservationists of the Choctaw horses today. The experience was captured in photography by my mother, Lynda Kay Sawyer, and is available as fine art prints (ChoctawSpirit.com).

I took literary license with the football game on the National Mall lawn in that the first forward pass in a football game was not until 1906.

Lastly, avid readers may have picked up the similarity of the corset and marriage proposals in Lynn Austin's "A Proper Pursuit." That novel did inspire the use of loosening a corset in this book! I'm a fan of Lynn Austin's historical fiction, and loved including a nod to her work here.

GLOSSARY OF CHOCTAW WORDS

~

Chihowa: God
Chi hullo li: I love you
Chi pisa la chike: I will be seeing you / I will see you again
Halito: A friendly greeting
Luksi: Turtle
Ome: Expressing a ready assent, agreement or acknowledgment
Pokni: Grandmother
Yakoke: Thank you

PHRASES

Issish ittimilaiyuka yvt Hattak Vpi Homma ikono kvt issish alotowa vlheha ya yakni holittoblichi kvt ohmi kiyo.
The mixed bloods are not Indian enough to love land like the full bloods.

Chim atoksvli yvt katiohmi?
How is your work?

Pim anumpa haklo ka achukma.
It is good to hear our language.

Mihma chim olbvlaka ya chi haksobish vt haklashke, "ilvppakosh hina, iakaiya, ibbak isht impa imma pit ish folotakma micha afvbekimma ish folotakma, achi tok.(Isaiah 30:21)
And thine ears shall hear a word behind thee, saying, "This is the way, walk ye in it, when ye turn to the right hand, and when ye turn to the left." (Isaiah 30:21)

THE EXECUTIONS (*CHOCTAW TRIBUNE SERIES, BOOK 1*)

Who would show up for their own execution?

It's 1892, Indian Territory. A war is brewing in the Choctaw Nation as two political parties fight out issues of old and new ways. Caught in the middle is eighteen-year-old Ruth Ann, a Choctaw who doesn't want to see her family harmed.

In a small but booming pre-statehood town, her brother owns a controversial newspaper, the *Choctaw Tribune*. Ruth Ann wants to help spread the word about critical issues but there is danger for a female reporter on all fronts—socially, politically, even physically.

But what is truly worth dying for? This quest leads Ruth Ann and her brother Matthew, the stubborn editor of the fledgling *Choctaw Tribune*, to old Choctaw ways at the farm of a condemned murderer. It also brings them to head on clashes with leading townsmen who want their reports silenced no matter what.

More killings are ahead. Who will survive to know the truth? Will truth survive?

The Executions is available on multiple retailer sites.

TRAITORS (CHOCTAW TRIBUNE SERIES, BOOK 2)

"Someone's going to be king in this territory.
No reason it can't be me. It sure won't be you."

Betrayed.

Someone is tearing at the fabric of the Choctaw Nation while political turmoil, assassinations, and feuds threaten the very sovereignty of the tribe. It stands under the U.S. government's scrutiny.

When heated words turn to hot lead, Ruth Ann Teller—a mixed-blood Choctaw—fears losing her brother who won't settle for anything but the truth. Matthew is determined to use his newspaper, the *Choctaw Tribune*, to uncover the scheme behind Mayor Thaddeus Warren's claim to the townsite of Dickens. Matthew is willing to risk his newspaper—and his life—to uncover a traitor among their Choctaw people.

But when Ruth Ann tries to help, she causes more harm than good—especially after the mayor brings in Lance Fuller, a schoolteacher from New York. How does this charming yet aloof young man fit into the mayor's scheme?

When attacks against the newspaper strike and bullets fly, a trip to the Chicago World's Fair of 1893 is the answer they need to save the Choctaw Tribune. The trip holds a key to Matthew's investigation.

But Ruth Ann must find the courage to face a journey to the White City —without her brother.

***Traitors* (*Choctaw Tribune* Series, Book 2) is available on multiple retailer sites.**

SHAFT OF TRUTH (CHOCTAW TRIBUNE SERIES, BOOK 3)

"Nothing to it but a stout heart."

On a mission to bring justice to the outlaw gang that murdered his father and brother, Matthew Teller leaves the *Choctaw Tribune* newspaper for his sister to operate and plunges into an unfamiliar world of darkness and danger. Working inside the coal mines of the Choctaw Nation—one of the most dangerous places in the country—he searches for a man who may have the answers to this six-year-old mystery. But after Matthew uncovers an earth-shattering truth that rocks him to his core, he must decide what right is, and what price he is willing to pay for it.

Ruth Ann Teller knows she can handle publishing the *Choctaw Tribune*—until she loses their biggest advertiser. Now, with Matthew miles away and the future of the newspaper resting squarely on her shoulders, Ruth Ann must make a bold move to keep the newspaper afloat in her brother's absence. She sets it on a course for new success or total disaster.

Striking coal miners. Outlaw gangs. An unsolved crime. And a Choctaw family that fights for one another, and for truth.

Shaft of Truth (*Choctaw Tribune* Series, Book 3) is available on multiple retailer sites.

~

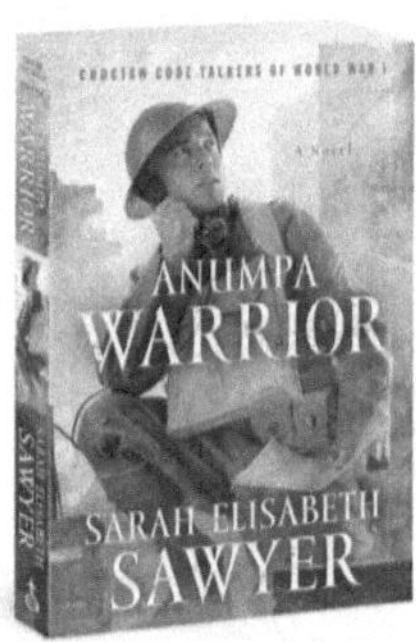

The day I betrayed Isaac, I vowed never again to speak my native language in front of white men.

When America enters the Great War in 1917, Bertram Robert Dunn and his Choctaw buddies from Armstrong Academy join the army to protect their homes, their families, and their country. Hoping to find redemption for a horrible lie that betrayed his best friend, B.B. heads into the trenches of France—but what he discovers is a duty only his native tongue can fulfill.

War correspondent Matthew Teller is ready to quit until an encounter with a fellow Choctaw sets him on a path to write the untold story of American Indian doughboys. But entrenched stereotypes and prejudices tear at his burning desire to spread truth.

With the Allies building toward the greatest offensive drive of the war, the American Expeditionary Forces face a superior enemy who intercepts their messages and knows their every move. Can the solution come from a people their own government stripped of culture and language?

***Anumpa Warrior: Choctaw Code Talkers of World War I* is available on multiple retailer sites.**

~

Touch My Tears: For this collection of short stories, Choctaw authors from five U.S. states came together to present a part of their ancestors' journey, a way to honor those who walked the trail for their future. These stories not only capture a history and a culture, but the spirit, faith, and resilience of the Choctaw people.

Tushpa's Story: Young Tushpa, his family, and their small band embark on a trail of life and death. More death than life lay ahead.

A continuation of the anthology *Touch My Tears: Tales from the Trail of Tears*, this story follows an original manuscript written by Tushpa's son, James Culberson.

Touch My Tears **and** ***Tushpa's Story*** **are available on multiple retailer sites.**

YAKOKE

This book was years in the making, and it never would have seen the light of day without the encouragement of my faithful readers, editors, and book team. Yakoke, truly!

Dear Catherine Frappier took time in between her constitutional law studies at Harvard to read and give me in-depth feedback on the earliest draft of the manuscript that I let seep out. Thank you, sweet friend. And the same thank you to my other sister-friend, Mollie Reeder, an extraordinarily talented writer, who helped get the book on the right track (and stay there) from the outline phase onward.

No one supports my work more behind the scenes and on-stage than my mama, Lynda Kay Sawyer. *Chi hullo li*, I love you!

Special appreciation goes to Dr. Ian Thompson, PhD, RPA (Director of the Choctaw Nation Historic Preservation Department, Wheelock Academy, and the Tuskahoma Capitol Museum) and Dora Wickson (School of Choctaw Language translation specialist) for their help in cultural and historical accuracies and Choctaw phrase translations. Yakoke!

Above all, I give praise and glory to Chihowa, the Great Jehovah, for gifting me with the ability to tell a story. His mercies are new every morning, and I long to always heed the Word behind me, whispering, "This is the way, walk in it."

ABOUT THE AUTHOR

SARAH ELISABETH SAWYER is a story archaeologist. She digs up shards of past lives, hopes, and truths, and pieces them together for readers today. The Smithsonian's National Museum of the American Indian honored her as a literary artist through their Artist Leadership Program for her work in preserving Choctaw Trail of Tears stories. A tribal member of the Choctaw Nation of Oklahoma, she writes historical fiction from her hometown in Texas, partnering with her mother, Lynda Kay Sawyer, in continued research for future works. Learn more at SarahElisabethWrites.com, Facebook.com/SarahElisabethSawyer

www.ingramcontent.com/pod-product-compliance
Lightning Source LLC
Chambersburg PA
CBHW031931110726
47902CB00001B/136